# Song
## *for my*
# FATHER

## J M STOLL

# PART ONE

# FEBRUARY 1951

TED SAT AT the piano, half playing, half conducting, his long thin wrists protruding from his air force battledress blouse. A dull afternoon light filtered through the high metal windows and the men huddled around the piano as if it would take away the chill. He signalled the end of the last note. 'Lovely, lads. Really lovely. Coming on ever so well. Same time next week, and we'll run through the Vaughan-Williams, so have a look at it if you can in the meantime.'

'Thanks Ted, see you next week.' As the nine men filed out of the hall, the lights came on. Ted looked up and saw Frank Bassett walking towards him, uniform immaculate as always, his boots reflecting the yellow lamplight.

'Very nice, Ted. I never realised we had such talent here.' Ted didn't know Frank well. He'd come to the station about a year ago from somewhere up north. They would occasionally meet in the sergeants' mess but Frank wasn't Ted's type. He was a bit of a show-off, a great one for a dirty joke, everyone's best friend. What on earth did he want? 'Are you thinking of joining us? I didn't know you could sing.'

'Don't look so worried, Ted. Tone deaf. Not a chance. But it is your musical help I'm after. It's my boy, you see.' Frank handed him a piece of folded newspaper. It was an advertisement: *Choral Scholarships – St Christopher's College Choir School, Cambridge.* 'I want to put him up for this. First-rate education. All paid for.'

Ted handed the cutting back. 'Can he sing?'

'That's why I'm talking to you. His schoolteacher told Sheila it were the one thing he were good at, but I don't know anything about music. I thought maybe you could try him out. See if he's up to it.' He took some duplicated sheets out of a buff envelope and gave them to Ted. There was an application form and a description of what was required for an audition. Scales, aural tests, performance of *O Rest In The Lord*, 'plus piece of applicant's own choice'.

'I'm not sure if I'm the right person. I'm only an amateur. This,' he waved towards where the choir had stood, 'is only a bit of fun. Applicants for St Christopher's need professional singing teachers I should think. I'd be out of my depth.'

'You're doing yourself down, Ted. I've talked to some of the blokes in the choir and they reckon you know what you're at. That's why I'm asking for your help. Anyway, you know I couldn't afford to get a professional teacher on a sergeant's wages.' Frank checked himself. 'Not that I'm asking you to do it on the cheap – don't worry I'll see you all right – it's just that I'd like your opinion, and maybe your help, as a friend.'

Ted didn't want to get involved but could see that it was going to be hard to say no. 'I still don't think I'm the right person but I suppose if you brought the boy around some time I could listen to him and see if he's worth getting some professional help for.'

'I knew you'd be the right man to talk to. That's capital. When would be a good time?'

FRANK BROUGHT THE boy to the hall after the following week's choir rehearsal. 'This is Geoffrey. Say hello to Sergeant Cunningham.'

The boy looked at the floor and mumbled, 'Hello, Sergeant Cunningham,' in a squeaky monotone.

'Hello, Geoffrey.' Ted tried to put some warmth into his voice. There was no response in the boy's expression, but maybe this was normal. He had no nieces or nephews and didn't know much about children.

'He's a bit shy. Might be best if I left you to it. Get to know each other, you know. Shall I come back in half an hour? I'll be in the mess if you need me.' And, over his shoulder on the way out, 'Behave yourself, Geoff.'

Ted looked at him properly. He did seem very small. And

thin – a sharp chin, fingers peeping out from the sleeves of his oversize blazer, stick-like legs appearing from billowing grey shorts.

'How old are you, Geoffrey?'

'Nearly eight.'

'Your dad says you like singing. Would you like to sing something for me?'

The boy stared at him blankly.

'What about a nursery rhyme, or a hymn, maybe? Your dad said you sing at school.'

'We sing hymns at assembly and then after that they sometimes play us the wireless and we sing along with it.'

'*Singing Together* on the Home Service?'

'I don't know.'

'Why don't I play something, and then, if you know it, you can just sing along a bit?'

Geoff nodded.

Ted took from his battered briefcase a piano book of nursery rhymes which he had been given when he was a boy and started to play *Sing a Song of Sixpence*. After a few notes Geoff began to hum along quietly, and then, as he found his voice, an astonishingly pure and accurate treble emerged. Ted played some more songs with similar results; then he tried an aural test, playing a few bars of a made-up tune which he asked him to sing back. Geoff repeated it note perfect. 'Well done, Geoffrey! Very well done.' The boy smiled briefly, then the blank expression returned. Perhaps smiling wasn't 'behaving himself'.

'Do you know why you're here? Do you know what this is all about?'

'My dad told me to come.'

'But do you know why?'

'No.'

'Would you like to know why?'

'I don't know. I mean…' Ted could see that he was trying to think what the correct answer was.

'Your dad thinks you might be able to get into a choir school. Do you know what that is?'

Geoff shrugged.

'It's like a normal school but as well as the regular lessons like English and arithmetic there would be a lot of singing, and you'd be singing with other boys in a choir in somewhere like a church. Do you go to church?'

'No.'

'Would you like that? To go to a special singing school? And you'd be boarding – living there, that is, away from home.'

'I don't know.'

'But you do like singing, don't you?'

'It's all right.' Hadn't his father discussed it with him at all?

Just then, Frank came back into the hall. 'So, how are you getting on then? What do you think, Ted?'

'There's no question he's musical.'

'So could he get into this school, then?'

'That's another matter. As I said before, I've no experience in this sort of thing at all.'

'But he's musical, you say, so couldn't we have a try? Get him up to scratch?'

'I still think you'd be better off with a professional.'

'But you'd have a go, to help me out, wouldn't you?' Ted was still silent. 'To start him off. And then we could get a professional in later on.'

'It might work, I suppose. And then there's also the question of whether it's what Geoffrey wants.'

'Don't worry about that. You don't have children, do you, Ted? He's only seven. How can he know what's right for him? That's a parent's responsibility. I want the best for him, like any parent, so if I tell him that this is best, he'll do what he's told. Won't you Geoff?' Geoff nodded.

THE LESSONS TOOK place every week. Frank would drop off the boy after the choir practice, and for half an hour Ted would go through voice exercises, aural tests and the other stuff required for the audition, dredging up boyhood memories of singing in his church choir. Geoff made rapid progress and in his timid way seemed to be enjoying the lessons and the attention he was getting. Ted enjoyed the lessons too, pleased at how the boy was coming on and resigned to the fact that no professional help was ever going to be sought, though it still irked him.

At the end of April, Ted told Frank that he reckoned Geoff would be ready for St Christopher's June audition date and Frank sent off the completed application form to the choir school. In due course a letter came back inviting Geoff to an audition on a Saturday afternoon in late June.

'I don't know how to thank you for everything, Ted.'

'Thank me if he gets in. I'm still not sure whether I've taught him the right way.'

'Don't worry, you've done a great job,' and he patted him on the shoulder. 'Look Ted, I know I already owe you and all, for what you've done and I hate to ask you for another favour, but I wondered if there's any chance you could take the boy up to the audition. You've got a car, haven't you? You see, for me to take him up by train is bit of a performance, and I think it'd give him more confidence too, if he knew you were there.'

Ted doubted it would really be so difficult for Frank and Geoff to go by train, but as Geoff was his protégé in a way, maybe it wouldn't be such a bad idea. To show he wasn't a complete chump he replied, 'Might be possible. Course I'd need something for petrol. Must be a good sixty miles each way, probably about five gallons would do it… shall we say a quid's-worth?'

'Of course, I was going to say that. A quid it is.'

# JUNE 1951

TED WAS WAITING for them outside his quarters dressed in civvies – a tweed sports jacket, grey flannels and cloth cap, his driving cap as he liked to think of it.

'You look different, Sergeant Cunningham – not in uniform, I mean,' said Geoff.

Frank was quick with, 'Don't be cheeky, Geoff.'

'Is this your car, Sergeant Cunningham?' said Geoff with more excitement in his voice than Ted had ever heard. It was an MG Midget in pillar box red with beige upholstery. The chrome gleamed like the silver in the officers' mess. It was a fine day and the roof was down.

'Nice motor, Ted. Oh what it is to be single and fancy-free. Fat chance a family man could own a car like this.'

'It was a bit of luck. One of the flight officers was posted to Rhodesia and needed to get rid of it quickly so I got it for a bit of a song, otherwise I could never have afforded it.' It didn't sound very convincing.

'In you get, Geoffrey,' said Ted, opening the passenger door.

'Wow!' Geoff was wide-eyed.

Frank gave Geoff a playful punch on his shoulder. 'Now do your best at the audition. Remember everything Sergeant Cunningham has told you, and behave yourself. The wife's made some sandwiches for you both,' and he handed a brown paper packet to Ted, 'and here's the quid for the petrol and another couple of bob to get some pop for the boy and a beer for you.' Would this be the extent of Frank's 'seeing him all right'?

As they drove off, Geoff was positively animated. 'I never knew you had an MG, Sergeant Cunningham. It's a TC, isn't it? One and a quarter litre.'

'You seem to know a lot about cars.'

'One of my dad's friends gave me a Motor Show catalogue. I read it every night. MGs are one of my favourites.' And so until the wind noise became too intrusive, they talked about cars, with Ted quite astonished at the small boy's encyclopaedic knowledge. In Baldock, Ted bought some lemonade and a bottle of light ale. Outside the town he found a lay-by and they sat on a grass bank to eat the sandwiches.

'How do you feel about the audition, Geoff?' Immediately the mood had been broken, and Ted saw it had been a mistake to leave the safe subject of cars.

'I don't know.' Geoff looked at the ground, shrinking back into his school uniform, the only clothes Ted had ever seen him in.

'Oh well, let's not worry about it. It's worth a try. You've a very good voice, you know, but if it doesn't come off it's not the end of the world, is it?'

'My dad'll kill me if I don't get in.' They finished eating their sandwiches in silence. Back in the car, Ted tried to distract him by explaining how the clutch and the gears worked.

They had directions on how to reach the choir school, which was on the edge of the city. Ted asked Geoff to read out the street names and tell him when to turn and they arrived at a building which had been designed to look more like a private house than a school. They entered through the panelled front door into a generous hall with a floor of shining black and white marble tiles. The domestic character was maintained by the grandfather clock and large oak settle, but the smell – a combination of disinfectant, furniture polish and boiled cabbage – betrayed that it was an institution of some kind and invoked in Ted strong memories of his own schooldays. In one corner there was a half-glazed door labelled 'Office' in gold paint, at which Ted knocked. It was opened by a neatly-dressed young woman who was clutching a clipboard. 'Interview?' she asked.

'Yes. Geoffrey Bassett.'

'Good. Now, Geoffrey, you just wait on the bench in the hall and someone will take you in shortly. Mr Bassett, I would suggest you come back in about an hour; we should be done by then.'

'Actually, it's Cunningham, Edward Cunningham, I'm...' he struggled for a moment with a suitable description, 'his singing teacher and a family friend. Won't you need me to accompany him for his pieces?'

'Just leave the music with Geoffrey and we can manage on our own.'

He knew that this was how it worked, it had been in the audition instructions, but he was worried about leaving Geoff by himself. 'Good luck, Geoff. Don't worry old boy, it'll all be all right.'

There was just time to take a quick stroll into the city centre and back. He'd visited Cambridge once as a boy but his memories were vague and he'd forgotten how pretty it was, especially on a sunny afternoon like today. Punters lazily drifted down the river, flower beds were full of colour, lawns were immaculate and the college buildings looked completely unaffected by the six years of war and privation suffered in the rest of the country. He wondered whether Frank Bassett had ever visited Cambridge.

When he got back he found Geoff sitting on the settle in the hall. 'How'd it go, Geoff?'

'I don't know,' came the predictable answer. Then a door opened and a portly bald-headed man in a three-piece tweed suit came out and walked towards them. He put out a hand to Ted. 'Mr Cunningham, isn't it? Claude Cowdray, headmaster.' Ted accepted an extremely firm handshake. 'So you've helped young Bassett prepare for the interview.'

'I'm only an amateur. I just did what I could.'

'I see. May I have a few words in my study?' Leaving Geoff on the bench, he followed the headmaster into a panelled room with desk at one end and sofa and easy chairs at the other. The headmaster waved him into one of the easy chairs.

'Quite an enigma, your boy. Sings like an angel, clearly very musical, reads well enough but otherwise academically very questionable. You see,' he stroked his chin, 'we expect a pretty high standard at St Christopher's as boys are expected to go on from here to one of the better public schools. Is your boy up to it?'

'The boy's father asked me to help with the singing. I just helped him prepare his pieces and the aural tests and so on; I wasn't aware of the academic requirements. He's just at the local school. I don't suppose their standards are particularly high. He's certainly a quiet boy, but perhaps that's simply a lack of stimulation.'

The headmaster carried on stroking his chin accompanied by some heavy intakes of breath. 'I'll need to think about it, but on the whole I believe I shall give him the benefit of the doubt. What's his father do?'

'Sergeant in the RAF. Like me. We're colleagues.'

'Oh, I see. Stayed on after the war.'

'Yes.'

'Well, we certainly owe you chaps a debt.' More chin-stroking. 'I'll be in touch in writing next week. Thank you so much, Mr…'

'Cunningham.'

'Yes, of course, Mr Cunningham, or should it be Sergeant Cunningham?'

'Either is fine for me.' He was keenly aware of the tone in which the headmaster had said 'sergeant', a tone carefully graded for NCOs. No doubt the headmaster had a full range of tones for all ranks from Able Seaman to Field Marshall.

'WHAT DID THAT man say?' They were back in the car and on the Trumpington Road.

'He said you sang very well.'

'Does that mean I've got in?

'They haven't decided yet.'

'Oh.'

There was no point in beating about the bush. 'Singing was good, but he was worried about the academic side.'

'What does "academic" mean?'

'Did they ask you other things, apart from the singing?'

'Yes, I had to do some sums and then read a story and write down answers to questions about it.'

'Well, that's called "academic" stuff. He thought that you weren't as good at that as you were at music and singing.'

'Oh.'

He tried to change the subject to cars but he could see that Geoff wasn't in the mood this time and in a few minutes he found that the boy was asleep.

Back home, he dropped off Geoff and told Frank about his conversation with the headmaster.

'Sang like an angel. Well you certainly did your bit, Ted, and I'm truly grateful. Angel,' Frank sniffed, 'by heck.'

Ted was at his desk on Wednesday when Frank rushed in waving a letter. 'He's got in, the little bugger, he's got in!'

'That's great news, Frank. Great news. You must feel very proud.'

'Over the moon, and it's you I have to thank.'

'No really, it's Geoffrey who did it. The boy has great natural talent. I didn't have to do much at all.'

'No, Ted, you're being too modest, and to thank you, the wife and I would like to invite you over to our house. Would tomorrow evening be all right for you? We thought we'd get in a nice steak and kidney pie from Newlands and have a few beers. Would 6.30 suit?'

'Are you sure? I was very happy to help – enjoyed it actually – there's really no need…' Having dinner with the Bassetts was the last thing he wanted to do.

'Oh no, Ted, you must come. We all want to show our appreciation.'

'Well then, thank you, that would be lovely. 6.30 would be perfect.'

'See you tomorrow, then,' and Frank bounced out.

THE MARRIED QUARTERS section of the station consisted of four rows of identical small houses like pieces on a Monopoly board, set in neatly mown lawns without flower beds. Frank opened the door. 'Nice to see you, Ted. You've met Sheila, haven't you?'

'Only briefly. Hello, Sheila. Very kind of you to invite me over.' They shook hands.

Sheila Bassett was the sort of woman that men's eyes would turn to watch as she walked down the street. Ted had heard someone say that she'd worked on the cosmetics counter of a large department store before the war. She didn't mix much with the other RAF wives who thought she'd got above herself. They had to put up with 'make do and mend' but she somehow had money to spend on new clothes and hairstyles.

'Right. Pale ale all right for you, Ted?' Frank poured glasses for Ted and himself and a sherry for Sheila. There was even some lemonade for Geoff, who was sitting quietly in the corner of the room, which was furnished with a utility dresser and a tired-looking three-piece suite. A print of two Spitfires hung over the mantelpiece. 'To happy days at St Christopher's. Well done, Geoff, and thanks to you, Ted. Cheers.'

Polite conversation followed in which Ted had to elaborate on his trip to Cambridge, which as he had suspected, neither Frank nor Sheila had ever visited. 'See how lucky you are, Geoff, to be going to a place so full of history and that.' Ted glanced at Geoff who remained expressionless.

The dining room was just large enough for the four of them, and Sheila passed the pie through the hatch from the kitchen. This was augmented with some runner beans and mashed potatoes. 'I'm afraid I'm not much of a cook, Ted, but the pie's from Newlands so it should be all right at least.'

'Everything's very nice, Sheila. Really.'

'So, what were you up to before the war, Ted?' asked Frank. Ted realised how little most of them knew about each other. 'Before the war' seemed a world away.

'I was in the printing trade, working for my father.'

'In London, was that?'

'Yes, Hammersmith. My father started it up with one of his chums after the first war.'

'Printing, that's always a good business, i'n't it? People always need stuff printed, come rain or shine.'

'I don't know about that. It has its ups and downs like everything else, but Father has been pretty lucky with it on the whole.'

'So that's how you learnt about draughtsmanship and photography and all that stuff.'

'My father and I agreed it would be good for me to learn the trade properly, so when I left school I went to college for three years to get fully fledged. Then I went to work for him for a couple of years and then war broke out and I joined up.'

'What happened to the business?'

'Oh, Father and his partner are still running it, although he's getting on a bit now. Mother died in '44 and that knocked him down a bit. What about you, Frank?'

'Parents? They both died in '44 too. The V1 Christmas Eve raid on Oldham.'

'Oh I'm sorry, Frank. That's rotten.'

'Oh well, that's war, i'n't it.'

'So is that where you're from?'

'Yes. And Sheila too. We were childhood sweethearts, weren't we, Sheila?' Sheila gave the slightest of nods.

'I were in the insurance business. Worked me way up from ledger clerk to salesman.' Talk of Oldham seemed to strengthen Frank's northern accent. 'It were a good job but I don't miss it. Walking round every night, collecting the shillings, even in the bleeding snow. Joining up were the best thing. The RAF's a great life. I'n't it, Sheila?'

'If you say so, Frank.'

'What about another beer, Ted? We're celebrating after all.'

Frank had a couple more pints over the tinned peaches and custard, whilst Ted sipped his one pint more slowly. Geoff was sent off to bed and Sheila went into the kitchen at which point Frank brought out a bottle of Scotch and poured out two glasses. He then proceeded to tell some anecdotes at which Ted laughed politely. Ted wondered what Sheila saw in him. Surely she wouldn't have been short of offers? Frank was good-looking enough, quite dapper and with the gift of the gab, but also something of a bore and the snobbier officers would definitely have called him 'vulgar'. There again, Sheila, whatever her looks, was hardly scintillating company either.

THE TELEGRAM CAME the following Tuesday from Ted's older sister: 'FATHER SERIOUSLY ILL STOP COME HOME SOONEST STOP BARBARA'. In less than half-an-hour he had secured compassionate leave and was driving to Hammersmith. He had been down to see his father about a month ago when he'd seemed pretty well, so it had been a shock to receive Barbara's wire. When he arrived at the house he met the doctor coming out. Dr Boyars had been their GP for about fifteen years and had been in and out a lot during Ted's mother's illness.

'Hello, Ted. I'm glad I've been able to see you. Barbara has all the details, but it's not looking too good. Your father has had a stroke, quite a serious one. It's possible he might recover, in which case you'll see him improve a good deal in the next few days, but it's also possible that he might not improve much at all and even have another stroke. Very hard to tell. I'm sorry, but I knew you'd want me to give it to you straight. I'd like to talk for longer but I have a couple of other urgent visits to do. I'll try to pop in again this evening if I can. Chin up.'

'Thank you, doctor. I understand.' He knew that behind the doctor's businesslike manner lay a well of compassion.

He went into the house, which had hardly changed since his childhood, in fact probably not much had changed in the sixty years since it had been built. Dark brown preponderated: woodwork painted in thick oily varnish, a worn stair runner in an indeterminate pattern of beige and maroon, the original encaustic tiles of black and burgundy in the hall leading to brown linoleum on the steps down to the kitchen and beyond.

Finding no one downstairs he went up to his father's bedroom. Barbara gave him a hug, possibly the closest physical contact since they had played together as children. 'He's sleeping,' she said. He glanced at the bed with its oversize mahogany bedhead. His father looked diminished with only his head above the sheets, his cheeks sunken and colourless, his chest hardly rising as he breathed. 'I heard you talking to the doctor, what did he say?'

Ted repeated the doctor's words. Barbara sighed. 'It would have been different if Mother were still alive, but I don't think he has much fight left in him.'

Ted held her hand. 'We'll see. Now what about a cup of tea? Shall I bring it up here or shall we go downstairs?'

'I think he'll be asleep for quite a bit longer, let's go downstairs.'

In the kitchen, Barbara filled him in on the details: Mrs T, the charlady, had found him moaning and unable to get out of bed that morning. She'd rung the doctor and Barbara. Thank goodness they'd had the phone put in. Barbara had organised a nurse to stay tonight.

'Poor old Mrs T must have had a shock,' said Ted, 'she must be quite a bit older than Father.'

'She certainly must be over seventy, but she always was a pretty tough old bird, didn't bat an eyelid during the blitz.'

They discussed all the contingency arrangements depending on the speed of their father's recovery but studiously avoided talk of what would happen if he died.

Ted went upstairs and sat by his father. Was he asleep or awake? He talked to him about anything that came into his head: the RAF, the choir, young Geoffrey Bassett, his car, the printing works. Sometimes his father's face twitched. Did that mean he could hear him and understand what he was saying, or was this wishful thinking? The doctor visited again in the late afternoon. The fact that Ted's father had not opened his eyes or moved his hands was not a good sign.

Later, Ted's father's business partner, Joe Peavey, called around. Joe looked much older than when Ted had last seen him. He took hold of Ted's father's limp hand. 'What ho, old friend,' he said. Ted looked into Joe's eyes and saw tears. Like Ted, Joe went through the motions of a normal conversation with Ted's father. A new order for perfect-bound booklets had come in, one of the old platen presses was playing up, a competitor had gone over completely to litho, and more in this vein. 'Must be going now, Ethel will be wondering where I am. I'll pop in same time tomorrow.' Ted accompanied Joe out of the room. 'Can't believe it, can't believe it, Ted. He was fit as a fiddle yesterday.' They made some light conversation but Ted could see that Joe's world was crumbling.

Rather than going home to Bromley, Barbara was staying the night and George, her husband, was coming straight over from the City and would sleep there too. Barbara was four years older than Ted, and George was six years older than Barbara and seemed to come from an earlier generation. He liked to dress for dinner, although that wouldn't be possible tonight.

'I think we all need a stiff drink,' said George after Barbara had briefed him. 'Any Scotch in the house?' Whisky, a soda siphon and glasses were procured from the drinks cabinet in the sitting room, and Barbara prepared an omelette using a tin of spam and some dried egg powder she'd found in the larder. The night nurse arrived and Ted, Barbara and George went to bed. It was still rather early – barely dark outside – but no one felt in the mood for conversation.

The night was warm and sticky. Ted opened his old bedroom window and looked up and down the street as he used to do as a boy, observing comings and goings and imagining the lives behind the windows of the other houses. Like missing teeth, there were two or three gaps in the road where houses had been bombed. He had slept in this room all his life until he'd joined up in 1939. He'd been a young man for some of those years but this still seemed like a boy's room: his model yacht and kite were on top of the wardrobe, shells and stones he'd collected were still on the mantelpiece, he knew that even his old school blazer and cricket kit, last worn seventeen years ago, were still in the wardrobe. If his father died, what would happen to this room? A knot of nostalgia caught in his stomach.

At about two in the morning the nurse knocked on Ted's door and asked him to come to his father's bedroom. Barbara and George were there too in their dressing gowns, sitting next to the bed, hand in hand. A dry clicking came from Ted's father's throat. The nurse said that it was the death rattle and it wouldn't be long now and that there was no point calling the doctor as there would be nothing he could do. He wasn't in any pain or discomfort, she was sure. Ted wondered how she was sure. Gradually the clicking grew softer and then it stopped altogether. 'He's gone,' said the nurse. Barbara wept silently. Ted felt numb. An image came into his head of a distraught woman he'd seen during the blitz, who had wailed uncontrollably as the firemen had brought a body out of a bombed-out house. He wondered how it would feel to be able to release his sorrow like that.

# AUGUST 1951

TED'S SERVICE WAS due to end in August. He had been considering staying on for longer but his father's death changed things and he decided that he would leave at the end of August after all, return to Hammersmith and go back to the printing works. The idea had always been that Ted would take over the business. Joe was struggling on his own and Ted felt an obligation to help him, and he was ready for a change.

A few weeks before his leaving date, he bumped into Frank Bassett. 'So, you're going back to Civvy Street,' said Frank.

'Yes.'

'And I've taken a posting in Cyprus. Did you know?' He hadn't known. 'It's worked out well, what with Geoff going to St Christopher's and all. The wife's looking forward to sunnier climes too. Geoff will be able to come out to us in the holidays. Ooh, that's a thought. You've done such a lot for us already I don't like to ask, but is there any chance you could do one more favour?'

'What?'

'Seems they have something halfway through the term, an "exit" I think they called it, where parents are expected to take their boys out for the day. It's a Saturday near the end of October. Thing is, we won't be here then, and as you know Geoff, and I think you're fond of the boy, maybe you could take him out on our behalf. Of course I understand if you can't do it. I suppose Geoff would just have to stay in on his own. Wouldn't kill him.'

'No, that's all right. I'm sure I could do that. Just let me have all the details.'

'And if the school need to contact anyone about Geoff while we're away, could I give them your name? Just for emergencies of course.'

'I suppose so.' Ted gave Frank his Hammersmith address and phone number.

The following week Ted received a letter from Frank with the details of the *exeat*. It also contained a typewritten page:

> *To whom it may concern. I, Frank Bassett and I Sheila Bassett as parents of Geoffrey Bassett appoint Edward Cunningham of 36, Mayhew St., Hammersmith, London to act In Loco Parentis for aforesaid Geoffrey Bassett while we are unable to do so through military duties, overseas posting, etc.*

It was signed by Frank and Sheila. In pencil at the bottom Frank had added: '*Have also sent copy to school.*'

*In loco parentis?* Was this really what he had agreed to? Frank Bassett, true to form, but what could he do? The thought of seeking out Frank and getting him to withdraw this document seemed more trouble than it was worth.

IT FELT STRANGE leaving the RAF station for the last time and even stranger entering the empty house in Hammersmith. Barbara and Ted had sorted out their father's personal belongings after the funeral. Most of his clothes had gone to an East End mission, quite a lot of stuff had been thrown out and memorabilia and other items, thought too good to throw out, had been put into packing crates and stored up in the attic. Goodness knows who or what they were storing them for. But as he came through the door, the house still smelt of his father, and his mother, and his own childhood.

He had decided that he would move into his father's bedroom. It seemed silly to go back to his own old room, with the model boat and the kite. He couldn't bring himself to sleep in the bed in which he had seen his father die so he had extravagantly bought a new one. To avoid it seeming as though it was someone else's room that he was sleeping in, he had also had the room redecorated and changed the pictures and some of the other furniture. He wanted this to be his own, new room. In due course he intended to set about changing the rest of the house, but this would have to be a gradual process.

As well as the oddness of returning to the stale familiarity of the house he would need to get used to living on his own. In the RAF he had had his own quarters but he ate most of his meals in the mess and was used to the company of the other men. In Hammersmith his daytimes were now spent at the printing works, which was busy and sociable. It was always a pleasure to spend time with Joe Peavey and there were other old hands whom he knew from his days working there before the war. There were also new employees he needed to get to know and a constant stream of customers and sales reps to meet. But in the evenings and at the weekend he was on his own in the house. He wasn't exactly lonely – he was happy enough in his own company – but it was quieter than he was used to. He would look around for a choir to join.

# SEPTEMBER 1951

GEOFF'S PARENTS DROPPED him off at the choir school as quickly as possible while the taxi waited outside with ticking meter. Sheila gave him a peck on the cheek and Frank's last words were, 'You'd better behave yourself,' with wagging finger for emphasis. Then he was by himself in the entrance hall watching other boys being hugged and cosetted by tearful mothers and stoical fathers.

Geoff learnt that he was a member of Junior House with about forty other boys aged between seven and eleven who slept in three upstairs dormitories. During the day they were joined for lessons by another forty or fifty day boys. Geoff was one of twelve new boarders to join the school that September. One had an older brother at the school so was able to impart a certain amount of information to the rest, but otherwise they had to learn what was expected of them by some mysterious process of osmosis. Transgressions of this unwritten code were dealt with either by a sharp kick in the shins by a more knowing boy, or by a master pinching their ears or giving them lines such as, *'I must remember to bring my geometry set to all mathematics lessons without fail'* to be written out twenty times.

It seemed that most of the boys had already attended other preparatory or dame schools before coming to St Christopher's. As Geoff had only attended local primary schools this immediately put him at a disadvantage. Much of the prevailing language, customs and procedures meant little to him – it was if he were a visiting foreigner. Up to now, Geoff had only ever written in pencil, at St Christopher's he was presented with a wooden pen with metal nib which had to be dipped into a porcelain inkwell recessed into a slot at the top of the desk. At his first attempt, he glanced around at the other boys and tried to copy them but only succeeded in spattering ink over his exercise book to the amusement of the other boys and irritation of the master. At mealtimes, rather than queuing up at a hatch, a plate of meat (or whatever the dish was) was served to each boy who then had to help himself to vegetables from bowls on the table. If you were too slow – which usually Geoff was – by the time the bowls got to you they were empty. Perhaps the most important thing at which he completely failed was the ritual of the Tuck Box. Favours, friendships, influence, protection could all be gained through judicious dispensing of the contents of a well-stocked tuck box. No doubt future successful careers in the City or the Diplomatic Service were built on the skills learned, but as Geoff had no tuck box and its significance was a mystery to him, he was condemned as forever an outsider and victimhood was his lot.

His chief tormentor was Macdonald, one of the older and larger boys in his class. Cocky and self-confident, Macdonald was bolstered in his role by a couple of sidekicks, whose fawning support – 'Give it to him Mac, the little squirt' – was their chief protection against being victims themselves.

Each day exposed Geoff to another degradation, another trap to fall into, another opportunity for punishment to be meted out by fellow-pupil or master. The staff were not all bad, but some of the weaker teachers especially, could not resist the temptation to make fun of his errors as an easy way to gain favour in a boisterous classroom.

He coped with all this by climbing into a shell of blankness. His face was expressionless, he uttered few words and never tried to defend himself. Whether the abuse was verbal or physical, he seemed to accept it as his lot in life, as if this was all he had any right to expect. It wasn't so different to life at home after all. After lights out, the darkness would overwhelm him with a feeling of utter emptiness. What was the point? Nobody liked him. Nobody wanted him. And he would sob into his pillow with the bedclothes over his head so that he wouldn't be heard, though often this didn't work and a pillow would be rammed down onto his head and 'Shut up, Bassett, or you're for it,' would be loudly whispered.

On his third morning he woke up to find that his pyjama trousers and sheets were damp. He tried to conceal what had happened but the boy in the next-door bed – one of Macdonald's stooges – noticed the smell of urine and saw Geoff's look of shame and terror. 'Bassett's wet the bed, Bassett's wet the bed,' and the chant echoed round the dormitory until matron came in. Quickly everyone resumed their dressing and bedmaking and she came over to Geoff's bed.

'Strip the bed and follow me.'

He waited outside the laundry cupboard and she gave him clean bed linen and a maroon rubber sheet. 'You'd better leave the mattress to air and then make your bed tonight with this underneath the bottom sheet. Try not to do it again.' Dazed that he wasn't to be punished, he went back into the dormitory. Knowing that matron was still outside, the other boys desisted from more chanting, but he was acutely aware of their smirking and contempt, and the hopelessness of his cause.

Amongst all this misery there was just one single ray of light, one solitary sanctuary providing an escape from the other degradations: choir.

The boys who had been at the school during the previous year were already singing in the chapel. Geoff, with the other new boys, was in a separate practice choir, which, wonderfully, was spared the malign presence of Macdonald. Two other factors also contributed to choir practice being different from all other activities. One was the fact that Geoff was good at it, the other was Mr Doughty.

Mr Doughty was different from the other masters. It was obvious that he loved what he did and he had a way of communicating his enthusiasm to the boys. He also seemed to understand how to get the best out of them without shouting or throwing chalk at them or pulling their ears or giving them detentions or beating them.

Geoff already knew the rudiments of reading music from the lessons he'd had for the audition. This, along with his excellent sense of pitch and time, meant that he was quick to pick up and remember a tune. He was clearly one of Mr Doughty's favourites and three weeks into the term the master asked him to stay on after one of their lessons.

'Bassett, I have an idea to put some treble solos into the carol service. It would need some individual lessons after normal school. As the best boy in the class I'm offering you first choice. Would you like to have a go?'

This was the first time any teacher had offered Geoff anything amounting to praise or encouragement. He was taken by surprise but managed to stammer out a 'yes, sir'.

'Good man. What about half past four this afternoon?'

Geoff nodded his assent.

As a single man, and junior choirmaster, Mr Doughty lived in the school in a set of rooms in the opposite wing to where the boys' dormitories were located. Geoff knocked tentatively at the dark polished door. 'Come,' shouted a muffled voice. 'Ah, Bassett, excellent.'

He entered a large sitting room, certainly large compared to the sitting room in the Bassett's RAF house. Instead of lino or worn carpet on the floor there were rugs with diamond patterns on them in red and black, the walls were crowded with paintings, there were shelves lined with books, a fire burning in the marble fireplace, velvet armchairs and sofa, little tables stacked with musical scores – the entire room exuded an atmosphere of warmth and comfort. He spotted Mr Doughty sitting at a small grand piano inside a velvet-curtained bay window. 'Over here, Bassett. I've just been fishing through some things that we could try out.' He handed Geoff some music, played an introduction on the piano and nodded him in. He sang diffidently at first, but then with increasing confidence as he caught the gist of the tune. 'Not bad for a first effort, well done, not bad at all.' They then worked on the piece in detail with Mr Doughty generous in his praise and encouragement.

'Good, very good. That will do for today. Shall we carry on this Thursday?'

He nodded.

'Excellent. Tell me Bassett, how are you getting on here? I've heard you've had some trouble settling in.'

'It's all right sir.'

'What about Macdonald? Has a tendency to be rather over-assertive I think. Hasn't been troubling you, has he?'

'No, sir.'

'Silly question anyway. You don't strike me as a sneak. You're not a sneak are you, Bassett?'

'No sir.'

'Good man. See you at practice tomorrow.'

# OCTOBER 1951

TWICE A WEEK Geoff went for his lessons with Mr Doughty. This did not go unnoticed by the other boys, generating further taunts, slaps and kicks. But Geoff didn't mind. Mr Doughty was his one friend and his private lesson was his haven.

The last lesson before the half-term *exeat* was to be a special one, Mr Doughty said. Rather than having tea with the other boys, the two of them would have their own tea in Mr Doughty's room to celebrate the good work Geoff had done. When he arrived he saw Mr Doughty through one of the three doors that led off from the sitting room. It was a tiny kitchen, with a sink and two gas rings. Mr Doughty was humming to himself as he stirred a large mixing bowl. 'Ah, Bassett, ready for tea?'

'Yes, sir.'

Geoff watched as Mr Doughty poured some of the mixture from the bowl into a frying pan on one of the gas rings. There was a sizzling noise and the smell of warm milk and hot butter. 'Pancakes. Hope you like them. Why not come in here and have a go? Watch me.' He flipped the pan and then caught the pancake. When it was done, he placed it on a plate which he then covered with a second upside-down plate to keep it warm. 'Now you try.' Mr Doughty helped him with the bowl and more mixture was poured into the pan. Geoff held the pan and Mr Doughty guided his hands so that the mixture evenly coated the base. As it began to dry out he teased a metal palette knife around the edge of the pancake so that it swished freely in the pan. 'Now, toss it like I did.' Mr Doughty stood behind him and held his forearms and together they flipped the pan. To Geoff's surprise the pancake landed neatly on its reverse. 'Bravo!' cried Mr Doughty and a feeling of pleasure coursed down Geoff's back. Two more pancakes were made and then they sat down at a small table in the corner of the sitting room and ate them, spread with jam, along with cups of tea. Geoff felt as happy as at any time he could remember.

'Now, just enough time for a little work.' Mr Doughty got up and went to the piano. There was room for two on the long piano stool and Mr Doughty patted the space next to him. 'Sit here, next to me Bassett. I'll put your music next to mine.'

When Geoff started singing, Mr Doughty continued playing just the left-hand piano part and put his right arm around Geoff's shoulder. It felt funny but he carried on singing. Then Mr Doughty began to stroke Geoff's side and then moved his hand to Geoff's knee which was just visible at the mouth of his voluminous shorts. Mr Doughty began to stroke Geoff's knee in time to the music. Geoff had never been touched like this before, not by his parents, not by anyone. But Mr Doughty was also different to anyone else he knew, so perhaps this was just another one of Mr Doughty's differences. Then Mr Doughty actually put his hand up the leg of Geoff's shorts. He stopped singing. 'No, carry on singing, Bassett, don't stop, and when you get to the end, do a repeat.' Now Mr Doughty's hand had crept through the bottom of his baggy underpants and began to touch his balls and willy. Geoff's voice squeaked with surprise. 'Did you like that, Bassett?'

Geoff had no idea what he was supposed to say. Mr Doughty was his friend. Was this just his way of being friendly? 'I don't know, sir.' Then Mr Doughty took Geoff's hand and began to rub it over the top of his tweed trousers, whilst with his other hand he unbuttoned his flies. Geoff saw the end of Mr Doughty's shirt sticking out of the fly opening like the corner of a handkerchief. Now Mr Doughty poked Geoff's hand through the flies and moved it up and down over his pants. Geoff felt something hard through the cotton material like a fat finger or a sausage. What was it? How could it be his willy? Willies weren't like that. He didn't understand. Mr Doughty started rubbing more vigorously and began to make short quiet moaning noises from the back of his throat, then Geoff felt the sausage jerk and the pants felt wet. Surely Mr Doughty hadn't done a wee in his pants? He didn't like this; a distant childhood memory came into his head: his father had found him with his hand down his shorts, he was holding his willy inside his pants, his father had pulled out his hand roughly and then smacked him on his cheek, hard.

'Dirty boy. Never do that again,' he had said. And now Mr Doughty was making him do the same thing. He didn't understand.

Mr Doughty got up and went through one of the other doors, evidently through to a bedroom. He came out a few minutes later looking calm and composed. 'Now Bassett. You and I are good friends, aren't we?'

'Yes, sir.'

'And you enjoyed the pancakes and the tea, didn't you?'

'Yes, sir.'

'And you like your singing lessons with me, don't you?'

'Yes, sir.'

'You wouldn't like them to stop, would you?'

'No, sir.'

'You see, what happened just now is something that good friends do, but it's also a sort of special secret thing, a secret just between you and me. Do you understand?'

'I don't know.'

'What don't you know?' and this was said with just a hint of irritation.

'So, it's a secret that I mustn't tell anyone else.'

'That's right. Good boy. It's a secret that we need to keep in order to carry on being friends. You want us to carry on being friends, don't you?'

'Yes.'

'So you will promise to keep our little secret, won't you? Otherwise we certainly couldn't be friends any longer and in fact, it would also get you into a great deal of very serious trouble if you told anyone our secret. Do you promise?'

'Yes, sir. Can I go now?'

'Of course you can, Bassett. See you at practice tomorrow. Remember your promise.'

'Yes, sir.'

THERE WAS A crowd of parents milling around the front door of the school when Ted arrived and he felt awkward both for being on his own, and – although the others would not have realised this – for not being Geoff's father. The door opened and a stream of boys bounced out ready to be hugged and kissed by their parents. Geoff was at the back looking worried until he saw Ted, whose tall frame was visible above the other heads.

'Oh Sergeant Cunningham, I wasn't sure if you were coming. My dad said you would but I wasn't sure. Maybe you'd forget.'

'Well, here I am, Geoff. How are you?'

'All right.'

'You don't sound too sure. I thought we could go out for a spin in the MG and then you can tell me all about it. How does that sound?'

'I'd like that.'

They started walking to the car. 'By the way, Geoff, now that I've left the RAF I'm not Sergeant Cunningham anymore, so it's Mr Cunningham.'

'Oh. All right, Mr Cunningham.'

In the car, Ted handed him a road map. 'As it's quite a nice day, I thought we could go to Ely. There's a big old cathedral there I've always wanted to visit. Can you map read?'

'I don't know, I've never done it.'

Ted showed him the route they would be following and explained the rudiments of the map. He already had a pretty good idea of where to go but thought it would be nice for Geoff to have something to do. With great concentration, Geoff looked out for the relevant signposts and guided him on to the right road.

There were only a few other tourists looking around the cathedral and as they gazed up at the roof they almost bumped into an elderly gentlemen who was showing around two young women. 'I'm just taking my young nieces from America on a tour. I'd be more than happy for you to join us.' Ted and Geoff gratefully tagged along. Evidently their guide had a long connection with the cathedral and explained various architectural and decorative features, leavened by a series of personal anecdotes.

After their tour, Ted found a tearoom. They sat in a corner and Ted ordered some sandwiches and some pop for Geoff.

'So, tell me all about school.'

'How do you mean, Mr Cunningham?'

'Well, why not tell me about your normal day? Getting up, breakfast, lessons, that sort of thing.'

Without much enthusiasm Geoff described his daily routine. From his factual description he gave few clues as to whether he was happy there or not.

'And what about the other boys? Have you made any friends?'

'They're all right I suppose. I don't know anyone very well yet.'

'And the masters?'

'Some of them get a bit cross if I do things wrong, except Mr Doughty, he's nice to me.'

'Really? Tell me about Mr Doughty.'

Geoff told Ted about the extra lessons. 'He says I've the best voice in the form, that's why I'm his favourite. At the last lesson we made pancakes and had them for tea, and then…' Geoff stopped.

'What?'

'Oh, em, nothing.'

There was something about Geoff's sudden mid-sentence stop that caught him. Ted had been a choirboy himself – just in his local church – that was what had started his interest in music. His first choirmaster had been perfectly nice but had then stopped because of illness and a temporary replacement had filled in for a few months. This was Mr Brewster, undoubtedly a fine musician, but all the boys thought that there was something odd about the way he would put his arm around them and tickle them under their shoulders. Ted had mentioned this to his mother and she had told him to stay away from Mr Brewster and never to be alone with him although she didn't explain why. And then Mr Brewster suddenly left. One of the other boys said that it was because he had been caught 'interfering' with a boy at a school where he gave singing lessons and had had to leave London. In adulthood, Ted had also noticed the stories in the more sensational press about choirmasters and schoolmasters molesting young boys and had even heard the odd snigger in the sergeants' mess when it was mentioned that he – a single man – was starting a choir. Perhaps this accounted for his heightened sensitivity.

Ted breathed in and out slowly and then asked, 'Did something happen between you and Mr Doughty?'

There was a brief pause before Geoff said 'No.'

'Now Geoff, you must tell me the truth. Or,' and now Ted weighed his words carefully, 'did Mr Doughty tell you that you mustn't say anything or you'd get into trouble?'

Geoff nodded slowly. 'I promised him.'

Ted paused. 'I know that breaking promises is wrong, but sometimes it can be less wrong to break a promise than not to. Let's say you saw a boy at school stealing something, and perhaps because you were scared of him you promised that you wouldn't say anything. But in that case, the stealing would be a worse thing than breaking the promise, so it would be right to tell someone about the stealing, wouldn't it?'

'I suppose so.'

'So perhaps Mr Doughty did something wrong, something that he shouldn't have done, and then made you promise not to tell, but it would be all right to tell because the wrong thing was worse than breaking the promise. Do you understand what I'm trying to say?'

Geoff nodded.

'Will you tell me then?'

'I'm scared.'

Ted paused for thought again. 'I know you're scared. Often doing the right thing is scarier and more difficult than doing nothing. I can't make you tell me. But if Mr Doughty hasn't done anything wrong then it won't matter anyway. And if he has done something wrong then you know it is the right thing to tell me, or at least someone, about it.'

Geoff told him what had happened. 'Was it a wrong thing that he did?'

Ted rubbed his hand across his mouth and breathed deeply. 'Yes, it was a wrong thing. You see, your private parts are called private because that's what they are, and apart from a doctor, it's not right for other people to touch them. It's a bit hard to explain because you're only young.'

'I thought it might have been wrong. Mr Doughty looked as though he knew he'd done something wrong. Are you going to have to tell on him?'

At that point the waitress brought their sandwiches. 'Let's have our lunch and I'll think about it,' said Ted. They ate in silence.

After lunch they walked back and when they were in the car Ted said that he would have to talk to the headmaster about Mr Doughty.

'I'm going to get into trouble, aren't I?' and Geoff began to sob quietly.

Ted patted him on the back. 'Don't worry old chap. I'm sure it won't be as bad as all that.' Geoff's little shoulders shook in spasms. 'Everything will work out for the best. I promise you. And that's a real promise.'

By the time they got back to St Christopher's, Geoff had stopped sobbing. He now simply looked red-eyed and miserable. 'Why don't you stay in the car and I'll go in,' said Ted.

It was mid-afternoon and everything seemed quiet. Ted tried the 'Office' but there was no response, so he then knocked at the headmaster's door, which he remembered from Geoff's interview.

'Come in!'

Mr Cowdray was behind his desk going through some correspondence and looked annoyed at the interruption. 'Yes, what do you want?'

'I need to talk to you about Geoffrey Bassett.'

'The *exeat* is until six. Can't it wait?' The headmaster looked up at Ted and began vaguely to recall their last meeting. 'RAF, isn't it? You taught the boy for his audition. Oh yes, and there was something from his father about *in loco parentis* if I remember correctly.'

'Yes, that's right.'

'Well?'

'Can I sit down?'

'Oh yes, I apologise. It's just that this is supposed to be a boy-free day and I was trying to get on with other things. But if it's important, by all means, sit down,' and he nodded to a chair facing him on the other side of the desk.

'It's about Mr Doughty.'

'Oh yes?'

Ted took a deep breath. 'Geoffrey told me that Mr Doughty had been giving him extra lessons, something about teaching him some solos. It seems that Geoffrey was visiting him alone in his rooms.'

'Well, what of it? Mr Doughty believes that the boy has quite a lot of potential but needs help having missed out, shall I say, on some of the advantages enjoyed by the other boys.'

'At his last lesson – just last Thursday – Geoffrey has told me that Mr Doughty… interfered with him.'

'Interfered with him? What do you mean by that?'

'Mr Doughty fiddled with his private parts and then made Geoffrey reciprocate – touch Mr Doughty, that is.'

'This is an extremely serious allegation, Mr, er…'

'Cunningham.'

'Mr Cunningham. But I find it extremely hard to believe. In fact, impossible to believe. Mr Doughty is a highly experienced and respected member of our staff. He has been here for many years and came to us with the highest references.'

'That's as maybe, but I am only telling you what Geoffrey has told me.'

'Well, that's the point, Mr Cunningham. This is only what the boy has told you and I am far more inclined to trust my own knowledge of Mr Doughty than your boy's completely uncorroborated allegations. Please wait a moment.' Mr Cowdray picked up the phone on his desk. 'Ah, Andrew, I'm so pleased you're there. Sorry to break into your *exeat* but could you possibly pop over to my study for a few minutes?... Yes, right now if you could.'

Mr Doughty was there in less than a minute. 'What's up, headmaster?'

'This is Mr Cunningham. He has responsibility for young Bassett.'

'Oh yes,' said Mr Doughty nonchalantly turning towards Ted, 'very fine voice, Bassett, great potential. I've actually been giving him some extra lessons to get him up to scratch.'

'I'm extremely sorry to broach this subject, but Mr Cunningham has some ridiculous story from the boy that you have been... molesting him in some way. Sexually molesting him.'

Mr Doughty looked completely taken aback. 'Molesting him, Headmaster? I don't know what to say, I'm lost for words. I have been trying to help the boy – giving up my own free time – and he has repaid me with this gross and disgusting allegation. Oh dear, oh dear. One does one's best, but these boys from...' he searched for the appropriate words, 'the lower orders simply cannot be trusted.'

'Well, Mr Cunningham,' said the headmaster, 'you have your answer. The boy has fabricated a malign accusation against Mr Doughty – goodness knows what his motives might have been – but I can assure you that it is groundless.'

'With respect, Mr Cowdray, all we have is a denial from Mr Doughty. Are you going to dismiss Geoffrey's allegations just like that? He gave quite a number of details which really are beyond his experience and imagination to make up. He's eight years old. He's an innocent boy. How on earth would he even know about such things?'

'Mr Cunningham,' asked the headmaster, 'do you have much experience of boys yourself?'

'No, I don't.'

'So young Bassett is the only boy you have had much in the way of dealings with?'

'Yes.'

'For all we know, you might be the one who has been "interfering" with the boy and given him these ideas which you say are so beyond his imagination. For all we know you may even have put the boy up to this.'

'That's an outrageous suggestion.'

'No less outrageous than the allegations you have made against Mr Doughty. And, as Mr Doughty is a man I know well and trust and in whom I have great confidence, I have no hesitation in believing him above you and young Bassett. Of course, I'm not for a moment genuinely suggesting that you have molested him, but I am just attempting to show you how flimsy the boy's allegations are. The point is, that you don't know boys, and I do. I have spent all my professional life in their close proximity and I think that I am pretty well-qualified to judge of what they are capable. And I can tell you, Mr Cunningham, that fabrications of this kind are well within the imagination of most of them, including Bassett. And, unfortunately, I am inclined to agree with Mr Doughty that allowing Bassett to come here, despite his undoubted musical abilities, was a mistake. I should have realised that he would be out of his depth and that, in one way or another, he was bound to come a cropper.'

'So there is nothing you are going to do about this.'

'Exactly right, Mr Cunningham. What were you thinking of? That I notify the police and that Bassett should repeat these gross calumnies to them and that the school's reputation be dragged through the mire, only to have Bassett's allegations – if it should come to that – laughed out of court under even the most incompetent cross-examination? Is that what you really expected?'

Ted could see that he was beaten. He completely and utterly believed Geoff, but the headmaster was right. It would be the word of a timid eight-year-old boy against the weight and reputation of St Christopher's College Choir School. It was a hopeless case.

Mr Cowdray observed Ted's silence. 'Well Mr Cunningham, it seems that you have at last seen sense. And now we must decide what to do. Luckily the school is empty now, so this can all be done without any fuss or attention. Bassett must collect his things and leave right away. I will tell the other boys and staff that he became ill and then we shall say no more of this. And Cunningham, if these lies are repeated by the boy, or you, to anyone at all, you will find yourself at the sharp end of a very unpleasant suit for slander. I will give you ten minutes to get the boy to clear his locker and there's an end of it.' He exchanged glances with Mr Doughty and then motioned Ted to the door.

'WHAT'S GOING TO happen?' asked Geoff, when they were in the car and driving back to Hammersmith. 'I knew I'd cop it. My dad's going to kill me,' and he began to sob again.

'Now Geoff, I promised you that it would work out for the best and I meant it. You did the right thing to tell me about Mr Doughty, and after you told me, I couldn't possibly have left you at St Christopher's knowing that he was still there and doing those sorts of things to you. Your dad said I was *in loco parentis* which is Latin for being in a parent's place, so I have to act as if I were your father. No father I know could have left you at that school and said nothing. I had to do what I did. But don't worry, whatever happens, I'll make sure it's all right for you.'

They sat in silence for the rest of the journey, preoccupied with the repercussions, both of them wondering whether it really would have been so bad if he'd stayed at the school, both of them conjuring up in their minds startlingly similar pictures of Frank's reaction to the news ('I warned him to behave himself. What's wrong with that boy?' Sheila impassive), both of them thinking: and what now?

Ted found it hard to suppress the voice in his head asking why had he got involved in the first place and what had he got himself into now. Then he looked at Geoff – small, alone. A stronger voice told him that it had been the right thing to do.

Geoff had no more tears left for the moment and instead had given way to his usual numb resignation. Whoever told him what to do – his father, Mr Doughty, the bully Macdonald, Mr Cunningham – he always copped it.

It was dusk when they arrived at Ted's house. As they went through the front door Ted thought how gloomy the house seemed and hoped this wouldn't upset Geoff, but on the contrary, he was rather impressed, having only ever been inside RAF houses. They sat at the kitchen table with its scrubbed pine top. Ted looked around the room: the gas stove that had replaced the coal range when he was a boy, and the butler's sink with the hot water geyser above, which had saved Ted's mother from having to fill up kettles from the tap in the scullery. It had seemed rather modern at the time, but now Ted was aware of how dated it looked.

Ted told Geoff the plan that he had formulated during the journey. 'First thing is I'll have to write to your parents and explain what's happened. I'll find out from them how we go about getting you over to Cyprus. In the meantime, you'll stay here. When we know how long it's going to take we might have to look for a school place for you somewhere around here, just till you can go back to your parents.'

'My dad's going to kill me.'

'You said that before but I know it's not true. None of this was your fault. You didn't do anything wrong, and telling me about Mr Doughty was the right thing to do. I couldn't leave you at St Christopher's with all that going on. Your father will understand – of course he will. He'll see that it wasn't your fault. The only people he'll be angry with are St Christopher's and Mr Doughty.'

'You don't know my dad. Whenever anything happens I get the blame and he gives me one. He'll never believe me, about Mr Doughty and that. He'll be like the headmaster and say I made it up. This is the worst thing that's ever happened.' His lower lip began to quiver. 'I'm scared.' And now he found his tears again.

Ted didn't know what to do. Should he put his arm around him? With the memory still fresh of what Geoff had told him had happened with Mr Doughty, he thought not. He knelt down on the floor next to Geoff's chair so that their eyes were level. 'I know things might look bad now, old chap, but we've got to get through it and then things will be better, I promise. Like in the war. Sometimes it was very, very bad. But it was all right in the end.'

Geoff said nothing.

They went up to Ted's old bedroom and he started making up the bed. 'Er, Mr Cunningham?'

'Yes, Geoff?'

'Em, sometimes I wet the bed.'

'Oh, let me think. Oh yes, let's just put a couple of towels on top of the mattress then, just in case. It happened to me a bit when I was your age and that's what we used to do. Soon grew out of it.'

There was a pile of old motor magazines in the corner – *The Motor* and *Motor Sport* – which Ted suggested he might like to look at. Both of them were happy for the distraction and Ted left him leafing through them on the floor, whilst he went down to write to Frank Cunningham. When he'd finished, he rang his sister and recounted what had happened.

'Ted, how will you look after him in the meantime? Given what's happened, I don't think it's a good idea for him to be living alone with you. Anyway, what will you do about cooking and that sort of thing? I worry about you anyway, on your own, but with this boy it's a different matter. And what about when you're at work?'

'I know. That's why I've phoned you. I think maybe I should get a maid or a housekeeper or nanny or something – just for a week or two whilst things are being sorted out – but I don't know where to start.'

Barbara agreed that would be a good idea and suggested he try advertising in *The Lady* or going to a domestic agency – there used to be one in King Street, maybe it was still there.

Ted went up to check that Geoff was all right. He was in bed now, still reading a magazine. 'What about if I read you something, to help you get to sleep?'

'A magazine?'

'No, a story.' Ted looked at his boyhood bookshelf with its collection of diverse volumes from comic annuals to school textbooks. He took out *The Wind in The Willows*. 'What about this?' Geoff looked at him blankly. 'Well, let's start and see if you like it.' He started reading, and for a few minutes Geoff looked completely transported to the river bank with the Mole and the Water Rat, and then he was asleep.

THE NEXT DAY was Sunday and Ted knew that he must keep the boy occupied and divert him from thinking about yesterday's events. He'd been to The Festival of Britain a few weeks ago – that would be ideal. He found his programme and then saw that it had shut at the end of the previous month. He glanced through the paper. Even better, the Motor Show was on at Earl's Court. He thought he would make it a surprise for Geoff so he didn't tell him where they were going. The tube journey alone seemed exciting enough for Geoff, but when they arrived at the exhibition he was transfixed. 'Wow, Mr Cunningham, look at that…' greeted his arrival at every stand. Both Ted and the exhibitors were surprised at the intelligence of the questions the small boy asked.

In the evening, Ted went up again to read him more of *The Wind in The Willows*. 'Mr Cunningham…'

'Yes, Geoff?'

'Thank you for taking me to the Motor Show. It was smashing.'

'I'm glad you liked it. I enjoyed it too.'

TED HAD NO alternative but to take Geoff into work with him on Monday. The printing works was less than a ten-minute walk away and some presses were already running when they arrived, filling the air with their clack-clacking. Ted explained that Geoff was a friend's son whom he was looking after for a few days because 'something had come up' and this seemed to satisfy Joe Peavey and the other men. Geoff had brought his Motor Show catalogue with him and Ted suggested that he sit in the office – a partitioned area at one end of the building – and read, but to Ted's surprise Geoff asked if he could look around the works and watch the machines. Joe offered to take him around, introducing him to the machine minders and explaining what each of them was doing and this gave Ted the chance to pop round to King Street to look for the domestic staff agency.

Sure enough, it was still there as Barbara had remembered, over a bakery. Ted climbed the narrow stairs and found himself in a small waiting room. He went up to the window in the timber partition through which he could see a wooden card-index filing cabinet and a middle-aged woman sitting at a desk. She came up to the window. 'Can I help you, sir?'

He told the same story about looking after an eight-year old boy for a few days on behalf of a friend. It had all happened rather suddenly and he needed someone to help look after the boy and perform various domestic tasks. He had feared that the woman would start asking more questions, but she seemed to accept what he had said at face value. 'Do you know how long you would need her?' she asked.

'I don't know. Shouldn't be more than two or three weeks I think. Maybe less.'

'Most of my people are looking for longer engagements.' The woman paused, sucking in her lips. 'There is someone, but the trouble is she doesn't have any references.' She explained that a young Irishwoman had come in that morning who was urgently looking for work. She had said that she had helped bring up her younger brothers and sister and knew all about looking after children as well as cooking, cleaning, laundry and so on. 'But you see, she hasn't actually worked as a domestic before, this would be her first job and so she has no references. You'd be taking a risk.'

Ted felt out of his depth and wished he had asked Barbara to come with him. 'What would you suggest?'

'Well, as you only need someone for a short time, she might be worth a try. Would you like to interview her?'

The girl had said she would be coming back to the agency later that afternoon to see if anything had come in. The woman at the agency had told her that she would probably be wasting her time but the girl had seemed desperate to find something. It was arranged that she would ask her to go straight to Ted's house for an interview at five.

A PETITE, MOUSEY-HAIRED young woman stood at the door, nervously holding her fingertips. 'I'm Mary Devine. The agency sent me. Are you Mr Cunningham?'

Ted introduced her to Geoff and then took her into the sitting room for a private chat. He explained that he needed some help looking after Geoff but didn't know for exactly how long.

'I've four younger brothers myself, so I know all about boys. Sure it would be no trouble to look after him. He looks like a quiet one anyway. Will he not be at school during the day?'

'He should be going back to his parents in a few days. They're abroad. I'm just waiting for them to say when he can go over to them.' It seemed enough to satisfy her.

'They told you at the agency that I have no references.'

'This would be your first job?'

'In England, yes, it would be, Mr Cunningham. I promise that you won't regret it if you give me a chance. I'm a good worker.'

Mary paused. 'You see, I decided to come over to England to make a fresh start. There's not much work in Ireland and it's very quiet. I wanted to see a bit more of the world, if you know what I mean, and I have to start somewhere.'

Ted could hear his sister saying to him: 'Your trouble, Ted, is that you always want to see the best in people and that's why they take advantage of you,' but there was something about Mary which made him trust her, a mixture of vulnerability and pluckiness.

'Well, I'm happy to give it a try if you are.'

'Oh bless you, Mr Cunningham. You won't be sorry. I promise.'

NOTHING COULD HAPPEN until Ted had received a reply from Frank Bassett, so for the next ten days everything seemed to be in a state of limbo. Being the week of the general election added to the atmosphere of uncertainty. Mary had started work the day after her interview and had moved into the room at the top of the house. Without any fuss, she just seemed to take over: shopping, cooking, cleaning – everything. She also struck up a rapport with Geoff, and Ted would be amazed to come home from work to hear them both laughing over some game – cards or snakes and ladders or even, once, hide-and-seek. To fill the days, Mary would get Geoff to help her with the cooking and do some of the household chores. 'It's not that I'm trying to get him to do my work, Mr Cunningham, but every boy needs to learn how to look after himself and also the devil makes work for idle hands, don't they say, so we have to keep him busy, don't we?'

In the evenings Ted was also giving Geoff some piano lessons. It had been Geoff's idea. Ted liked to play every day, even if it was only for ten minutes, and Geoff would sit and listen. Ted hadn't wanted to suggest that Geoff do some singing, which might hold unwelcome memories for the boy, but when he'd asked if he could have a go at the piano, Ted had said that he would be happy to show him what to do. He found some of his old piano tutors and got a high stool so that Geoff would be at the right height to play the Challen upright in the front room. At first the array of white and black keys seemed bewildering but Ted showed him which was middle C and for future reference Geoff saw that this lined up with the middle of the lock mechanism for securing the piano lid. Then Ted pointed out which notes on the keyboard corresponded to the marks on the musical stave. As he could already read music, he was quick to pick it up and needed little encouragement to practise during the day and then show off to Ted in the evening what he had learned.

AT LAST, FRANK's letter arrived in the morning post

> *Dear Ted,*
> *Thank you for your letter but I must say that I was very concerned to hear of this turn of events. I find it hard to believe what you have told me about St Christopher's. You told me that the headmaster did not believe Geoff's story and in all likelihood I think he was right. I'm sorry to say that there have been quite a lot of occasions when the boy has lied to me over the years and generally I don't think he is very truthful. It is a great shame that you took the boy's word for it and then had to talk to the headmaster. It would have been much better if you had written to me first before taking such drastic action. Still, I am not blaming you, Ted, because you weren't to know that Geoff was probably lying and I expect you thought what you were doing was for the best.*
> *However, I do think that what has happened is very much of your making and that you must take responsibility for the consequences. At the moment it is impossible for me and Sheila to have Geoff with us in Cyprus. From what I understand, there would be no school place here for Geoff until next September so there is nothing for it but for you to have the boy stay*

*in your care until then. I am sure it will be easy for
you to find a school for him in London and as before I
leave you in sole charge In Loco Parentis.*
  *Yours truly,*
  *Frank Bassett*

Ted read through the letter three times and then sat quietly
to absorb its contents. Different emotions competed: disbelief,
outrage, self-doubt, fear of the future, guilt, regret. He decided
it would be best to wait until the evening to let it sink in. When
he was back from work he rang Barbara.

'Surely that can't be right, Ted? The boy's not your
responsibility; they can't simply land him on you.'

'Well, they have.'

'But what about the authorities? Shouldn't they be the people
to take him? Make the parents have him back or put him in a
children's home or something?'

'Possibly. I suppose I could make enquiries.'

'I really think you should.'

'The thing is, I do feel some responsibility for him. After all,
it was me who took him away from the school.'

'Well if the boy was telling the truth…'

'I was never surer. If you'd seen the way the headmaster and
the other master had reacted. It was so harsh and so one-sided.
There was something going on there, I know there was. I could
hardly have left him there.'

'All right, I agree you had to take him away. But you were
doing his parents a favour, it's outrageous that they should
blame you and then, quite literally, leave you holding the baby.
What a nightmare. It's just like you, Ted, to get yourself taken
advantage of.'

Dazed, Ted went into the sitting room where Geoff had just
started practising the piano and Mary was putting away a set
of Ludo. It looked like a normal domestic scene. A small boy,
a very young mother, perhaps. Happy. Comfortable. He knew
that Barbara was right: he was being taken advantage of, but he'd

also promised Geoff that it would be 'all right'. He'd given his word. Surely 'all right' couldn't mean just washing his hands of the boy by sending him off to a children's home, especially after what had happened at St Christopher's? Frank had said that he and Sheila had no relatives. Who else but Ted could look out for Geoff? The only other option would be to enter into protracted and acrimonious negotiations to force Frank to take Geoff back, but that might take weeks or months anyway. Maybe it was true that there would be no school place for him in Cyprus. Even if Frank eventually agreed to take him back, what would happen to Geoff in the meantime? If Ted was going to have to look after him for several more weeks, he'd have to find a school place for him anyway, so maybe it would be less disruptive for the boy if he stayed till the summer. Would that really be so bad?

'Mary, could I have a word?' They went into the kitchen. 'There's been a bit of a change of plan. Geoff is going to be staying with me for quite a bit longer. Probably till next summer. Would you be able to stay on, while he's still with me?'

'Oh, Mr Cunningham, I'd like nothing better. He's a grand boy. I don't mean to speak out of turn but I have the feeling he's been short of a bit of mothering.'

'I think you may be right. Will you come with me when I tell him?' And then with Mary at his side, Ted went in to talk to Geoff.

'So I won't be going to Cyprus?'

'Probably not till next summer.'

'So I won't see my mum and dad till then?'

'Well, of course they'd like you to be back with them sooner, but it looks like that won't be possible.'

'Will I be sent away to another school?'

'No. You'll be living here, but I'll find a school for you to go to in the daytime, like you did before you went to St Christopher's.'

'And you'll be looking after me?'

'Yes. Mary and I will be looking after you, just like we are now.'

Geoff looked up at them. 'Can I carry on practising now?'

'Yes, of course.'

Ted and Mary went back into the kitchen. 'How do you think he's taken it?' asked Ted. 'He didn't say much.'

'When I think of my little brothers… well, he's different. There were so many of us, there was always noise and games and fights, but you couldn't be quiet, even if you wanted to. But Geoff, he's a quiet one. He has his own world in his head.'

'But you've brought him out of himself. I've seen him laughing and playing with you, he's like a different boy.'

'When there's something else, something to occupy his mind, yes, maybe he forgets, but then he remembers, and he's back in his own world again.'

'So, has he taken it all right – staying here till the summer? I know so little about children.'

'He needs time, Mr Cunningham.'

'Is he still wetting the bed?'

'Yes.'

'I wonder if it's something medical. I'd better speak to the doctor.'

LORINERS' WAS TED'S old school. He'd started at the junior school aged seven and moved to the senior school at twelve, staying until sixteen when he'd taken his School Certificate. Thanks to their successful trade in bits, bridles, stirrups and spurs, the Worshipful Company of Loriners had generously endowed the school and the fees were comparatively modest. The boys were generally the sons of professionals and better-off tradesmen, such as Ted's father. Ted had read a few years ago in the old boys' news that one of his classmates was now teaching at the junior school, so the following morning he left a message with the school secretary asking if Mr Denston could telephone him either at work later that day or at home that evening. He then remembered that he'd said he would speak to the doctor about the bed-wetting and rang the surgery. Ted printed the surgery stationery so the receptionist made a 'special exception' and put him straight through to Dr Boyars.

'Hello, Ted, what can I do for you?'

He explained that he was looking after a friend's son for a few weeks, that the boy was wetting the bed, and asked whether this was anything to worry about.

'There can be medical reasons for bed-wetting, but they're rare. It usually happens when a boy's upset or nervous about something. Anything can set it off, a new school, a parent dying or ill, that sort of thing. Maybe it's just being away from home.'

'What should I do?'

'The less fuss, the better, in my book. When they're feeling happy and more secure, it nearly always stops.'

Michael Denston called at lunchtime. 'Fancy hearing from you, Cunningham, after all these years. How the devil are you?'

Ted asked if they could meet as soon as possible, ideally later that day, and it was arranged that he would come over after school had finished.


TED ENTERED THE junior school lobby. Little seemed to have changed since his schooldays apart from everything seeming smaller. Michael Denston was also much as he remembered him from almost twenty years ago, still boyish and with a twinkle in his eye.

'Is there somewhere we can talk in private?' asked Ted.

'This is all very mysterious. Let's go to my form room.' The desks with their cast iron frames and flip-up bench seats were still there, along with the wall maps of the British empire and diagrams of steam engines and posters of the 'Trees of England'.

'Wasn't this old Tommy's form room?'

'Yes, and I know you're going to say it's hardly changed, but don't worry, it's due for refurbishment very soon. Even Loriners' has realised we're now in the 1950s. So, what's this all about?'

Ted went through the whole story, including exactly what had happened at St Christopher's.

'Can't say I'm completely surprised. Over the years I've heard some pretty ghastly stories. Trouble is that these buggers just get passed on from school to school. Nobody wants to make a fuss as it might get back to the parents, so they give them a good reference just to get rid of them. I suppose if your predilection is for little boys, a prep school is something of a magnet. We've nearly had our fingers burnt here but we've got a good network of spies and luckily have filtered out some bad 'uns before we gave them jobs. If you like, I can see what I can find out about your Mr Doughty.'

'They said they'd sue me if I mentioned it to anyone.'

'Just trying to frighten you off, old boy.'

'I know, that's why I've told you, but they had a point about poor Geoffrey being destroyed if it ever went to court.'

'Quite right. No one would want to put a boy through that.' There was a pause. 'So, now you've been left holding the baby.'

'Those were exactly the words my sister used. I suppose they do lend themselves to the situation. Yes, and I need to get him into a school as soon as possible. That's why I'm here.'

'Always tricky starting in the middle of a term but it might be possible. Thing is, Cunningham, is he going to be trouble?'

'I can't see why he should be. I don't think he had a very easy time when he was living with his parents. I get the feeling that his father used to knock him about a bit. They seemed very happy to send him off to St Christopher's – couldn't wait to get him off their hands. But if he's treated with kindness he's a delightful boy, and bright too, I think, if he's given a chance. I've been giving him a few piano lessons and he's picked it up in no time.'

'I'll have to talk to the headmaster, and we'll need to have a look at the boy, but I'd like to help you out of your predicament if I can. How do you feel about being left *in loco parentis*?'

'When his father first asked me to help with his singing, I thought to myself: don't get involved. And now, almost a complete stranger, no blood ties, I find myself responsible for Geoff. It's outrageous really, and my initial reaction was anger. My sister said I should simply hand him over to the authorities to deal with – let them take responsibility. But the thought of their sending him off to some children's home while they argued with his parents. I just didn't have the heart. He seems such a lonely little chap.'

'Quite the Good Samaritan, Cunningham.'

'Are you married, Denston? Any children?'

'Sadly no. I got engaged during the war, but when I came back, she'd gone off with someone else. Bloody ARP warden. They used to go out fire-watching together but evidently spent most of the time watching each other! Still, Cunningham, we're not over the hill yet. There's still hope for us.' They laughed. 'So, you stayed on in the RAF. Did you say you were a sergeant? I remember doing Corps with you, why no commission?'

'I never felt too comfortable about being put in charge of a load of other chaps just because I did Corps at school. Preferred to work my way up.'

'You'll be telling me next you voted Labour last week!'

'And you'll be telling me you voted Conservative!'

MICHAEL DENSTON TELEPHONED Ted the next morning. An appointment had been made for the following afternoon for Geoff to see Mr Denston and the Headmaster. 'Look, Denston, I need to warn you that Geoff might be a bit behind in some of the curriculum. Can you make some allowances?' Then he had an idea. 'Does the headmaster have a car?'

'Yes, a…'

'Don't tell me, otherwise you might think I'm cheating. Just ask your headmaster to ask Geoff what he thinks of his car.'

'Never been asked that before. But all right, I'll mention it to the beak.'

AFTER GEOFF'S EXPERIENCE at St Christopher's, Ted felt bad at having to put him through another interview, but it couldn't be helped; one way or another Geoff was going to have to go to a new school. During the previous few days, Ted had felt that Geoff was becoming a bit more self-confident, but he knew that with people he didn't know he tended to become shy and withdrawn. And he was still wetting the bed. 'Just be yourself, old boy, there's nothing to be afraid of. Mr Denston's an old friend of mine and wants to help us out if he can.'

The interview was an informal affair. Michael Denston suggested that Ted stay in the room with them so that there was a familiar face. The headmaster, Mr McKinnon, was very different from St Christopher's Mr Cowdray – young and approachable. To Ted's surprise he addressed Geoffrey by his Christian name and then explained that he wanted to get to know him a little to make sure that Loriners' would suit him. 'You see, Geoffrey, every school is different and every boy is different, so we want to see whether we are both going to get along all right. Now, Mr Denston has told me you're interested in cars. Is that right?'

'Yes, sir.'

'I drive a fairly new Rover 75. What do you think of that?'

'Wow! A P4? They're brilliant. Do you have the full hydraulic brakes? I think they're quite a lot better than the older ones.' There then followed a discussion on various features of the Rover and other modern cars. Geoff's enthusiasm and knowledge was impressive.

'And you're keen on music too, I hear?'

'Mr Cunningham's teaching me the piano. It's quite difficult to play one thing with one hand and something different with the other, but I'm beginning to get the hang of it.'

After successfully reading a passage aloud from, of all books, *The Wind In The Willows*, the headmaster asked Ted and Geoff to wait outside. A few minutes later both the headmaster and Mr Denston came out and told Geoff that they would be happy to take him and suggested he start the following Monday.

THE NEXT AFTERNOON, they drove to Whiteleys to buy the school uniform. As she had younger brothers, Ted thought it would be a good idea if Mary came too. She was pleased to be included and didn't let on that her brothers had worn nothing but hand-me-downs. They entered the palatial building, Mary and Geoff wide-eyed. Elegant inanimate leather-clad hands on the glove counter seemed to beckon them towards the heady scents of the perfumery. They reached the lift, and Geoff was mesmerised by the liveried operator who turned a shining brass handle to open and close the doors and proclaimed the names of the departments at each floor. In the boys' department a man in a dark suit asked if they needed help. He found the required tie, cap, socks and games shirts in the drawers of a long counter and then went to a stock room, returning with a couple of blazers to try on, of which the first fitted perfectly. Recalling Geoff's oversize St Christopher's blazer, Ted asked, 'Is there enough growing room?'

'It's a false economy, sir. Boys generally wear out their clothes faster than they grow out of them.'

Mary whispered something to Ted, who then asked the assistant to add two pairs of pyjamas. He carefully packed the purchases in a flat cardboard box which he tied with string. 'The total comes to seven pounds, eighteen and four, sir.'

'Will you take a cheque?'

The assistant looked at Ted's tie. 'RAF, sir?'

'Yes. Only packed it in a couple of months ago.'

'Royal Marines, myself. Of course, a cheque will be fine, sir.'

As they walked back to the lift, Geoff said, 'My dad's going to kill me when he finds out how much it's cost.' Now Ted understood why he'd been so quiet during the transaction.

'Oh, your dad won't have to pay me back. While you're with me, I'm paying for any stuff you need. Cheer up, we can hardly have you going to Loriners' in a St Christopher's uniform, can we?'

'I'm sorry I'm costing you so much, Mr Cunningham. Can you afford it?' Ted wondered where he had he picked up his notions of affordability? An overheard conversation between his parents? A motor journalist's comparison of different cars?

'Yes, I think so.'

'Are you rich, then?'

'No, not rich. After all, I'm not driving a Rolls Royce, am I? But I'm better off than quite a lot of people, and I try never to forget that.'

MICHAEL DENSTON RANG Ted that evening. 'In these situations, before he starts, we try to get a new boy to meet someone who'll be in his form. I've spoken to the parents of a boy called Eric Lazarus, and they've said they'd be happy for Geoffrey to come over to them this weekend to meet their son. Break the ice.' Ted agreed that sounded like an excellent idea. Then Mr Denston asked, 'Are you giving him any pocket money?'

'No, I hadn't thought of that.'

'It's only that I've had a few boys who were a bit worried when they started school – new place, new people and all that – and I've found that pocket money seems to perk them up a bit, give them an interest.'

'I'm a bit out of touch. How much do you suggest?

'Oh, I think a shilling a week should do.'

TED TOOK GEOFF around to the Lazarus's for tea on the Sunday afternoon before his first day at Loriners'. Their house was on the river, a twenty-minute walk away. The first thing that struck Geoff was the noise. It seemed that a musical rehearsal of some kind was going on in one of the upstairs rooms, audible even before the front door was opened. Mrs Lazarus, an elegant woman wearing slacks and a black-and-white striped top ushered them in. 'Sorry about the racket, my husband's murdering Mozart upstairs. Mr Cunningham, isn't it? And you must be Geoffrey. Do come in.'

The house was large and untidy. Piles of books, old newspapers and magazines seemed to cover every surface. The walls were lined with artwork, most of them oils with thickly applied paint which Ted described to Mary that evening as 'modern art, but not abstract'. They later found out that Mrs Lazarus was the artist.

The music stopped and there was the sound of many feet tramping downstairs. Everyone crowded around the large kitchen table. Along with Mr Lazarus – a thickset man whose receding hairline, spectacles and moustache gave him a passing resemblance to Groucho Marx – were a couple of musical friends, Eric and his three older siblings, Adam, Ruth and Nicholas. Everyone was introduced and Mrs Lazarus started dispensing cups of tea and hot buttered crumpets. Eric sat down next to Geoff. 'Sorry, it's a bit noisy here. Shall we go next door?' With this he beckoned Geoff to bring his tea and crumpet into the sitting room. It certainly had been rather overwhelming in the kitchen and completely out of Geoff's realm of experience.

'That's better,' said Eric. 'Do you have any brothers or sisters?'

'No.'

'Must have seemed like the lion's den to you, that's what Mum calls it when we're all in there talking at once. Sorry.'

Geoff would normally have been tongue-tied, but there was something about Eric's matter-of-fact tone that made him feel comfortable and that their conversation would not end with a rebuff or worse. 'No. I liked it. It was… exciting.' That was the best word he could think of.

'I don't know about that. I'd call it exasperating.' This was one of Eric's new words, which he'd picked up from his older sister. Geoff didn't know what it meant, but it didn't matter, he got the sense.

'Mr Denston said your parents are abroad.'

'Yes, they're in Cyprus. My dad's in the air force.'

'Who's Mr Cunningham?'

'I'm staying with him. He was in the RAF with my dad. My parents can't have me back in Cyprus with them for a bit, so Mr Cunningham is looking after me instead.'

'Crikey! And is he all right? He's not like some wicked guardian, is he?'

'No. He's nice. And there's Mary too, she helps look after me,'

'Is that his wife?'

'No, she's our housekeeper.'

'Gosh, sounds like *The Secret Garden*.'

'What's that?'

'Hang on, I'll lend it to you.' He came back a minute later with a book. 'It's really good. And now you're starting at Loriners'. Where were you before?'

'St Christopher's College choir school in Cambridge. But it wasn't very nice there so Mr Cunningham's sending me to Loriners' instead. He was at school there himself and knows Mr Denston.'

'Denston's all right, and Mr McKinnon, the headmaster.'

'Yes, I met him. We talked about his Rover.'

'Are you interested in cars?'

'Yes.'

'You must talk to my dad then. He's got a Lagonda.'

'Wow!'

# NOVEMBER 1951

LORINERS' WAS WALKING distance from Ted's house. On his first day, Ted and Mary walked with Geoff to school and Mary was there to walk back with him afterwards. After that, he was safe to walk on his own. Mr Denston had been right, the pocket money did perk him up. He was able to buy *The Beano* and a few sweets from the shop near the school – luckily he still had his ration card – and had money to buy tuck at break. But Loriners' was altogether a more cheerful experience than St Christopher's anyway. In some ways it was similar. The building was from the same era and the classrooms were similarly furnished. At morning assembly they sang the same hymns from the same hymn book and recited the Lord's Prayer as they had done at St Christopher's. The content of the lessons and the teaching were also much the same, but in other ways the school felt very different to Geoff. Being a day school was part of it – the feeling of freedom of having somewhere else to go to at the end of the school day – but the other boys were also friendlier and there was no bullying Macdonald or his equivalent. Another difference was that he'd already met Eric Lazarus.

Geoff had had no close friends at his old primary school. That had been his third school and each time no sooner had he started to make friends, his father was re-posted and he had to start again. The village children had also been stand-offish towards the RAF children, and the other RAF children had been stand-offish towards Geoff because his father was a sergeant. A more confident boy would soon have cut through these tribal prejudices, but Geoff was already shy and withdrawn and in this hostile environment he had simply withdrawn further into his own world. Even though he was a bright child, he had struggled with the different expectations of new teachers and varying syllabuses. St Christopher's had been even worse; its customs more arcane, its masters more exacting, and although not all the boys were his enemies, he hadn't made friends with anyone either. But now Eric Lazarus was his friend, and that made him 'all right' and he began to make other friends too. And, of course, there was Ted and Mary.

When he came back from school Mary would give him tea and he would tell her the day's events. This was a complete novelty to Geoff, whose own mother had shown no interest at all in his school day. Mr Denston had said that his handwriting was awful and given him a book of writing exercises to copy. Loriners' had long ago jettisoned the old inkwells and boys had to use Osmiroid 65 fountain pens. Mary would patiently sit next to him as he practised straight lines, curvy lines, lines of joined up V's like the teeth of a saw, or U's like waves in the sea. Then she would dictate silly rhymes for him to write out: *'Geoff's new pen is as black as a hen'*, *'A boy who is grand must write a good hand'*. They would laugh and it was fun and he found that as he practised he got better at it, and she would tell him how clever he was. He would ask her about when she was at school, and she'd do impressions of her teachers and he would laugh so much that he had to lie down on the floor to recover. And sometimes she'd talk about her younger brothers and her little sister and the naughty things they used to do and she'd laugh too but then she'd look sad, and for no reason she'd give him a hug, and he'd feel warm and safe.

Then Ted would come back from work and would also ask about school and then most days he would give him a piano lesson. That was different from doing writing with Mary. Ted would explain something very carefully and Geoff would concentrate hard to get it right. It didn't matter if he got it wrong, Ted would still say 'well done, old chap' but he knew when he got it right because Ted would say 'excellent' or 'brilliant', but Ted didn't tell stories about when he was a boy and there weren't laughs like there were with Mary.

# DECEMBER 1951

GEOFF BROKE UP the week before Christmas and Ted received his end of term report in the form of a letter from Mr Denston, the gist of which was that Geoff was becoming more confident and was well on the way to making up the deficiencies in his former education. His contribution to the choir was especially commented on. Ted thought of sending the report on to Geoff's parents but was upset on Geoff's behalf that they had not sent any communication to him at all. He couldn't understand it, but as he said to Mary, 'If they can't be bothered to ask, I don't think I should be bothered to tell.'

Now it was the holidays, Geoff and Eric would meet at each other's houses, although Geoff preferred going to Eric's home, where there was always so much going on. It would seem very quiet when Geoff got back to Ted's house. When Eric came to visit Geoff they would tell Mary that they were going to the park. In fact they would creep into a bombsite and play out make-believe confrontations between British and German soldiers, taking it in turns to be goodie or baddie.

Ted also suggested that Mary take Geoff on a few outings in London. As well as keeping him occupied, this was as much for Mary's benefit as Ted recognised that she hardly knew the place. They visited the Tower of London and the Natural History Museum. As a special treat, Mary also took Geoff to the cinema. He had seen films before at the RAF station, where there had occasionally been screenings on 'family days', but he had never been to a proper cinema. They went into the dark auditorium and were directed to their seats by a uniformed usherette with a torch. The seats tipped up and down. There was a tall woman in the row in front but Geoff found that he could see the screen over her head by sitting on the edge of the unfolded seat. The film was *Never Take No For An Answer* about a small Italian boy in Assisi and his quest to get the pope to let him take his sick donkey into the crypt of the basilica to be blessed by St Francis. Both Mary and Geoff were in tears at the end of the film.

'I don't know what made me cry,' Mary told Ted that evening at the kitchen table after Geoff had gone to bed. 'It was a piece of nonsense. If only it were true that the pope and the Catholic Church was so full of compassion that they would even help a poor boy with a sick donkey.'

He didn't want to pry but it seemed that her remark expected a response. 'Have you found the Catholic Church to be lacking in compassion, then?'

'Oh, Mr Cunningham. I don't know how to answer. You've been very kind. Don't think I haven't noticed that you've been careful not to ask me anything about my family back home. And I'm grateful, Mr Cunningham. Grateful for that, and for giving me this job and for treating me like a human being. I know how some people treat servants – like they're dirt…'

'You may be working for me, but Mary, you know I don't think of you like that, like a *servant*.'

'I know you don't, Mr Cunningham, but there are others who would do,' she took a deep breath, 'and have done.' She took a longer pause. Tears began to fill her eyes and she wiped them away. 'I hate being secretive, but I don't want to burden other people with my troubles either.'

'I don't know what it is, but if you want to tell me, I'm ready to listen. I won't say anything to anyone else. Not that there is anyone else I talk to much, apart from my sister I suppose.'

'Well then… I'm here because I got myself pregnant by some good-for-nothing charmer. And then I had the baby and lost it. And the shame and guilt that's drummed into us by those bloody priests and nuns – sorry for my language, Mr Cunningham – meant that I couldn't face my family any more. So here I am.'

Ted waited for her to go on.

'I was the oldest. After me there was Eamon and Liam and

Eugene and Pat and then the baby, Bridget. My daddy spent most of the time working in England – building and labouring work. He was doing the best for us he could and we lived on the money he sent back. I helped my mam with the younger children until I left school. I wanted to be a nurse and my teacher said I'd done well enough to go to nursing school, but we had no money for that, so I started doing cleaning work around the villages. Then a girl I met working in one of the big houses told me that she'd worked in a hotel in Roscommon and that the money was much better. She'd had to give it up because her mother was ill and she needed to be at home, but she said she would write to them if I was interested. So sure enough I got the job and it was grand. The work was hard: cleaning, laundry, scrubbing potatoes – whatever I was given – but I was used to hard work so it didn't trouble me. We slept four to a room in the attic, but we each had our own bed which was more than I'd had at home. And the food was good and there was plenty of company. We even had a half-day off each week, so we could walk about the town or get a bus to visit home.

'And then I met this boy. He was a driver, a chauffeur, with a smart suit and a peaked cap. He was working for a rich American who'd come back to Roscommon to look up his poor Irish relatives. Even though he was only a driver, they paid for him to be treated like any other guest at the hotel with his own room there and everything. He couldn't believe his luck. He was a good-looking boy with all the blarney you could find, and he saw me sweeping the carpet outside his door one day and he set his cap at me, as they say, and I fell for him like Cinderella and Prince Charming. Course, it was only supposed to be a kiss and a cuddle, but we got carried away and I spent the night with him, and a few more nights after that. I was a fool. And then a week later, he'd gone. It wasn't as if I didn't know the facts of life. One of the girls at school had got hold of a banned book called *Married Love* and would lend it out at a halfpenny a day. But a book is one thing and real life is something else, so I couldn't quite believe it when I found I was actually pregnant.'

'What did you do?'

'What could I do? One of the other girls at the hotel told me about the sisters' laundry in Galway and I went there. They take you in, you have your baby, and if you can't look after it – which most can't – they take your baby away.'

'What about your family? Couldn't they help?'

'Perhaps there are families in Ireland who would have helped, but I couldn't ask mine. In the village I came from I would have brought the deepest shame on them, so the laundry was the only place I could go. I thought I could stay there, have the baby and then start again in Galway or back home. But then my stupid brother came looking for me. He'd come to Roscommon looking for work and tried to find me in the hotel. They told him I'd gone home, but when he said that I hadn't, they found one of the other chambermaids and he made her tell him where I was. Of course, men weren't allowed within miles of the laundry, except doctors and priests, but Eamon is a devil when his blood his up and somehow he managed to get to see me for five minutes. He told me I was a disgusting whore and I was to stay away from home. Can you imagine it? I'd been like a mother myself to the little ones, Pat and little Bridget. It broke my heart, Mr Cunningham, it broke my heart.' Tears welled up again, but again she wiped them away. 'It was like hell in the laundry. Not so much the work, but the sisters. They hated us. They treated us like dirt. And then three weeks before my date, I stopped feeling the baby kicking. The other girls told me not to worry, but I knew something was wrong, and then, a week later the baby came and it was born dead, stillborn. They took him away from me. I never saw him but they told me it was a boy and that they gave him a Christian burial. And the sisters said it was a punishment for my sins. A punishment. That helpless baby. That's what I thought of when I saw that film, with the pope and all the priests and brothers showing the compassion of Jesus himself to a boy and his sick donkey, and there was us sinners at the laundry being treated like worthless dirt by the Sisters of Mercy, of *Mercy* would you believe, and that little baby dying as a punishment for *my* sins.' And then Mary could no longer hold back her tears.

There'd been bad times in the RAF – planes lost, aircrew killed or maimed – where 'stiff upper lip' had served as the expected sympathetic response, but he could hardly say this to Mary. He got out of his chair and put his arm over Mary's shoulder; she turned her head and wept into his breast, whispering 'I'm sorry, I'm so sorry,' between her sobs. Then she composed herself and gently pushed him away.

'What about a cup of tea, then?' asked Ted. Mary nodded. By the time he'd set the teapot on the table, Mary seemed to have recovered and Ted felt that it would be better to change the subject.

'Mary, I'd like to talk to you about Christmas.'

'I'm sorry Mr Cunningham, it would have been better if I hadn't said anything. I don't know what came over me.'

'There's no need to say sorry. I only hope that telling me what happened may have made things easier for you, lightened the load perhaps.'

'Yes, Mr Cunningham, it has.'

Ted poured the tea. 'And Mary?'

'What, Mr Cunningham?'

'Do you think you could call me Ted?'

'I don't know. Would it be right? I mean, you are my employer. Is it allowed?'

He smiled. 'I don't think there's any law. This isn't exactly Buckingham Palace.'

It was a release for Mary, to laugh after her tears. 'All right then… Ted.'

'Now about Christmas. Is there anything else we need?'

'No, Ted. Everything is ready.'

Barbara had rung him about Christmas a few weeks earlier. After the death of their mother, Ted and his father had gone to Barbara's for Christmas dinner, but this year Barbara and George had been invited to George's sister's in Broadstairs. 'I'm sure if I asked her she'd invite you too.'

'That's kind, Barbara, but don't worry, we'll manage fine here. It'd be nice to have Christmas in Hammersmith after all these years.'

'If you're sure. What about Boxing Day? Why don't you and the boy come and have lunch with us then?'

'That would be lovely. Would it be all right if Mary came too?'

'Really? Is that appropriate?'

'What do you mean?'

'Well, she is *staff* so to speak.'

'Don't be so ridiculous, Barbara, this is 1951. Mary is looking after me and Geoff, we think of her as our friend. And anyway, she's nowhere else to go.'

'Well, I suppose so, if we must.'

Barbara had visited Ted twice since Geoff and Mary had come to live with him. She thought Mary was perfectly nice for an Irish housekeeper and Geoff was harmless enough as little boys go, though she couldn't quite understand the obvious affection Ted had for him. It seemed rather irregular to be entertaining Ted's housekeeper to lunch, but as there would only be the five of them she was prepared to indulge her little brother, after all, it hadn't been an easy year.

Christmas held no particularly warm memories for Geoff. The best thing had been the RAF station communal children's Christmas parties where a Santa had given out some presents and there had been sandwiches, cakes and orange squash. But Christmas day at home with his parents had seemed little different to a normal Sunday. The previous year Geoff had made gifts at school for his parents: a cigarette box for his father made from a tobacco tin covered in coloured paper and a dress hanger for his mother where Geoff had cut up an old jersey and sewn it on to the wooden bar. Neither gift had been greeted with much enthusiasm. His parents had given him a set of happy family cards and a gyroscope. Frank said that the man in the toy shop had said it was the latest thing, you pulled a string to get it spinning and then it would balance on the top of a lead Eiffel tower. Try as hard as they could, it just fell off. Frank was cross: 'I paid good money for that,' and vowed to take it back to the shop, though he never did. Still, it soured his mood for the day, and they ate their festive meal of turkey rissoles and boiled potatoes in silence.

With such low expectations, Geoff was surprised at the preparations Ted and Mary were making. Ted bought a tree and found a box of tree decorations in the attic. Mary and Geoff dressed the tree and then Mary had the idea of making some decorations for the house which they produced by folding and cutting old newspaper to make chains of Christmas trees, snowmen, snowflakes and stars, which they strung from small tacks nailed into the picture rails. There were also Christmas cards – not many – that had been put up on the mantelpiece. Geoff surprised Ted by asking whether he could send a card to his parents. Ted thought that would be an excellent idea. Geoff bought a card with this own money, it said 'Merry Christmas' on the front with a drawing of three ringing bells tied with yellow ribbon entwined with holly. Inside, Geoff wrote: *'Best wishes for Christmas. Mr Cunningham is looking after me very well and we have a housekeeper called Mary who is very nice. I am at a new school which is also nice. I hope that you are well. Is it nice in Cyprus? Love, Geoffrey.'* No card came for Geoff.

On Christmas morning Geoff found an old woollen stocking at the end of his bed and with great excitement he took out each item – a sweet or small toy – savouring the moment and exclaiming 'wow' and 'crikey' as he went along. Later on he unwrapped the presents waiting for him under the Christmas tree. From Ted there was *The Motor Yearbook* and from Mary, a set of colouring pencils. Geoff had been saving some of his pocket money and had augmented this with a small loan from Eric enabling him to buy a chamois leather cloth for Ted, for whom cleaning his beloved MG was a weekly ritual, and a pair of woollen gloves for Mary, whose current ones he had noticed had holes.

After their Christmas dinner the three of them played snakes and ladders and then propped up on his elbows, Geoff lay on the floor and started to read his new book whilst Ted played the piano.

Boxing Day lunch with Barbara and George went much better than Ted had expected. When they arrived, George seemed very excited and immediately asked Geoff and Ted to follow him upstairs. There, in one of the many large spare bedrooms, he had pushed the furniture aside and set up what turned out to be his boyhood model railway set. 'I thought it would be nice for Geoffrey to see it. It was all boxed up in the garage. Used to spend hours playing with it when I was a boy. It's one of the original 1920 Hornby clockworks. Couldn't bear just to get rid of it.' Ted thought what a blow it must have been for George that they had been unable to have children.

Geoff and the two men sat on the floor as George pointed out the level crossing, the station and stationmaster, the tunnel, the bridge and various other important elements of the track. Geoff was captivated and George showed him how to wind up the trains and change the points as the two engines whizzed around.

Downstairs, Mary helped Barbara in the kitchen. 'My brother says that you have been a great help to him, looking after Geoff and keeping house.'

'Thank you, Mrs Manton. I've tried to do my best.'

'It's quite an odd thing, a single man like my brother suddenly being landed with taking care of an eight-year-old boy. I just can't understand why he isn't with his parents.'

'I don't know, Mrs Manton, it's not for me to say.'

'Quite right, Mary. And what about you? What brought you to London?'

'It's very quiet where I come from; I suppose I wanted to see a bit more of the world.'

On the way home, Geoff was full of talk about the train set, which had kept him and George fully occupied before and after their lunch. 'I've never seen George so animated,' laughed Ted.

'What does animated mean?' asked Geoff. 'Like an animal?'

'No, it means lively or excited, like "animato" in music.'

'Oh. Yes, he did seem excited. It was more like playing with Eric. He didn't seem like a grown-up when he was playing with the train, but at lunch he reminded me of the headmaster of St Christopher's.'

It was already eight when they got back to Hammersmith. It had been a long day so Geoff just had some milk, and bread and butter and then went straight up to bed. Ted suggested to Mary that they could listen to the wireless and he lit the coal fire in the sitting room and waited for her to come in

'Mary, I've been wanting to talk to you. You remember before Christmas when you told me about what had happened to you back home and how you didn't like having to be secretive.'

'I do.'

'Well I feel the same. You see I haven't really told you how Geoff comes to be living with me.'

'It's really none of my business. You don't need to tell me anything.'

'No, but I want to.' And then Ted told her the whole story. 'It was when he mentioned George reminding him of the headmaster at St Christopher's, do you remember, in the car? That made me want to tell you.'

Mary said, 'They didn't even send him a Christmas card or letter,' and then she paused, 'but I don't suppose I'm in any position to talk. I wrote to my parents to tell them I'd gone to London to start afresh, but I never expected them to write back. Eamon would have made sure of that. The two of us never got on so well. I think we were jealous of each other. He was my mam's favourite and I was a daddy's girl…' She stopped. 'Sorry, we were talking about Geoff.'

'The thing is, I worry about what will happen to him when he goes back to them. Of course they blame me for taking him out of the choir school, but how could I have left him there?

They just seem to want to get rid of him; I'm not sure if they feel much affection for the lad at all. I feel responsible. He should be nothing to me. It's not as if his father was even a friend of mine, but… well, someone has to look after him.'

'But he isn't nothing to you, is he?'

'Well… It's just that I hope they'll… well… give him a bit of love.'

# JANUARY 1952

Ted was sitting near the gas fire reading some printing machinery catalogues. He'd lit his pipe and thin wreathes of smoke rose from the bowl releasing a sweet, dry aroma. Geoff had gone to bed and Mary was doing some sewing in the kitchen where the light was better. There was a ring at the doorbell and Ted got up to answer.

'Hello, Ted. Sorry to give you a fright.' It was Frank Bassett.

Ted's face had gone white. 'Just a bit of a surprise… quick, come in out of the cold.' He showed Frank into the sitting room. 'Cup of tea?'

'Something stronger would be nice, if you've got it.'

'Whisky?'

Frank nodded. 'Neat is fine.'

Ted poured the drink and took a better look at Frank. He was holding a cigarette between his thumb and forefinger and taking nervous puffs. His fingers were nicotine stained and they were shaking a little. The skin on his face looked waxy and yellowish. There were large bags under his eyes. Frank had always prided himself on his appearance but Ted noticed that his collar was grubby and his suit – he was in civvies – looked creased, with a dark stain on his left lapel. Frank took a large sip from the glass. 'Aren't you having something, Ted?' He didn't want to seem impolite so poured himself a small tot.

'P'r'aps I should have written, but it would only have been to say that I needed to see you. I'm not too good at letters. You see, something's come up.'

'Oh.'

'Well, a few things, in fact. Sheila's left me for one.'

'Oh, I'm sorry to hear that.'

'She's run off with a bloody Greek, would you believe? I

thought it would work in Cyprus, that we'd be able to make a go of it, specially without Geoff around. Fresh start. See, things hadn't been too good between us, and I thought the change might make things better. But then she met this Greek, plenty of money, shipowner or some'at, and she's bloody run off with him.'

Ted didn't know what he should say. Frank continued: 'So I've chucked it in with the RAF and I'm emigrating…' he half-laughed, half-sniffed. 'I'm going to South Africa. New life. "Turn over a new leaf" isn't that what they say?' Frank drained his glass and held it out. Ted refilled it.

Ted felt an ache at the bottom of his stomach. 'What about Geoff? Are you taking him with you?'

'That's what I need to talk to you about; that's why I'm here.' He leaned back in the armchair and stared vacantly into the middle distance. 'I'm not blaming the boy – it weren't his fault I suppose, but it were never right, right from the start.' He took a swig of his whisky. 'You might as well know the whole story. Me and Sheila had stepped out a bit before the war, but I knew she weren't serious about me. She had her eye on better things. Cor, she were a stunner, and she knew it. Though I say so myself, I were a cut above most of the lads we knew, but even I weren't in her league. Anyroad, then the war came and I joined up, and then blow me if a couple of years later I bump into her at a dance. She were packing parachutes at another RAF station nearby. So we had a few dances and it seemed like old times and she said she'd see me again but I didn't hear from her till months later. Then, out of the blue, I get this note from her. She were sorry she hadn't been in touch and could she see me now. I should have smelled a rat, but the truth is, I were soft on her – always had been. So then we meet and she says she'd come to her senses and I were the one for her, and, what with the war and everything, why hang around? I couldn't believe me luck. So of course I said yes and we were married two weeks later in the register office. Her parents wouldn't come. Didn't approve of me, or Sheila for that matter. Against their religion, you know, hell and brimstone chapel folk they were. So it were just Sheila, me and my pa and ma, and a mate of mine were best man.

'For a few weeks, everything were good. We found some digs and Sheila got a transfer to my station. She weren't feeling too well some of the time, but she blamed it on the mess food. And then one day we had a little argument over summat, nothing important, but she snapped, and then she said, as I were going to find out sooner or later, it might as well be sooner, and she told me that she were expecting. First I thought that were great news, but then I saw she were crying and she says: "It's not yours."

'It were like I'd been punched in the gut. I asked what she meant and then it all came out. She'd been with this Yank. They'd come over just after I met her at that dance. She'd taken up with one of them, and that were it.'

Ted was trying to take all this in. 'You mean you're not Geoff's father?'

'It's my name on the birth certificate, but no, I'm not his real father.'

'But what happened to his real father?'

'He were called out on one of the first Yank bombing raids. Missing in action. Sheila'd written to him, but she'd heard nothing and then she went to his station and they checked and told her. She knew her parents wouldn't have her, so what could she do? And then she thought of me.'

'But even after she told you, you still stayed with her?'

'As I said, I loved her and she knew it. So we patched it up and I said I'd be the child's father. I knew she were using me, but if it meant I could be with her, what the hell? I knew she didn't love me, but I thought that she must like me, and that over time we'd get closer. At first it were all right, but after Geoff came, she seemed to go off me. In fact she went off everyone.'

'What do you mean?'

'Well, the birth were a tricky one. Went on for hours. I were allowed to wait outside to start with, but then her screaming got so bad they told me to go home as they could see I were getting upset. They had to cut her open in the end. Scarred for life, she said she were, and she blamed everyone. Me, the midwife, the doctor, the father I suppose, but mostly the baby… and herself. I never thought she were going to be the maternal type, but she really took against Geoff. She went through the motions of course, when other folk were around, but when we got back home I don't think she'd even have fed the baby if I hadn't been there to make her. That bloody baby. She hated him.

'Later on, she pulled herself together a bit and got into some sort of routine. I don't think she hated him then as much – it were more like she just had no interest in him, as though he were nothing to do with her. Truth is, Ted, I can't say I were much better.'

Frank drained his glass and held it out for another refill. 'But you like him, Ted, don't you? Oh, sorry, I don't mean you're like that choir chappie – if it were true, which I still doubt – but like an uncle or summat.'

'I am fond of Geoff. Yes.'

'Well, that's why I've come. You can have him. He's yours. For keeps.' Frank then pulled some crumpled sheets of paper from the inside pocket of his jacket. 'Here you are. All official.'

The first sheet was Geoff's birth certificate with its numbered columns in red ink. '1', 'When and where born', *'Twenty-eighth of March 1943, Kettering General Hospital'*; '2', 'Name, if any', *'Geoffrey Arthur'*; '4', 'Name and Surname of Father', *'Frank Sydney Bassett'*; and so on. The second sheet was typewritten on the lines of Frank's original *in loco parentis* page:

> *I, Frank Bassett, of no fixed abode, formerly of RAF Akrotiri, Cyprus as father of Geoffrey Bassett, currently residing at 36, Mayhew St., Hammersmith, London do hereby transfer all parental authority to Edward Cunningham of 36, Mayhew St., Hammersmith, London so that the said Edward Cunningham is henceforth and permanently to adopt the said Geoffrey Bassett as his own son.*

'I wanted to make it official, like.'

Ted was completely taken aback and found it hard to form any coherent words.

'Don't you want to take the boy then?' asked Frank.

'It's so sudden,' Ted stammered, 'I don't know what to think.'

'Well, if you don't want him, I can take him to Barnardo's. He can't come with me.'

'No, Frank… I'll take him. It's all right, I'll take him.'

'Good. Now there's summat else.' Frank made it sound like a commonplace transaction had just been agreed, as if he'd just sold Ted a lawnmower and was now going to offer him a garden roller. 'I'm a bit hard up for one reason and another, and I need some dough to get me ticket and keep me going for a bit. Could you lend me a couple of hundred?'

'A couple of hundred?'

'Well, whatever you can manage. I'll pay you back when I'm on me feet again.' Even Frank realised how this might sound. 'Look, this is nothing to do with you adopting Geoff. Ted, I'm begging you. I've been having a bad time. When Sheila left I went to pieces.'

Ted's eye caught the stain on his lapel again. 'I suppose you need cash. I don't keep much. I'll just look upstairs and see what I've got.' In fact a customer had paid Ted in cash that day and he'd taken the money home for safe-keeping, but how much should he give Frank? He knew he'd never get the money back and there was also that unpleasant feeling that he was buying Geoff in some way, but… He came downstairs. 'You're in luck. I can let you have ninety pounds.'

There was a huge look of relief on Frank's face. 'Oh, Ted, that's great. I won't forget this. As soon as I've sorted things out, I'll get in touch about cabling you the money.'

And that was it. Frank seemed in a hurry to leave and Ted had no intention of delaying him. Knowing what Frank had told him, he wasn't surprised that he hadn't asked to see Geoff nor enquired about how he was. Ted mumbled something about wishing him good luck, they shook hands and Frank was gone.

Ted went into the kitchen. Mary said nothing, waiting for him to tell her whatever he wanted to. He sat down. 'That was Frank Bassett.' He handed her the birth certificate and his typewritten adoption statement. She read them and looked up at him with a look of confusion. Ted went on, 'He said that he wasn't Geoff's father… yes, I know it says he is on the birth certificate but it turned out that Sheila – Geoff's mother – was already pregnant when they got married.' He gave her the rest of the story. 'He said if I didn't want Geoff, he'd take him to Barnardo's. What could I say?'

'What did you say?'

'I said yes.' He put his face in his hands. 'What have I done?' Then he took his hands away from his face and looked at her. 'Please, Mary, tell me if I've done the right thing.'

'It's not for me to say. I don't want to speak out of order.'

'Please, tell me what you think.'

'You've done the right thing.'

'Have I? Really? What do I know about adopting an eight-year-old boy, about becoming his father? I know we talked before and I said I was worried about what would happen to Geoff, but I didn't expect this. It's such a responsibility. Maybe he would be better off at Barnardo's; at least they know what they're doing. And what about Geoff himself? What if he doesn't want me to adopt him? Surely he must have some say in it?'

'Ted, in a children's home he'd just be one of hundreds. Look what you've been able to do for Geoff, like teaching him the piano and reading him stories. And I've watched you. You already look as if you could be his father – a good father. And I've watched him too. He's happy here. If you adopt him he really would become your son. Wouldn't that be the best thing for both of you?'

'I don't know. I suppose it might.'

'Think if Frank had turned up and just taken him away. You yourself said that they didn't seem to show any love for him and that Geoff was frightened of his father. You'd be able to give him the love he needs, which they would never have given him.'

'But even if I did adopt him, can he really give Geoff away like that? It doesn't seem right. I'll have to talk to someone who knows about these things.'

'Are you going to say anything to Geoff?'

'No, not yet. I have to think this through first. Find out what the legal position is and then decide what's best.'

TED WENT TO see his solicitor the next afternoon. Harold Pearce hid a shrewd mind behind an avuncular exterior. Ted had seen him several times to discuss his father's probate and he knew he could trust him. He briefly explained how Geoff had come to be living with him, recounted his meeting with Frank and showed him the 'adoption' document.

'This is quite a bit outside my area of competence, Mr Cunningham. I think we may have to consult counsel. I'll make some enquiries and get back to you.'

The next afternoon, Harold Pearce rang Ted at his office. 'I think I've found someone who can help on this. Apparently he's the top man on this sort of thing, so top prices too, I'm afraid. A conference – meeting with him, that is – will cost twelve guineas. Is that all right?'

'Well, if he's the top man I suppose I have no choice.'

TWO DAYS LATER Harold Pearce and Ted were sitting opposite Peter Crempel at his chambers in the Middle Temple. Both ends of the desktop in front of them were covered in neat rows of folded papers tied with thin pink ribbons and the great man was leaning back in his chair with his fingertips pressed together, his black jacket and striped trousers, wing collar and dark tie exuding exactly the austere aura of authority that was intended. He had a reputation for being a fierce advocate in court, but it was mainly put on for effect and he found it delightfully amusing that he was known behind his back as 'Crempel of the Temple'.

After the introductions, Crempel picked up the letter he'd received from Harold Pearce and Frank's 'adoption' document. 'Thank you for these, most useful. I wonder, Mr Cunningham, whether you could briefly outline the position in your own words.'

As he had done for Pearce, Ted told how he had come to prepare the boy for the St Christopher's entrance, how Geoff had been extremely unhappy at the school, how Geoff's parents had asked Ted temporarily to look after him, and the gist of Ted's recent meeting with Frank.

'You say that he was unhappy at the school. This is not unusual – a new school, away from his parents for the first time in unfamiliar circumstances and so on. Wasn't it rather drastic to withdraw the boy from the school? Surely he would have settled in sooner or later?'

Ted realised that he would have to explain what had happened. 'Geoffrey told me that he had been molested by one of the masters. When I learned this, it was impossible for me to leave him at St Christopher's.'

'I see. And you believe the boy's story?'

'Absolutely.'

'Did you inform the police?'

'I decided that this would not be in Geoffrey's best interest.'

'Very well. And do you believe that Geoffrey is now happy living with you?'

'I do.'

'And what are your domestic arrangements?'

'I engaged a housekeeper when Geoffrey came to live with me and he is now attending Loriners' junior school in Hammersmith.'

'Why there?'

'It's near to my home, I was a boy there myself and an old classmate of mine now teaches there and helped me get Geoff a place at short notice.'

'All this at your expense?'

'Yes.'

'Good. Good. And, most importantly, you definitely want

to adopt him.'

'That's why I'm here. I need to know all the facts before I can make a decision. I have to act in Geoffrey's best interest.'

'But if you thought it were in his best interest, would you be willing to adopt him?'

Ted paused. 'Yes. I would.'

'You realise that under the 1949 Adoption Act this would mean that he would become your heir and would have exactly the same legal status as if he were your own biological son.'

'So Mr Pearce has told me.'

Crempel rocked back on his chair. 'This,' he picked up Frank's typewritten page, 'of course is of little value. I would not recommend that we use it to obtain an adoption order.'

'Is that because Frank Bassett has said that he is not Geoffrey's real father?'

Crempel made a grunting noise. 'The law is never so simple. The court would require evidence that Bassett was not the father. We only have his word for it. He would certainly not be the first father to deny paternity. The fact that the child's conception predated the marriage ceremony is so commonplace as to be of no relevance whatsoever. Furthermore, he was clearly caring for the boy as if he were his own son, so natural father or not, he was the boy's *de facto* guardian. But the crux here is that we don't have the mother's consent. Whatever Bassett might have said or written, it is the mother to whom the court will defer.'

'But as far as we know, she has run off with another man, and has certainly shown no interest in taking back the boy,' said Pearce.

'So Bassett says. But what if he were wrong? Imagine the boy's mother turning up in the next few weeks, months or even years. It will be hard to get an adoption order with such a sword of Damocles hanging over our heads. We would have to be certain that she has genuinely abandoned the child or at any rate cannot be found. No, this is my advice: apply for the boy to become a ward of court, and then ask the court to appoint you, Mr Cunningham, as his legal guardian. I can't see their objecting.

You are already fulfilling this role perfectly respectably. Then wait two or three years, and assuming neither parent appears, but especially the mother, you would then be in a strong position to apply for the adoption order, as long as you can show that this is what the boy wants.'

'Two or three years?'

'That is my advice. It would be better, of course, if you were married by then.'

'Married?'

'This is usually preferred nowadays, although not a legal requirement as long as the welfare of the adopted child is not affected.'

Harold Pearce now asked, 'You have said we should wait in case either parent appears, does that include Frank Bassett if he changed his mind?'

'Conceivably, though from what you say this sounds unlikely. Assuming Bassett was truly not the biological father, I take it we have no idea whom that might be.'

'Frank said that he was an American airman, missing in action,' said Ted.

'Well then, we can discount him.'


BEFORE GOING THEIR separate ways, Harold Pearce and Ted went to the A.B.C. Tea Rooms around the corner in Fleet Street to discuss the implications of their conference with 'Crempel of the Temple'.

Ted sighed. 'It's all quite a lot to take in.'

'I can see that, but he is regarded as extremely sound in this area of the law. We could always seek a second opinion if you prefer.'

'Oh no, I'm not doubting his opinion, it's just that's it's such a momentous decision to take. A human being's future in one's hands. I need to be sure that it's the right thing to do. And aside from that, it's knowing how to explain all this to Geoff.'

'What's the boy like?'

'How do you mean?'

'Well, is he highly-strung? Slow on the uptake? That sort of thing.'

'Certainly not slow on the uptake; his school report said that he's a very bright boy, but he's not had an easy time of it and I'd be lying if I said that he wasn't affected by all this. What eight-year-old wouldn't be? Leaving aside the incident with the choirmaster, he was plainly very miserable at St Christopher's. He wets the bed. I spoke to my GP about it and he said it's probably to do with him being sent away from home. But since he's been with Mary and me, he does seem to be becoming more confident and generally happier. His greatest fear always seemed to be that he'd "cop it" from Frank, and at least he won't need to worry about that any more.'

'So you don't think he has been damaged by the way his parents treated him.'

'It's outside my realm. Who knows how these things affect you? You'd have to ask a psychiatrist, but I think with time, he'll be able to put all this behind him.'

'And love.'

'Yes, and that too.'

'And you love him? Sorry, it's not a very English thing to ask.'

'Well, I do care for him, if that's what you mean. I'd just imagined I'd be looking after him for a few weeks initially, and even when it looked like it might be eight or nine months, I was prepared to do that because there was no one else. It had never crossed my mind to adopt him.'

'And now?'

'I'm not religious, but… it does seem that fate has rather drawn us together. It's as if there's a magnetic pull. Do you have children?'

'Yes, two girls. Twenty-two and twenty-five.'

'And did you love them from the moment they were born?'

'Unreservedly. But of course, adoption is different. It would be unusual, I imagine, if it was love at first sight as it were. And that's not to say that all parents automatically love their natural children. In my line of work, one soon sees that this is far from universal. But can you picture yourself in the future loving him as a father should love a son?'

'Put that way, yes. I'm pretty certain of it.'

'And in due course he would be able to love you?'

'Up to now, there's no reason why he should. I'm just the chap looking after him.'

'Nothing more than that?'

'I'm pretty sure he trusts me, but I don't think it would enter his mind to love me. Maybe with time, if I really do become his adopted father. I'm pretty sure he loves Mary though.'

LATER THAT EVENING when Ted knew that Geoff was in bed, he told Mary what Crempel had said. She said, 'So you've decided that you will try to adopt him.'

'I suppose I have. I just wish I knew for sure that it was the right thing.'

'You needn't worry, Ted. I can't think of anything better for him.'

'But Mary, you're as much a part of this as I am. You will be able to stay, won't you? Till he's settled.'

'Of course I will. I'm here for as long as you need me.'

'Thank you, Mary. The solicitor asked me if I thought Geoff loved me, and I said maybe he would with time, but that I was pretty sure he loved you. You've certainly given him more love than his mother ever did.'

'And you've given him more love than Frank ever did.'

'I feel I must say something to Geoff. I hate doing things behind his back.'

'He's only eight, Ted. There's only so much he would be able to understand.'

'Maybe, but I need to explain that whatever happens, his future's safe.'

THE NEXT DAY was Saturday. It surprised Ted how everything now seemed clearer in his mind. 'I need your help today, Geoff,' he said over breakfast. Geoff looked up at him. 'I think I need a new car.'

'But Mr Cunningham, I thought you loved your MG.'

'I do, but with the three of us it's not a very practical car. You have to squeeze into the back. It's not a real seat. I thought we could visit a few showrooms and see what might suit us better. It would have to be something second-hand that I could part-exchange for the MG. Oh, and something else, Geoff. I think it's time you stopped calling me Mr Cunningham and started calling me Ted instead.'

'Ted,' Geoff voiced the word slowly as if he were tasting an unfamiliar food for the first time. 'I don't know if my dad will think that's right. He might say it was cheeky.'

'I think it'll be all right. I'll explain when we're in the car.'

They walked around to the mews where Ted kept the car garaged. Geoff sniffed the scent of leather mixed with oil and petrol as they got into the MG. 'I do like this car, though, Mr… Ted.'

'I do too, but let's start driving and I can explain why it's time for a change.'

Ted headed up the Great West Road where he knew there were several motor dealers. It would be easier to explain about Frank's visit with Geoff next to him in the car than it would be sitting face-to-face.

'Your father came to see me last Monday night. You were in bed and he didn't want to wake you.'

'My father?' There was panic in Geoff's voice.

'He's asked if you could carry on living with me for longer.'

'Longer? Till after the summer?'

'Much longer. You see he's left Cyprus. He's going to South Africa, and he thought it would be better if you stayed here with me.'

'What about Mum?'

'I'm sorry Geoff, but they're not together any more. Your mother has met another man and is staying in Cyprus.'

'I don't understand.'

'I know. It's not easy. Sometimes these things happen. People get married but then things don't go the way they'd hoped.'

'Oh. So I'm not going back to my mum or my dad?'

'I don't think so. It's a bit complicated. You see, your father asked if I could adopt you instead.'

'Adopt?'

'You know, it's when someone takes over officially as your father or mother.'

'Oh. Forever?'

'Yes, forever. It can't be done right away. We'd have to get permission, and that will take a couple of years, maybe longer, but in the meantime you would carry on living with me just the same as now. And of course, with Mary – she's said she'll stay on for as long as we need her. But you have to agree too. That's part of the permission. They'll only give permission if it's what you want too. Ah, here's the first showroom. Let's park and see what they've got.'

There were a number of possible vehicles, their virtues and shortcomings discussed earnestly between Ted and Geoff, but not convinced that any was just right, they drove a mile further to another dealer. Here they saw a smart 1947 Riley RMA in two-tone dark brown and cream, which the dealer offered to exchange for the MG plus a hundred and seventy-five pounds. It was more than Ted wanted to spend, so he said he would think about it. Then the dealer said he'd take a hundred and fifty, and seeing Geoff's wide eyes, he accepted the offer, leaving the MG and driving off home in the Riley.

'I don't know which of you is worse,' Mary scolded as they showed her the new car and listed its attractions. 'As long as it has four wheels and goes, the rest all sounds like nonsense to me.'

'Five wheels, Mary. Don't forget the spare,' said Ted.

'Six. You've forgotten the steering wheel!' chimed in Geoff, who then ran upstairs to check references in his motor magazines.

'He seems chirpy. Did you tell him?' asked Mary.

'Yes, but he hasn't said much about it. I don't suppose it's sunk in yet. He'll need time. That's why I thought it would be good to go to the motor dealers, so that he'd have something else to occupy his mind for a bit.'

'You're a very thoughtful man. You really understand him.'

'You understand him too.'

'I suppose so. It's funny how something can happen and change a life completely, how giving Geoff some singing lessons can end up with you adopting him…'

'It's not settled yet.'

'I know, but I think it will be. Anyway, what a different world it is for him here in Hammersmith when you think of that loveless home he had on an RAF station somewhere. And if I'd never met that chancer in Roscommon I'd surely still be there, working in the hotel.'

GEOFF HAD SEVERAL conversations over the weekend with Ted and Mary about the proposed adoption. He was straightening it out in his mind – what it all meant, what were the implications, how this man whom until recently he'd been calling Mr Cunningham, could become his father. He also asked what would happen if Ted didn't adopt him. Ted wasn't sure. Probably he would go to a children's home or maybe to foster parents who would look after him like Ted and Mary were now. Or someone else might adopt him. On Sunday night Ted came up to read him his bedtime story. They had finished *The Wind in the Willows* long ago and Ted was now reading the *Just So Stories*. Before Ted started reading, Geoff said, 'I do want to stay here, with you and Mary. I like it here. Will that be all right?'

'Of course it will. We want you to stay too.'

In the morning, Geoff found his sheets and pyjamas were dry.

TED RANG HAROLD Pierce from his office and asked him to set

in motion the application for Geoff to become a ward of court and for Ted to be appointed his legal guardian. No sooner had he put down the phone, it rang.

'Ted Cunningham, please.'

'Speaking.'

'Ah, Ted. This is Phil Vine.'

'Hello, sir.'

'No need for the "sir", you're in civvies now. Sorry to call you out of the blue but I need to talk to you. I rang your home and was given your work number. I hope that's all right.' Phil Vine was the urbane RAF Police flight lieutenant from Ted's old station.

'Of course.'

'It'd be better if I could come to see you. Would this afternoon be possible? I could come to your workplace if there's somewhere private we can talk.'

'Yes, that should be all right.' Ted gave him the address.

'SORRY IF THIS all seems a bit cloak and dagger,' said Phil, when they were alone in Ted's office. 'It's about Frank Bassett.'

'I'd wondered if it might be.'

'Oh?'

'Frank came to see me a week ago. No doubt you'll want me to tell you what it was about – which I will in a minute – but there was something odd, too. He was in a bad way and some of what he said didn't quite make sense, like how he'd left the RAF so suddenly. When you called I just naturally thought it was probably something to do with him.'

'Well, you were right. So what was his visit to you about?'

Ted started with the choir school audition and then saw that he had no choice but to explain why Geoff had left St Christopher's, and why he hadn't informed the police.

'I can't condone what you did,' said Phil. 'The only way we can stop these pederasts is by exposing them and bringing them to justice.'

'I know you're right in principle, but the thought of Geoff

85

having to testify in court. He wouldn't have stood a chance. They would have made mincemeat of him. What would've been the point?' He then gave a detailed account of Frank's visit.

Phil whistled. 'Quite a story. I wouldn't normally go into details, but seeing I know you and how you're connected with Bassett, I think I might as well put you in the picture. You're right, Bassett is officially AWOL. He did a bunk from Cyprus without telling anyone. But there's more to it. Firstly, I was already investigating him because of financial discrepancies. We recently had a station audit and found quite a lot of evidence that he'd been misappropriating funds. It's just small amounts, that's why we hadn't picked it up before, but it had been going on for more than a year, so the total mounted up. Might have been doing it at his previous postings too. We're checking that now.'

'Did he know he was under investigation?'

'Well we didn't tell him – we were still gathering evidence – but he might have got wind of it somehow. Then there's this story about his wife leaving him. A couple of days before he did a bunk, he got pretty drunk in the mess and started telling anyone and everyone that she'd left him. When he went AWOL this was the first line of enquiry that the RAFP in Cyprus followed. It turned out that Sheila had been seeing a Greek fellow and that Bassett had been heard rowing with her several times recently, so things evidently not too good between them. The Cyprus chaps got hold of the Greek man, who didn't deny that they'd been carrying on, but he also claimed that he hadn't seen Sheila for several days and was actually quite worried about her because she'd failed to turn up for their last assignation.'

'Are you suggesting that Frank did away with her?'

'Anything's possible. It would certainly be one explanation for why he left in such a hurry and how he's gone to pieces.'

'Good Lord.'

'We then found out that his son was living with you, and thought that he might try to make contact, although far from wanting to see his son, from what you've said, the reason he came to see you was the very opposite, he simply wanted to be rid of the boy.'

'I genuinely think he had a guilty conscience about Geoff, but I won't deny that he might have also seen me as a soft touch to give him some money. What I don't understand is why he needed money if, as you say, he'd been successfully stealing for a few years.'

'Well you must remember that Mrs B had rather expensive tastes. She did get noticed. Even my own wife had wondered how she was able to dress in the latest fashion, while…' he stopped. 'Perhaps now is not the time to go into domestic discussions chez Vine. Anyway, what you've told me is extremely helpful. I just hope we're in time to stop him before he gets on a ship to South Africa, if that's really what he intended to do. I know it's unlikely, but if he contacts you again please ring my office.' Phil wrote his number on a slip of paper.

'Would you be able to keep me up to date if anything happens?' asked Ted.

'Of course.'

THREE DAYS LATER there was another call from Phil Vine. 'I'm afraid our bird has flown. Embarked on the *Warwick Castle* to Cape Town last week. We've cabled the South African police to hold him at the other end. I'm off to Cyprus to see what I can glean there.' For Geoff's sake, Ted hoped the less that could be gleaned the better.

The next news came by letter. Sheila had been seen leaving the RAF station on the bus to Akrotiri town. She had also been seen meeting her Greek male friend but that was the last sighting. Things were now further complicated by the apparent disappearance of the Greek man too. *'Our boys and the Cyprus police are working together on the case. Nothing more for me to do here.'*

And then another phone call from Phil. 'Frank didn't get off the ship at Cape Town and the police couldn't board without a warrant. Seems he's not been well – or that's his story. My hunch is that he'll disembark at Lourenco Marques or Beira, knowing that he'll be much safer in Mozambique. He's no fool.'

Finally, a second visit to Ted's office. 'I wanted to talk to you in person. Bad news, I'm afraid. Frank Bassett is dead.'

'Dead?'

'Sorry to shock you. As I thought, he was making for Mozambique. He left the boat at LM but then immediately collapsed. They got an ambulance and one of the ship's officers went with him, but he was dead on arrival. Reckon his liver packed up. He'd spent the whole voyage pickled by all accounts.'

'Poor blighter.'

'Maybe, maybe not.'

'What about Sheila?'

'Complete blank. Seems the Greek fellow was waiting for a cheque to clear so that he could clean out his bank account. Amounted to more than two thousand pounds. Took the money and that's the last anyone's seen of him.'

'Does that mean Sheila did go off with him after all?'

'Who knows? They've both vanished into thin air.'

'But wouldn't they be logged at some border crossing or need to show their passports somewhere?'

'They could be in Greece, or on one of the islands or God knows where. These places are still recovering from the war. There are all sorts of people floating around who've left their pasts behind. If you spread a bit of cash around, people are happy not to ask questions.'

TED TOLD MARY about Frank's death and then went up to Geoff's room, where he was doing his homework. Ted explained that Frank had become ill on the ship to South Africa and had died.

'So I wouldn't be able to go back to him, even if you weren't adopting me.'

'Not now, no.' And then he went back to his homework.

Ted came downstairs.

'What did he say?' asked Mary.

'Nothing. Well only that it meant he couldn't go back to Frank now, whether I adopted him or not.'

'Oh the poor boy. To think he was still frightened that could happen.'

Geoff was a bit quieter than usual at supper, but didn't seem upset when Ted read him his bedtime story – they were now on to Rider Haggard's *King Solomon's Mines*. In fact it was Ted who was almost in tears when he came down. 'It's not as if I liked the man. Even before I knew how he treated Geoff, there was something snide, cocky, about him. And it doesn't surprise me either that he was fiddling the books. But Sheila? I can't believe that he could have done away with her, however cruel she might have been to him, I really think he did love her. And maybe he did genuinely feel bad about how he'd treated Geoff too. He might not have been a good man, but… poor sod, to end like that.' He put his face in his hands, his elbows resting on the table. 'Sorry.'

'No need to be sorry, Ted,' and she put her arm around his shoulder as he had done to her when she had told him about losing her baby in Ireland. And then she kissed him, her cheek brushing against his wet stubble. 'Let's go to bed,' she whispered. Ted felt in a bit of a daze. He hadn't been expecting this at all, but her closeness, the feel of her skin against his, suddenly made him aware of her as a woman and it just seemed the most natural thing to do, and hand in hand they went upstairs.

The next morning she slipped out of bed early fearful of being discovered by Geoff. Ted usually left the house for work before Geoff left for school, but claiming that he wanted to do some paperwork at home, he waited for the boy to go so that he could speak to Mary.

'Mary, we need to talk about the future.'

'Oh, Ted, I'm so sorry. I don't know what came over me. What you must think of me. Oh Ted.' She paused to wipe her eyes. 'I'll ring the agency and tell them to send someone else to look after you both and I'll leave as soon as she's here.'

'What are you talking about?'

'Last night. All I hope is that one day you'll find it in your heart to forgive me.'

'Forgive you? But what for?'

'God, you'd think I would have learned from Roscommon. What was I thinking of?'

'Mary, I don't understand. Was last night a mistake? Is that what you're saying? It certainly wasn't a mistake for me.' Fighting his natural reserve, he grabbed her hands, 'It was wonderful. Don't you understand? I thought it was wonderful. Are you telling me you made a mistake? You seemed happy.'

'Oh Ted, I was happy, of course I was, but it was wrong. People will say I seduced you.'

'More likely they'll say *I* seduced *you*. But it's nonsense – we both felt it was right.' He paused as he gathered his thoughts. 'Look Mary, I know it's sudden. Is it three months you've been here? But we've got very close to each other, and – after last night – I, I… You must stay. I need you to stay. I want you to stay… always.'

'Always?'

'Yes. As my wife. Sorry, that wasn't much of a proposal. Mary, will you marry me?'

'Because you feel sorry for me, or guilty about last night, or...'

'No, because I love you.'

'But Ted, I'm twenty and you're thirty-three. I'm nobody from nowhere, a fallen woman from the Irish bogs. Can't you see that everyone will say I've seduced you for your money, that you're a weak-willed fella that I've wrapped around my little finger…?'

'Stop! Is that what you think of me?'

'Of course not, but it's what other people will say.'

'No more than they'll say I was an employer taking advantage of a defenceless young woman. And anyway, who cares what they say if we really love each other? Or is it that you don't love me, that's why it was a mistake?'

'No Ted, I do love you. You'll think me silly, but after I told you about why I left Ireland, and I was crying and you held me, I knew then. But I never thought anything would happen. How could it? How can it? We're miles apart, can't you see that?'

'I can't. If we both love each other what difference does anything else make – age or where we're from or anything? But if you really think that I'm too old, that…'

'No, no…' she held her face in her hands.

'Don't cry, Mary, please don't cry. I want to make you happy, we should be happy, this is our chance.' He held her and she sobbed into his chest, and then breathed deeply and regained her composure.

'Do you mean it, Ted, really? Do you really want to marry me?'

'I wouldn't have said it if I hadn't meant it. Most people who marry haven't lived together even for the few months that you've been here, and most haven't slept together either. When I think about people like my sister and George, I'm sure they loved each other, but they didn't know each other nearly as well as we now know each other. They really couldn't have known what it was going to be like, living together and so on.'

'"So on". You're so sweet, Ted.'

'Well, you know what I mean.'

'But what about Geoff?'

'Geoff? But this would be the best thing for Geoff – he'd have a mother then too.'

'Are you sure that's not why you're wanting to marry me? Didn't you tell me the lawyer man said they prefer people who adopt to be married?'

'But that's not why I want to marry you, I promise. Whatever happens with Geoff, even if, heaven forbid, I can't adopt him, I still want to be with you.'

'I don't know, Ted. I'm still not sure if it's the right thing to do.'

'I am sure, but I want you to be sure too. Look, let's give it some time, so you can get used to the idea. We won't say anything to anyone and we'll just go back to the way it was, and then if you really think it's not what you want, we can just try to forget that any of this happened. I know I won't be able to, but that doesn't matter.'

For the next two days, Mary and Ted tried to behave exactly as before, but whenever they caught each other's eye, it was obvious what they felt. On the third evening, after they'd gone to bed, there was a light tap on Ted's bedroom door. 'Ted, can I come in?' She heard a muffled 'Mary?' and came in, closing the door softly behind her. 'I can't stand this any longer. I try to sleep but can't stop thinking about you, what I want to do with you. Please, can I get into bed with you?'

'God, Mary. It's been torture.'

'I POPPED INTO the town hall this morning, to check how it works.' Geoff had just gone to bed and Mary was doing the washing up. Ted carried on, trying to be matter-of-fact but his voice betrayed both nervousness and excitement. 'Without your parents' consent you have to be over twenty-one.'

'Parents' consent? I'm not going to ask them for anything. I told you I wrote to them when I started here with you, told them this was my address, but I heard nothing from them. No, I won't ask them for anything.'

'But don't you think you should write to them anyway, just to tell them?'

'Maybe afterwards.'

'I don't like to think of your being at war with them.'

'Nor me, but that's how things sometimes are, especially in Ireland. But Ted, I'll be twenty-one in September anyway. Surely we can wait till then?'

'Yes, of course, but should we tell people now, like Geoff, or my sister?'

'They're going to know sooner or later, but your sister's not going to like it.'

'Don't worry, she'll come round, but perhaps it's no bad idea for her to have some time to get used to it. I'll ring her tomorrow.'

'HELLO, BARBARA.'

'Ted?'

'Yes.'

'Hello, darling, how are you and your little household?'

'Well, that's mainly why I'm calling, and also to find out how you and George are.'

'Now come on, Ted, you know you hardly ever call me unless it's to ask me for something…'

'That's not altogether fair.'

'All right, then. George and I are perfectly well, thank you. Now, out with it – why are you really ringing? Is it about the boy?'

'His name's Geoff as you jolly well know. No, he's fine. It's actually about Mary.'

'Don't tell me she's leaving you. It doesn't surprise me…'

'No, it's nothing like that, in fact it's just the opposite actually.'

'What do you mean?'

'Well, she's staying – forever, I hope.'

'Forever? I don't understand.'

'We're going to get married.'

Seconds of silence ticked away on the other end of the phone. 'Ted Cunningham, are you mad?'

'Now come on Barbara, I was worried you might take it like this, but I'm going to explain and you're going to have to listen and then you're going to have to behave like the reasonable, intelligent woman you are.'

Ted heard deep breathing. 'All right, I'm listening.'

'It won't take long. We love each other and we want to stay the rest of our lives together. That's it. She's everything I want. She'll be a wonderful wife and she already looks after Geoff as if he were her own son…'

'Younger brother, surely?'

'All right, younger brother then.'

'How old is she, Ted?'

'She's twenty, and that makes me thirteen years older than her and George is six years older than you, and we both know lots of long and happy marriages where…'

'But it's not just that. What do you know about her? She's

from some Godforsaken corner of Ireland, they're pig ignorant peasants and Catholics to boot. She's come over here, come to work for you and knows a good thing when she sees it. I suppose she got you into her bed too, and…'

'Now look, Barbara, if you're going to carry on like this, I'm going to put down the receiver.'

'So I'm right, aren't I? Oh Ted, can't you see it? You're such an innocent.'

'Barbara, you've got it all wrong. It's not like that at all.'

'Ted, darling, I can see the attraction. There you are, confirmed bachelor, with the added responsibility now of the boy…'

'Geoff.'

'All right, Geoff then. Anyway, this young woman comes along and uses her feminine charms – and I'm not blaming you, Ted, because I expect nine out of ten men in that position would have done exactly the same as you – but can't you see it? How can it work? You're from such completely different backgrounds. Just because you haven't had much success with girls of your own class, doesn't mean you have to stoop this low.'

'Barbara, say one more thing like that and I'm hanging up.'

'But, darling, you know I'm only thinking of you. I just can't bear to see you make a fool of yourself and throw your life away.'

'Look, I can see this is a bit of a surprise. It would have been nice, of course, if you'd congratulated me and wished us both every happiness for the future, but knowing you as I do, I expected your initial reaction was going to be exactly like this. Funnily enough, when I asked Mary to marry me she said a lot of the same things and that people would think that she'd entrapped me in some way. She actually offered to leave, but I persuaded her to stay and my hope is that when you've had time for it to sink in, your better nature will prevail and you'll see Mary not as member of the untouchable "lower orders" but as a kind and decent human being and as someone who will make me happy.'

Another deep intake of breath. 'All right. I've said my piece and you know what I think, but it's only because I don't want you to make a terrible mistake.'

'I know that. But please Barbara, just for once, put all your prejudices aside and give her the benefit of the doubt.'

'I'll think about it.'

# MARCH 1952

IT WAS THE week of Geoff's ninth birthday. Ted was at work and a telephone call was put through to him.

'Is that Edward Cunning-ham?' It was an American man's voice, pronouncing the last syllable of Ted's surname with a hard aitch. 'You won't know me, my name is Art Shiner. I'm over here from the US for a few days. I understand that you know Sheila White, sorry, I mean Mrs Sheila Bassett. I'm a friend of hers from the war. Could I meet you? I'd sure like to talk to someone who knows her.'

Ted knew instantly that this must be something to do with Sheila's liaison with the American airman, but more than that he couldn't guess. He saw little point in protesting that he hardly knew her. 'Of course. I'd be happy to meet you. When would suit you? You said you were over here for a few days.'

'That's right, and I'm travelling around a bit too. I don't want to impose myself but I wonder whether there is any way we could meet this evening.'

'Yes, I could manage that.'

'I'm staying at The Cumberland, Marble Arch. What about meeting in the bar at six?'

'All right, six at The Cumberland. How will we know each other?'

'I'll tell the barman to expect you and he'll point me out, I guess. My name again is Art Shiner.'

'Thanks. See you tonight.'

'I'm the one who needs to do the thanking, Mr Cunningham. I really appreciate this.'

Ted let Mary know that he'd be home late and then after work took the tube up to Marble Arch. The barman indicated a good-looking man with slicked-back dark hair sitting at a corner table.

He stood up as Ted approached. He was tallish – only a couple of inches shorter than Ted – and wearing a smart double-breasted brown suit. He held out his hand to Ted. 'Mr Cunningham. I'm Art Shiner. So pleased to meet you. Drink?'

'Well, a whisky and soda, then. Thanks.'

Art gained the barman's attention and ordered the drinks.

There were a few seconds of uneasy silence and then Ted said, 'Look, I think you should know that I don't know Sheila White very well, but through a rather unlikely set of circumstances I am currently looking after her son and I wonder whether this is anything to do with that.'

'I guess it is. Say, can I call you Edward?'

'Yes, of course, but it's usually Ted.'

'And I'm Art. How did you know it's about the kid?'

'Frank Bassett came to see me a few months ago and told me that he wasn't Geoff's real father and that Sheila had been seeing an American airman at the time. When you rang, I put two and two together. I'm guessing that you must have known him.'

'Known him? Fact is, I'm the guy.'

'But I thought he was missing in action.'

'Took them some time to find out, but I survived after all.'

'Oh.'

Art smiled. 'I can see it's a bit of a surprise, me being raised from the dead and all.'

'Well, of course it's very good news, but not quite what I had expected.'

'I can understand that. I guess I owe you an explanation.'

'I expect there's quite a bit of explaining I may need to do too, but you go first.'

'OK. Phew, where to start? I thought I'd practised this in my head but I'm kind of confused now. OK if I smoke?'

'Of course.'

Art offered the packet to Ted, who declined. He lit up himself, inhaled deeply and breathed out the smoke in a thin stream. 'I came over in '42 and only met Sheila in June. Just happened that

I ran into some fellow-musicians on my base and we put together a little jazz combo. Our first date was for some RAF dance and that's where I met Sheila. I could see her eyeing me up when I was on the bandstand and then during our break she started a conversation and we ended up spending the night together. Then we met a few times after that and then I was moved without warning for my first mission. I was a navigator and had to replace a guy who'd taken ill. That's why I never even had a chance to say goodbye to Sheila. I felt bad about that.

'It was my first mission and it all went wrong. It was a bombing raid on some enemy airfields in Holland but the Germans must have gotten wind of it somehow cos they were waiting for us. We were the first plane to get hit and everything went up in flames. I managed to bail out but they saw me coming down and organised a welcome party nice and quick. I tried to leg it but they caught me in twenty minutes. I'd twisted my ankle in the fall so I wouldn't have got far anyway.'

'Bad luck.'

'On the contrary, I was the lucky one. There were three of us in the plane. The pilot was killed in the fire and the third guy bailed out without a chute. I saw him sailing past me as my chute opened. The look on his face still gives me nightmares.

'I then got moved from one stalag to another. I guess I had something of a reputation as a troublemaker. Eventually me and some of the other Jewish guys were picked out and sent to a labour camp. That really was bad.'

'So you're Jewish?'

'Not practising, but good enough for a Nazi.'

'But surely that was against the Geneva Convention?'

'Trouble was, I didn't have my attorney with me. Sorry, I didn't mean to get smart. You're right. Generally the Jewish GIs were treated the same as everyone else, but this time I wasn't so lucky. But I made it, so I was lucky after all. Although, when I finally got back home I was not in a good way. Still, "time the great healer" they say, and I got over it.'

'Did you make contact with Sheila?'

'I wish I could say that I had. Truth is I hardly knew her. We had some fun – she was a good-looking girl – but it was wartime. I was young, trying to act tough though really scared as hell. It wasn't a love affair, at least I didn't see it that way. Anyway, I didn't even have her address. By the time the war was over my mind was on other things. I had some rehab, got back on my feet, got a job in the aero industry in Seattle, met a swell girl out there, got married and started a family. Let me show you.' He took a wallet from his inside jacket pocket and pulled out a photo of him standing next to a pretty blonde woman. Art was carrying a small boy and she was cradling a baby. 'That's Beth holding Carol – she's almost one now – and I'm holding Charlie. He's three.'

Ted studied the snapshot. The perfect American family. 'So why the interest in Sheila now?'

'Last year, my folks decided to sell their house and move to an apartment. They live in Boston. That's where I'm from. I went to help them pack up and among their stuff I found a box of things they'd put by for me, old school books, photo albums, that sort of thing. And when I went through it I found a letter from Sheila. It must have been forwarded from my base in England when I was missing. You see, it was quite a few months till they knew I'd been taken prisoner. I guess the letter was forgotten about. In it she said that she was pretty sure she was pregnant and asked to see me so we could decide what to do. She said she loved me and I'm guessing she hoped we'd get married. Boy, you can imagine how I felt when I read it.

'My wife, Beth, is an amazing woman and I have no secrets from her. So I took the letter back with me and asked her what I should do. We agreed that I had to find Sheila and see if she'd had the baby and do whatever I could to make things right. It turned out this was more difficult than it sounded. The Veterans Association and air force welfare people weren't much help, but one guy I spoke to said why not try a private detective agency.

Sounded crazy, like something out of Raymond Chandler, but I had to try everything. They worked with another agency based in London. They found out that Sheila had married and had a kid, but they checked the marriage record and the birth certificate and the dates fitted the time I was seeing Sheila. They traced Sheila and her husband to Cyprus but then both of them vanished from sight. But they did find out what happened to the boy. I guess I could have written to you, but I thought it would be better if I came to see you and then I could also meet,' he paused for a moment, 'my son. Luckily for me there was a sales trip to Europe due to come up, so I waited till then and... here I am.'

'So you know why Geoff is with me.'

'Not sure if I know all the details. Maybe it's your turn now.'

Ted then told his story: what happened at St Christopher's, Frank's visit, his plan to adopt Geoff and what he knew about Frank and Sheila from Phil Vine of the RAF police.

When Ted finished, Art gave out a whistle. 'This is the craziest thing I ever heard. They just abandoned Geoff with you? How could they do that?'

'That's how I felt, but when I found out that Frank wasn't really Geoff's father I could begin to understand.'

'Yes, but Sheila! For God's sake, this is her son.'

'I know. Frank said that she wasn't the maternal type and she also blamed Geoff for forcing her to marry Frank.'

'That's ridiculous. How could she blame a baby who had no part in anything?'

Ted shrugged.

'So tell me about Geoff. My son. I just can't believe this.'

Ted did his best to describe what Geoff was like, the progress he'd made since starting at Loriners', his musical abilities, his interest in cars, the friendship he'd made with Eric Lazarus. Art listened intently, closely observing Ted's face. 'You'll be really proud of him, I know,' said Ted, 'you couldn't ask for a better boy.'

Art felt his throat tighten and he wiped his eyes. 'I don't know what to say Ted. Seems to me he couldn't have asked for anyone better to take care of him. Thank you, thank you for doing what you did.'

'You don't need to thank me, really you don't. To say I've enjoyed every minute isn't the right word, but you know what I mean. I'm just so grateful that I had the opportunity to know Geoff and to help him. When he goes back with you, I don't quite know what I'm going to do.' And now it was Ted's eyes that were moist.

'Go back with me? Hold on. Did I ever say that? I've got to think this through. The idea was just that I would find Sheila and, well, make sure she and the kid were OK. I thought you'd know where she was. This has all been quite a shock. I don't know what I'm going to do.' Art closed his eyes, and let his chin rest on his collarbone. Eventually he lifted his head again. 'This is too much. I need some time.' He paused again and then leant forward. 'Could I meet Geoff, maybe tomorrow? Don't say I'm his father, just introduce me as a friend of his mother's.'

'I'm sure we could do that. He gets back from school at about a quarter past four. What about coming round for tea?'

'Tea, so very British,' Art laughed, a welcome release of tension. 'I have a meeting near London tomorrow and then I go to Paris for two days. I'm sure tea tomorrow would be OK.'

ON THE TUBE back home, Ted pictured Art and Sheila together. They would have made a handsome couple. Then images of Art bailing out of a burning plane, then a dark cell in some stalag, then the snapshot of Art and his new family, so wholesomely American. Then Geoff. Did he look like Art? A resemblance about the eyes, the hair? Or was he imagining it?

Home, Mary said that Geoff had gone to bed but was waiting for him to say goodnight. Ted went upstairs. The bedroom was still little changed. Ted's old model boat and kite still on top of the wardrobe, still the piles of old motor magazines, now augmented by some more recent editions and copies of *The Beano*.

'Sorry I wasn't here earlier. I had to meet someone after work. How was school?'

'Usual I suppose. But in music Mr Barlow asked if anyone was interested in learning an instrument.'

'Would you like to, as well as the piano?'

'I think so. Not sure. Eric says he wants to do trumpet.'

'What about you?'

'Not trumpet. Maybe clarinet. Or do you think violin would be better?'

'Difficult. Both would be good choices. When do you have to decide?'

'Not for a few weeks I think.'

'Well, give it some time and then see what you think.'

Ted said goodnight and went downstairs.

'Are you all right?' asked Mary, 'You look as if you've had a shock or something.' He recounted his meeting with Art.

'Oh, Ted. Do you think he's going to take Geoff back with him? What would we do?'

'He is Geoff's father, he has every right. He's made the effort to find him.'

'But you said he just wanted to straighten things out with Sheila.'

'Maybe, but now he knows what's happened perhaps he'll feel it's his responsibility to look after Geoff.'

'I can't bear to think of losing him. He seems so happy now, settled in his new school and… well… as if we were his real family.'

'But we're not his real family, are we? After all, a father is a father.'

'But you're the one who's been a father to him.'

'For a few months, that's all. I keep on thinking if it were the other way around, if I found my own son with a stranger with no blood ties, how would I feel?'

'But you're not a stranger. You love him and he loves you.'

'But if Art wanted to take him back, and I fought it and won, can't you see how eventually Geoff would find out and he'd hate me forever?'

'Oh, Ted.' And they held each other.

WHEN GEOFF CAME back from school the next day, he was surprised to find Ted home from work and a full tea laid out by Mary with home-made scones and cake. 'But my birthday's not till Saturday.'

'Don't worry,' said Mary, 'this is something different. We have a friend of your mother's coming for tea.'

'A friend of my mother's?' Geoff screwed up his eyes in an effort of concentration but simply couldn't think of anyone who could be described as a friend of his mother's. Then the doorbell rang. Ted got up and Geoff stood in the kitchen looking along the hall corridor to see who it was. Ted brought Art into the kitchen and introduced him to Geoff and Mary.

'Geoff, this is Mr Shiner.'

Art leaned down so that he could make closer eye contact with Geoff and shook him by the hand with a firm grip. 'Pleased to meet you, Geoff. I'm Art, an old friend of your mother's.'

'How do you do?' Geoff mumbled, looking at the floor.

Mary broke the silence with, 'Let's have tea.'

'Gee, this looks great. Scrumptious, isn't that what you say in England?'

They chatted for a bit about Art's work and what Ted had done in the RAF. Knowing it was rude to stare, Geoff tried to take surreptitious glances at the glamorous American. With embarrassment he found Art was looking at him too.

'Ted tells me you play the piano.'

'I'm only a beginner really.'

'Maybe you could play a bit for me later.'

Geoff looked at Ted, who nodded.

Geoff then surprised everyone, including himself by asking, 'How did you know my mother?'

'Oh, er, I met her before she got married. I was over here with the United States Air Force.'

'Oh.'

'But I left England before you were born.'

'Mr Shiner was shot down over Germany and taken prisoner,'

Ted added.

'Wow.'

Art was persuaded to tell them what had happened to him in the war. 'Hey, that's all in the past. What I'd really like is to hear Geoff play some piano.'

Geoff was bursting with questions about Art's wartime experience but could see that the moment had passed. They went into the sitting room and opened the lid of the piano. 'Why not try one of the Bach pieces?' said Ted. Geoff found the music and played one of the minuets, stumbling at first but then getting into his stride. At the end they all applauded and Geoff blushed.

'How long you been playing, Geoff?'

Geoff counted the months on his fingers. 'About five months I think.'

Art whistled. 'Gee, kid. You're good,' then, turning to Ted, 'and you have a great teacher too.'

'Do you play, Mr Shiner?' asked Mary.

'Hey, everyone, please just call me Art. Well I play a little piano, but clarinet is really my instrument.'

'I might be learning the clarinet,' said Geoff with excitement. 'No kidding!'

'Did you play professionally, Mr... Art?' asked Mary.

'I guess I sometimes got paid to play, if that's what you mean, but I never earned my living that way. Just played in bands when I was a kid and then with some guys in the air force.'

'What kind of music,' asked Ted.

'Well, I started classical. I even had lessons at the Boston Conservatory, but then I discovered jazz and never looked back. When I joined up I had an audition for one of the air force bands but those guys were too good for me and they thought I'd be more use as a navigator.'

'You said you played a bit of piano. Could you play something for us?' asked Geoff.

'It's been a long time, but, sure, I could try a little.'

Art sat down on the piano stool and started a left-hand

boogie-woogie pattern, slowly at first, but then speeding up like a locomotive getting up steam, then in came the right hand with the tune. It was *Honky Tonk Train Blues* Geoff later found out. He was captivated. More applause.

'Now Ted, what about you?'

As the others had played, Ted had no choice. He was an accomplished pianist but hated the limelight, especially following Art. He picked a Mozart sonata, a slow movement, not too flashy. At the end, Art nodded slowly. 'You're a fine musician, Ted, as well as a fine teacher.'

On the way out, Art whispered to Ted that he'd be in touch. When Art left, Geoff could talk of nothing else. 'I never knew my mother knew an American. What did he play on the piano? Is there music for it? Do you think the Germans tortured him? He must have been very brave.' Ted tried to hustle him along to get his homework done and get ready for bed.

On Saturday, Geoff had his birthday party. Eric came and another three friends from school. They played pass the parcel, musical chairs (with Ted playing the music on the piano), consequences, and hide and seek. Then there was a full birthday tea with jelly, sandwiches and birthday cake with candles. Geoff blew them out and everyone sang Happy Birthday. Geoff had never had a birthday like it.

At seven o'clock the doorbell rang. The guests had left and Geoff was doing a jigsaw on the sitting room floor. It was one of his birthday gifts, the Flying Scotsman, with two hundred pieces. He heard Mary: 'Art, what a surprise, how nice to see you again.'

Art came into the room. Ted jumped up from his newspaper and they shook hands. 'I'm sorry to have busted in like this. Is this a bad time?'

'Of course not, you're most welcome. Can I get you a drink? Cigarette?'

Art took a cigarette from the case proffered by Ted. 'A Scotch and some soda or water, whatever you have.' He was carrying something under his arm. 'Thing is, I have something for Geoff, for his birthday.' He handed him the package.

Geoff untied the string and took off the brown paper. Inside was what looked like a small leather-covered suitcase. 'Go ahead, open it,' urged Art.

Geoff pressed the two brass buttons on either side of the case and the hasps sprang open. Inside it was lined with red crushed velvet with five fitted indentations each holding a piece of black wood with metal attachments. A small metal plate attached to the velvet near one of the corners said 'Selmer'. Geoff looked at it for some time. He didn't want to seem ungrateful. He knew it was something special. 'Thank you. It looks marvellous. Thank you.' He paused. 'What is it, exactly?'

Art laughed. 'I'll show you.' He slotted the five sections together. 'Any ideas now?'

'It's a clarinet! I never knew they came to pieces like that.'

'You got it, kid. Let me show you.' He took out from his pocket a small cardboard box. 'These are reeds. You have to check them and try them. You'll be lucky if you get four good ones in a box of ten.' He held them up to the light one by one. 'This one looks good – see, the pattern's nice and even.' He put it into his mouth and licked it, then fastened it to the mouthpiece, carefully positioning it and tightening up the two brass screws on the ligature. The whole process seemed to Geoff like a magic trick. Then Art played. Scales, arpeggios, what Geoff later on found out were called 'licks' and some snatches of tunes. 'Now you try.'

Art showed him how to hold the instrument and the shape to make with his lips and mouth. Geoff blew. First nothing, then a horrible squeak, then something like a note. 'Atta boy, you got it. Your teacher will show the rest, but just one bit of advice from your Uncle Art in case the teacher forgets, every day you gotta start with long notes. Play them like you love them, like you're standing out front of the Philharmonic Orchestra. When you can play the long notes, the rest is easy.' Art turned to Ted and Mary. 'I guess I should warn you that you're going to have to get used to some pretty strange noises for the next few weeks until Geoff gets going.'

'Don't worry about that,' said Ted, 'it's a wonderful present. Thank you, Art.'

'Well, I was in Paris and I walked past a music store and there it was.'

Had it really been quite such a chance purchase? Ted said nothing, but anyway, there was no denying it was an inspired choice and he could see that Geoff was enchanted. He and Mary had given him a bicycle. It was second-hand but in good condition. Ted had overhauled it and touched up a few scratches. Geoff had been thrilled. It would get good use but Ted knew that any place it might have had in Geoff's heart had been quickly supplanted by the clarinet.

While Geoff was trying the clarinet, Art asked Ted if he could have a private word with him. 'Come into the kitchen, he won't hear us there.'

'Ted, I've spent the last three days thinking about what to do. I'm his father and the last thing I want to do is not to face up to my responsibilities. Sometimes I think, sure, he should come back with me to the US. Beth is a great mother and he'd have a kid brother and sister to play with, and I think I could be a good father to him. But then I think, boy, that kid has been through an awful lot. If he's happy here, why rock the boat? And Ted, would it be that easy for me take him? Wouldn't we have to get lawyers involved? And it could all take time and… well, I don't know, but it might upset him a lot. Hell, what do you think?'

'Mary and I are both very fond of Geoff. It's not official yet, so please don't mention it to anyone, even Geoff, but Mary and I are planning to get married next year.'

'Hey, that's swell. Congratulations.'

'Thanks. I think he already sees Mary as a sort of mother figure so I think he'd be pleased to know that she'll always be here, but that's really by-the-by, he's your son. If you want to take him, of course we'd miss him – desperately – but I'd support you if there's anything legal to deal with.'

'I really appreciate that. You're a very fair guy. Look, I couldn't take him right now even if I wanted to. A few days to think about this ain't gonna make much difference, so I'd like to discuss this with Beth and then I could write you.'

They all said goodbye to Art and he kneeled down and gave Geoff a hug, who looked surprised but happy. 'Thanks very much indeed for the clarinet. I promise I'll practise like you told me.'

# MAY 1952

TED HAD BEEN dreading Art's letter. Weeks went by with no word so it was something of a relief when at last an airmail envelope with United States stamps landed on the mat in the middle of May. At least the waiting was over.

> *Dear Ted,*
>
> *First, sorry for taking such a long time to get this letter to you. It hasn't been easy to think what to do and I wanted to make sure I took enough time to look at every angle.*
>
> *Beth and I have finally decided that it would be best for Geoff if we left him with you. I could see that he was happy in your home and it would put him through a lot to uproot him and make him start all over again. Just trying to explain how I come to be his father would be quite a big deal for a kid of nine to take in. It breaks my heart to think that I won't be taking care of my own son but I know I will be leaving him in the very best hands. Thanks to you and Mary for caring for him. I couldn't think of better people to leave him with. Even Frank and Sheila were right on that one!*
>
> *Maybe someday, when he's older, I might be able to meet him and then you and I could tell him this story and why I took this decision. I only hope that he won't think badly of me and will believe me when I tell him that I only wanted to do what would be best for him.*
>
> *I will still keep in touch, as the family friend he thinks I am, and I would appreciate any news you can send me of how he's getting on.*

*Yours sincerely,*
*Art*

Ted showed the letter to Mary. When she got to the end she embraced him and he felt his shirt become damp from her tears. She wiped her eyes. 'I don't know what I would have done if he'd taken our boy away.'

'I know,' said Ted.

'And when he told us about what happened to him in the war, and then playing the piano, and coming back with the clarinet, I could see Geoff slipping away, as if he was stealing him from us.'

'But Mary, Geoff is his son. He had every right.'

'But Geoff is happy with us. He loves us and we love him. How could we have been sure that Art would really have loved him like we do?'

'He says it breaks his heart not to be taking care of him. And anyway, he left him here because he could see it was for the best. Doesn't that show he loves him?'

# SEPTEMBER 1952

'You can open your eyes!' Ted and Geoff had somehow secretly managed to bake a cake, ice it and decorate it with twenty-one candles, which Geoff had just lit under Ted's careful supervision. Now Ted rushed over to the piano and he and Geoff sang a rousing chorus of Happy Birthday.

'Silly boys,' said Mary, the tears now rolling down her cheeks. 'Will you look at me? I'm such a blubber.'

'Quick, blow them out, otherwise they'll melt the cake,' said Geoff. Three puffs later, they were all out. Ted handed her a cake slice and she carefully cut three slices. Remembering from his own birthday in March, the first at which he'd had birthday cake, Geoff said, 'And don't forget to make a wish!' They watched carefully as Mary took a small bite of her slice, her tongue moving around her mouth and then licking her lips.

'Not bad – for beginners!'

They gave her their presents and then Ted said that he and Mary had some news they wanted to tell Geoff.

'Mary and I,' and he held her hand now, 'are going to get married,' and they looked eagerly at Geoff for his reaction.

His mouth opened and shut as he gulped for words. All he could say was 'gosh'. Seeing Mary and Ted smiling encouragingly he knew that wasn't enough. 'Er… bravo!' Bravo, he remembered, was what Mr Doughty had said to him when he'd tossed the pancake.

'You are pleased, aren't you?' said Ted. 'It'll mean that Mary will definitely be with us forever. And, when the adoption comes through, she'll be your mother.'

'Oh, yes.' He could see from their faces that they had expected a more enthusiastic response. 'It, it sounds very nice.'

'You look worried, Geoff,' said Mary. 'What is it? What's the matter?'

'It's just…'

'Go on.'

'Well, if you're married, won't you have children, your own children, and, and, you won't really need me then, will you?'

'Oh, Geoff.' Mary came and kneeled next to him, taking his hands in hers. 'Geoff, we'll never leave you. You're our boy. Even if there are other children, we'll still love you the same as before. You do understand that, don't you?'

Geoff nodded slowly.

'Oh, my boy.' And she hugged him tightly.

# PART TWO

# MARCH 1961

My eighteenth birthday. As usual, a package arrives from America. The first one had come a few days before my tenth birthday with instructions on the back of the brown paper parcel saying '*Not to be opened until March 28th*'. The shape of the package had rather given it away, but it had still been exciting to unwrap it and find the 78 sandwiched carefully between two sheets of plywood. The green label on the record said 'CARELESS LOVE – JOHNNY DODDS with Tiny Parham' and there was a card enclosed.

> *Dear Geoff,*
> *Happy Birthday. I hope you're well and still practicing your clarinet. Johnny Dodds was one of the first guys I ever listened to. He was one of the greats and you can learn a lot from him. Careless Love is a sweet number and I recommend you try and learn it off the record. There's no better way.*
> *Send my regards to Ted and Mary.*
> *Your good friend,*
> *Art*
>
> *P.S. Keep blowing those long notes!*

I followed his instructions to the letter, spending hours carefully lowering the needle on to the record and painstakingly learning the song until I was note-perfect. Of course, I didn't tell my clarinet teacher who was strictly classical.

I remember telling Eric about Art's visit at the time, in fact for a few weeks I could talk of little else until I saw that everyone was getting a bit fed up. Even if he hadn't sent me *Careless Love* and then the other records, I would never have forgotten him, but they made him seem yet more special to me.

I carefully unwrap the brown paper and pull out this year's record. It's Art Pepper – *Gettin' Together*. Art smiles out from the sleeve: he's wearing a black, button-down collar, short-sleeve shirt to match his dark hair. He's good looking. In fact there's almost a hint of my Art – Art Shiner – about him, although Art Pepper looks shortish and my memory is of Art Shiner being tall. I take the record out of the sleeve, clean it with the anti-static sponge, put it on the spindle and flick the start switch. The pick-up arm knocks the disc, it drops onto the turntable and there's a crackle as the stylus makes contact with the vinyl. The first few birthdays they were 78s, but then an LP came on my fifteenth. That year's present from Ted and Mary was my own gramophone, a Dansette Junior which could play 33s. Coincidence?

As usual Eric's with me. He's sitting on my bed and I'm on the floor. The music starts and at the same time I lay out all the previous birthday records on the carpet, starting with the five 78s: Johnny Dodds – *Careless Love*, Sidney Bechet – *Blame It On The Blues*, Artie Shaw – *Nightmare*, Benny Goodman – *Flying Home* and Benny Goodman – *I've Found A New Baby*. Then the LPs. The first is a ten-inch with the words *Classics in Jazz* as if handwritten onto a scrap of paper and paper-clipped to the sleeve. Below this 'Miles Davis' in capitals and a pen-and-ink sketch of him in full flight on his trumpet. Underneath are the track titles as if randomly piled on each other: *Deception, Rocker, Moon Dreams, Jeru, Venus De Milo, Godchild, Israel, Rouge*. Then the twelve-inch LPs: John Lewis – *Grand Encounter*, Sonny Rollins – *Way Out West*, and finally I put the sleeve of this year's record on the floor with the others: Art Pepper – *Gettin' Together*.

Eric picks up the family snapshot enclosed with this year's present. 'It's funny,' he says, 'but you look quite a bit like him, you know.' The first track finishes and the next tune starts.

I take the snapshot from Eric. 'Don't you think it's a bit strange that he's sent me a present every year? I mean, he's the only person I've ever met who knew my mother, apart from Ted, and then he sends me presents every year, and bought me a really expensive clarinet.'

'Maybe. I don't know. Perhaps he just took a shine to you or something. His name's Shiner after all!'

'That's pathetic. But, seriously, I've never told this to anyone but I've been going over it again and again in my head for ages, thinking about it every night before I go to sleep. There's only one explanation: the resemblance in the photo is because Art must be my real father.'

Now Eric turns and looks me in the face. 'Your father? Seriously? You told me your father had been in the RAF with Ted.'

'You mean Frank. But what if he wasn't my real father? What if Sheila – that's my mother – had an affair with Art, then he went off to fight and she lost contact with him? He told us when he visited us that he'd been shot down and taken prisoner. She then found herself pregnant and as she couldn't find Art she decided to marry Frank. At some point, maybe years later, Art must have found out. That's the bit I can't work out, but anyway, eventually he started looking for me and traced me to Ted. And surely he must have told Ted that he was my father and that's why he wanted to see me? What other reason could he have had? And look at the records. *Grand Encounter,* then *Way Out West,* and he lives in Seattle, about as west as you can get.'

'I'm not with you.'

'It's a message. He wants me to visit him: *Grand Encounter, Way Out West, Gettin' Together.* And look at the first ones: *Careless Love* and *Blame It On The Blues* would be describing my conception and then *Nightmare* what happened to him in the war perhaps and then…'

'*Flying Home,* after the war and *I've Found A New Baby,* his new wife…'

'Beth. Yes.'

'What about the Miles Davis? That doesn't make sense.'

'Well it's such a good record maybe he just couldn't resist sending it, but the first track is *Deception* and there's also *Godchild* and *Israel.*'

'What's *Israel* got to do with it?'

'Well, when he told us about being a POW in Germany, he said he was picked on because he was Jewish. Like you.'

Eric puts on an exaggerated Jewish accent, 'Welcome to the faith, my boy.' We laugh. He says, 'This is like Sherlock Holmes. Are you really sure? How would he know you'd get it?'

'I suppose he didn't, but if I am his son, maybe he thought I'd think the same way. And you know, my middle name is Arthur. It took me years to connect that with Art, but he must be Arthur too, so my mother named me after him. And now, with no prompting, you've mentioned that I look like him, and this year's record is *Gettin' Together* by *Art* Pepper.'

'Blimey! Have you told Ted and Mary you think Art's your father?'

'No. As I said, you're the only person I've told. If I'm right, then they must already know, but they don't know that I know.'

'So why not tell them now that you've worked it out?'

I think for a few moments. 'There must have been a reason why they didn't tell me, and it must have something to do with Art not taking me back with him. Wouldn't that have been the obvious thing? After all, I was only with Ted because Frank had dumped me on him. Art had taken the trouble to find me, came to see me, gave me a birthday present, really seemed to like me, but then leaves me behind. Why? I was his son, for God's sake.'

'Perhaps it just wasn't possible. Maybe the authorities wouldn't have let him take you. How could they have been sure he really was your father?'

'Seems a lot of trouble to go to just to kidnap a nine-year-old nobody wanted.'

'But you were wanted. Ted and Mary had decided to adopt you.'

'Yes. But still. It does seem odd, especially if I'm right about him now sending me a coded message that he wants me to go out to America to meet him.'

'And would you have wanted to go back with Art, if they'd told you he was your real father and he'd been able to take you?'

'Even though it was nine years ago I remember exactly how I felt. There was something so exciting about him. And the fact that he gave me the clarinet. It was like winning a prize you never expected to win. And he actually hugged me, which Frank certainly never did and even Ted hasn't ever done, and I remember wondering at the time what it would be like to have a dad like him. So the answer's yes, I would have gone with him.'

'I still don't understand why you can't talk to Ted and Mary about it. Maybe there's a simple explanation.'

'It seems disloyal. Ted doesn't have a selfish bone in his body, he'd always have been thinking of what was best for me and that's the only reason I can think that they decided it was better not to tell me. But if I tell him now that I've guessed it, it might upset him; he might think I'm angry that I wasn't told the truth years ago. And he might blame Art for sending me the message too, and, I know it sounds mad, but I don't want to get Art into trouble.'

'And are you angry with Ted about not telling you?'

I shake my head. 'It's pretty impossible to get angry with Ted. That's the trouble with him. I sometimes wish he'd stand up for himself more. He's almost too kind for his own good. So, not angry with him, I mean, look how things have turned out. I know I'm adopted but I really think I love Ted and Mary as much as you love your parents. And they've loved me back, and looked after and educated me and, well, given me all that I could have wished for, but at the same time I keep thinking: why should my life have depended just on the luck that Frank got Ted to give me singing lessons? I know you can argue that everyone's birth is an accident – who your parents are, how they treat you and everything – but at least if they're your real parents it's a sort of genetic destiny. When you're adopted it's just a matter of chance.

So I can't stop thinking about what it might have been like if I'd gone to live with Art.'

'Couldn't you just talk to Mary about it?'

'I've thought about that, but then it would be a sort of conspiracy, going behind Ted's back, and I don't think either of us could do that.'

'And would you really go to see him in America then – *Way Out West?*'

'Well, if I try for Cambridge, I'd have to stay on till the end of December and whether I get in or not, I'd still have nine months off till the next October, so I thought that maybe I could work most of the time and then earn enough to get over to America.'

'Have you told Ted about going to America?'

'Not yet.'

'What would he think?'

'I can't think he'd have any reason for discouraging me. He'd probably say "wonderful idea, old chap".'

'And would you tell him that you'd go to see Art?'

'No.'

'Wouldn't he guess?'

'I don't know.'

'And when you come back?'

'I suppose it depends on how it goes. But yes. I would tell them then.'

'Geoff – I've got to ask you, and just tell me to shut up if you don't want to talk about it – but what happened to your mother? Aren't you curious about her too? After all, she's also fifty per cent of your "genetic destiny" as you put it.'

'You mean Sheila.' I don't want to call her my mother. I want to disconnect her from me. 'All I'd been told was that she'd met someone else in Cyprus and had left Frank, so when I began to suspect Art was my father, I did ask Ted if he knew any more about where she was. He was very embarrassed, but he said he honestly didn't know for sure. The story was that she'd gone off with a Greek chap in Cyprus, but they'd both sort of disappeared.

The thing is, I was with her for the first eight years of my life and it's hard to think of any happy memories. She just didn't seem to like me. And if I was the reason she married Frank, then I can't really blame her. I'd see other children at school whose mothers were all lovey-dovey with them, which seemed peculiar to me. Sheila hardly ever touched me, so at the time I thought that was normal. Now I'm older, and after the way Mary treats me, and seeing people like you with your mother, I see that the way she treated me wasn't normal at all. But the fact is, unlike Art, she's never tried to contact me once in all these years, and she's known where I am all along, so I can't think of any reason I should go looking for her.'

# SEPTEMBER 1961

I'M BACK AT school for the Oxbridge scholarship term. Knowing that I'll be at university soon, Mary is worried that she won't have enough to do, so she's decided to go on a course to work with handicapped children. First she needs to pass O-level maths. She's forgotten a lot of what she did at school so I'm helping her to revise. I say that it seems funny, me helping her when she gave me so much help when I was small.

'But you're doing a grand job.'

'If I am, it's because I learnt from you. Don't you remember helping me with my handwriting when I started at Loriners'? I was so behind. And then later even with French, when you didn't know a word of it, and Latin.'

'Well, I knew a little from church.'

'And now I'm trying for Cambridge, and I wouldn't have been able to do any of this without you.'

'It's you who's done it. You were so clever, I saw it right away. You just needed someone to encourage you. And anyway, it wasn't just me. There was Ted too, he was always helping you. And your teachers at school.'

'But you showed me what to do. Before that, I used to panic if I didn't understand something. I remember when I started at the choir school, I didn't have a clue what to do, and no one would help me. It was pretty much the same at the other schools before that.'

'But did your parents never help you?'

'Frank and Sheila? Not that I remember.'

'But you learnt to read and write.'

'I was lucky. There was one teacher at my first school who used to help me, and when I left she gave me a children's dictionary so that I could look up words I didn't know. Not that there was anything to read at home, but then Frank's friend gave me the Motor Show catalogue and I'd read that for hours on end.'

'And even your mother? Did she never ask you about what you were doing at school?'

'I don't think so. That's why it was so different when I came to live here with you and Ted.'

'Well we had fun, didn't we? But still, you seemed so worried sometimes. We thought it must be because you missed your mother.'

I pause, trying to remember how I felt when I first came to Hammersmith. 'No, if I was worried, it wasn't because I missed Sheila, it would have been because I was scared I might have to go back to living with her and Frank.' And as I say this, I'm planning to go behind Mary and Ted's backs and meet Art. And I sort of know it's wrong, but I can't help it. It's a compulsion, like gamblers or alcoholics or drug addicts have I suppose.

# DECEMBER 1961

'THE POST'S HERE,' calls Mary, 'and there's a letter for you.'
Ted's already left for work. I come downstairs. The letter has
a Cambridge postmark. I take the letter into the sitting room
whilst Mary goes back into the kitchen. My hands are shaking and
sweaty as I open it. *'Dear Mr. Cunningham, we are sorry to inform you
that you have been unsuccessful in the recent scholarship examination and we
have filled all the places in engineering at this college…'* Bugger. Bugger!
Wait, there's more, *'But we have passed your papers to another college
in our group and I understand that they will be contacting you directly with
an offer of a place.'* What? I read it through again, and again, and
a fourth time. God. I've got in, I've got in! I go into the kitchen
and hand the letter to Mary. 'I think I've got in – somewhere.'
She reads the letter and hugs and kisses me.

'I can't believe it. Our boy going to Cambridge.' Overcome,
she begins to cry. She's always blubbing, but I don't mind, it's
one of her most endearing features. Between her sobs, 'Quick,
you must ring Ted.'

'Well done, old chap! Well done.' I imagine Ted in his office.
I can hear how excited he is. I think I'm almost happier for him
than for myself.

'I suppose I'll get a letter soon from the other college. I didn't
know it could work like this.'

The afternoon post brings another letter. It's from St
Christopher's College. I skim through it: *'…high standard, unusual
distribution of applicants to other colleges… very happy to welcome you to
the college next Michaelmas Term.'*

St Christopher's. I'd seen the name in the same group of
colleges but hadn't thought much about it. My physics master
had suggested the other college, they had a good record of taking
Loriners' boys, it never entered my head that applications might

be passed on from one college to another. But no matter. Why shouldn't I go to St Christopher's? They had made the offer. It must be all right. I ring Ted again.

'St Christopher's. That's a bit of turn up.' He pauses. 'But it's all right, isn't it? It's still Cambridge.' I wonder how much he thinks I still remember.

'Yes, of course. Just a bit of a surprise.'

'Is Mary there? Can I have a quick word?' I hand the receiver to her and she shushes me out of the room.

The conspiracy is revealed that evening. Ted comes up to my room and knocks on the door. 'Supper's nearly ready, but come down first into the sitting room.' When I get there I see that Mary's changed into her best dress and there's a tray with three glasses on top of the drinks cabinet. Ted disappears into the kitchen and returns with a bottle. It has gold paper around the neck with 'MOET' in black capitals, two dots over the E. Gold print on the label proclaims 'Dry Imperial, Moet & Chandon'. Ted carefully levers off the cork using his two thumbs. There's a pop and he catches the escaping foam in one of the glasses. He fills the glasses slowly, allowing the foam to subside. 'To Geoff!' We clink glasses. 'Well done! The last time I drank Champagne must have been Barbara's wedding. What do you think?'

Mary and I move our tongues around inside our mouths. It has a musty taste, almost nutty, but the bubbles also give it a lightness and sharpness. 'It's already going to my head,' laughs Mary, who hardly ever drinks.

Ted puts down his glass and comes over to me and shakes my hand, holding my arm with his other hand. I say, 'Thank you, Ted. I owe you so much.' This double handshake is already close physical contact for Ted and I know that he wouldn't feel comfortable if I hugged him. Is it because after what happened to me at St Christopher's he's always wanted to be careful not to do anything 'inappropriate'? More likely he's just not the hugging type.

'Don't be silly. You did this on your own. I'm so proud.' He turns his head away; I know it's because he doesn't want me to see that he's near to tears.

As USUAL, THERE are Christmas Eve drinks at the Lazarus's. They started the tradition of a Christmas Eve 'soiree' in 1952, so this will be their tenth. We've been to all of them and most of the other guests are regulars too. Eric says that it's the only way his father can commandeer an audience for his string quartet, as their performance is the centrepiece of the evening's entertainment.

Eric left school in the summer and is now doing medicine at Edinburgh. He's in the kitchen entertaining the younger crowd with anecdotes about dissecting cadavers, and eccentric lecturers.

'So you've got nine months before you start at Cambridge. What are you going to do?' It's Eric's older sister, Ruth. I like her but she's a bit scary. I'm always worried I'm going to say something stupid.

'Not sure yet. I think I'll try to get a job and earn some money and then maybe go abroad for a few weeks. Up to now the furthest I've ever been is Devon.'

'I've got a friend who went grape-picking in France. He had a wonderful time.'

'Or Greece.' Now it's Eric's brother, Adam, who's wearing a large knotted red-and-white spotted handkerchief around his neck. Eric says he fancies himself as a bit of a Bohemian. 'Apparently you can live on next to nothing on the islands. I know lots of people who went there last summer.'

'Maybe,' I say, 'but I had this notion of going to America.'

Ruth says, 'America! Golly, why America? Wouldn't that cost the earth to get to?'

'I thought perhaps I could work my passage. It's just somewhere I've always wanted to go to. And they speak English, so that would be easier.'

'Work your passage. How romantic.'

'What's this about working your passage?' says Eric's father, who's wandered into the kitchen to get some more wine.

'To America. It's just an idea. There was chap at school last year who went on a freighter. I think he helped in the kitchen or something like that.'

'Mmm. Let me think about this. Maybe I can help you.'

# JANUARY 1962

IN THE NEW Year, out of the blue I get a phone call from Mr Lazarus. 'Geoff, you said something at our party about working your passage to America. I have some contracts to provide bands for some of the liners. What about if I could get you into a band?'

I knew he was a music agent but thought he just organised classical concerts and that sort of thing. 'A band? But I've only done stuff at school. I don't think I'm qualified.'

'Nonsense. You're an extremely talented musician – and I know what I'm talking about. You'd be able to pick it up easily enough. You've sight-read some very tricky stuff at my house without any difficulty. This would be more-or-less the same, with a bit of jazz thrown in.'

'Gosh, jazz? I really think I'd be out of my depth.'

'But you and Eric played in that band at the Speech Day concert. You were very good.'

'But…'

'Look, this is what I want to suggest. The chap who puts the bands together for me is Les Bunting. He's a reed player himself. He's a grumpy old sod, but he's a first-class musician and one of the best band leaders in the business. I've had a word with him, and on my recommendation he's willing to give you an audition, but the decision is his. If he thinks you're up to it we'll have to get you into the union but I don't foresee any problems. You'd then have a free passage to New York and back. He could see you on Thursday morning at eleven. He's in Willesden. Not far.'

'Well, I suppose it's worth a go.'

'That's the spirit.'

'I don't know how to thank you, Mr Lazarus.'

'Happy to help. But remember, don't pack in engineering and go pro on me!'

This is a standing joke. For the last few years I've been playing the odd clarinet part at their Sunday afternoon 'scrapings' as Mr Lazarus calls them. 'You're too good for us, you know Geoff, but please don't go professional. I spend all day trying to get work for brilliant musicians. It's such a hard life for most of them and what was once a great pleasure can simply become drudgery. Better to stay a gifted amateur and choose when and what you play and who you play with.'

I FEEL MY heart thumping as I walk down the long curved street of small terraced houses with tiny front gardens. I check the house number and ring the bell. I see a shadow approach through the dirty coloured glass in the front door and it's opened by a bulky man with a greying short-back-and-sides haircut. 'Mr Bunting?'

'You must be Geoff. Call me Les.' He's wearing a threadbare cream shirt and dark grey flannel trousers slung underneath his beer-belly so that the trouser ends sit in folds over his grease-stained suede shoes. His voice has a gruff London accent and he's holding a lighted cigarette. 'Come in then.'

The front room is lined with shelves stacked with sheet music and records. Instrument cases and music stands are scattered on the bare floorboards along with a couple of grubby rugs. An upright piano and some plain dining chairs complete the furnishings. 'So you want to work on the boats. I'm only seeing you cos Jack Lazarus asked me and he thinks you can play.' There's an intake of breath. 'OK. Let's hear you.'

I open my clarinet case and self-consciously assemble the instrument. 'Here you are,' says Les, 'try this.' It's the clarinet part of a band arrangement of Benny Goodman's *Air Mail Special*. The tempo instruction at the top says Fast Swing. 'I'll count you in. One, two, a one-two-three-four.' I get to halfway down the page when Les interrupts with 'That'll do.' I think I haven't played it too badly.

'OK, I know it's your first look at it, but tell me what you got wrong.'

I feel six inches high. What do I say? 'Em... I think I might have fluffed a couple of notes in this run,' I point to somewhere on the page.

Les shakes his head. 'No, it's not the notes. You read the notes well, bloody well for a first go. Something else.'

Now what? My mind goes blank.

'It's the *feel*. "Fast Swing", it says. You've got to swing it. Listen to me.' Les opens a case and puts his own clarinet together and then plays the same section, accentuating the second note of each pair of quavers. 'Now, try again like that.' Of course. I was reading it like a classical piece. Why didn't I realise that? I try again. Les says, 'Better. But you're thinking too hard.' He's right. 'You've got to *feel* it. And tongue it on the off-beat too – that'll help. Play along with me and do exactly what I do.' We play it again. 'Got the idea?'

'I think so, yes.'

Les waves at one of the chairs, 'Sit down.' He takes puffs of his cigarette and strokes his chin with the other hand. 'Thing is, it's not just reading, you know, I need a jazzer. After the strict tempo stuff the punters like a bit of a jam session. Have you done any blowing?' I'm not sure what he means and stare blankly. 'Blowing, busking... improvising.'

'Oh. Well only a little. Me and some other chaps at school got together a band and played at Speech Day and some birthday parties.' Why did I say that? I sound like something out of P G Wodehouse. I look at Les's face and can see he thinks I'm a public school idiot. I say desperately, 'But... I can practise. I play along with records at home. I'll do whatever you tell me.'

Les rocks back in his chair. 'What records?'

'We started a record club at school. Eric, Jack Lazarus's son is in it. Even though we've left school, we still meet when we can. We swap records, all sorts of stuff, Louis Armstrong, Lionel Hampton, Lester Young...'

'Do they all start with an L?'

'No... sorry...' He's making fun of me but at least he's

130

smiling now.

'It's OK. Let's hear you then. Something you've busked on.'

Our band only has a repertoire of three numbers. I pick up my clarinet, mentally count myself in and start on the theme of *I Got Rhythm*. I then improvise for one chorus, and then finish with the theme again. I think I get the swing feel and put in some impressively fast runs. It feels better than how I usually play it.

Les has been rolling a cigarette as he listens and now he lights up and inhales deeply. 'When I started playing, nobody would tell you nothing. The old geezers said they'd had to learn it themselves and us young'uns would have to do the same. They were worried we'd take work away from them I suppose. Well I don't hold with that, so let's start with a few basics. First thing is, don't try to play so many notes. Play less and you'll say more. You've got to mean every note, you see. Playing fast is all well and good but it's what you say that counts. I'd rather hear three notes that mean something than twenty which say nothing. You say you've been listening to stuff – that's good – but how *hard* were you listening, and as well as the notes they played did you also hear the notes they didn't play? People need a chance for what they've just heard to sink in. Give 'em space. You with me?'

'Yes, I think so.'

'Oh, and one more thing: start strong. It's like Mark Antony, you know, "Friends, Romans" and all that rubbish. Get your first phrase in your head before you start, and play it like you really mean it – chances are it'll carry you through to the end.' He pauses. 'Do you want to try it again? Just the first eight. I'll bang out the chords. Take it slowly. Tell me when you're ready and I'll count you in.' He goes over to the piano. 'Remember,' he jabs his finger for emphasis, 'good first phrase.'

I close my eyes and try to concentrate for a few seconds. 'OK. Ready.' My first phrase is just seven notes spread over two bars. I then repeat it with only the last two notes changed. As Les has said, the last four bars just seem to find their own way home.

'Maybe, maybe,' Les mutters under his breath. 'All right. But it's going to take a bit of time. Can you come back for lessons? It's fifteen bob an hour, mind.'

'That's OK. I'll be working at my father's printing works and he's going to pay me.' I've done it again, it sounds so pathetic.

'Very nice,' with sarcasm. 'All right. Here's what I want you to do for next time.'

I don't think of jazz musicians being great at writing out music, but incredibly quickly and neatly he jots down some exercises for me on a sheet of manuscript paper. 'Practise these in every key till they're second nature.' Then he looks through a pile of sheets on top of the piano. 'You've got to learn the standards. Let's start with these,' and he gives me *All The Things You Are, Just Friends* and *Body and Soul.* They're on manuscript paper with just the melody lines and chord symbols above them. 'Do you know what the chords mean?'

'Sort of,' I lie.

'Well, just listen to some records of these and with your ears you should be able to work it out. These dots are in concert by the way, so you'll have to transpose to B flat, but best to learn them by ear so that you can play them in any key. Got to keep the bloody singers happy, haven't we?'

I don't really understand what any of this means but I nod anyway.

'The main thing is to listen to everything you can. And when I say *listen* I mean *listen.* At the end of the day that's the only way you can learn to play jazz.'

DURING THE DAYTIME I work at P V Cunningham and in the evening I try to practise for at least two hours. At the weekends I practise six hours or more. This isn't just about earning Les Bunting's respect and getting the job on a ship. There's more to it. I just want to be able to do this – to master it, to get as good as I can. With the band Eric and I performed in at school, I know that the applause was more for effort than for quality. Now I want to do it properly.

The public library has recently opened a record section and I can borrow three LPs at a time. I choose records which have versions of the standards Les has asked me to learn, and following his advice, I listen to them over and over again, playing along with them and trying to understand the notes that go into each musician's solo. I also sit at the piano and work out the chords and what they're called – minor sevenths, flattened ninths and so on. I think I'm getting the idea.

I LEAVE WORK early to get to my first lesson. I feel pleased with my progress but I'm still full of trepidation. Les opens the door. A smell of boiled potatoes and tobacco smoke hangs in the air. I get out my clarinet and place on the music stand the sheets of manuscript paper he gave me last time. Les looks over my shoulder and points at one of the exercises. 'Try this one first.' It's an arpeggio going up one octave and then coming down a semitone higher, then up again another semitone higher and so on. 'And with the swing tonguing like I showed you. Start on your low C. I'll count you in.' I play as instructed and I take Les's nod as a note of approval. 'Do it again, but this time starting on your high C and coming down.' I do this without incident. 'And the other exercises, how d'you get on with those?'

'OK, I think.'

'Well then, let's try one of the charts. *All The Things You Are* in A flat concert as written. I'll bang out the chords for you.' Les goes to the piano and counts out a medium tempo. I concentrate as hard as I can but there's so much to think about I start fluffing notes and then stop altogether.

'Sorry. I played it OK at home but it won't come now.' I expect a gruff response but Les is gentle.

'We all have that sometimes. Just take a few deep breaths. You're trying too hard. Trust yourself. Trust the music.' He counts in again.

I get to the end and look questioningly, almost pleadingly at Les. Les nods slowly, talking to himself more than to me, 'Yeah, you might just be getting the hang of it.'

AFTER ABOUT SIX weeks of lessons I notice an absence of strong criticism which I take to mean that Les is reasonably happy with my progress. Then comes a minor bombshell. 'Course, clarinet isn't going to be much use on the boats. It'll be all right for the odd arrangement but you'll need to be on sax for most of the time – alto would probably be best.' Even Les takes in my crestfallen expression. 'I've got a spare alto I could lend you while you get it together.' He rummages around and presents me with a worn case. 'You'll want to get a better mouthpiece, but it'll do to start with. Let's see what sound you can make.'

The alto feels completely different to the clarinet and my first attempts are pretty rough. 'Don't worry. You'll get there. But you need to hear the sound you want in your head to give you something to aim for. You'll need to practise lots of long notes – at least fifteen-minutes-worth every time you practise. It's the only way.'

'That's what I was told when I first started the clarinet.'

'Well whoever told you that, knew what they were talking about.'

AFTER A FEW weeks I begin to feel that I'm making a halfway decent sound on alto. It also fits the sort of music I want to play. Then Les asks me if I'm free the following Friday evening. 'I've got a gig down at the Feathers. Maybe you could sit in for a couple of numbers.'

'Oh,' my heart starts beating faster, 'am I ready?'

'We'll see.'

Some numbers are selected and I practise them inside out for the next couple of days. The Three Feathers is near Shepherd's Bush. It's seen better days, but it has a large back room which is a regular venue for British jazz bands with the occasional American guest. I've been there with Eric two or three times to see some leading lights. It's arranged that I'll play two songs with the band at the end of their first set. I haven't told anyone else about it and am relieved to see it's a thin audience. Fold-up wooden chairs and small round tables are crammed into the room. It seems that most of the people are regulars and I sit on my own at the back of the room slowly sipping a pint. The band leader is nominally the trumpet player but the line-up has been put together just for tonight. All the musicians play regularly with each other in various outfits – dance bands, orchestra pits, studio ensembles – and the way they communicate makes me think of some foreign ex-patriot community getting together simply for the joy of speaking their own language in alien surroundings. A list of songs has been agreed in advance, but each number is preceded by a short discussion just to confirm intro, 'outro', solo order, rhythm and tempo.

Les is on tenor saxophone. This is the first time I've heard him playing properly and I'm in awe of his sound, technique and inventiveness. The other musicians are of a similar standard and the crowd, although small, is appreciative, applauding at the end of each solo and grunting 'yeahs' and giving knowing nods when one of them plays something particularly nice.

The trumpeter has been giving brief introductions, sometimes with a witty play of words in a deadpan delivery. Now he steps forward and waves towards me. 'Unlike us old geezers who have great futures behind us, for the last two numbers of our set I am going to invite to the stage a young debutante (there are wolf whistles from the audience) who my old pal Les, here, says may soon be taking the bread from our mouths. And you will be able to say that you heard him here first. Please welcome to the bandstand, Geoff Cunningham.'

I try desperately to avoid eye contact with the applauding audience as I pick my way to the front and retrieve my instrument from where I've left it assembled on a chair behind the drummer. My first number is *Just Friends*. I line up with Les and the trumpeter, who whispers, 'Don't worry, you'll be fine. You play the theme and Les and me will do some noodling. You count us in.' I look around and smile grimly at the pianist, bass player and drummer and then call out 'one-two-a-one-two-three…' as I've heard Les do a hundred times.

I have no memory afterwards of how I played, but I recall that after my two-chorus solo there was enthusiastic clapping, a cry of 'good on you, boy' and, most unexpected of all, a pat on the shoulder from Les. After the others have soloed, I lead off the theme again and then to my own amazement when I get to the last-but-one bar I spontaneously nod to the others to indicate that I want to slow to half the tempo and they all follow me exactly.

At the end of the set I shake hands with the musicians. 'Nice playing,' says the drummer. 'Is this really the first time you've played in public?'

'Pretty much, apart from some stuff at school, but it was nothing like this. I can't believe that I've played with you chaps. You all made it so easy for me. I don't know how to thank you enough.'

'It was a real pleasure,' says the trumpeter. 'Any time.'

At my next lesson, Les tells me that there isn't much more he can teach me. 'When Jack Lazarus asked me to see you I don't mind telling you I thought it was going to be a complete waste of time, but I suppose I should have known better. I've got a lot of time for Jack. He's nobody's fool. Anyway, now we've got to find a way of getting you a job on the boats. Course, it's not what it was. Used to be only the cream could get a job on a boat, but now with these jets, they're having to cut back on entertainment and they've dropped the rates. That should help you though. Even then, they've got their standards and you'll need to show you've got some experience. Not much, just something for a reference, so what about a week or two at a Butlins at Easter? I know someone who could probably fit you in. It'd be mainly reading, easy enough, and you'd earn yourself a bit of dough to get your own alto. You'd have to join the union too, but I can pull some strings.'

On my birthday, another LP comes in the post from Art. It's Miles Davis – *Someday My Prince Will Come*.

# APRIL 1962

THERE ARE ONLY two of us in the compartment by the time we get to Bognor. He's a middle-aged man and he holds the door open for me as we get off the train. There's a hissing noise and a cloud of steam as we walk down the platform. 'You should remember this sight for your children,' he says. 'It'll be all diesel next year.'

The other band members already know each other; they're civil enough but I'm back to being the new boy at school. We have a rehearsal for the opening event tonight and I acquit myself well enough to relax a bit. Most of the others are in their forties and fifties but there's a saxophone player and a trumpeter in their early twenties who decide to take me under their wing. Mike, the trumpeter, explains: 'The great thing about this gig is the birds. They're desperate for it and they love musos. Good-looking lad like you will have them crawling all over. Course, consorting with the punters is officially frowned on, but as they say, "what the eye can't see" and whatnot.'

'And don't forget the Redcoats,' added Billy, the sax player, 'there's some crackers.'

Mike sees the lost look on my face and adopts the character of a smarmy Dickensian cockney. 'Ah, William, I think we have an innocent on our 'ands. Might I assume that you are unfamiliar with matters carnal, young Geoffrey?' We're leaning on the terrace balustrade in front of the miniature golf course with a grey sea in the background. Mike and Billy are smoking but I've declined the offer of a cigarette. I feel the blood rush to my face. 'Ah, say no more,' continues Mike, 'just count yourself fortunate that you have found yourself in the company of a couple of muckers who will see you all right. Will we not, William?'

'Indeed we will, Michael.'

'Now, have you got protection?' I'm too self-conscious to say anything. 'I take that as a no.' He reaches into his trouser back pocket and hands me a tiny maroon and white envelope marked Durex Protectives. 'With the compliments of the house. There's a couple here to be going on with, but you'll need to get your own, soon as. There's a Boots in the town.'

'Er, thanks,' I mumble.

Mike puts his arm around my shoulder. 'Don't look so glum. Blimey, you queer or something?'

'No. It's just that I haven't met many girls.'

'Ah, shy. Don't worry, we'll soon put that right, won't we William?'

THE HALL IS already packed when we take up our places on the bandstand. The audience ranges from young teenagers to pensioners, with one toothless old codger in a double-breasted suit complete with medals. After some introductory banter from one of the Redcoats, the music starts and people flood on to the dance floor. To avoid the flashes from the revolving mirror ball, I keep my eyes down and concentrate on the music in front of me and only occasionally raise my gaze to look for cues from the band leader. This is serious. I'm being paid to perform. A professional. Although I'm sure nobody is looking at me, the part demands that I appear cool and nonchalant. But inside I feel the excitement, the energy, something infectiously animal in the smell of smoke, beer, cheap scent and sweat.

After a bottle of whisky is awarded to the raffle winner, the last dance is called and then at midnight the campers are told to return to their chalets with the expectation of another fun-filled day tomorrow. In the band room behind the stage, instruments are put in their cases, dinner jackets are changed out of and hung up in lockers, and civvies are donned. Billy and Mike catch me outside the fire door which opens on to the tarmacked parking area behind the hall. 'Right, you're on,' says Mike nodding over his shoulder to the far corner of the car park where I make out three figures huddled next to some bushes. We walk over. With mock formality, Mike introduces me to Doreen, Pam and Jean and we all shake hands. There are mumbles of 'pleased to meet you' and 'how do you do'.

'These beautiful and charming music lovers have expressed to me their desire to pursue philharmonic conversation around the perimeter fence of Stalag Bognor. Is that not so, m'ladies?' There are giggles. 'Right. Let's go.' Mike grabs Pam's hand and amid shrieks and the clatter of heels he pulls her into the darkness.

'One for all and all for one!' cries Billy and similarly runs off with Doreen, which leaves Jean and me. I know I'm blushing deeply.

She turns to me. 'Your mates are right comedians, aren't they?' She has a slight West Country burr.

'I suppose so. I only met them today. I don't know them that well.'

'They told me you might be a bit shy. You're not shy are you? Not really?'

'Em…'

'Come on, give us a kiss, handsome.' And then she grabs my head and pulls it down so that our lips meet and she pushes her tongue into my mouth. 'Now, that weren't too bad, was it?' She waits for a reply. 'Well, was it?'

'Er, no.' Not knowing what I'm supposed to do, I put my arms around her and kiss her back.

'Now that's better, in't it?' and she presses me hard towards her and rubs my back and then grabs my buttock. 'Let's find somewhere more comfortable, shall we?'

The bushes mark the edge of a small shrubbery and we scramble under the low branches to a soft patch of ivy and slightly damp leaves. 'Cor, it's a bit parky, in't it? I need warming up.' She pushes me on to my back and climbs on top of me and then we roll together on to our sides.

'You're gorgeous, you are. I was watching you when you was playing in the band. I said to the other girls, he's the one I'm having.'

I've no idea what the etiquette is, but I manage to stammer, 'You're smashing too.' In fact I've hardly taken her in. Blonde curly hair, I think, dress a bit too tight, holding in a plumpish figure.

'Come on, lover boy. This your first time, is it?'

There's no point feigning experience. 'Yes.'

'Don't worry. I'll show you what to do. I won't bite – at least I'll try not to.' And she nips my neck in a fit of giggles.

I GET BACK to my four-berth chalet and creep into my bed whilst my older room-mates snore. At breakfast Mike and Billy catch up with me. 'How d'you get on, Romeo?' asks Mike.

'OK, I suppose.'

'OK, I suppose,' Mike mimics me. 'Well did you or didn't you?'

'I did.'

'That's my boy. Extra sausage for you this morning!'

JEAN GOES HOME on Easter Monday. Then there's Maggie and then Susan. They all seem to know the rules of the game: intimate physical contact with talking restricted to Anglo-Saxon expletives and snatches of polite conversation innocuous enough for a vicarage tea party. I know nothing about them and they know nothing about me. They seem to find it satisfactory and I certainly enjoy it at the time, but that's the extent of it – something transient and forgettable. After all the hype, I was expecting something more. The rest of the time I find a quiet corner where I can practise and I put in a good six hours a day. This also gives me an excuse to get away from Mike and Billy who've wheedled out of me that I've got a place at Cambridge and now refer to me as 'the professor'.

# MAY 1962

'THIS IS THE best I can do.' It's a Monday morning and Les has rung the P V Cunningham number I'd given him. 'One of my blokes wants to take off three weeks while his wife has a baby. That would give you six days to New York, five days there and then six days back.'

'Only five days in New York?'

'I said, that's the best I can do. I'm not a bleeding travel agent. We're lucky this has come up. But I need to know right away as the boat leaves on Friday and if you can't do it I'll have to find someone else.'

'I'll do it.'

'Good. You got an alto yet?'

'Yes, it's just being checked over at the shop. I'm picking it up tomorrow.'

'What you get?'

'An old Conn underslung.'

'How old?'

'The man thought it was around 1946.'

'Rolled holes?'

'Yes.'

'Good. Nice horn. What you pay for it?'

'Seventy.'

'Reasonable enough.'

'Oh, I've just thought of something. Is there an address in New York I can give for someone to write to me at? There's somebody I'd like to see when I'm over there but if they write back to me here it won't arrive in time.'

'We always stay at Mrs Grady's place.' He gives me the address.

I GIVE THE news to Ted and Mary, who is in a high state of

excitement. 'I've always wanted to go there. There was someone I was at school with who went to live in New Jersey. You could look them up, I'm sure they'd love to meet you.'

'I'm only going to be there for five days. I'm not sure how much I'll be able to do.'

'Course,' says Ted, 'you can leave that for your next trip, old chap. You'll want to see the sights and my goodness you'll need a bit of a break I should think, and you'll have earned it too.'

I go up to my room and write an airmail letter.

> *Dear Art,*
>     *I have managed to get a job playing in a band on a transatlantic liner. I will have five days in New York from 24th to 29th May. Is there any way I could meet you? It's already too late for your reply to get here before I leave, so please write to me c/o Mrs Grady, 296, Manhattan Avenue, Brooklyn, NY.*
>     *By the way, I have a place at Cambridge University to read engineering, starting in October.*
>     *Hoping we will meet again soon.*
>     *Love to you and your family,*
>     *Geoff*

I fold the blue airmail form, lick the gummed flaps and press them down. My saliva leaves a dark smudge along the edge of the paper and it slightly puckers as it dries.

On the way back from the post box I'm wracked with guilt. I've gone behind Ted's back, the man who's given so much to me, who's shown me such kindness, and yes, whom I love as his son. Another voice says: you have to do this on your own.

TED AND MARY insist on driving me down to Southampton on the Friday morning. Ted has replaced his old Riley RMA but has stayed loyal to the marque and now owns a Riley Pathfinder. When I was younger the three of us would sit cosily on the front bench seat with me watching in the middle as Ted changed gear, but now I'm too big and Mary sits in the back.

Most people arrive by train and the car park seems something of an afterthought. It takes us nearly fifteen minutes to walk to the passenger terminal, passing warehouses and goods wagons. The terminal building looks just like another warehouse from the outside but inside it's rather luxurious, with a bar and comfortable seats. A uniformed attendant checks my ticket and passport and points me towards a designated waiting area. As it's only for those embarking, I have to say goodbye there to Ted and Mary, who is dabbing at her eyes with a small handkerchief. Ted and I shake hands and he pats my shoulder. 'Good luck, old chap. I'm sure you'll have a wonderful time. A real adventure.' He then takes something out of his pocket. It's a small package wrapped in brown paper. 'Something from Mary and me.' Mary gives me a hug and then waves me away, clenching her lips so as not to break down.

'I'll be fine, Mary. Don't worry.'

Mary nods back behind her tears.

I walk over to the waiting area and count to ten before I look back and watch them making their way slowly out of the terminal arm in arm. I turn back towards the benches and see Les with some other men, whom I assume are the other band members.

'Ah, Geoff. Come and meet the gang. You know Ron, our pianist from The Feathers, and this is Sid, our drummer, Terry on bass, Mick on trumpet and Bluto on trombone.

'I'm Alf really,' says the trombonist, putting out his huge hand. He's a giant of a man with a large black beard and wild hair whose nickname is based on his close resemblance to the villain in the Popeye cartoons. 'Very pleased to meet you, Geoff, Les has told me all about you. Welcome aboard.'

The Tannoy starts calling passengers and embarkation begins. The ship is bigger than I'd imagined and it takes almost half-an-hour for us to board. I find that I'm sharing a cabin with Les in the bowels of the ship and I follow him down countless stairs and corridors till we reach it. Once inside, there's barely room for us both to stand at the same time. 'You hop on to the top bunk while I get organised and then it's your turn.' Whilst Les unpacks what he can into a small built-in cupboard, I open the package from Ted. It's a camera. I smile as I read the name *Reid* engraved in a handwriting script on the top. Ted has told me about Reids – they'd used them in the RAF, a Leicester-made copy of a Leica but in Ted's opinion even better made. There's a note from Ted. *I've already loaded it with a colour film. F8 on a 250th should cover most situations. Take plenty of pictures to show us when you get home.'* More pangs of guilt course through my body for not telling him about writing to Art. But then maybe Art won't write back to me and then it won't matter.

Les has finished unpacking. He looks over my shoulder at the camera. 'That looks nice.'

'Yes, it's a present from my father.'

'You're lucky. The only thing my dad ever gave me was a clip round the earhole. Here, I've left some space for you to hang up your dinner jacket.'

'Gosh, quite tight, isn't it?'

'There's worse, I can tell you. But the food's usually OK. You don't get seasick, do you?'

'I don't know, I've never been on a ship before.'

'Here, you'd better take one of these then. We're playing tonight and I can't have you throwing up all over the shop.' He rummages around in the cupboard and hands me a packet of Dramamine sea-sickness pills. 'They might make you a bit drowsy but that's better than being sick.'

I take one of the pills, swallowing it without water. Just as well. As soon as the ship enters the open sea, I start feeling queasy. The pills numb the nausea but I can still feel the dull ache and can't bring myself to eat anything. The band meets at six for a run-through of the evening's song list. I've already looked through my parts earlier and despite feeling pretty awful I manage to get through the rehearsal all right.

After dinner the passengers – first-class, I assume – come into the saloon in evening dress and the band kicks off. Luckily it's a thin crowd, as many are also in the process of getting their sea legs, and we're able to finish without any requests or encores.

The next morning I feel quite a bit better but Les advises me not to eat much breakfast and gives me some plain chocolate to stave off my hunger as I watch the others tuck into bacon and eggs. Then it's time to practise and I'm surprised that even though the musicians are experienced pros, they still go through daily routines of scales and exercises. Les says, 'If you don't practise one day, you'll know; if you don't practise for two days, I'll know; and if you don't practise for three days, everyone'll know.'

That evening the crowd is much livelier, drinking more and as it gets later, they urge us on enthusiastically. Then the requests start. Sometimes the numbers are in our pad and we can play a stock arrangement, but for others we simply agree a key and improvise harmonies as we go along. The budget hasn't stretched to a singer so Bluto doubles on vocals with a gravelly but surprisingly sensitive delivery, and the incongruity of this wild-looking giant gently crooning make him a particular hit with the audience. Les signals who should take a solo and I'm acutely self-conscious when it's my turn. The audience become irrelevant as I know that the only discerning critics in the room are my fellow band members, who will notice any wrong note or stumble. All I can do is concentrate, with Les's words 'play less, say more' echoing in my head. At the end of the evening as we pack up our instruments, Les says, 'Good work,' and then looks in my direction, 'everyone,' and I began to relax.

THE ROOMS IN our digs in Brooklyn are spotlessly clean and Mrs Grady is famous for her large breakfasts. She asks which one of us is Geoff Cunningham and hands me a Western Union telegram. 'GREAT YOU ARE COMING TO NYC. CALL ME COLLECT 206-655-2121 AS SOON AS YOU CAN AND WE CAN ARRANGE TO MEET. LOOK FORWARD TO

SEEING YOU SOON. LOVE ART'

Mrs Grady lets me use her phone to call 'collect' and I give the operator the number Art has given me. I'm connected to the switchboard at Art's work. 'Mr Shiner, please.'

'Putting you through.'

A female voice answers, 'Mr Shiner's office.'

'Can I speak to him? This is Geoff Cunningham. I'm ringing from New York. I've just arrived from England.'

'Geoff, yes, Mr Shiner said to expect your call. I'll transfer you now.'

'Hey, is that really Geoff?'

'Yes. Hello.'

'Wow, I can't believe it. You made it.'

'Yes, no icebergs luckily.' We laugh.

'So you still only got five days here?'

'Yes, I go back on Tuesday.'

'Too bad you can't stay longer. I expect you'd like a day to see the city but then you could come out here for the weekend. Today's Thursday, so I was thinking I could book you on the Friday evening flight from Newark. It leaves at 5.45 and gets in around 8.30 our time. Then you can go back on Monday some time.'

'Well, if you're sure...'

'Great. The tickets will be waiting for you at the Northwest desk at Newark. I suggest you get there an hour before take-off. Where you staying?'

'Brooklyn.'

'Fine. Get a cab to the airport. Have you got money?'

'Yes.'

'Good. I'll pay you back of course. This is on me.'

'That's OK.'

'No, you're my guest. I'll be waiting for you at Sea-Tac.'

'Sea-Tac?'

'Sorry, Seattle airport. It's really Seattle-Tacoma you see. So it's the Northwest 5.45 direct flight from Newark, tomorrow,

Friday. You got that?'

'Yes. I've got it.'

'Hey and we can go to the World's Fair too. It's something else.'

'Thank you. I don't know what to say.'

'Don't worry, you don't need to say anything. Can't wait to see you tomorrow. Oh, I nearly forgot to say, you've been playing in the band on the ship. Clarinet?'

'Alto sax mainly.'

'No kidding. Make sure you bring your horn with you. So long.'

'Bye.'

On Les's recommendation, I go to Manny's on West Forty-eighth Street and buy a new mouthpiece for my alto and then walk south to the Empire State Building to take photos for Ted and Mary. In the evening I go out with Les and Bluto to a jazz club to hear one of our idols. But, exciting as it all is, all I can think of is what it's going to be like meeting Art tomorrow.

I INSTANTLY RECOGNISE Art as I enter the Sea-Tac arrivals concourse. I wave to him tentatively. Art takes a moment to make eye contact as he confirms to himself that it must be me because of the saxophone case and then puts out his arms. I've only been expecting a handshake, but realise in time to put down my cases and accept Art's embrace. It's the first time I've been hugged by a man since Art's visit on my ninth birthday. As we break apart, I notice that there are tears in his eyes.

'Let me take a look at you.' Art holds me at arms' length and looks me up and down. 'Gee, I can't believe it. That scrawny little kid I met in London. And now...' He takes my alto case and we walk out to the car park. 'So tell me how you got to play on a liner.'

I explain about Jack Lazarus and Les.

'And you picked up the alto, just like that. Good boy. And the jazz, too?'

'Well, you'd got me started when I learnt *Careless Love* off the record.'

'You did that? No kidding.'

'Yes, but I didn't really know what I was doing then. It was Les who got me on the right track. It was hard at first, but then I sort of got the hang of it. Well, I think I did, anyway.' We reach the car. It's an enormous thing with fins, twin headlights and a bullet-shaped chrome mirror mounted on the driver's door. 'Gosh, is this yours?'

'Yup. Buick Electra. What do you think?'

'It makes our cars look so tiny. It's more like a plane or a rocket than a car. Have you seen the Morris Mini-Minor? It's about a quarter of the size.'

'Our cars may be big but I read about that Mini-Minor. That's some neat engineering. Front-wheel drive, transverse engine, rubber suspension. You English are innovating, while under the hood our autos hardly change. It's just styling here. That's what sells, I guess. Hey, you're going to study engineering at college. Are you thinking of working in the auto industry?'

'Actually I'm more interested in aeronautical engineering.'

'You don't say, and me working for Boeing.' The car starts with a throaty hum. 'So you were saying this guy Lazarus said maybe he could help you get a job on a liner, but why not just play in a band at home?'

'Well, the liner job was really just so that I could get over to America. It would have been too expensive otherwise.'

'Why America?'

I think for a few moments before answering. I've rehearsed this speech many times but I don't want to rush into it. 'I suppose it was as much to see you as anything.'

'Me?'

'Er, yes. Well, it was the way you came to see me when I was a boy and then getting me the clarinet and sending me the records. I feel connected with you I suppose.'

'Connected?'

'And you knew my mother too.'

'Yeh.'

'And the records,' I pause again, 'well, I might be imagining it, but it seemed like there was a message.'

'A message?'

I swallow. 'That you wanted me to come out and visit you. *Grand Encounter, Way out West, Gettin' Together, Someday My Prince Will Come.*'

We stop at some traffic lights. The lights change and Art moves the car away slowly. 'You know, I never thought in a thousand years that you'd get that. I don't even know why I did it. I guess that first number…'

'*Careless Love*, you mean.'

'Yup, *Careless Love*, I guess that gave me the idea and then I just couldn't stop myself.' He exhaled a long breath through loose lips.

'*Careless Love* because that was you and my mother?'

'I guess so.'

'So you are my father.'

'Yeh,' he was nodding slowly, 'I am your father.' We drive the next block in silence. 'And did you tell Ted what you thought?'

'No. It was as if your message with the records was maybe supposed to be a secret between you and me.'

'Yeh, I can see that now.' Art says nothing for another block. 'The thing is, I'd promised to myself and Beth that I was going to tell you before we got to the house – get things out in the open right away, start right, you know – but I couldn't imagine how I was going to do it and you beat me to it anyway. Hey, we're here.'

It's a tree-lined road with neat two and three-storey houses on either side. Some are clapboarded, painted in white or pastel shades, others have brick walls, some a mixture of both. Their porches look out onto tidy lawns without any walls, fences or hedges separating one front garden from the next. Art drives the car up a short driveway and parks in front of a white-doored garage. The front door of the house opens and two children run out whilst a woman stands in the doorway. The children stand next to the car as I get out. The boy puts out his hand, the seriousness of his demeanour contrasting with the excited way they've run to the car.

'Hi, I'm Charlie, and this is my sister, Carol.' We shake hands.

Carol smiles. 'Are you truly our brother?'

I'm taken aback. 'Um, yes.'

She puts out her arms. 'Then, may I kiss you, please?' I lift her up and she puts her arms around my neck and gives me a noisy kiss on my cheek. 'He smells like you, Dad!'

Art's laughing. 'Hey, give Geoff a chance.' I put her back on the ground but she insists on holding my hand as we walk up to the front door.

'Welcome, Geoff, I'm Beth.' She also extends her arms and hugs me tightly. She's only a little bit taller than Mary, and my chin rests on her soft blonde hair.

'Hey, you kids should be in bed,' says Art.

'But Mom said we could stay up and meet our brother. There's no school tomorrow,' says Carol.

'Sure, but now you've met him, it's time to turn in.'

Beth waves them inside. 'Come on children, into your pyjamas.'

'Geoff,' asks Carol, 'will you come up and kiss us goodnight when we're in bed? Can he, Mom?'

'Would you?'

'Of course.'

We're in the hall now. While the children file upstairs with Beth, Art takes me through to a spacious living room which looks out onto a terrace and a large back garden. 'Sit down and relax. Sorry I should have warned you that we'd told the children. I meant to tell you a whole load of stuff in the car, but it didn't seem to go to plan.'

'They're lovely children. But, yes, it was a bit unexpected. What did you tell them?'

'I said that I'd been married to someone else in England during the war and she'd had a son but we then divorced. That seemed to satisfy them, but Charlie is thirteen now so I guess he might start asking more questions soon. Right now they just love having a big brother from England.' Art looks hard into my face. 'Are you OK? You look kind of pale.'

'It's just a lot to take in.'

'Don't I know it.'

Beth comes into the room. 'They're ready for you to say goodnight.' She leads me upstairs. There are five doors opening out from the landing. She points at one of them. 'This is your room, and that's the bathroom, and this is Carol's.' I go in. The walls and curtains are pink, there is a pink quilt on the bed and she is wearing pink pyjamas. Rows of predominantly pink dolls sit on some shelves above the bed, and the room smells of pink soap.

'Could pink be your favourite colour?'

Her mouth opens wide and she gasps. 'How did you know?'

'Must be because I'm your brother, I suppose,' and I pan my head around the room.

'Aw, you're kidding me, aren't you?' she giggles, but then earnestly, 'I love you, Geoff.'

I think she must have a crush on me. What should I say? 'Em, and I love my new little sister too.' She beams. I give her a kiss on her forehead and say goodnight.

Charlie's room is painted pale blue with curtains featuring a repeating pattern of cars, planes, trains and rockets. Pennants are pinned to the wall next to his bed advertising the Seattle World's Fair and the Seattle Totems. A collection of model airliners is neatly arranged on a small desk. Charlie is lying in bed reading a magazine.

'What are you reading?' He shows me the cover: *Seattle World's Fair 1962* in large capitals. 'It's the Official Souvenir Program. Dad says we're going on Sunday, to show you. I've already been twice before. It's the swellest thing I've ever seen.' I think of myself reading Motor Show catalogues.

When I come down, Art goes up himself to kiss the children goodnight. I wait for him in the living room. It couldn't be more different from my home in Hammersmith. Airy and modern, with two rectangular blue sofas at right angles to each other, geometric patterned curtains and a large cream rug on top of a polished wooden floor. I sit down on one of the sofas.

Art comes in and sits down next to me. 'You must be starving. Beth is getting some food ready. Seems you've made a hit with the kids.'

'It's just so strange suddenly to have a brother and sister when I've always been on my own.'

Art gets up. 'I have to explain what happened. Hold on, I need to get something.' He leaves the room and comes back two minutes later holding an envelope. 'You'd better read it.'

I pull a letter out of the envelope. It's written on cheap lined paper which is now yellowing at the edges. The handwriting looks vaguely familiar, slightly untidy with looped g's and y's.

> *Darling Art,*
>
> *I went to your station but they told me you were on a mission and they didn't know when you were coming back. They said they would forward this to you. I wanted to speak to you first but it can't be helped. I'm not much good at letters. I think I'm pregnant. I can't be completely sure but I'm two weeks late, which never happens with me. I don't know how you will take this news but I think this was meant to be. I love you. I knew it the moment I first saw you. I'm praying it's the same for you. I've never felt like this for anyone. Please come to see me as soon as you can. I can't bear to be without you. I love you so much.*
>
> *Sheila*

'God.'

'I'm sorry. Oh maybe this was a mistake. To show you your mother's letter. I'm so sorry.'

'No. It's OK. Just a bit of a shock.'

'Yes, but you see, I never got the letter. I was shot down and taken prisoner.'

'Yes, you told us that when you first came to my house.'

'But I was reported as missing in action. It was months before anyone knew I was still alive. So your mother must have gone back to my base and they would have told her I was missing and then I guess she married Frank. And I never got the letter, so I didn't know anything about it.'

'But you have the letter now.'

'It must have been forwarded to my folks with my other personal stuff and then it was put in a box and forgotten about and I only found it in 1951 when my parents moved house. I had to use a private investigator to find out what had happened to your mother. They found out where you were but they never found her. So I came to see Ted, and you know or you've guessed the rest. Ted told me you'd had a tough time but that things were getting better for you, and when I came to visit you I could see that you were happy there and Ted was doing a great job. Right from the moment we first met, he thought I'd want to take you to live with me, and he said that as I was your father he was fine with that, even though I could see he liked you so much. I didn't know what to do. And it wasn't as though I could just take you off with me then, there would have to be some legal business to make it all kosher, so I asked Ted to give me some time to think about it. I came back to the States, and Beth and I talked it over. We would both have loved you to come live with us, but the question was what was best for you. It was the most difficult decision of my life. But after all that you'd gone through, and seeing that you'd settled so well with Ted and Mary, and how they felt about you, I… Well, you know what happened anyway. And once we'd decided on that, it seemed kinder not to say anything to you. Better to wait till you were older. We all thought that. Did we do wrong? I can't tell you the number of nights I've woken up in a cold sweat thinking about it.'

'Excuse me, I hope I'm not interrupting,' it's Beth, 'but the food is on the table.' We go through from the living room into a dining room which is divided from the kitchen by a long counter. A selection of salads and 'cold cuts' is laid out on a dining table spread with a red cloth.

'So what do you think of the States?' asks Beth as she fills my plate.

I feel completely drained of energy. Why had I come here? Thousands of miles from home, sitting down to eat with complete strangers. 'Um, I've seen so little, I can't really say.'

'Course you can't,' says Art. 'You look beat. Plane trip takes it out of you.' He looks at his watch. 'It'd be two in the morning now in New York. Let the kid eat. By the way, Beth, did I tell you that I ran into Stan Clark at the airport when I was picking up Geoff?' Conversation continues in that vein leaving me to my thoughts, I eat just enough to be polite and go to bed straight afterwards.'

THE CHILDREN ARE already having breakfast when I come down. 'Mom told us not to wake you. Gee, you were asleep for ages.'

'Sorry, I was pretty tired I suppose. Thanks for letting me sleep in.'

'Are you good for waffles and eggs? How do like them?' asks Beth.

'Fried please.'

'Sunnyside up or easy-over?'

'Oh, em, sunnyside up. Can I do anything?'

'Thanks, I'm good. You just sit there and they'll be coming up presently.'

Art comes in. He'd been wearing a suit the previous night, but now he's in blue jeans and a check shirt and looks younger.

'Sorry if this sounds stupid or rude, but Art, how old are you and when's your birthday?'

'I think you have every right to know,' he laughs. 'Charlie, you tell him.'

'Dad was born on July fourth 1923 which makes him thirty-eight years old right now.'

'Fourth of July? Isn't that Independence Day?'

'Yup, that's me. A true-born American. Now, this is the plan; let me know what you think. This morning I thought we could drive downtown and we could show you something of the city, and then drive out to Alki so you can have a good look at the Pacific. The weather forecast is that it'll brighten up this afternoon. Then I thought we could have a barbecue back here tonight.'

'Yeah!' cheer the children.

'Then tomorrow we'll spend the day at the World's Fair. How's that sound?'

'Sounds tremendous. Thank you so much, Art and Beth. It's terrifically kind of you to have me and lay so much on.'

'You English are so polite,' laughs Beth, 'we love having you, you're family.'

'Then Sunday night,' continues Art, 'I have a proposition. Me and some guys have a regular gig at a bar in town. How'd you like to sit in with us?'

'Gosh, but would I fit in all right? I mean, would I know the things you play?'

'We just do standards pretty much. I guess you must know what you're doing if you've been playing on a liner, but why not you and me have a blow this morning and we can see how we get on?'

'That would be great. I have to practise anyway. I've missed two days' practice already and if I miss another day…'

'Everyone will know! Huh, I know that one! Me too. You ready? Get your horn and we can go now.' Art leads me out through a door in the kitchen into the garage. In the back corner there's another door. 'This is my den. It was originally a workshop but I converted it into a music room. Soundproofed it with offcuts from the plant, airframe grade material, the best there is.' Art goes to a shelf and pulls out a large instrument case.

'Do you not play clarinet anymore?'

'Hardly ever. I moved over to tenor around five or six years

155

ago. Clarinet just didn't suit the kind of stuff I wanted to play.' We take out our instruments. 'Hey, a Conn, me too. Father and son.' Art starts warming up, playing runs of notes up and down the instrument and I do the same, feeling like I've undressed in a changing room and am having my naked body inspected. 'Nice sound. If I played alto that's exactly how I'd like to sound.'

'I was going to say the same to you. I got a new mouthpiece in New York. It still feels a bit strange.'

'Sounds OK to me. What you get?'

'A Meyer five.'

'I use a Link. OK, long notes now. Start soft, build and then down again. Any note you like. Hey, what am I saying? You must know all this already. Let's go.' We each choose a note at random. It happens that they make a major third. We blow a further nine notes, sometimes making chords, but even when we pick notes a semitone apart the discord doesn't sound bad. 'What shall we try now? Hey, why not *Someday My Prince Will Come*?'

I smile and nod.

'B flat concert so that'll be G for you. Know the head?'

'I'll have a go.'

'I'll count you in.'

I know this song backwards having played along many times with the track on the last LP Art had sent me. As I start the theme, Art joins in playing harmonies softly in the background. The notes sound so right, it's as if I'm accompanying myself. After a chorus of improvisation, I nod for Art to take over and it's now me who plays the harmonies. Art holds up four fingers to indicate a chorus where we alternate improvising four bars each. After we complete the thirty-two bars, Art shouts 'together' and we begin improvising together, weaving lines between each other, calling and answering, echoing and embellishing, and then Art brings back the theme for the last eight bars. 'Hey man, that was something. Did you ever think of going pro?'

I tell him what Jack Lazarus said about just staying a gifted amateur. 'Isn't that what you did?'

'Sure. Stupid question. No money in it, just late nights, booze and drugs. Stay as you are. Boy I'm proud. I remember when I first met you and you played the piano and I could see you were musical but I would never have imagined that little kid would end up being able to play like that. Nice.' He nods his head several times. 'Nice.'

We go back into the kitchen where the children are helping Beth make sandwiches for the picnic on the beach. I watch as she wraps them in transparent plastic film which she tears from a roll. 'What's that?'

'This? It's just Saran Wrap. Don't you have it in England?'

'I don't think so. Well, I've never seen it.'

'And look,' Beth tears some off and uses it to cover a bowl of coleslaw, 'this will keep it airtight and fresh in the icebox.'

'Where do you get it?'

'Any supermarket or food store, I guess. Why?'

'I'd love to get some for Mary, she'd be amazed.'

'Well, we'll be stopping off at the supermarket later anyway to get some things for the barbecue, so you can buy some then.'


AFTER THE BARBECUE, Beth takes the children upstairs, and Art and I start washing up the dishes. He starts the conversation. 'When we were talking yesterday I never got to hear your answer about whether I did wrong not to take you back with me after I'd found you. You'd have every right to hate me for that.'

I take a dirty plate and rinse it in the sink. 'I guessed most of what happened: you and Sheila, and then your finding me with Ted; but I thought that maybe Ted didn't want you to take me. Or maybe because I'd already said I wanted him to adopt me, you wouldn't have been able to take me, and that's why he'd made you agree not to tell me that you were my father. That's why the records were a sort of secret message – so that Ted wouldn't know.'

'No, it was nothing like that. Like I said, Ted was the first one to say I could take you. We both just thought it might upset you, to tell you I was your father. Better to wait till you were older.'

'But why? Why not tell me? Why not ask me what I wanted?'

Art puts his face in his hands, shakes his head and mumbles 'Oh man, oh man.' He lifts his head up and looks at me. 'I don't know what to say. We just thought it was for the best. All of us, Ted and me and Beth and Mary, I guess, too. You'd had a hard time of it. To rip you out from where you seemed happy – new family, new country, new everything – just seemed too much to ask. And Ted was already your guardian. We'd have to go through legal stuff too. They might not even have believed you were my son. How could I prove it? They might not have let you go. Could have taken months, years even.'

'But why send me the records, then?'

'It was the only way I could think of staying – what did you say in the car? Oh yeh, "connected". As for the message, I'm sorry, Geoff. I didn't seriously think you'd get it,' and he puts his head in his hands again.

I put my arm around his shoulder. It seems so strange. He's weeping now and I'm comforting him. *I'm* comforting *him*. He rubs his eyes and takes deep breaths. 'I'm OK. I'm OK now,' he says.

'I'm sorry. It's my fault. I can see that you and Ted meant everything for the best.'

'Your fault? You're not to blame in any way, you understand?' And he puts his outstretched hands on my shoulders and looks me in the face.

'I understand.'

'Good.' He takes his hands off my shoulders. 'But everything was OK with Ted and Mary, wasn't it? You were happy with them, weren't you?'

'Yes, I was happy. They've been marvellous to me; I couldn't ask for better parents. Really.'

'I never stopped thinking about you, how you were getting on. My own son. Even with everything here, and Charlie and Carol, I knew I was missing out on so much. But we're together now. Thank God, we're together now,' and he hugs me, patting

158

his hand on my back. We break apart. 'Now, what about these dishes?' He takes a rinsed plate from the draining board and starts drying it. I put some more dirty plates into the dishwater and start swishing them with the washing-up brush. A long minute passes. 'And you really know nothing about your mother, where she is or who she's with?' he asks.

'You probably know more than me. Ted said that she'd left Frank to go off with a Greek man and that they've left no trace. I suppose she wanted to start afresh.'

'I can't understand how she's never tried to contact you, just to check you're OK.'

'I suppose she just didn't like me. It was because of me that she'd married Frank…'

'Hey, that wasn't your fault. If it was anybody's, it was mine.'

'It wasn't anybody's fault, but looking back I can imagine she blamed me for how things turned out. Frank was pretty horrible and even as a child I could see that they didn't get on, but at the time I just thought that was normal.'

'And what about her folks? Didn't they know about you?

'Before I was officially adopted by Ted and Mary, there was a children's officer who had to check whether any relatives wanted me. Ted explained it all to me in case they asked about it at the adoption hearing, because I'd be there too. The children's officer had contacted my mother's parents, and Ted said that they felt it was better that I stayed with him because I was settled. I think he was just being kind. I never even knew I had grandparents till then. I seem to remember that I once asked Sheila about them and she said they were dead.'

'Boy! But you're not even a little curious about them and about what happened to your mom?'

'Sometimes, a little, but most of the time I don't think about it. But what about you? I know nothing about your parents – my grandparents – do they know about me?'

'I feel bad about this. The answer is no. But I'm going to tell them about you now. See, I was a bit wild when I was a kid. Not

159

in a bad way, but, you know, hanging around with other musicians, underage drinking and smoking stuff I oughtn't have. I never did any hard stuff. I saw what it did to other guys, but I was young and a little crazy. Then the war came and I was sent to Europe and then what happened and all, and I learned to be an adult. So when I found the letter from Sheila I didn't want them to know what a klutz I'd been so I didn't say anything and then, after I met you, and decided to leave you with Ted, I couldn't bring myself to tell them. I did tell my sister though, but she agreed it was probably best not to say anything.'

'Your sister? So I have an aunt?'

'Sure. Joan. She still lives in Boston.'

'And cousins?'

'Yeah. She's married to Gersh. He's a surgeon. They have two boys. Let me see, Ryan is a year older than Charlie, so he's fourteen and Jimmy must be sixteen. Yeah, he's nearly through his sophomore year.'

'And my grandparents?'

'Well they're pretty good. Dad's retired, he's going to be seventy this fall. Mom's sixty-eight.'

'But what are they like? Where do they live? What did he do?'

'Hey that's a lot of questions. Maybe I should start at the beginning. Dad and Mom were both born in Lithuania. Well it was actually part of Russia then. Things weren't too good for Jews, they weren't allowed to move around without a permit, just had to stay in the one area. They were invaded by the Germans in World War One and then after the war Lithuania became independent and Jews were free to go where they wanted, so they got out as soon as they could and came over to America, the promised land. Lucky for them. Some of the family stayed on in Lithuania. They were all killed in the next war.'

We've finished the washing up and Beth comes in to say that the children are ready for us to go up and say goodnight. Goodnights said, we come down into the living room.

'Can I get you a beer?' asks Art.

Beth says, 'Is he allowed?'

'Under Washington State law you're too young to drink, but seeing you're English I don't suppose it counts.'

'Art, you know that's not true.'

'Well either way, I reckon it's time for a beer. Do you want anything, honey?'

'I'll have a glass of lemonade. There's still some left in the icebox.'

'Now, where was I?'

'You were telling me about your parents, my grandparents.'

'Oh yeah. Well they were lucky, they got to America in 1920. My dad had some cousins in Boston and they helped him out. He started working in a drapery store and then after a few years he opened his own store and then some more branches. Then he sold up and retired. He and Mom do pretty good. They have a nice apartment, good friends. They play golf, bridge, go to Miami in the winter for some sun. We try to see them twice a year. They come to us, we go to them. They love the grandchildren.'

'Do you think I could meet them one day?'

'Sure. I've just got to find the right time to tell them about you.' Art takes a swig of his beer and lights a cigarette. 'I guess it's a bit embarrassing to tell them I got some poor English girl pregnant. They love Beth, don't they honey? But as she's not Jewish it took some time for them to get used to the idea.'

'So are they religious?'

'Not really. They go to temple maybe two or three times a year, which believe me is not much. If you were an orthodox Jew you'd go twice a day. But still, they mix mainly with other Jews, it's more a kind of social thing.'

'So they might be anti me on principle.'

'No, it's nothing like that. Just they'll need some time to get accustomed.' He gives me a light punch on the chest. 'Don't look so worried. It'll be OK.'

'Ted has a sister but she has no children. Their parents are dead. Mary has a large family in Ireland but she fell out with them for some reason years ago. I don't know if Sheila's parents are still alive. And even Frank's family were all killed in the blitz. Suddenly I've got a brother and sister, aunt, uncle, cousins, grandparents. I don't know how to put it. Of course, I'm pleased. More than that, much more than that, but it just seems so odd suddenly to have a whole family I didn't have before. I'm sorry, I'm not expressing myself very well. I suppose I knew about you and Beth and Charlie and Carol, but it was all in theory. Now it's real.'

Beth comes over and sits next to me on the sofa, putting her arm around my shoulder. 'You just need some time. We're so pleased to have you in the family.'

'Thank you. Both of you.'

I go to bed but can't get to sleep. I keep on thinking of what might have happened if they'd asked me when I was nine if I wanted to go to live with Art. Would it have been so difficult for me to have coped with? I would have had a younger brother and sister, barbecues on the beach, grandparents… And yet Ted and Mary gave me everything I could have wanted, including their unqualified love. I feel such guilt at imagining any other life, for being seduced by the apparent glamour of Art and Beth and America, for making unfavourable comparisons between dull, cold, wet England – do I really mean dull, cold, wet Ted? – with exciting, modern, suntanned America; exciting, modern, suntanned Art. And Ted, the gentlest, fairest man I know. Ready to adopt me because he and Mary genuinely wanted me to become their son, and then ready to return me to my natural father because that was the right thing to do. Now I wonder more about Art. In his position, what would I have done? And who am I like? Art, Ted, my mother? None of them? All of them? Not Frank, at least, that I know for sure.

AT BREAKFAST CHARLIE has his World's Fair programme ready. 'I know what we need to see. I'll show you here in the program…'

'Hey, why don't we make it a surprise?' interrupts Art.

I can see that Charlie is disappointed and say, 'But I want

you to be my official guide and tell me about everything when we see it.'

'Gee. Yes, I can do that. Official guide. Wow.'

Art points out landmarks as we drive into the city. Then we park the car and walk to the monorail station where a conveyer belt, like an escalator but without steps, takes us up to the platform. Posters proclaim that we are on our way to *Century 21*. We've already seen the Space Needle in the distance, and in less than two minutes we're at the fair terminal with the tower looming above us. I think how much Ted would enjoy this, but despite Charlie's enthusiasm and the rest of the family's pride, I feel that I am only playing along for their benefit. It's all very impressive but I can only feel the novelty and strangeness of being with Art, the rest is just a colourful backdrop. Tomorrow evening I'll be back in New York. Will I ever see Art again? What does it mean? So much effort to get here, and now what? The feeling comes over me in waves. For a few minutes something in the fair distracts me – the view from the top of the Space Needle, a ride on the Ferris wheel, some exhibits in the science pavilion – but then it returns, an ache in the pit of my stomach. Luckily Art and the children are engrossed in the things they are seeing and don't seem to notice, but Beth takes my arm and holds me back for a moment.

'You're quiet. It's hard for you, isn't it? Don't worry, I understand. It'll be OK.'

'Sorry, I hoped nobody'd notice.'

'Nobody has, except me. It's just that sometimes you're so like Art and I just sensed something – the way you're feeling.'

'Like Art? Am I?'

'In some ways, yes. In other ways, though, you couldn't be more different. That's the way with all kids I guess. But when I saw you listening to Charlie at that last exhibit, I just saw a look in you, a look that Art has when I know he's pretending to be interested but his mind is actually on something else.'

'It's just that I'll be going back tomorrow. It's been such a short time. It seems like one of the most important things in my life has happened, and then in a flash I'm moving past. Like my ship sailing past the Statue of Liberty.'

'It won't be like that. You're family now. There will be other times, longer times. It'll be OK.' She holds my arm tightly. I feel as if I'm going to cry, but I swallow a few times and it passes.

Everyone is tired when we get home. We eat a quick snack and then the children go up for their baths. Beth won't be coming to hear Art and me play at the club. 'I'm a bit tired and we haven't got a sitter, and maybe this one is best just you two together.'

'But honey, I'm sure Mary Anne could sit for us, the kids just love her.'

'No, don't worry about me, I just want you boys to have a great time, father and son.'


THE VENUE IS a bar in downtown Seattle, quite smart compared to The Three Feathers in Shepherd's Bush. From the street we enter a long narrow room with a bar running down its length, which opens into a larger room at the back with tables and chairs and a small bandstand. A coloured man is setting up a drum kit. He waves to us as we come in. Art and he put their arms around each other's shoulders. 'This is Geoff, my long lost son from England, and this is Lenny Levitt, the best drummer in the Pacific North West.'

'He's just kidding me. Pleased to meet you Geoff.' As we shake hands, I realise that this is the first coloured person I've ever touched. 'Art says you're going to sit in with us. That's great. Welcome to Seattle.' Two other men now enter and come up to the bandstand.

'This is Lars Stenson, and this is Geoff my son from England.' A tall, very blonde man puts down a double bass and shakes hands. 'And this is Lou Feldstein, our pianist.'

Instruments are taken out of their cases, which are then put out of sight into a tiny changing room behind the stage. We tune up and play a few warm-up exercises, each of us momentarily isolating himself in a private world. Art looks at his watch. 'OK, we've got twenty minutes before Dave opens the doors. Shall we do a set list?' They gather around the piano. I'm not sure whether I should join them or stay back. 'Geoff,' Lenny beckons me towards them, 'hey man, relax, we don't bite, we're all friends here. You make the first call.'

I look questioningly at Art, '*All The Things You Are?*'

'Great choice,' says Lenny. 'Lou?'

'Sounds good to me. Up tempo, though. Then maybe a slow blues in B flat. *Blue Monk*?'

A provisional list of twenty numbers is drawn up. There have been a couple of suggestions that I don't know but Art insists that I'll be able to pick them up easily enough. 'I'll play the head and you can blow a couple of choruses later on. The changes are nothing fancy.'

The doors to the room are now opened and a few people, mostly men, began to drift in. The band members nod and exchange greetings with them as they make their way towards the bar where they order beers for themselves and a Coca Cola for me. Art has briefed the other guys and they ask me about playing aboard ship and my jazz favourites.

'Have you heard *Kind of Blue*?' asks Lou, the pianist.

'Yes, my teacher lent it to me.'

'Bill Evans is something else, huh? Did you hear *Sunday at the Village Vanguard*?

'No, not yet.'

'You got to listen to that, man. Those left-hand voicings. That's like listening to the future.'

An attractive woman whom I guess is in her late thirties walks up to the band stand. 'Hi, guys!'

'Hey, Donna, great you could come.' Art gives her a big hug and she kisses the other musicians. 'You won't believe this, but this is my son, Geoff, from England.'

Donna does a double-take. 'England?'

'Yeh, well, it's a kinda long story. Let's just say I wasn't much

165

more than a kid, and it was during the war, and, well you know…
but the main thing is that Geoff has come all the way over here
just to look up his old man and I couldn't be happier about it,
and – and this is the killer – he plays alto and he's going to blow
us off the stand tonight, isn't that right Geoff?'

'I don't think so, Art…'

'English modesty. Just you wait. And Donna, I hope you're
going to do some numbers with us. What do you say, guys?'

'Sure, Donna,' nod the other musicians.

'Just try and stop me!'

Art turns to me. 'Donna is something else. She's sung at
Birdland, The Lighthouse…'

Donna interrupts, 'Well, a long time ago, I'm kinda retired
now, but I can't help making an exception for you guys.' She
turns to me, 'I just love these guys, especially your daddy,' and
she shoots a glance at Art. I look more closely at her and decide
she's more like early forties.

'What you want to sing, Donna?' asks Lou.

'What say *Spring* in the first set and maybe *Too Close* in the
second?'

'Sounds good to me. I got C and G – that OK with you?'

'That's just fine.'

'Come on guys,' says Art, 'we better get started. Donna, I'll
bring you up after three or four numbers, OK?' Donna blows
him a kiss.

The room is about half-full now. My mouth is dry. I sip
some Coke and feel the familiar emptiness in my stomach as
the cold liquid descends. I hear Les's words in my head – 'start
strong' – and say them over to myself.

On the bandstand, Art looks at Lenny and they begin to
synchronise the nodding of their heads to agree a tempo. Art
counts in. The standard bebop introduction to *All The Things You
Are* is a repeated three-note phrase. The timing is tricky and I'm
a tiny bit out for the first phrase, but I correct myself and then I
launch into the theme and now I'm feeling more confident. Art

harmonises behind me. I know objectively that the members of Art's band should sound no better than Les and the other chaps on the boat, but there seems to be an extra energy, an intangible quality of jazz being played in the country where it was invented. Lenny's drumming in particular seems to propel us forward but without ever losing control. I improvise two choruses and then nod to show that I want to hand over the baton and Lou takes over. The audience applaud my solo and the other band members grunt and nod their approval. Art whispers to me, 'You were flying, man. It was a knock-out. Every note meant something.' I'm on a high. Everyone's playing is superlative; Art's, the other guys' and mine. It's on a different level to anything I've known before. At the end of the number, Art takes the microphone. 'Good evening everyone. Wasn't that great?' Whistles and 'yeahs' from the audience. 'And now I'd like to introduce the band members. Lenny, this is Lars, Lars this is Lou, and Lou this is Lenny.' The three men ham it up, shaking hands as if this is the first time they'd met. It's an old joke, but even though they've seen it before, the audience loves it. 'But you may be wondering, folks, who this young man is. Well, for one night only, we have been able to bring over all the way from England a stellar alto player and name to watch: Geoff Cunningham.' Everyone cheers. 'Geoff is the son of an old family friend of mine, and I've got to say that I was mighty surprised that someone from over the pond knew how to play jazz, not only knew, but is right now blowing us old guys off the stand – ain't that right?' More cheers. 'But I think I may know his secret. I'm guessin' that to play like that he must have some American blood in there. What d'you think folks?' Yet more cheers.

Donna comes on to do our fifth number *Spring Can Really Hang You Up The Most*. The lyrics of a lovelorn and jaded woman seem to come effortlessly to her. Her voice has a touch of sandpaper to it, perfect pitching and despite the slow tempo, she still swings. The audience are impressed and so am I. Although the chord changes are not too challenging, as I've never played it before, I decline a solo and leave it to Art to improvise an impeccable half chorus before Donna comes back for the final sixteen bars.

The penultimate number of the first set is to be a my slow ballad 'feature' *But Beautiful*. 'I'm going out back,' says Art. 'Take it easy, you got plenty of time. Stretch out, man, stretch out.'

I play the theme but find my reed is squeaking a bit. 'You take the first solo,' I whisper to Lou and point to my reed. I quietly creep round the side of the stage and out through the curtain to reach the small changing room to get a reed from my instrument case. I open the door to the room, which is little more than a glorified broom cupboard but just large enough to hold a dressing table, a cupboard and a couple of chairs. The sight that greets me is Art's bottom with his trousers around his ankles as he thrusts into Donna who is leaning against the wall with her dress hitched up. Donna smiles at me with a sort of 'life's crazy, isn't it?' expression and I flee the room, pulling the door shut behind me. I take some deep breaths to try to calm myself, but I know my face is red and I'm sweating. When I get back on stage, Lou is just nearing the end of his first chorus, so I realise that I couldn't have been away for more than thirty seconds. I nod to Lou to take another one, but Lou turns his head towards Lars, who takes over instead. Somehow I manage to get through my own solo, but with a squeaky reed and a feeling of anger. This is not the ballad performance I had envisaged, although the audience don't seem to mind. And then Art is back on stage, calm and smiling, and leading the applause. The last number of the set is *Cherokee* and I count in a furious tempo and play like a man possessed. I solo first, then Art, Lou and Lars. Then I hold up eight fingers to indicate that Art and I should alternate eight bars with the drummer. After two choruses of eights, I hold up just four fingers. At the tempo we're playing, each four bars takes around three seconds to play. Thinking of Les's dictum 'play less, say more' I realise I'm not saying much, but there again it doesn't take many words to express how I'm feeling. There's wild applause at the end of the number and then Art gently guides me backstage. I don't know whether I want to cry or to punch him. 'How could you?' I shout.

Art puts up his hands. 'Hey, hey, take it easy, man.'

'But how could you? I mean, Beth, the children. How could you do that?'

'OK, OK, I know it doesn't look good.'

'*Look?*'

'OK, already. It *isn't* good. But… I don't know how to say this… the thing is it don't mean anything. It's just, mm… well something physical, like eating or drinking. I love home cooking, home cooking is the best but every once in a while I go to a restaurant, for a change, that's all, it doesn't mean home cooking isn't still the best.'

'I can't believe you're saying this. *Home cooking!*'

'Look, just try and take it easy and we can talk about this in the car. I wanted this to be a great night for us, and you're playing a storm…'

'Hardly surprising.'

'Please, Geoff. I'm begging you. I know I'm not perfect…'

'*Perfect!*'

'You're getting it all wrong. Please, just give me a break till we finish here tonight and then we can talk. *Please!*'

I heave a sigh. 'OK.'

'Thank you, Geoff.' Art puts his arms out as if to embrace me, but I push past him and walk round to the bar.

Lou is there getting beers for the band. 'You want something?'

'I'd love a beer.'

'Sorry, Geoff, you know the rules. State of Washington, no alcohol for minors.'

'OK, then another Coke.'

'What happened just now, on the stand, you seemed a little upset when you came back? Was it the reed? You still sounded great.'

'No, not the reed.'

'Then what? Oh, shit! You went to the dressing room and

169

found Art and Donna…'

'Yes.'

'Holy shit.'

'Does that mean they do it all the time?'

'Hey man, it's not like that, it's just…'

'But they've done it before?'

'Look, Geoff, it ain't my business. I don't know what they do back there…'

'But you've guessed?'

'Kinda. But it doesn't mean anything. I know them, known 'em both for years, it's just their way of saying hi, I suppose.'

Before I can say anything, Lenny joins us at the bar. 'Just came to help you carry those beers. Hey Geoff, I wanted to tell you man, you're one hell of a player. Real talent, real talent, man. Ain't that right, Lou?' Lou nods. 'Didn't think there were guys in old En-ga-land who knew how to play like that, and you're only a kid. How you get to play like that?'

I feel myself going red. 'Thanks, Lenny. I don't know what to say, I…'

Lou comes to the rescue: 'These English are so modest, Lenny, and now you've put him on the spot.'

I say, 'But playing together with all of you, honestly, if I am playing well then it's all down to you. It's as if up till tonight I'd been running and tonight I started flying…'

'Well you certainly were flying,' says Lenny, 'especially *But Beautiful* and then *Cherokee*, almost angry-sounding, I loved it.'

'Geoff was just telling me, he was a bit worried about his reed,' says Lou.

'Man, they could charge double, no triple, for reeds that make you play like that and there'd be a line outside the music store till Christmas!'

WE'RE DRIVING HOME. 'So,' says Art, 'you still mad at me? You seemed to have cooled off on that second set. You played great, man. I mean that, really great.'

'So did you, and I really mean that too. Those guys make it so easy.'

'Ain't they something? But, Geoff, we still friends?'

'I don't know. I just can't understand how you could do that to Beth.'

'Look Geoff, like I said, Donna means nothing to me. It was just something physical – nice, yes – but no emotion. She's lonely, a good-looking dame, we like each other, but I like ice cream too. It means nothing. I was just doing what millions of married men do all the time and millions more would do if they got the chance. You made it yet with a girl?'

'Yeh.'

'You going steady with someone?'

'What?'

'You know, dating someone?'

'Oh. No.'

'But you made it with some girl, or girls maybe?'

'A few.'

'So it was just the four F's then?' I look blank. 'Find 'em, feel 'em, fuck 'em and forget 'em?'

'No, it wasn't like that, I…'

'So you still seeing them all, writing them love poems?'

'No, but… I suppose you're right.'

'Right. So me and Donna is the same.'

Of course it's not remotely the same. 'What about Beth? You haven't told her about Donna. What would she think?'

'You're right. I haven't told her because it means nothing.'

'But if she found out?'

'She'd get mad all right, but she knows I love her more than anything and we'd get over it. I know we would. So, are we friends again?'

'I suppose so,' I say, but I'm not sure anymore.

'Look, Geoff, I gotta tell you man, you coming out here to see me, it means so much…' Art wipes his eyes, 'see, now you've got me started, and I got to concentrate on the road,' he pauses to turn left. 'When I first saw you, at Ted's house, and you were just this little kid, and you looked scared almost, but when I played piano for you, the way your eyes sparkled and seemed to come alive, boy, it was something special for me, and I knew, then, that you really were my son. And then me sending you the records, like a message in code, I guess, and you break the code and here you are. Man, oh man. I want so much to be a father you can love and be proud of and then I go and fuck up with Donna and everything. Please, Geoff, you gotta give me another chance.'

Now I was wiping my eyes. 'Yeh, of course. I'm sorry.'

'You don't need to be sorry. It was my fault. I'm sorry, truly sorry to have messed up. Please say you forgive me.'

I say, 'I forgive you.' What else can I say?


MY FLIGHT LEAVES at 8.30 on Monday morning. The children have insisted that they be woken up to say goodbye. Bleary-eyed, they hug and kiss me. 'You will come back soon, won't you?' asks Carol.

'Of course.'

Then it's Beth's turn. 'You do mean it, you will come back, Geoff?'

'I mean it. I might even be able to get another job on a ship later this summer.'

In the car, Art and I are silent, then start speaking at the same moment. 'You first,' says Art.

'It's just that as soon as I leave you, I know there'll be a thousand things I wanted to say, but right now my mind's gone blank.'

'Me too.' He pauses, 'I can't tell you how swell it's been having you here. Over the years, I've thought of you so much. Felt so guilty. Asking myself over and over, did I do the right thing, leaving you behind with Ted. Thinking how can I ever make it up to you. Wondering what would have happened if I'd found Sheila's letter earlier. So many things. And now, we've had two days. Two days in nineteen years. Boy. I don't know where I am.'

We sit in silence as we pass from the suburbs to the industrial hinterland of the airport.

Art resumes. 'I just gotta say how proud I am. You turned out so great. When you were playing last night I was boiling with pride. And I could see the looks on the faces of the guys thinking, "who is this kid?" and the audience too.' He pauses again as we turn into the airport. 'But you know, it wouldn't have mattered if you couldn't play a note. You're my son, that's the thing.' He parks the car and we walk over to the terminal building. 'Write me when you're home. I get deals with the airlines that fly Boeings, I can get you a ticket. We can plan a proper visit. You could visit my folks; yes, we could all meet in Boston maybe.' We've reached the check-in counter.

'Thank you. That would be great. I'll get very long holidays at Cambridge. I'd love to come again, soon.'

Art smiles.

'What is it?'

'I'm thinking, you're like me, but you're also like Ted. Very British I suppose.' The thought makes me smile too – thinking of Ted and the ways in which I'm like him – but when we embrace, un-Ted-like, both of us have tears running down our cheeks.


IT'S EARLY EVENING when I get back to Brooklyn. Les is sitting in the front parlour – as our landlady calls the room where breakfast is served – and he sees me as I pass by the open door. 'How'd it go?'

'Um, fine. Very well, thanks.' On my second or third lesson, Les asked me why I wanted to go to America. I'd been vague, saying that it was just somewhere I'd always wanted to visit and that I also wanted to look up an old family friend.

'I'm meeting up with the other blokes later in Greenwich Village – want to come?'

'Yes, please.'

'Fancy a bite first? I thought of going down to Chinatown.'

At the restaurant Les explains the menu and shows me how to use chopsticks. When we order, he asks for two beers. 'How old you are?' asks the waiter.

'Twenty-one.'

'You got ID?'

'No... well, yes. Sorry, I'm only nineteen.'

The waiter roars with laughter. 'That's OK. New York State you can drink at eighteen.'

Les is laughing too. 'Tastes like gassy dishwater anyway, but it's all you can get here.'

The waiter puts some hot plates fuelled by small candles on the table and then brings over the food.

'In Seattle you had to be over twenty-one to drink.'

'So that's where you went.'

'Yes. I played a gig there. They were really good.'

'Oh, yeah. Tell me more.'

I take a deep breath. 'You see, the chap I went to see – he plays tenor actually – he's more than an old family friend, he's actually my father, although I didn't know that for sure before, but now I do.'

Les dips a piece of chicken in some plum sauce. 'I'm listening.'

I take a sip of beer. 'He met my mother during the war. He was in the air force, stationed in England. They hardly knew each other really, but, you know, wartime and all that, and then he had to leave on a mission and he got shot down and was taken prisoner and my mother thought he was dead and married someone else. She was pregnant with me, you see.'

'How did you find out about him?'

I tell him the rest of the story.

'And he's the one who got you on to clarinet, you say.'

'Not exactly. My music master at school had suggested it, but Art bought one for me and that decided it I suppose.'

'So that's where you get your music from.'

'And Ted. Ted Cunningham, who adopted me. He taught me singing and piano, but he doesn't play jazz.'

Les has finished eating now and lights a cigarette. 'I've got a son, you know. He's a bit younger than you. Thirteen. In fact, he's in America too. His mother was a singer I used to work with. We were never that serious. But anyway, she got pregnant and we had a go at living together, and then he was born. We called him Lester. Nice little baby he was. But I was no good at it. And then she met an American bloke working in London – trumpeter, nice player – and they came over here together. He was about two then. That's the last time I saw him. They're in Louisville, Kentucky. Bloody miles away. I have thought about visiting them. There's no hard feelings, you know, but… it might upset him. Better to wait till he's older. Like you did. Yeah.' He looks at his watch. 'Christ, look at the time. We'd better be off.'

TED AND MARY are waiting for me when the ship docks, brimming with questions about my trip. Have I been seasick? Have I eaten enough? Was my cabin comfortable? Have the other musicians been friendly? What did I do in New York? I wonder when the right moment will be to tell them about Art. In the car I try go through my trip chronologically, so it isn't until we hit the South Circular that in an as matter-of-fact way as possible I say that I decided to look up Art Shiner and flew out to see him in Seattle.

'You flew out to see him?' asks Mary in amazement.

'In a jet. He works for Boeing and got me a free ticket.'

'But why?'

I take a deep breath. 'Before I say any more, I know that Art's my father.'

'Ah,' says Ted.

'In fact, I'd pretty much guessed it some time ago.'

'We'd wondered whether you might, but we were going to wait till you were twenty-one to tell you.'

'And it doesn't change anything about how I think of you both. You know that your adopting me was the best thing that ever happened to me. You know that, don't you?'

'Well…'

'It was. As far as I'm concerned, you are my parents, and I love you both. Not *like* a son, I *am* your son.'

'Oh, Geoff...' croaks Mary.

'Now Mary, don't start being soppy.'

'I can't help it,' and she lapses into quiet sobs.

'Cheer up, old girl,' says Ted.

'Not so much of the "old", Ted Cunningham,' she laughs through her tears.

When we get home, I give a detailed account of my time with Art, Beth and the children, but obviously leaving out the episode with Donna. 'I should have told you I was going to see Art. Looking back, I can't quite understand why I didn't. I was worried you might be upset, but it was silly. I know you would have understood. I'm really sorry. Please forgive me.'

'Nothing to forgive, old chap,' says Ted. 'We should be saying sorry to you for not having told you earlier. I was never comfortable about keeping it a secret, but we all thought it might upset you, you see, especially when you were so young. And then before the adoption hearing, we had a meeting with the barrister – Crempel of the Temple, he was known as – very starched collar sort of chap. I told him about Art Shiner coming over and showed him his letter – he'd sent us a letter, you see, saying that he thought it was best that you stayed with us – and Crempel said to tear it up. I didn't of course, I've still got it, but he said it would only complicate things. After all, Art wouldn't be able to prove he was your father and anyway it was only the mother they were interested in. And I said, but shouldn't we tell you in case you said you wanted to go and live with him. And he said it wouldn't have been up to you. All you could say is whether you wanted to be adopted by us or not.'

'You were right. It would have upset me. You did the right thing.'

'You don't know what a weight it's been on our minds.'

Then Mary says, 'We knew in our bones that you would be happier with us...'

'Now, Mary...'

'No Ted, I've got to say it. We could see how impressed you

were when Art came to see us and played the piano and the clarinet, and that we were very dull in comparison, but I thought there was something about him…'

'Please Mary…' interrupts Ted again, but Mary carries on.

'You can't imagine, Geoff, how much we wanted you to be with us, how much we loved you, and I was so worried that he'd take you away, but we truly wanted what was best for you and I just wasn't sure about him, how it would be with him, whether we could trust him, but Ted kept on saying that it was a father's right to have his son with him…'

'Well, his right to choose.' says Ted, 'And if I'd tried to stop him and you'd found out later, you would have hated us for it, and I couldn't have lived with that.'

'It's funny,' I say, 'Art asked me whether I hated *him* for not taking me back with him to America. But Mary's right, maybe it wouldn't have worked out and anyway he agreed it was better to leave me here with you, and you've been the most wonderful parents I could hope for, so everything's been for the best. So I don't hate anyone for anything. But I'm still pleased I went to see him.'

'Of course you are,' says Ted.

'Heavens, I nearly forgot!' Mary jumps up from the table and runs into the scullery. She comes back carrying a cake with 'Welcome Home Geoff' spelled out in white icing on a chocolate backing. 'I'll bet you must be starving. I'm sure they didn't feed you properly on that ship.'

A FEW DAYS later Eric comes around. We go up to my room. 'Here's something I got for you from New York, I don't think you can get it here yet. I played with these guys in Seattle and the pianist recommended it to me.' I hand Eric the white paper bag from the New York record shop.

He says, 'I like the bag.' It has a drawing on the front of a girl in a rah-rah skirt holding up a disc as if it were a basketball under the banner *I FOUND IT! at the Colony*. He takes out the

LP. '*Sunday at the Village Vanguard.* Bill Evans. Wow, thanks.'

'Sorry but I've taken the liberty of playing it. It's fantastic.'

'So, how'd it go?'

I give a quick rundown of the trip and meeting Art and his family, up to the night in the jazz club.

'And?' asks Eric.

'What do you mean, "and"?'

'Am I your best friend?'

'You know you are.'

'And I know you pretty well.'

'Course.'

'Well I just sense there's an "and", that something else happened.'

'Did you say you were thinking of psychiatry?'

'Maybe, eventually.'

'I can see why. Either that or forensic medicine or mind-reading.'

'Very funny. So what did happen, really?'

I recount how I'd found Art and Donna in the dressing room and my exchange with Art.

'I didn't know you'd done it with a girl.'

'Medical term is that?'

'How, where?'

'It was when I was playing at the holiday camp. Everyone was at it, well all the young people anyway, but that's not what this is about.'

'Sorry, but, Christ! I think I need to book a holiday at Butlins right away.'

'I thought you wanted to know about me and Art.'

'Well, seems you're a chip off the old block.'

'Meaning?'

'You and Art, both getting your leg over whenever the opportunity presents itself.'

'Look Eric, this isn't funny.'

'Well it does have its funny side.' I glare at him. 'Sorry, but seriously, maybe Art had a point. Why should you be so surprised at what he was doing, when you were doing the same thing yourself in Bognor?'

'Because I'm not married with two kids, that's why.'

'But it's not a crime. Loads of married men behave like that.'

'That's what Art said, millions of men do it and millions more would if they had the chance.'

'Exactly. And you said you told him that you forgave him.'

'What else could I say? But I wanted Art to be better than that. That's the point. I mean, do you think your father's having it away on the side? His secretary or one of his artistes?'

'Oh God, I hope not. His secretary is about sixty and has a bit of a facial hair problem.'

'Eric, this isn't funny!'

'*So-ree!* Let me think. Seriously, I don't think my dad's the type.'

'And that's what I'm saying, I didn't want Art to be the type.'

'So what now?'

'I don't know. I suppose I had an image of him in my mind, and when I met him and Beth and the children, and then played some music together, it was like a dream come true. I really felt close to him, more than that. And then he goes and… I don't know.'

'What don't you know?'

'It's just that I was disappointed, that's all.'

# OCTOBER 1962

TED TAKES A lot of persuading not to drive me up for my first term. The memory of being dropped off in Cambridge by Sheila and Frank is still surprisingly vivid and I've decided that I'd rather arrive on my own. I load what I can into a rucksack and a suitcase. With my saxophone too, it's all rather unwieldy and I relent as far as allowing Ted to drive me to Liverpool Street but draw the line when he suggests I use a porter to take my luggage down to the platform.

'You've turned into quite a stubborn lad, haven't you? Just because you're off to Cambridge doesn't mean you can have it all your own way, you know.'

'I wonder where I picked it up from.' We laugh and shake hands. 'Good luck, old boy. Remember to phone us when you get a chance.'

'I will.'

I find a compartment with some vacant seats and manage to squeeze my baggage onto the shelf with some help from another passenger. I thank him.

'Pleasure. Am I right in thinking that you're getting off at Cambridge?'

'Yes.'

'University?'

'Yes, it's my first term.'

The man puts out his hand. 'Adrian Hadley. Third year, history at Trinity.'

'I'm doing engineering at St Christopher's.'

'Nice college.'

'Good, I mean thanks. Sorry, it's all a bit new. Not really used to the idea yet.'

'It won't take long, don't worry. By the way, what's in that case?'

'Alto saxophone.'

'Thought so, but didn't want to presume in case it was a theodolite or a wooden leg or something. Classical or jazz?'

'Jazz, I suppose. Though I do play classical clarinet.'

'Any good?'

'Um, well, pretty OK I suppose.'

'I detect false modesty. Smell it a mile off. Well, we can soon put it to the test.'

I look around in panic and see that the other occupants of the compartment are an elderly couple.

'Not here, old chap,' he laughs. 'You see, I play too. Piano. In fact, I'm president of the University Jazz Club, so spot of luck running into you. We're a bit thin on the ground this term.'

We spend the rest of the journey talking about jazz and unintentionally I mention who I heard in New York and then I have to admit that I played on the liner.

'Crikey, a pro. I'm worried now you'll be out of our league.'

'No, I bet you're all better than me.' The train is pulling into Cambridge now. We help each other with our luggage and then share a taxi into the town. I get out first and I promise to get in touch when I've found my feet.

My interview had been at the other college, so this is my first time at St Christopher's since I was eight. I remember walking from the choir school to the college via the Backs. The choirmaster had a key giving access to the Scholars' Garden, through which we would be led, then crossing over the bridge into the main college precincts. The street entrance to the college is new to me, or at least I have no recollection of it. I enter through the small door within a giant door, into the arched gatehouse. A bowler-hatted man with a moustache stands in a doorway marked Porters' Lodge.

'Afternoon, sir.'

'Hello, my name's Geoffrey Cunningham. Hold on.' I take out the letter I've been sent with instructions on getting to the college and so on. The porter finds my name on a list and gives me a key. 'Go to the far left-hand corner of Old Court, through the archway on the left into Cowling Court and you'll find D staircase on the opposite corner.'

When I get there, I find my name on a list just inside the doorway, neatly sign-written in capitals with a wooden slider next to it to indicate whether I'm in or out. I move the slider to 'in'. My room is on the first floor, with my name sign-written again above it. The room is gloomy but serviceable. A bed, a desk, a chest of drawers, a wardrobe, a bookshelf and two chairs. A sash window looks out onto Cowling Court. I explore the staircase and find the lavatory, bathroom and a tiny kitchen with sink, kettle and two gas rings.

At six o'clock the freshmen assemble in the Junior Common Room – the JCR – to be addressed by Mr Hemstall, the head porter. Most look nervous and homesick, as I imagine I must look too, but a handful of extroverts are breaking the ice. There's a hush when Mr Hemstall enters. Though of middle height, his presence suggests a bigger man. Like the first day at a new school, he takes a register of names. One poor chap is called Presley. 'Oh, Elvis, is it?' I am grateful that 'Cunningham' is innocuous. There is then a pep talk in which Hemstall tells us the various rules by which we are expected to abide, and the sanctions for transgressions. I wonder if he has children and if so, I pity them.

Mr Hemstall leaves the room and we relax a bit and begin to chat in groups. Then we go into dinner in the candlelit hall and I find a space next to some of the chaps I've been talking to. The Master and fellows appear through a door within the panelling and file up to the high table. A Latin grace is said and we negotiate getting our legs into the narrow space between the long bench and the table. Boys of more-or-less our age wait on us. Some ignore them but I look them in the eye and say thank you. It seems very Them and Us, Town and Gown.

On a Saturday afternoon, a couple of weeks after I've arrived, I go over to Trinity to look for Adrian Hadley. I find his room but he's out, so I push a note under his door asking him to get in touch about the Jazz Club. The weather's fine, so I decide to cross the river and walk back along Queen's Road. Thinking that perhaps I might find a new route to the University Library, I turn off into one of the streets of large redbrick villas and then to my surprise find myself in front of a board proclaiming 'St Christopher's College Choir School for boys from 7 to 13'. Without a moment's thought I find myself walking purposefully and a little angrily through the front door and am assailed by the familiar smell of disinfectant, polish and cabbage. The office door is half open and I see a grey-haired woman at work behind a desk. She jumps when I put my head around the door and ask whether the headmaster is in.

'Yes. I mean, no.' But I have already opened the door marked Headmaster and march in.

'What the blazes!' says the man behind the large desk. But instead of Mr Cowdray it's someone else, balding but with a young face still.

'Mr Denston!'

'Yes, but who are you, and what are you doing bursting into my room like this?'

'I'm Cunningham, Geoffrey Cunningham. No, I was Geoffrey Bassett when I was in your form, it was before Ted Cunningham adopted me and I changed my name.'

'Bassett! How extraordinary. Why are you here? What's it all about?'

At that moment the school secretary comes in. 'I'm so sorry, headmaster, he just walked straight in. I didn't have time…'

'Don't worry, Miss Taylor, it turns out it's an old friend of mine, though for the life of me I still don't know why he's here.' He turns to me. 'What about a cup of tea?' I nod. 'Would you do the honours, Miss Taylor? And then you really must go. You know you shouldn't be here on a Saturday.'

A chastened Miss Taylor leaves the room. 'Sit down, Bassett. Sorry, Cunningham. Now tell me what's going on.'

'Gosh. I don't know really. I was just walking up the street – you see I've just started at Cambridge, I'm at St Christopher's of all places, engineering…'

'Well done.'

'And I saw the board for the school, outside, and something took hold of me and, I couldn't stop myself. Did I say? I'd been a boy here. Only for a short time, before I was thrown out. And that was the point, I suppose. I just had to tell the headmaster, the one who was here when I was a boy, that I'd done all right.'

'Good for you! But you found me instead.'

'Yes. And now I feel a complete ass.'

Mr Denston smiles and then starts laughing and then Miss Taylor comes in with the tea and finds us both in hysterics.

'So you're headmaster here. Congratulations, sir.'

'Yes, been here six years now.'

'Can I ask what happened to Mr Cowdray?'

'Retired to Malta.'

'And Mr Doughty?'

'Ah, now I remember. When I applied for the job I knew there was something about St Christopher's that I'd been told, but I couldn't for the life of me remember. Suppose I'd put it out of my mind. But I now recall exactly what it was. Ted Cunningham came to see me about you, didn't he? That's why you started at Loriners' in the middle of the term. Was it Doughty who you'd had a run-in with?'

'I suppose you could call it that.' Then with panic, 'He's not still here, is he?'

'No, he's dead. Killed himself. Jumped in front of a train. About seven years ago.'

'God.'

'He was up for trial. He'd moved on to another school by then of course. Gross indecency. Couldn't face it. Did he take the coward's way out, or was he a brave man sparing everyone a lot of unpleasantness? Never could make my mind up on that one. Still, either way it was hell for the train driver. Are you all right?'

'Em, sorry, yes, I'm fine, just a bit of a surprise.'

'Yes, I can see that. Bad memories.'

'That's the funny thing. I've hardly thought about it for years. I don't think what happened to me was really that terrible. It only happened once. He put his hand down my trousers and then I had to do the same to him, but, you know, he didn't actually hurt me or rape me or anything. Now I'm older I know that, well, it can be much worse than that. And of all the people at St Christopher's – this is the odd thing – he was actually the one who was nicest to me, made me feel special – and he was easily the best teacher too.'

'Yes, but Cunningham, ask yourself why he was being nice to you.'

'I suppose so.'

'What do you think might have happened if Ted hadn't rescued you, so to speak? Might have ended up much, much worse.'

'Yes, I see that now. What does still make me angry, though, is the way they wouldn't listen to Ted. Just trying to brush him off. I suppose that's one of the things I wanted to tell Cowdray.'

'Understandably. I can assure you that I would deal with this sort of thing very differently, but I'm sorry to say that it's still going on in plenty of places. Prep schools are magnets for these people, but when something happens, there are lots of heads who will do anything they can to avoid a fuss, so the offender is quietly asked to resign, given a reference and then goes somewhere else.'

'That's awful.'

'I agree. Now, tell me more about yourself. Engineering did you say? And how's Ted?'

At the end of the conversation, Mr Denston asks, 'There's no hall lunch tomorrow, is there?'

'No, not on Sunday.'

'So what about coming over to have lunch with us? I have a niece visiting us so the more the merrier.'

'But I don't want to put you or your wife to any trouble.'

'No trouble, it'll be a pleasure really, Cunningham. Oh perhaps that's a bit formal now; Geoffrey, isn't it?'

'Everyone calls me Geoff.'

'Geoff it is. And I'm Mike.'

THAT EVENING, I ring home on the public phone in what must have been a converted broom cupboard in the JCR. I drop in my three pennies and wait for someone to answer. 'Hello, Riverside double four, one, two.' It's Ted. I press button A and the coins clatter through the mechanism.

'It's Geoff.'

'Hello old boy. Call box? Hang on, I'll ring you back.' I give him the number and hold the receiver cradle down with my finger so that I can answer immediately. I have already written with news of my first week, but Ted wants to know what's happened since and any other details he's missed out on, and I tell him about meeting Michael Denston.

'How extraordinary.'

'He was very friendly. He sent his regards to you. In fact he's invited me to lunch tomorrow. He's married now, two small children I think he said.'

'That's nice of him. He always was a nice chap. It's thanks to him that you went to Loriners'. So Doughty killed himself. Good Lord. I wouldn't be surprised if the headmaster wasn't up to the same thing. Thick as thieves. No wonder he's made himself scarce. Malta, did you say?'

THE DENSTONS' HOUSE is next door to the school, a large Victorian villa in a similar style to the main building. I ring the bell and a small girl of about four heaves open the wide front door. 'Are you the deaf boy? Or p'r'aps you can't hear me.'

A woman in her mid-thirties appears. She has slightly wild reddish hair and an infectious laugh. 'Sorry about Frances. She's got a bit confused about the name Geoff and thinks you're deaf. Frances, dear, I've explained to you, he's called Geoff, it's short for Geoffrey and he's not deaf.'

'Oh, all right.'

'I'm Georgina, Mike's wife, but everyone calls me Georgie. Maybe that explains why Frances finds names confusing.' She holds out her hand. 'So pleased you could come, Geoff.'

Mike appears. 'Ah, Geoff, do come through.' We go into the drawing room which is startlingly similar to my memory of Mr Doughty's room at the school. A pretty girl who looks about seventeen is sitting on a sofa with a toddler on her lap. Her long brown hair is swept back and held in place with a black velvet Alice band and she's wearing trousers and a white blouse. 'This is my niece, Julia, and this young rascal is Roland, isn't it?' and the little boy chuckles with glee as his father tickles him under his arm. 'And this is Geoff, who's just started at St Christopher's.' I shake hands with Julia. 'Julia's thinking of applying for Cambridge herself next year and wanted to have a look around.'

'Well, I'm not sure, actually. As well as probably not having a cat in hell's chance, I'm also wondering whether it might be a bit stuffy and one of the new universities might be more fun. Are you finding it stuffy, Geoff?'

I'm bowled over by her self-confidence, not to mention her looks and am momentarily tongue-tied. 'Em, it's a bit too soon for me to judge. It is a little overwhelming but I suppose I'll get used to it.'

'The trouble is that I live in Oxford anyway, and although the town itself is different, once you go into a college it's exactly the same and I'm not sure if I wouldn't rather have a change.'

'Julia's father is professor of classics at Oxford, you see, married to my sister.'

'Gosh,' I say, and too late realise how much I sound like a schoolboy.

'Bit fierce, isn't she? Father's daughter, you see.'

'N… no, not at all,' I mumble.

'Uncle Mike, don't be ridiculous, I'm not at all like Daddy. I'm a lamb and you know it.' I've always found Eric's older sister a little scary, but Julia is in a different league, she sounds more like twenty-five than seventeen, and yet I can't take my eyes off her. 'So what are you reading?'

'Engineering.'

'The engineering fellows I've met at my father's college seem to be either stupendously interesting or mind-numbingly boring. I hope you're not the boring kind. Sorry, that was terribly rude of me. You really mustn't take any notice of me, I just run away with myself sometimes. It's only that in my experience they do seem to fall into one of those two categories.'

'I think you might be being a bit unfair.' I'm absolutely desperate to make a good impression. As usual Les's 'start strong' echoes in my head. 'Have you ever heard of Paul Dirac?'

'No, I don't think I have.'

'He's a professor here. He's an engineer – well that's how he started out. He won the Nobel Prize in 1933 for theoretical physics, for work to do with atomic theory and quantum physics. Some people think he's one of the most brilliant minds of all time, up there with Newton and Einstein, but by all accounts he's also a bit odd. No small talk, socially awkward, so if you met him you might find him mind-numbingly boring too, but that's only because his mind is working away all the time on things that he thinks are more important – fundamental truths about the universe, things that might make inventions possible in the future that we can't even imagine.'

'Touché,' laughs Mike. 'I think you might have met your match, my darling niece!'

'Don't talk such rubbish, Uncle, this isn't a fencing match. You're not to listen to him, Geoff, he can be very silly sometimes. Come and sit next to me and tell me more about this strange man, Paul…'

'Dirac.' I sit down and something that feels like a spark of electricity runs through my body now that I'm closer to her. 'Maybe we've talked enough about engineers, what about you, what subject are you thinking of doing?'

'French I think, and perhaps another language, Italian or German, if they'll let me.'

'And then what?'

'Not sure. Teaching maybe.' Seeing he is no longer the centre of attention, little Roland begins to pull faces and smack Julia, so Mike takes him away leaving the two of us alone. And as we talk she sounds less and less scary and begins to sound just like any other seventeen-year-old, with the same uncertainties and vulnerabilities that I had when I was seventeen (and still have now, I suppose) and we carry on talking until Mike calls us in to lunch.

Although they ask me to stay on for tea, I don't want to outstay my welcome, I also have quite a lot of work to finish for a supervision tomorrow. 'It was so kind of you to invite me, I've had a lovely time, really.'

'And we've so enjoyed having you,' says Georgie, 'you must come again. I know it can sometimes be lonely when you're away from your family so you must treat us as a home from home, mustn't he, Mike?'

'I should say so, but I think we might need to have Julia here if we are to tempt him away from his work.' Julia and I both blush.

# MARCH 1963

A BIRTHDAY LP comes from Art: Milt Jackson – *Invitation*. The letter with it says that it's going to be his fortieth birthday that year and he's planning a trip over the Independence Day weekend to see his parents in Boston. Beth and the children will be coming too and they will all be able to stay in the empty apartment of some neighbours of Art's parents. *'It would be so great if you could make it. I have talked to my airline contacts and I can get a ticket for you, changing at Newark. You could even stay on for a few days longer if you wanted to do any sightseeing or visit some other places.'*

I admit to myself that the passing of time has lessened my anger and disappointment about what happened with Donna, and that I still want to see him again and also to meet my grandparents and the rest of the family. Partly it's curiosity, but it's more than that; it's 'connection'.

Ted, Mary and I have a birthday tea together. Eric can't come. My term has ended but his term is longer to allow him extra time to work in a hospital. I tell them about Art's invitation. Ted says, 'That's kind of him to invite you. I think it's a very good idea for you to meet his family, and it says a lot for them that they all want to meet you.' Mary says nothing and I can see that she looks worried.

I write back to Art to say that I would love to come, and maybe stay some extra days to see more of New York and some other places. Art writes back giving me details of tickets I can pick up from the TWA office in London. He also says that he's spoken to one of his cousins who lives in New York and I would be able to stay with them in their Manhattan apartment.

# MAY 1963

I'M WALKING BACK to my room when I run into Mike Denston in Old Court. 'Hello, old chap, we thought you'd disappeared or been sent down, perhaps!'

'I feel dreadful, sir, I mean Mike. I just don't know where the time's gone and now it's exams and nearly May Week and the end of term. And you were so kind to me. Maybe I could pop in to see you the weekend before we go down.'

'Of course, it would be lovely to see you and hear how you've been getting on, but it's really my niece who keeps asking for news about you.'

'Really? Julia?'

'I should say so. She'd kill me for telling you, but you made quite an impression.'

'Did I? Gosh. How is she?'

'Well I think she's up to her ears in A-levels right now, but she's coming up to stay next week, still thinking about applying and wanted to see some plays and the bumps and so on.'

'Em, em is she going to a May Ball?'

'Not that I know of.'

'Do you think she'd come if I asked her?'

'But St Christopher's aren't having one this year.'

'But I'm in a jazz band that's playing at King's, Jesus and Christ's, you see, so I'm sure I could get a ticket for one of them.'

'But can you do that if you're playing too?'

'I don't actually play for more than an hour and a half, so we'd still have plenty of time to enjoy the rest of the ball.'

'You keen on her too, eh? I thought so. No need to be embarrassed Geoff, I was twenty once myself, though it seems a long time ago. As for the May Ball, you'll have to ask her that yourself.'

'Oh, yes, of course, but I don't know her address or her phone number.'

'Have you got a piece of paper? Good.' I write down her number.

'And I don't even know her surname.'

'Edge.'

'Hedge?'

'No, Edge you dope, no aitch. Did you think I was Eliza Doolittle?' And he claps me on my shoulder and roars with laughter. 'Sorry, must rush, seeing your senior tutor five minutes ago.'

That evening, with my heart beating, I ring the number. A gruff male voice answers. 'Seven one nine two eight, yes, what do you want?'

'Could I possibly speak to Julia Edge?'

'Who wants her?'

'You won't know me but my name's Geoff Cunningham.'

'Geoff Cunningham, oh, but we do know you! You're the young man Julia met at her uncle's in Cambridge, aren't you? Goodness, for three weeks we heard little else but your name from that ridiculous daughter of mine.'

'Oh, I'm terribly sorry.'

'And so you should be. And then she went into an awful sulk because she heard not one further word from you.'

'I don't know what to say.'

'Preferably nothing. That's my usual recommendation to anyone thinking of talking to my daughter. Oh well, I'll see if she'll speak to you. Hold on.'

At that point the pips go on the phone and I hastily feed all the change I have into the slot.

'Hello, are you there?' It's Julia.

'Yes.'

'So what's Daddy said?'

'Not much, just that... well, actually he recommended I say nothing.'

'God, he's such a bore. Can you imagine having to live with him? No, don't answer, that was a rhetorical question. But why have you called after all this time?'

'I didn't have your number and... I ran into your uncle today... and he said you were coming up to Cambridge and I wondered whether you'd like to come to a May Ball.'

'Oh, that's a bit sudden. Well, yes, all right. I'm just in the middle of exams right now...'

'So am I, but I can get tickets for any night that suits you.'

'That's impressive, I thought they were like gold dust. All right then, make it the Friday.'

'OK, that'll be Christ's. Should be a nice one but it's not on the river of course, so there won't be punts at midnight.'

'I live in Oxford, remember. I never want to go on another punt again.'

'Right. Shall I pick you up from your uncle's? It'll have to be on the early side; I have to be there a bit before it starts because I'm playing.'

'Playing?'

'Yes in a band at the ball. I'll explain...' the pips start going again, 'The pips are going and I haven't any more change. I'll see you at 6.30 on the Friday at your uncle's and I'll explain... I'll write!' The line goes dead.

'You all right, Geoff? You look like you've just had a heart attack.' It's one of the other engineers in my year.

'Thanks, I'll be OK in a sec. Rather stressful phone call.'

'Not bad news I hope.'

'No, the opposite.'

Before I write to her, I'd better make sure I can get the May Ball ticket. I walk round to Christ's and go to the room of the ball committee member I've been dealing with. Luckily the name slider says 'in' next to his name: Tim Lerner.

'Sorry to intrude, but I'm after a favour.'

'Geoff Cunningham, isn't it? The wizard saxman.' He looks at a timetable pinned above his desk. 'Your band is playing in the small marquee at nine and then in the JCR at eleven. I hope that's still OK, all the timings are pretty final now and the programme's being printed tomorrow.'

'Yes, that's all fine, but it's something else actually. I'd like to bring someone with me.'

'What sort of someone?'

'A girl.'

'I had a hunch you were going to say that. The only way you can bring a girl is if you have a full ticket to the ball and I'm afraid they're all sold now, so the answer is no.'

'There must be some way. I know I'll have to pay, but I've made a promise now and I've just got to have a ticket.'

'Well you just shouldn't have made a promise you couldn't keep.'

'Oh, God. Please, Tim, there must be something you can do. What about people who don't turn up on the night, surely there are always one or two of those? We could skip the meal, or promise not to drink, anything. Please.'

'God, she must be someone pretty special, huh, or specially pretty! That was rather good, wasn't it? You of all people. I heard you at the last jazzsoc concert and credit where credit's due, you were simply stupendous. I've heard you described as the coolest man in Cambridge, truly, and now you're begging me to help you get a girl into the ball. Quite a turn-up.'

'Please, Tim, you've got to get me that ticket.'

'I'll do my best but I wouldn't hold out much hope.'

'When will you know?'

'I wouldn't think much before the date of the ball. I suggest you pop over here on the Monday and we'll see how we stand.'

'Nothing sooner?'

'God, you are desperate. Well, if I do know any sooner, I'll put something in your pigeonhole. That's the best I can do.'

'Oh.'

'No, not "oh", you're supposed to say "thanks Tim for being an absolute brick".'

'Sorry, thanks Tim.'

I walk slowly back to St Christopher's. What on earth am I going to say to Julia? Why did I offer her any night? Why hadn't I remembered that Tim Lerner is a prat and would be the worst person to ask for a favour? There's certainly no point writing to Julia now, not till I know for sure. I start crossing Bene't Street, head down, and jump out of my skin as a bicycle bell rings and someone shouts 'idiot' in a Scottish accent. I stop in my tracks as the bike skids to within an inch of me.

'God, I'm so sorry, I wasn't looking, my fault completely.'

'You're a bloody idiot, we could have both got seriously hurt... wait a minute, I know you, you're Geoff Cunningham.'

I desperately tried to place him. 'I am Geoff Cunningham, yes. Look, I'm awfully sorry – and for nearly causing a crash just then – but have we met somewhere?'

'I saw you playing at the Jazz Society. I'm a fan. In fact, we've booked you and your band for our May Ball, I'm James Mackie, Christ's.'

'Oh. In fact I've just come from talking to Tim Lerner.'
'Really?'

'I was asking him if he could get me a ticket for the ball. I want to take a girl I know. But he said there wasn't much chance. It wasn't a free ticket I was after, I want to pay, but he said you were sold out. That's probably why I wasn't looking properly where I was going just now. It's put me in a bit of a fix.'

'Tim Lerner is an arse. I admit he knows about music, but beyond that he's a bloody pain, but you know, we try to make the May Ball committee democratic and accept any help where we can. I've had three returns this week from old members who can't make it now. If I can sell their tickets, they can get their money back, so of course you can have one. It's twelve guineas.'

'James, I'm lost for words. You've saved my life, I...'

'Don't worry, I'm happy to have helped. Do you want to come back and get the ticket now?'

'Could I? But I don't have any money on me.'

'We can deduct if from the band's money if you like. You're getting twenty-five quid for the five of you, aren't you? That's plenty to cover it.'

'I don't know how to thank you.'

'Just play your heart out at the ball. That's all I need.'

WITH THE GOLD-EDGED numbered ball invitation safely in my pocket, I run all the way back to St Christopher's – looking out carefully for any traffic. The college library is still open for late-night crammers, and with shaking hands I start shuffling through the index cards in the drawer marked 'Eaton-Goldstein'. I find 'Edge', look for the latest title and find *Cicero at the Senate* published in 1961. I search the designated shelf and, thank God, the volume isn't on loan. I turn to the title page. *Hugh Edge, Professor of Classics, University of Oxford and Fellow of Radnor College.*

*Miss Julia Edge,*
*c/o Professor H Edge,*
*Radnor College,*
*Oxford*
*Dear Julia,*

*I must apologise for cutting you off on the phone this evening. I was on a public phone and I ran out of change. I can't imagine what you think of me, not being in touch for all this time and then out of the blue asking you to the May Ball. I wish I could claim to have a brain like Paul Dirac's to justify my flouting all the rules of polite society, but as you know, I'm just an idiot. The truth is that I thought you'd completely forgotten about me, but when I ran into your uncle he mentioned your name and that you had asked about me, so that gave me some hope that when we'd met for lunch last October, you hadn't thought me too much of an ass. You certainly made a big impression on me and so I thought I might be able to make amends for not*

*having written before, by taking you to a May Ball,*
*especially as you'll be in Cambridge anyway.*

*I think I said when we met that I played the*
*saxophone, and I'm lucky enough to have been booked*
*to play in a jazz band at some balls this year. You said*
*the Friday of May Week would suit you, so I've got a*
*ticket for the Christ's May Ball. The only snag is that I*
*have to play two sessions of 45 minutes each during the*
*evening, but all the rest of the time I would be able to*
*spend with you. We also have to get there at 7.00pm so*
*that I can help set up. I do hope you don't mind.*

*Like you, I'm in the middle of exams. I hope yours*
*are going OK. Mine have been a mixed bag so far, but*
*I don't think I've completely fluffed anything – yet!*

*I can't tell you how pleased I am that you can come*
*to the ball.*

*Love,*
*Geoff*


I agonise how to sign the letter: 'Your affectionate admirer',
'Warmest regards', 'Yours ever', but settle for 'Love'. How much
will she read into it, how much do I want her to read into it? I
seal the envelope, put on a stamp and take it to the post box in
the porters' lodge.

# JUNE 1963

THE DOOR IS open when I arrive at Mike Denston's house. 'Anyone home?'

Georgie shouts from the distance, 'Come through to the garden.' I walk through the hall and the drawing room and then out through the open French windows. Mike, in shorts, and Georgie, in a sun dress, are sitting on deckchairs and the children are running round the garden playing some game of their own invention. 'It's so hot, we left the front door open to get a through draught. I say, Geoff, you're looking very smart. But you must be boiling. Do take off your jacket. Wouldn't you like a glass of something cold?'

'Thank you, I wouldn't mind.' Georgie pours me a glass of homemade lemonade. 'Are you all well? I am sorry again for not being in touch for such a long time.'

'Don't worry about that – oh, I can see you're looking around. She's just putting on some finishing touches and will be down in a sec.'

'How did Tripos go?' asks Mike.

'Not too bad, actually. I got my results today.'

'And?'

'2.1.'

'Well done old chap. Good for you. I say, look who's coming.' I turn to look behind me as Julia comes through the French windows. It's hard to take it all in. The dress seems creamish with embroidery at the front and a skirt which must have petticoats I assume, because it sort of sticks out a bit all around. Her hair looks like it must have been plaited and then wound round her head.

'So Cinderella *is* coming to the ball!'

'Stop being silly, Uncle Mike. In your own way you're almost worse than Daddy.'

'You look absolutely lovely, Julia,' says Georgie, 'take no notice of him. Mike, why don't you get your camera and take a snap of her?'

Julia turns to me, 'Well?'

'I'm speechless. You look amazing.'

She smiles coyly, 'Do you really think so?'

'Gosh, Julia, how could I not?'

'Well you look very nice too.'

Mike runs back into the garden with his camera. 'Come on Geoff, put your dinner jacket back on and I'll take some snaps.'

'Wouldn't it be better if it was just Julia?'

'Don't talk rot – got to have both of you in the picture. You're taking her to the ball for God's sake.'

After Mike has taken what seems to be at least half a roll of pictures I look at my watch. 'Julia, we'd better go. I ought to be there at seven. It's a twenty minute walk, is that OK?'

'That's fine, but I'd better change my shoes and then I can put these back on when we're there. Hang on, I'll get them.'

When she's out of earshot, Mike turns to me confidentially. 'Now, Geoff, you realise Julia's still only seventeen, and while she's staying with me, she's my responsibility. I'm putting a lot of trust in you because I think you're a sound chap, who wouldn't abuse his position. Do you get my meaning?'

I look down and almost say 'yes, sir' as if I were back at school. 'You can trust me. I promise.'

'I want her back here no later than two. Is that understood?'

'Yes, Mike.' At this point Julia appears with a duffle bag slung over her shoulder.

'Good chap. Now I hope you both have a wonderful evening.'

When we're out of the drive, Julia turns to me. 'What did Mike say?'

'That I mustn't "abuse my position".'

'What, have your wicked way with me? Do you realise, we haven't even kissed each other yet?'

'Oh.'

'Let's do it now.' She turns to me, grabs my head with her hands and presses her lips on to mine, she then opens her mouth and her tongue touches mine and we spend what seems like minutes imitating the screen kisses that are only found in X-certificate films.

'Wow!'

'Wow, indeed!

'God, Julia, I feel a bit weak.'

'Don't be such a wet. You could hardly take me to a May Ball without ever having kissed me, could you? Come on, or you'll be late.'

We arrive at the college and are let through to the marquee where the band members are setting up. As well as the four musicians there is another girl in a ball dress. The trumpeter comes forward to greet us. 'Hello, Geoff,' he says in his Birmingham accent, 'this is Julia, my girlfriend from home, I'm taking her to the ball.' I shake hands with a tall girl with dark hair, wearing a black dress.

'That's a bit of a coincidence because I'm Julia too and Geoff is taking me to the ball. Where are you from, Julia?'

'Birmingham. What about you?

'Oxford.'

'Oh.'

'Funny, everyone in Cambridge says "oh" when I tell them I'm from Oxford. Why shouldn't anyone from Oxford want to visit Cambridge? People from Manchester visit Birmingham and vice-versa, so I can't see why people are always funny about Oxford and Cambridge. Look, these chaps need to set up, let's go and sit down over there and talk.'

The drummer comes up. 'Hello, Geoff. Is that your girlfriend? Cor, she's a bit of all right, where d'you find her?'

'Behave yourself, Keith.'

'Sorry. Do you know who else is playing tonight? I haven't even seen a programme.'

'The big names are the skiffle band and the pop group, they're a real Mersey band apparently. And they've got some good trad jazz, you now, whatshisname and the something stompers.'

'We're in good company then.'

'Now, let's do a quick soundcheck and we can practise some of the tops and tails.'

'OK, boss.'


AFTER THE BRIEF rehearsal, I come down to the two Julias who are deep in conversation. 'You'll never guess, Geoff,' says my Julia, 'but Julia has done exactly the same A's as me and she's already got a place lined up at Girton to do French as long as she gets her grades. Her French is absolutely brilliant. You should hear her.'

'I wouldn't be a very good judge, I'm afraid. I didn't get past O-level. We're done here, what about a walk around till we're on at nine.'

'How did your exams go?' asks Julia.

'I found out today. 2.1.'

'Brilliant. You are clever. You get a kiss for that.'

'Julia!'

'Just a little one.'

'OK.' Someone passes us and wolf whistles. 'Thank goodness this isn't my college or I'd never hear the end of it. What about your A's?'

'I think they went OK. I won't hear till August. But if they're good enough, I am going to do the scholarship term for Cambridge.'

At nine, my band starts playing and the two Julias sit at the far end of the marquee. There are some people dancing, but most are just standing around and listening, with plenty of applause at the end of the numbers and sometimes after the solos, especially mine.

'God, Geoff, I had no idea you were that good. You're like one of the bands on the radio. How did you get to play like that?'

I smile. 'Well I had some good teachers, and I practise like hell. I was playing for you, you know. I wasn't bothered about anyone else.'

'Oh, Geoff. I feel another kiss coming on.'

DESPITE HER PROTESTATIONS, I insist on leaving the ball at twenty-five to two. It's cooler now and she's wearing a black velvet cape that had been in her duffle bag.

'You look amazing, Julia. Where did you get the dress?'

'It's my mother's. We're about the same size, and we've got a friend who's wonderful at sewing and she did a few nips and tucks for us. Do you really think it's nice?'

'Julia, you really are the most extraordinary person I've ever met. One moment, you're a bundle of energy, whisking off that poor girl – the other Julia – and putting everyone in their place, and the next moment you're asking me if I really thought your dress was nice when you know full well that you were the prettiest girl at the ball and all the other chaps couldn't keep their eyes off you.'

'Do you really mean it, really, really?'

'Of course I do.'

'I don't know. You see, I don't think I'm particularly pretty, I think there were much nicer-looking girls than me there, and then I can't stop being pushy – it's my father's fault, I suppose – and then nobody likes me. Oh Geoff...' And she hugs me in tears.

I hold her tight and taste the salt on her cheeks. 'Julia, you know that's not true. Everyone is in awe of you.'

'But I don't want people to be in awe of me,' and she's sobbing now, 'I want them to like me.'

'Please, Julia, stop crying, or you'll make me cry too. I promise you everyone likes you and more to the point I've completely fallen for you.'

Mike is waiting at the front door when we arrive home. 'Gosh, Uncle, have you been waiting up for me?'

'It was so hot I couldn't get to sleep anyway, but I wanted to make sure that you were back safe and sound.'

'You are sweet. I take back anything horrid I've ever said to you.'

'Are you all right, Julia? Your eye make-up looks as though it's run. Have you been crying?'

'Yes I have, because I've just had one of the most wonderful evenings in my life.'

'Have you, by Jove? Well done Geoff!'

# JULY 1963

I LAND IN Boston in the early afternoon. It has just stopped raining and the airport tarmac now starts steaming as the sun reappears between the clouds. Art, Beth and the children won't be arriving from Seattle until later, so it has been arranged that Art's father and sister will be there to meet me. Art has sent them a photo so they have no trouble recognising me. They wave to me as I come out of the arrivals door, the man I assume to be my grandfather in a check sports jacket and a straw trilby, shorter and stouter than Art, and Joan, unmistakably Art's sister, tall and slim in an elegant white suit and white stilettos. They both embrace me.

'Geoff, Geoff, I'm your grandpa Max and this is your Auntie Joan. Look at him, Joan. Remind you of anyone? Geoff, you are the spitting image of your old man when he was your age. Ain't that right, Joan?' Max speaks with a slightly foreign American accent with his Rs coming from the back of his throat. Traces of his Lithuanian origins I assume.

'It's true, Dad.'

'Spitting image. Let me give you another hug. I can't believe it. So, Geoff, what you goin' to say to your old grandpa?'

'I'm so pleased to meet you – sorry, I'm a bit overwhelmed.'

'Listen to that, Joan. A real English gentleman. I have a Limey grandson who speaks like the Queen. What do you think of that?'

We walk out to the car park in the sunshine. Max, is shaking his head the whole time and chuckling to himself 'Limey grandson'.

'How was the flight, Geoff?' asks Joan, and then more quietly, 'Sorry about Dad, he's just so excited, I know he never let you get a word in. Welcome to Boston and welcome to our family.'

'Thank you, Joan. I think I know how your dad…'

'Your grandpa.'

'Yes, my grandpa feels. It's pretty much the same for me.

Hard to take in.'

'Sure it is. How could it not be? Oh, here's the car.' Joan puts a key into the driver's door of a gleaming white Lincoln. There is a click. 'Geoff, put your case in the trunk – it's open. Dad, you get in the front with me and Geoff can go in the back.'

'How did you do that with the key?' I ask. 'Open the doors and the boot, sorry, the trunk, all at once?'

'That. Oh it's just central locking. Don't you have that back home?'

'I've never seen it. But then we don't get many American cars in England.' Then more quietly, 'Wait till I tell Ted.'

'What was that?'

'Sorry, nothing.'

'So, Geoff,' says Max, 'what do you think of Boston so far? Nice place, eh?'

'Give him a chance, Dad, we're not even out of the airport.'

'Yeh, but I'm only asking.'

'No, it looks really nice. I know there's masses to see too, Harvard and museums and everything. Art said he'd be able to show me around.'

'Art, schmart! He doesn't even live here anymore. Your old grandpa will show you around. Nobody knows Boston better than me, ain't that right, Joan?'

'Sure, Dad.'

'See, Geoff, Harvard is not really in Boston, it's in Cambridge. Other side of the river. And you're at the other Cambridge, in England, right. So what's that like?'

I start explaining the collegiate system but see I'm losing my audience.

'Hm, sounds interesting,' says Max with a note of scepticism. 'Joan's husband Gersh was at Harvard, you know. Harvard Medical School. That's got to be the best medical school in the world, ain't that true, Joan?'

'Well that's certainly one thing you and Gersh can agree on. Ah, here we are.'

We've been driving through a suburb of substantial houses set in well-tended grounds, and now we enter the drive of an apartment complex consisting of three enormous ten-storey blocks, finished in brown brick and crowned with Hampton-Court-style towers. We stop outside one of the blocks and Joan says, 'I'll drop you here and park out back. Just take your suitcase, Geoff, and I'll see you upstairs.' A porter in a booth waves to Max as we come into the vast lobby. It's like the nave of a cathedral and has a thick red carpet and potted palms and rubber plants around the walls. We take one of the three lifts to the third floor and then walk down a wide corridor. Max's flat is at the end. 'Welcome to the Shiner residence, Geoff.' The white front door opens on to a large hallway. Double doors on the left lead to a living room and to the right I see doors to a dining room and a kitchen, the source of a faint smell of fried fish and onions. We go through to the living room, which must be three or four times the size of the sitting room at home. The thick white carpet is partly covered by large oriental rugs – Chinese I think – and there is an enormous L-shaped leather sofa in the centre of the room with brass and glass tables in front and at either end. Oil paintings of eighteenth century rustic scenes in curly gilded frames adorn the walls, and a pair of Empire-style marble-topped walnut cabinets stand to attention on either side of the double doors.

'Geoff!' exclaims a slim woman in an apron as she runs into the room. She has the same smile, the same dark hair and energetic bearing as Art and Joan, and the same accent as Max. She hugs me, and then wipes her eyes. 'I can't believe this.' She holds out her arms and stands back. 'Let me look at him. Oh my God, it's Art, you're just like Art when he was your age. Spitting image.'

'Spitting image. Just what I said, ain't that right, Joan? And listen, Annie, he talks like the Queen, a real Limey.'

'But too thin. Just like Art. You eat anything on the plane? You must be starving. Let me get you something. Bagel and *lox*, some potato *latkes*, maybe? I've got a ton of food.'

'No, really, I ate on the plane.'

'He's been flying for hours, Mom, and there's the time difference. Would you like to lie down and have a rest, Geoff?'

'No, I'm fine, really.'

'But something to drink and eat, just a little something. Cup of tea! You English love tea. A cup of tea and some honey cake. Please, Geoff, to make your grandmother happy.'

'That would be lovely. Thanks.'

Annie hugs me again. 'And so polite, too.'

'That's what I said. An English gentleman.'

I follow Annie through to a kitchen, which at half the size of the living room still seems enormous. Everything inside is to scale: a restaurant-sized range and a fridge the size of a wardrobe. Annie puts a kettle on the range and lays a cup and saucer and plate on the table in the centre of the room. 'Looking at the kitchen, eh, Geoff? Nice, isn't it? When we moved from our old house, I said to Max "I'm only moving to an apartment if the kitchen is at least as big as the one I'm leaving behind." What do you think?'

'It's amazing.'

'You think so, huh. But let me tell you Geoff, we weren't born with silver spoons, you know what I mean? Life in Russia was hard. In the war – World War One, I mean – the Russians made us leave our homes to get away from the Germans. Max and I hadn't long been married. All we could take with us was the clothes we were wearing and our cooking pots. Then the Germans overtook us and sent us back to our village, but when we got there our house had been looted and everything had gone. That's when we decided; whatever happened, one day we'd get to America. Everything you see here we made from hard graft. But Art told us, you didn't have it too easy either. Your mother and stepfather just walked out on you when you were a kid, isn't that so?'

'Did Art tell you about that?'

'Sure, and you being adopted by Mr Cunning-ham.'

'Ted, yes.'

'Ted! Sorry, he told us the name, but I couldn't recall it.'

'He and his wife Mary brought me up. I couldn't have asked for better parents.'

'Yes, but Ted Cunningham, he's not your real father. Now you've found Art, or he's found you, whichever way around it is, you've got a real father and all of us too, your real family.'

I change the subject. 'Would you like me to call you Grandma or Annie?'

'The other grandchildren call me *Bobbe*, it's Yiddish for grandma, it's what I called my own grandma.'

'*Bobbe*.'

'Geoff, you are a sweetheart. We'll make a *mensch* of you yet.'

'What does *mensch* mean?'

'It means a proper man, a good man – a good Jewish man,' and she places a cup of tea and plate of cake in front of me.

Joan comes in. 'I'm going to collect the boys now, Mom. I'll see you later.' She kisses Annie and me, whispering 'I'll see if I can get you a break', then aloud to her mother: 'Maybe you should take Geoff round to the Caplins' apartment soon, he might want a rest and a shower before Art arrives.'

'Whatever he wants, but at least let the poor boy finish his tea and cake. So Geoff, Art told us you play the saxophone too, really well he said, better than him.'

'That's not true, he's much better than me.'

'Well, you can argue that with him, but he says you played on the *Queen Mary* so you must be good.'

On safer territory now, I explain that the ship I'd worked on was a long way from being the *Queen Mary*, and then I talk more generally about music and Cambridge. Annie listens and nods her head. I've finished the tea and cake so she takes the cup, saucer and plate away and puts them into something that looks like another fridge, but has a door that pulls down and two racks on rails inside. I get up to look at it more closely.

'Is it to clean the crockery?'

'Sure, it's a dishwasher. Don't you have them in England?'

'I'm not sure.'

'Well, they're not so common here I suppose. Between you and me, Geoff, I prefer to wash up in the sink, but Max likes me to use the machine. Says, for what it cost, he's tempted to get in it himself and save having a shower!' We both laugh. 'It's funny, you laugh just like Art and you look so alike, and you play the sax like him, and he says you're keen on aero engineering like him, and yet you're different too. Maybe it's just your English accent. I just can't figure it out.'

Max comes in. 'Hey, what's the joke? What's going on here? Aren't you going to cut your grandpa Max into the game?'

'I just told Geoff you said you'd use the dishwasher to have a shower in.'

'Did I say that? No, I said that for what it cost, you could put your head in it and save going to the hairdresser. What d'ye think, Geoff? Ah, I'm only joking, and she knows it, don't you, sweetheart?' and he gives her a kiss on the lips.

'I'll take you over to the Caplins' apartment, Geoff, like Joan said and you can have a rest or a shower or whatever. Art and Beth should be here around six and the party's at seven.'

'Party? I thought we were celebrating Art's birthday tomorrow.'

'We are, but tonight's party's for you – to welcome you to the family.'

'Oh, gosh, I didn't realise. I do hope you haven't gone to any trouble…'

'Trouble!' says Max, 'Listen to him, Annie. Course it ain't no trouble – Annie loves any excuse to have everyone here and get us round the table – but even if it was trouble, so what! What kind of family would it be that couldn't get together to welcome a new grandson?'

Annie takes me round to the Caplins' flat, which is on the same floor but at the opposite end of the corridor. 'Here's the key, so you can let yourself in and out, I'll give the other one to Beth. Now, let me see, Rosie said to put you here, turn left and first door on the right.' The flat is very similar to Max and Joan's but smaller. We go down a corridor and she opens a door. The room has a double bed with beige velvet curtains hitched up in a fan shape on the wall behind and a matching velvet bed cover. There's a cream coloured dressing table in front of a window which looks out on to the back of the building. It reminds me of what I'd seen of a 'state room' cabin on the ship when I'd passed by an open door. 'The bathroom's through there,' says Annie pointing to another door. 'Nice room, isn't it? When they moved here they set up two bedrooms for their children and another for the grandchildren, for when they visit, but so far they only came once all together. And now Abe's not too good, they spend most of the time in Florida anyway. That's where they are now. Hope you have a good rest. See you later, Geoff,' and she comes up to me and gives me another hug. 'We are simply so happy to have you here.'

I lie down on the bed and try to rest, but my mind is racing and I know I'll never be able to get to sleep. After an hour or so I get up, have a shower in the palatial bathroom, get dressed and then go back to Max and Annie's flat. I ring the buzzer at the front door and it's opened by a middle-aged coloured woman dressed in a white dress and white stockings – for a moment I think she might be a nurse.

'I'm Geoff.'

'Come in, I heard all about you. I'm Estelle.'

I hold out my hand, 'Pleased to meet you.'

'And pleased to meet you too, Geoff. Max and Annie are just changing for the party right now. Why don't you just sit down and make yourself comfortable?'

I sit down in the enormous sofa and look around the room, but I feel restless and get up and walk to the kitchen, tentatively putting my head through the door. Estelle is there, cutting up fruit. 'Is it OK if I sit in here? I feel a bit lost on my own in that big room.'

'Sure, honey, know what you mean. It is a big room. You

make yourself at home here. Can I get you anything? Coffee, lemonade, Coke?'

'Thanks, but I'm fine. Can I do anything to help?'

'Why that's real kind of you to offer, but there's not much left to do now. Annie's got pretty much everything done. You OK? You look kinda, I don't know, worried about something. Sorry, I don't mean to speak out of turn.'

'It's probably because I was on the plane for a long time. I flew in from London this afternoon. But, well, it's all hard to take in. This is the first time I've met my grandparents. I didn't know what to expect.'

'Got to tell you, Geoff, your grandparents are the nicest people. You got to go a whole long way to find better.'

'I didn't know they lived in such a… em, nice place.'

'Sure is a nice apartment. I'm with you there. But, hell, why not? They can afford it. No point having the money if you can't enjoy it.'

'I suppose so.'

'Anyways, Max earned it. I know he started with nothing, but he worked hard and done good, and good for him I say. He can't help you people bein' good at making money.' And she roars with laughter so infectiously that I can't help joining in. 'But see, your grandparents never forgot where they came from. When I first started working for them – that was in the old house – your grandmother said to me, "If I'm going to call you Estelle, you got to call me Annie, I'm not having any of that Mr and Mrs stuff, and Max is the same." Well I can tell you there's not many white folks round here who think like that. May have been a long time ago your people was slaves too, but they ain't never forgot it.' At that moment, there is a long sound of the buzzer and a shout of 'They're here!' from the other end of the flat.

'That must be Art. I'd better go. Thanks for looking after me, Estelle.'

'It was a real pleasure.'

When I reach the lobby the door is open and Art and the

others are coming through. Carol sees me first, rushing up to me and hugging me for dear life. 'Geoff, Geoff!' Then she blushes, hunching her shoulders in embarrassment and hiding her face in her hands. I gently guide her back to me.

'Carol, it's so lovely to see you again, let me give my kid sister another hug.' I realise that the little girl with a crush is now nearly a teenager. I hug Art and Beth, and then Charlie is last in the line. Fifteen now, he has shot up and is taller than Beth and will probably soon be the same height as Art and me. His body shape is the same as ours but his face and colouring are like his mother's.

'Hi, Geoff,' he says in his now broken voice. For a split second it looks like he might put out his hand, but then he hugs me like everyone else.

Max and Annie are both there too now, Max in a dark suit and Annie in a black evening dress with a gold and diamond brooch on her breast, a pearl necklace, pearl earrings and wrists which rattle with gold bracelets. Everyone hugs each other. 'How's my sweetheart?' says Max lifting up Carol. 'Hey, how's your poor *zeide* going to be able to lift you up if you carry on growing like this?'

'You're looking lovely, Annie,' says Beth.

'Why, thank you. And look at Geoff in his suit. He could pass for an American.' Everyone laughs. 'Now, quick, you guys have to get changed; Joan, Gersh and the boys will be here soon. This is the key to the Caplins' apartment – you'll work out where everything is.'

'Come on, Geoff,' says Max, beckoning me into the living room, 'time I fixed us some drinks.' On the way in he picks up a cigarette box from one of the marble-topped cabinets. 'Cigarette?'

'No thanks. In fact I hardly smoke at all.'

'Good boy. I used to be a twenty-a-dayer, but, you know, Gersh – he's a heart surgeon, see – he told me, "Max, you are killing yourself, literally killing yourself smoking those things", so you know what? I gave up there and then, never smoked a thing after that, cigarette, cigar, nothing. And you know what?

I never missed it, not for one moment. Boy, I said to myself, what a load of money I could have saved if I'd never started! I wish your dad would do the same. Ah, I hate to see him with a cigarette, but he says he can't stop. Stop, I tell him. I did it, anyone can do it. But your dad, when did he ever listen to me? So, what's it to be, Martini, Scotch, Bourbon, Gin? I got everything here.'

'I don't know, we don't drink much at home. What is a Martini, actually?'

'You came to the right place, Geoff. Just watch me and learn.' He opens a black lacquered cabinet inlaid with swirling red and gold Japanese dragons, revealing shelves lined with glasses and bottles, and a counter top stocked with cocktail shaker, ice bucket, a saucer of sliced lemon and a bowl of olives. He mixes the cocktails and pours two glasses adding a slice of lemon and an olive to each glass. '*L'Chaim*! Do you know what that means? To life.'

'*L'Chaim*. Wow, quite a kick.'

'I hope you were watching carefully. You'll have to do the next round.'

There is another long buzz at the front door, I run to answer the door but it opens just as I get there. Art, Beth, the children, Joan, a middle-aged man, presumably Gersh, and two teenage boys tumble in. 'We pressed the buzzer,' says Carol, 'but just then Auntie Joan came with the key.'

Joan kisses me. 'Geoff, this is Gersh.' Gersh is wearing heavy black-rimmed glasses and has a goatee beard and moustache. He holds out his hand and firmly shakes mine. 'And these are your cousins, Jimmy and Ryan.' Eighteen and sixteen, the boys look like each other and like their father, though Ryan is taller. Both are in dark suits. I shake hands with them. Max and Annie are there too now. Max and Gersh hold each others' arms and kiss each others' cheeks, but the boys hug their grandfather.

Max reaches up and pinches Ryan's cheek. 'Will you look at this, Annie? What you feeding him, Joan? He'll be auditioning for the Celtics next! Come in everybody, let's have a drink.' He goes

213

over to the kitchen door. 'Hey, Estelle, time for the Champagne.' Estelle comes in with two bottles of Champagne in an ice bucket and twelve coupe glasses. He turns to Gersh, 'Surgeon, remove the cork!' Gersh fills the glasses and Estelle comes round the room with the tray. 'The last one's for you Estelle.'

'Thank you, Max, but you know I can't drink when I'm working.'

'Estelle, just once, go on, even half a glass already. How many times do I get a new grandson?'

'OK, Max, you win, but only a sip.'

'I'm not sure if the children should have any,' says Beth.

'Oh, Mom, please?' says Carol.

Max holds out his hands as if to beg. 'It's only a thimbleful, Beth. For their new brother.'

'OK. But just a taste. No more than that.'

Max taps his glass with his fingernail and the glass rings. 'Now everyone, you know I'm not one for speeches,' I hear Gersh murmur something to Joan, 'so all I want is for you to raise your glasses to the latest addition to the family. To Geoff!'

Everybody echoes: 'To Geoff!'

'Now, Geoff,' says Max, 'a few words, maybe?'

Everyone turns towards me. I smile back trying to disguise my panic. Reading my face, Art says, 'Dad, give him a break.'

I can't let them down. 'No, it's OK, I'd like to say something.' I desperately think of an opening line that can carry me through. 'You can imagine that coming here is quite something for me. Christopher Columbus came over the Atlantic, but all he discovered was a new continent, my journey has been much more special, I've discovered a new family. And not just any family, it's you, all of you. Thank you for all your kindness and hospitality and for welcoming me into the Shiner clan. I will do everything I can to live up to the honour you've given me.'

'To Geoff, *L'Chaim*!' shouts Max, who comes up and hugs me. 'I'm so proud of you. Shiner clan, I like that. Should I get a kilt or something?' and he roars with laughter.

'Enough of all this talking, doesn't anyone around here want to eat?' says Annie. 'Dinner is served.'

She ushers us out of the living room and through the hall to the dining room. The oval table is laid with eleven labelled places and there are two silver candlesticks towards one end. Annie shows me to my chair between Beth and Joan.

'Now, before everyone sits down, I have to make an announcement,' says Max. 'I think I'm right, Geoff, that this is the first Jewish meal you've attended. Now, as you probably know, we're not orthodox here, but we do like to keep up some of the traditions like lighting the candles and saying *kiddush* – the wine blessing, Geoff – on a Friday night. Trouble is, today is a Wednesday night. The other thing is, on a Friday night we like to eat *cholla* – that's the special bread for sabbaths and festivals, Geoff. So I go yesterday to the Jewish bakery and I say, "Sol, I need *cholla* for tomorrow night." And Sol says, "Max, you know I can only bake *cholla* for *Shabbus* and *Yomtov*." That's Saturdays and Festivals, Geoff. So I say, "But Sol, my long-lost grandson is coming to eat with us on Wednesday night and he's never eaten *cholla*, surely the rabbis would allow an exception so that the first time my grandson breaks bread with us he breaks *cholla*? And on top of that, Sol, I'll pay you a dollar, no one dollar fifty a loaf." They're normally thirty cents, Geoff. So Sol thinks and he says, "You know what, Max, Thursday is July fourth, which is a festival after all, so in some ways we could say that Wednesday night is *Erev* July fourth," *Erev* means the night before, Geoff, like Christmas Eve, "So" – this is still Sol speaking by the way "I think I can make an exception after all, but it will cost you two dollars a loaf." Can you believe that, two dollars a loaf? So I say to Sol, "Look Sol, you are a thief and a swindler, but for my long-lost grandson, no expense can be spared," so everybody – Estelle, bring in the *cholla*!'

Estelle brings in a silver salver with something on it covered in a white silk cloth, which she puts down on the table in-between the candlesticks and Max's place, where there is also a decanter of red wine and a silver goblet. '*Yarmulkes*, everybody!' A drawer is opened in the sideboard and velvet skull caps with gold embroidery are handed around to the men and boys and there is a cheer as I put mine on. Then Annie lights the two candles in the silver candlesticks and Max pours red wine from the decanter into the silver goblet and starts incanting the blessing until there is a final loud *Amen*, then the goblet is passed around and everyone takes a sip of the sweet wine. 'Who'll do *Motzi*? Come on Ryan, you only just did your Barmitzvah.'

'It was three years ago, *Zeide*.'

'You forgot already?'

'OK.' And then Ryan sings another short blessing, after which the white cloth is removed from the bread and the two plaited loaves are revealed. As we sit down, Beth catches my arm and whispers, 'You're doing fine.' Conversation then starts around the table as slices of bread are passed round and then Estelle and Annie bring in plates of smoked salmon, chopped chicken liver and chopped pickled herring. Next comes chicken soup with what Beth tells me are matzo balls. The children get up to help bring dishes and plates in and out of the kitchen and I start to get to up to help too, but Joan pushes me down. 'Sit down, Geoff, take it easy, you're the guest of honour, let the others do the work.'

Annie announces, 'I know it's not Pesach, but Art wasn't here then and it's his birthday tomorrow and matzo balls are his favourite. Any objections?'

Everyone shouts 'No'.

In a pause between courses, I turn to Beth. There is enough hubbub for us to have a private conversation. 'It's all so new. Actually my best friend, Eric, is Jewish, but I don't think they do any of this. I suppose it must have been all quite new to you too.'

'You can say that.'

'Was it a problem that you weren't Jewish then, when you and Art got married?'

'When Art told his parents, they weren't too happy, but he told them he was going to marry me anyway, so they saw there was no sense in trying to stop him, and then gradually they got used to me and now we get along fine. And they adore the children so that helps.'

'But Max and Annie aren't very religious, are they?'

'Thankfully. For some of the orthodox Jews, marrying out is treated like a death in the family, you're cut off forever.'

'So do you think they'd want me to marry a Jewish girl?'

'There's the funny thing. It goes through the female line – being Jewish – so you and Charlie wouldn't count as Jews anyway, well, except for Hitler.'

At the end of the meal Max stands up. 'Shiner clan – I really liked that Geoff – time to raise our glasses to the most important lady in the room, sorry Joan and Beth and Carol, but I think we all have to agree that tonight Annie has excelled herself as she always does. To Annie! Now what about *benching*?'

'Do we have to, Dad? The kids are tired.'

'Come on, how else will Geoff get to hear his great-great-grandfather's tunes? And you sing them best, Art, anyway. Gersh, you do the mumbling and we'll do the singing.'

Beth sees my blank expression. 'It's the grace after meals. They always used to do it when Max's dad was alive. Max's grandfather had been a cantor, you know, singing stuff in *shul*, huh, listen to me, *shul*, it's like temple or synagogue.' *Yarmulkes* are put on again and small prayer booklets are passed around, which at least have an English translation. Gersh leads with some monotonous recitations, like anarchic Gregorian chants to my ears, but then come snatches of other tunes, some like Mendelssohn or Brahms, others with middle-eastern scales that sound centuries older than any written music I know of.

'WHAT ABOUT A nightcap, Geoff?' Joan, Gersh and their sons have gone home and Beth has taken Carol and Charlie to the other apartment. Estelle has left some time earlier and Annie is putting the last things away in the kitchen, so it's just Max, Art and me slouched on the big sofa.

'Thanks, Max, but I don't think I can keep my eyes open much longer.'

'Sure, it's been a long day. But before you go to bed, tell me, what did you think?'

'Hey, Dad, give Geoff a break.'

'No, really Art,' I say, 'it's OK. It's like nothing I've ever known. Just so different. Ted has a sister, but she and her husband have no children. Mary, well, Mary's lost touch with her family.'

'Lost touch, how can that be? Family's family.'

'Irish families are not the same as Jewish families I suppose.'

'Ah, if she's Irish, that I can understand. You don't need to tell anyone from Boston about the Irish.'

'So it's pretty much just the three of us: Ted, Mary and me. Sometimes people have come around for a meal, but not often and never eleven people at the same table. So tonight has been like nothing I've ever experienced, and it's been wonderful, and the way you've included me…'

'Included you? Geoff, you're my grandson. How can we not include you?'

Art puts his arm around my shoulder. 'Come on son, time to hit the sack.'

THE ARRANGEMENT FOR the fourth of July is to have a 'brunch' at Max and Annie's flat and then go into Boston for the celebrations. I vaguely perceive someone putting their head around my door, but when I wake properly at around 10.30 the flat seems empty. I quickly dress and make my way to the other flat.

'We were about to send out a search party,' says Max, who opens the door for me.

'Sorry, I didn't think to ask for an alarm clock.'

'It's good. A young boy should get his sleep. I only wish I could still sleep like that.'

'I hope you weren't all waiting for me.'

'We just had some orange juice and coffee. We're in no hurry – today's a holiday.'

'Happy Birthday, Art.' I go over and hug him. 'I've got something for you.'

'We all have,' pipes Carol, 'but Mom said we had to wait for you.'

There is room for everyone on the sofa and one-by-one the presents are handed over to Art: a gold watch from Max and Annie, a gold tie pin and matching cufflinks from Beth, a pair of binoculars from Charlie and a leather attaché case from Carol.

'Hey, I almost forgot this,' says Max, handing Art a small envelope.

Art opens the envelope. 'Dad, that's great.'

'And I'm telling you, they weren't easy to get either. I thought maybe you and Geoff and Charlie could go.'

'Look everybody,' says Art. 'Three tickets for tomorrow evening at the Newport Jazz Festival – Maynard Ferguson, Dizzy Gillespie and Gerry Mulligan.'

There had been great discussion between Ted, Mary and me about a present for Art, and now I feel intensely embarrassed at how pathetic my gift appears. Art unwraps it and opens the cardboard box.

'Hey, Geoff, this is beautiful.' It's an aluminium beer tankard inscribed *'To Art on the occasion of his 40th birthday from his son, Geoff.'*

'It's handmade using parts of an actual Rolls Royce aircraft engine. It's done by someone Ted knows from when he was in the air force.'

'I hope they told the pilot!' laughs Max.

'And there's something from Ted and Mary too.' Art unwraps a silk tie with a Harrods label.

'Harrods. Isn't that where Queen Elizabeth shops?' says Max. 'See children, your brother Geoff is as good as royalty, ain't that right Geoff?'

'Because of the baggage, I could only take quite small things, I'm afraid. I know it's Art's birthday but I've got presents for everyone else too. I hope that's OK, Art?'

'Sure it is. It's very thoughtful of you.'

To Max and Annie I give a small framed print of St Christopher's College. 'That's swell. Hey, Annie, this would look just great in the den on the wall behind the TV, then whenever we're watching TV we'd be reminded of Geoff.'

Beth's present is a Liberty silk scarf; Charlie's, a Swiss army penknife; and Carol's, a leather writing case. Everyone expresses their gratitude and appreciation. I hope they aren't just being polite.

'Oh, and I've got something else for you,' and I hand Art something unmistakably an LP. Art pulls off the wrapping paper and reads the title of the record.

'*Liner Notes.*' He smiles. 'I get it.' The photo on the cover is of a man holding a tenor saxophone, leaning on the taffrail of a large ship with the New York skyline behind him. '*The Les Bunting Septet* – hey that's the guy you came over with, your teacher, no?'

'Yes. He wrote most of the arrangements on the ship.'

Art turns over the sleeve. 'And it really has liner notes too! Alun…'

'Yes, he's a friend of Les's, he's quite well-known.'

'Hey, says something about you: "The youngest member of the band is twenty-year-old Geoff Cunningham, who shows a maturity in his playing beyond his years. This is his first recording date and he also composed two of the numbers – the brooding *Ars Gratia Artis* and the jaunty *Enchanting Mud* – which Les has arranged making full use of Geoff's tone, somehow warm and cool at the same time. I'm sure we'll be hearing much more of Geoff in the future. I should also mention that Geoff took the cover photo."'

'What does *Ars Gratia Artis* mean?' asks Carol.

'Art for art's sake,' says Art, 'like round the lion at the start of MGM movies.'

'So did you compose that for Dad?'

'I did.' I don't mention that *Enchanting Mud* is an anagram of Ted Cunningham.

The children are now looking over Art's shoulder. 'Wow, you're famous, Geoff!' says Carol.

'We'll be lucky if we sell even a few hundred,' I say, 'I'm afraid jazz seems to be on the way out.'

'Hey Annie, we got time to go in the den and listen to Geoff's record?' asks Max.

She looks at her watch. 'Sorry, but we should start brunch, there's a lot to do today. I sure want to listen to your record, Geoff, but is it OK if we do it later?'

Annie leads us out to the dining room as Max describes the plan for the day. 'First we go into town and catch the parades and show Geoff some of the sights. Then we have a birthday dinner for Art at Marinelli's – do you like Italian, Geoff? This is the best Italian food in Boston – and then at ten we can take in the fireworks.'

'That's going to be quite late for the kids,' says Beth.

'Aw, come on Mom, we're big enough to stay up now,' pleads Carol.

Max says, 'Beth, give them a break. It's July fourth.'

'OK, but straight home after that.'


THERE IS MORE sightseeing the next day and in the late afternoon Art, Charlie and I set off in Max's car to drive the hour-and-a-half to Newport. Only on the way back at nearly midnight, with Charlie fast asleep in the back, do Art and I have a chance to talk alone. Art starts, 'It means everything to me that you came over, and the presents and all. And your record, and the song you wrote for me.'

'When I saw all the other presents you got, like that amazing watch from Max, I was rather embarrassed at what I got you.'

'Believe me, your gifts meant much more to me than Dad's watch.'

'Thanks.'

'I know last time we didn't maybe finish on the best note…' he glances behind him to make sure Charlie is still asleep, 'what with Donna and everything. You made me think. You were right, I have a lovely wife and children – including you – and I have to live up to them, so, look, Donna is history. I'm keeping my zipper zipped up from now on. I promise.'

'I shouldn't have said what I said. It was none of my business.'

'No, you're wrong there. It is your business and you were right to call me out. Look, I've been thinking about the future. I talked to a personnel guy I know at Boeing, told him you were studying engineering at Cambridge and wanted to go into the aero industry. Man, he was very interested. I feel sure you could get a position. What do you think?'

'In America? Is that possible? Am I allowed?'

'I've been thinking about that too. There are blood tests they can do now that can be used as evidence of paternity. With that, and the dates I was in England and just looking at the two of us together, I think I could get it made official that I'm your father and that would give you citizenship here. You could come over and live with us – the whole family together.'

'I don't know what to say.'

'Sure, sure. There's no hurry. Just an idea you might want to think about.'

THE FINE WEATHER breaks on Monday and there is steady rain as Max drives me to the railway station, Carol and me in the front and Beth, Annie and Charlie in the back. Art flew back to Seattle on Sunday but Beth and the children are going to spend a few more days with Art's parents. The farewells are emotional and I feel quite drained as I board the train to New York City. I expect to see countryside but it's mainly suburbs and industrial areas. I think about Art's suggestion – coming to live in America, officially becoming his son. I try to imagine what it would be like, how a future in America would be different from a future in England. One voice says 'take a leap into the unknown, what have you got to lose?' another says 'why risk what you have now?'

Max has told me that on no account should I take the subway carrying my suitcase, so I take a cab to the address on East Seventy-eighth Street, doing my best to converse with the driver who seems obsessed with the Profumo affair, convinced that England is seething with 'Ruskie' spies.

Art has arranged for me to stay with the Liedermans. Sam Liederman is Annie's first cousin. Sam and his wife will be away at their house in Long Island, but their daughter Rochelle will be at the New York apartment. It is in a large red-brick block with a narrow white awning that stretches across the pavement. I tell the doorman who I'm visiting and he tells me to take the lift to the third floor and he'll ring to say I'm on my way.

'Hi, you must be Geoff. Great to meet you.' She is about my age, black hair, tanned skin, a perfect smile, barefoot with long brown legs and short shorts. 'I'm Shelley.'

'Er, hello,' and I hold out my hand. Why do I always feel so intimidated by girls? She looks nice. Not as pretty as Julia, of course, but pleasant and friendly. Then I feel bad at even thinking of judging her on her looks and comparing her with Julia.

She shakes my hand. 'Very English!'

'It's terribly kind of you to let me stay here. I do hope it's not putting you to any inconvenience. Art just arranged it and I feel a bit bad that I haven't written to your parents or anything.'

'I promise you it's no trouble. My parents are always having people to stay – they're only sorry they're not here to meet you, they've gone to Long Island with my kid brother. Come in. Can I get you something? A cold drink maybe? You must be hot. Lucky you weren't here last Monday, we hit ninety-seven, everyone was going crazy.'

'Thanks, a cold drink would be lovely.'

I follow her down a dark corridor, illuminated at intervals with sunlight coming from open doors on the street-facing side. Abstract paintings and bookshelves line the walls. Unlike Max and Annie's vast kitchen, the Liedermans' is normal size, with a small table and four chairs.

'Coke or beer?'

'Maybe a beer, if that's OK?'

She opens two beers. 'I hate washing up, are you OK out of

the bottle?' I nod. 'Let's take them somewhere more comfortable.' We cross the corridor to a living room which is turning orange from the setting sun. Two comfortable-looking sofas are on either side of a coffee table covered in newspapers and magazines. There are more bookshelves, one with an impressionistic sculpture of a man vaulting over a bar. She sees me looking at it. 'I like that one, too.'

'It really captures the movement. It must be wonderful to be able to create something like that.'

'It's by one of Dad's patients. It's a maquette, you know a small version, to try out the idea. The real one is life-size, they exhibited it at the Museum of Modern Art here. Cigarette?'

'No thanks.'

'Mind if I do?'

'Course not.'

She finds a cigarette packet and matches under the heap of newspapers and lights one. 'So, my folks told me you're Art's son, from someone he met in England during the war. How come we never heard about you before?'

I tell her about Frank and Sheila, and Ted rescuing me from the choir school because I was miserable there, and Art using a detective to find me.

'I don't know what to say. It all sounds so crazy.'

'It is a bit, I suppose. But God, I've been an awful bore, just spouting off about everything. What about you?'

'Me? Booringsville! Typical middle-class, Jewish, New York. Dad's a psychiatrist, Mom teaches English lit at Columbia, my brother Daniel's still at high school and I'm just out of my second year at Radcliffe, majoring in history. Nothing as exotic and mysterious as you.'

'I promise you there's nothing exotic or mysterious about me. Living in Manhattan, to me, that's much more exciting. My parents and my life at home really are very quiet, dull even. Your life sounds much more exotic.

'HEY, IT'S PAST eight. Shall we get something to eat?' asks Shelley. We've been talking for over two hours. She's just so easy to talk to. Would it be like this if I had a sister? 'I think my Mom left some food in the fridge, or otherwise we could go out. There's a good cheap place a couple of blocks away, they do kebobs and stuff. I'm sorry but I'm not much of a cook.'

'Nor me. Going out would be fine.'

'I can pay if you like. My parents left some money here for me.'

'No, really, the least I can do is treat you. I'm pretty OK for money – I've been working at my father's printing works and I also earned a bit playing at some balls in Cambridge.'

When we've finished eating and the bottle of wine is nearly empty Shelley asks, 'Are you dating anyone?'

'I suppose I am, yes.'

'You don't sound too sure.'

'It's just that it's quite recent. Not very official yet.'

'So British! What do they call that? Stiff upper lip?'

'Perhaps not quite the right context, but, yes, we do say that. What about you? Do you have a boyfriend?'

'Kinda.'

'You see, you're no better than me. What does that mean?'

'It's a guy I met in Cambridge.'

'Cambridge?'

'Cambridge, Massachusetts I should have said. My college is right next to Harvard. We've been seeing each other for a year but it's,' she flutters her hand up and down, 'you know, a bit hot and cold.'

'Oh.'

She looks down at the table. 'Don't get me wrong, I like him… a lot, and I guess he likes me. He's a real fun guy to be with, he's funny and clever and cute-looking, and the sex is great, but I'm not sure if he's serious about me, or about anything.' She looks up at me. 'Oh, sorry, did I shock you, about the sex, maybe?'

'No, that's… fine.'

'Not that they make it easy, the college I mean, but I guess that's the same where you are. Are you and your girlfriend making it? Oh sorry, none of my business.'

'She's three year's younger than me, and as I said, we haven't known each other that long.'

'Oh. Hey, you shouldn't mind me, I've got a reputation for saying dumb things. I guess my parents are pretty liberal about sex and everything. I forget other people might not see it the same way.'

WHEN WE GET back to the flat she shows me to the spare room. There is a bookshelf with some carefully chosen books and more paintings and prints. We stand next to the twin bed nearest the door and then with no warning she leans over and kisses me – a deep, sensual kiss. 'We could push the beds together and I could sleep here,' she whispers.

'Er…'

'You OK?'

'Sorry, just a bit surprised. Look, Shelley, I think you're lovely, but could we talk? Maybe some coffee?'

'Sure.'

I follow her into the kitchen and watch her as she fills the pot, gets two mugs from a cupboard and puts a bowl of sugar and bottle of milk on the table. 'So?'

'God, this is hard.' I take a deep breath. 'Shelley, I really like you, and you're very attractive – I mean to say, I'm really attracted to you, and I'd be mad not to want to sleep with you…'

'But?'

'I'm finding it hard to explain.'

'Is it your girlfriend? What's her name?'

'Julia. Yes, but there's more to it.'

'What's she like?'

'It's funny, in some ways you remind me of her. Like you, she can be what I suppose people would call "direct", but her directness is more of a defence mechanism. Underneath she's

226

not as sure of herself as she sounds. I don't think that's the case with you.'

'Maybe, maybe not. What else?'

'You'd think she was very English. She's very pretty. Funny. Very clever. Thoughtful… I can't put it into words.'

'Sounds like you're in love.'

I nod my head. 'Sounds like that, doesn't it?'

'I kind of understand, but you're not engaged or anything.'

'No.'

'And you haven't even had sex together.'

'No.'

'So, if we had sex, just cos it would be nice, and we'd enjoy it. No strings. Would it matter? Or are you saving yourself for her?'

'God, you make it sound like I'm a real prude. No, nothing like that. I'm not a virgin. It's more complicated. Look if I tell you something will you absolutely promise not to tell anyone else?'

'You know I wouldn't.'

I tell her about Art and Donna.

'You know, it doesn't surprise me. I hardly know Art, maybe I've met him two or three times. Max and Annie always look us up if they're in New York, and I've seen them a couple of times in Boston, but Art's never been around.'

'But you're not surprised.'

'There's something about him. He's handsome and he knows it. He knows how to charm people, women and men. He's nice, people like him.'

'Is that all?'

'Well, he's what I suppose they call a "ladies' man". Might not be the easiest guy to be married to. But, Geoff, you're not like him. Is that what you're worried about? Why you don't want to sleep with me?'

'It's not that I don't *want* to, it's just I don't think it would be a good idea, it would make everything more complicated.'

'Would it matter that much?'

'Yes and no. it's more than just not wanting to be like Art

– well, the way Art is with women – it's… it's a feeling. Oh, God, how can I explain?'

Shelley pours out two mugs of coffee and passes the sugar and milk over to me, she then goes out of the kitchen and comes back with a cigarette.

'OK,' I say, 'you see, I'm here – I exist – because of the way Art is with women. When I talked to him about Donna, he said it didn't mean anything, but I'm proof that it might end up meaning a lot.'

'But aren't you pleased you exist?'

'There were times when I was small when I wasn't sure. But I've been incredibly lucky. If it weren't for Ted and Mary anything might have happened.'

'So you're worried I'd get pregnant?'

'That's not what it's about. I don't care what other people do, and I know lots of people are like Art and Donna and it's just something you enjoy like having a nice meal, but I don't think I can be like that.'

'But you said you're not a virgin, so you must have had sex with someone.'

'Some other guys sort of pushed me into it. Not that I wasn't a willing participant, but now I feel different.'

'Because of Julia?'

'And Art. And Beth. Art talked to me about it just on Saturday and said he felt bad too and he wasn't going to do it again.'

'Do you believe him?'

'I really want to. In so many ways I feel incredibly close to him. He even sort of invited me to come to live in America and work for Boeing; officially become his son.'

'And?'

'It would certainly be exciting, and I could really get to know him and all the rest of my family. Everyone's been so welcoming. It's like nothing I've ever experienced before. Everything seems so much less stuffy in America. In England it's all about who your parents are, where you went to school, where you went to university, but in America it seems different. Just look at President Kennedy compared to Harold Macmillan.'

'The land of opportunity, huh.'

We drink our coffee in silence for a few moments. 'Sorry, I've been an awful bore. You're so easy to talk to, that's the problem. Can I just hug you?'


THE FLIGHT BACK to London leaves at ten in the morning. When I check in they see that I have a complimentary ticket. 'Do you work for TWA?' asks the young woman in her neat navy-blue uniform.

'No, but my father works for Boeing. He got me the ticket.' I see her questioning look. 'He's American but I live in England. My parents divorced when I was young.'

She smiles. 'Oh, I get it. Hold on for a moment please.' She goes over and talks to an older woman and then comes back. 'We love our friends at Boeing. We have room in first class today so I'm going to upgrade you from economy. Enjoy your flight.'

TWA call it Royal Ambassador First Class and I sit down on the wide seat and stretch my legs imagining I am a titled diplomat on a special mission for the Queen. There is a large man on the seat next to me, reading through a thick sheaf of typewritten papers. After take-off, the air hostess comes round with coffee but he remains engrossed in his reading and only when lunch is served does he put down his papers. We eat in silence but when he sees that I haven't touched my chocolate pudding he leans over. 'Excuse me, but are you planning to eat that?'

'No, I'm already full.'

'Would you mind if I have it? As you can see,' and he pats his generously-proportioned stomach, 'I just can't resist anything chocolate.'

'Of course not.' I pass over the pudding.

'I hope you won't think I'm being rude, but I don't often see guys your age in first class.'

I tell him the same half-truth I told the check-in woman.

'So your father's with Boeing. Seattle?

'Yes. Marketing and sales.'

'Hah. Coincidence. I'm an attorney and my biggest client is Boeing. I look after legal business for them in New York.' He asks me what I'm doing and I tell him that I'm reading engineering at Cambridge.

'And then?'

'I'm not completely sure, most likely aeronautical engineering.'

'And your old man at Boeing too. No question, that's the place to be. Look where we're sitting right now: Boeing 707, best jet in the world, no one else comes near it. You British were ahead of us with the Comet. Too bad you had those crashes. Handed the whole world to Boeing on a plate. My advice to any young man setting out in this business, is learn from the best. You should get your pop to pull any strings he can and find you an opening.'

He gets back to his papers and I close my eyes and try again to imagine working in Seattle. First I'd live with Art and Beth, then maybe Julia would come over. Would we have to be married? But anyway, we'd get a place of our own, a small neat clapboard house painted cream with a lawn in front. And I'd be Geoff Shiner, and every weekend we'd go out with Art, Beth and the children to the beach or the forest or the mountains.

# AUGUST 1963

THE PHONE RINGS. 'It's for you, Geoff. A young lady.'

'Oh, thanks Mary. Hello?'

'It's Julia.'

'Hold on… sorry, I just wanted to close the door.'

'Am I a secret?'

'No, of course not, but I can't say all the things I want to if my mother is listening. I mean, is your mother in the room with you?'

'Fair point. Anyway I've got my results. Three A's.'

'Seriously?'

'Seriously.'

'You are brilliant.'

'Steady on, you got three A's too, I think I managed to wheedle that out of you.'

'Yes, but that was in sciences. Everyone knows it's much easier to get A's in science subjects. That's fantastic news. What next?'

'I'm going back to do the Cambridge scholarship exam, but even if I don't get in, I should be OK for somewhere else.'

'Pick anywhere you like, I would think. Are you celebrating?'

'Well that's the other reason I called. My parents want to take me out to dinner, and my brother, of course, and I've asked if you can come too.'

'And what did they say?'

'They said of course you should come. What do you think they would say?'

'Oh, Julia, but your father will think I'm an absolute fool, I mean, I just scraped through O-level Latin and I don't know a word of Greek.'

'And he doesn't know a neutron from a n…, I can't think of an appropriate alliteration, but he certainly doesn't know what a neutron is, so you have that on him. Anyway, you've got to meet them some time. And they really are very nice and my mother's perfectly normal. So can you come? It's going to be tomorrow evening, sorry for the short notice. You could stay the night at our house.'

'What?'

'They've got a spare room. Why, what did you think? Anyway, will you come?'

'Yes… of course.'


At supper that night I ask in a matter-of-fact a voice whether it would be OK if I left work early the next day and came in late on Friday. 'You see, I've been invited out to dinner in Oxford and then I'll stay the night there.'

'Of course,' says Ted. 'Anyone we know?'

'Well, sort of. Actually it's the girl who rang me this afternoon. She's Mike Denston's niece and I met her at their house, and then, later on, I took her to a May Ball.'

'She sounded very nice on the phone,' says Mary. 'Does that mean that she's your girlfriend then?'

'Yes, you could say that.'

'That's lovely news, Geoff. Would you like to tell us anything about her?'

'Em, well, she's done her A-levels and got three A's and will be trying for Cambridge herself in December, and the dinner tomorrow is to celebrate her results, and her father is a professor of classics and her mother is Mike's sister.'

'That all sounds very nice, Geoff. Don't you think so, Ted?'

'I should say so. And do you like her? Sorry, silly question. Do you like her a lot?'

'I suppose I do.'

'Jolly good.'


The Edges live in half of a large converted Victorian house in north Oxford. Although a bit older, it would not look out of place next to Mike Denston's house in Cambridge. Julia lets me in. I'm wearing a suit. 'You look nice.'

'So do you.'

'Mummy's lent it to me.' It's an expensive-looking black cocktail dress, not that I know anything about these things. In a whisper Julia confides, 'She bought it second-hand from a dress agency to wear for a college dinner.'

'Oh,' I whisper back.

'We're all in the kitchen. Come through.'

The kitchen is large and old-fashioned. A handsome man of my height, with a shock of white hair and wearing a double-breasted suit, stands up and puts out his hand. 'Aha, the young man, at last we meet. Hugh Edge.'

'Geoff Cunningham. Very pleased to be here. It's awfully kind of you to invite me.'

'Is he nervous, Julia? Have you told him I'm an ogre or something?'

'I've told him you're much worse than that.'

'Incorrigible girl. Geoff, don't listen to a word she says. I am a philanthropist – in the literal sense of the word – *par excellence*. A friend to all mankind.'

'Now do you see what I have to live with?'

'Hello, Geoff. Please ignore these two people, to whom I am only distantly related. I'm Margaret, Mike Denston's sister and we're really delighted you could come. And this is Peter, Julia's younger brother.'

'Hello.' Peter is fourteen and is completely different to Julia. He's sitting quietly with his shoulders hunched, and makes me think of myself at the age of seven when I first met Ted. Margaret, on the other hand, is an older version of Julia, an attractive woman still in her prime.

DINNER AT THE Randolph goes better than I feared it might. It's a warm evening, so Hugh decides we should walk there. The food is nothing special – by now I've been spoiled by enough dinners at St Christopher's to have a yardstick against which to measure restaurant food – but Hugh Edge, once I get over the bombastics, is certainly good entertainment and a better listener than I imagined he'd be. I feel immediately at ease with Margaret, who is calm, interested and interesting. Of course, Julia sets things off by proclaiming that I'd been in America the previous month visiting my new grandparents, and so I've no choice but to tell my life story, to which both Margaret and Hugh listen intently. Julia later tells me that as they are going to have to find out the story sooner or later, I might as well get it out now, and as it is territory on which I am the expert, at least it will stop her father dominating the proceedings. Peter says almost nothing. Even Julia is quieter than usual as she watches me 'winning them over' as she puts it.

It's still mild outside, so we decide to walk back. I try to talk to Peter, but the conversation is so one-sided that Julia has to rescue me. The rest of the walk is spent talking mainly to Margaret, who paints, and by coincidence knows Eric's mother.

Julia shows me to the spare room and at last we're alone. Julia silently closes the door and then we roll on to the bed and start kissing. 'I can only stay a moment or they'll smell a rat,' she whispers. 'God, I wish I could spend the night with you. You were brilliant, by the way. I can tell they liked you, well who wouldn't? But honestly Geoff you were brilliant with them.'

'I liked them. Your father's not nearly so bad as you make him out to be. He's a bit like you, or I suppose it should be the other way around. Underneath the bravado, he's a lot more sensitive and sensible that one's initial impression.'

'So that's what I'm like, is it? Thanks.'

'Well, you are marginally sexier.' We kiss again.

'I've got to go.'

'Is Peter OK?'

'Can't talk now. Wait till tomorrow morning. I'll walk you back to the station.'

WE TAKE A circuitous route to the station so that Julia can show me some of the sights. We start dissecting the previous evening and when we get to the Radcliffe Camera I again ask, 'So is Peter OK?'

'Not really. He's very clever, he eats up his school work, especially Maths, but he doesn't have any friends and as you've seen, he's very withdrawn.'

'When I saw him yesterday, he so reminded me of myself before Ted rescued me. But I realise now that I was unloved. That isn't the case with Peter.'

'No, we all love him dearly, but look, you accuse me of being like my father…'

'Not accuse you.'

'No, that was unfair, but you're right. My way of dealing with Dad is to give back as good as I get. Peter's way is to withdraw into his shell.'

'Won't he grow out of it?'

'We all hope so.'

I wonder why it was that I grew out of it so easily while Peter still seems troubled. Is it something I inherited from Art, or even from Sheila? Or is it simply that Ted is so different from Hugh Edge?

When we reach the station we hug and kiss like wartime sweethearts. 'When will I see you again?' asks Julia. 'I'll be back at bloody school in a matter of days.'

'Why don't you come and stay with us in London? We could go out to the cinema or theatre or even a concert or some jazz. Whatever you want. And you could meet Ted and Mary. What about Saturday?'

'No, I can't do this Saturday, but I could do the next.'

'Great, I'll ring you soon. I think my train's about to leave. Bye.'

MARY OPENS THE front door. 'You must be Julia, I'm Mary. Please do come in.'

'I'm so pleased to meet you Mrs Cunningham.'

'You must call me Mary, please.'

I come bounding down the stairs. 'Sorry, I didn't hear the bell go.'

'That's all right, we've already introduced ourselves. Please do come through, Julia. I hope you won't mind having tea in the kitchen.'

'Course not, we always have tea at home in the kitchen. It's awfully kind of you to have me, Mary.'

'We've been longing to meet you.'

'Have you?'

'Geoff's told us so much about you, but that's not the same as really meeting someone, is it?'

Mary has laid a cloth on the table – an honour usually reserved for birthdays and Christmas – and the table groans with a plate of scones, a fruit cake, a Victoria sponge filled with red jam, and a selection of sandwiches made with neat squares of white bread.

'I hope you're hungry, Julia.'

'Em, yes. I hope you didn't go to a lot of trouble on my account.'

'Of course not. I always like to make a nice tea for Geoff, don't I?'

'I'm afraid it's true. Mary spoils me rotten, but I think even you've excelled yourself today.'

'Well, it's nice to have a special occasion, every now and again, isn't it? Oh, I think that's Ted now.'

'Sorry to be a bit late. Something I needed to get in King Street. You must be Julia. Delighted to meet you. I'm Ted.' They shake hands. 'Geoff tells me that you're trying for Cambridge too. French is it?'

We talk about France and then Cambridge, and Julia does her best to do justice to Mary's tea, although she tells me later that she wasn't really hungry at all.

I turn to Julia, 'I've booked cinema tickets for tonight. I hope that's OK. *Billy Liar*. It hasn't been out long, it's meant to be really good. Oh gosh, you haven't seen it, have you?'

'Don't worry, it hasn't hit Oxford yet.'

'What time does it start?' asks Mary.

'7.30.'

'Well, you won't have time to eat beforehand, so you'd better make the best of the tea.'

'THEY'RE AWFULLY NICE,' says Julia. We're walking to the tube station. 'They seem devoted to each other. Ted's quite a lot older.'

'Thirteen years. Mary told me a couple of years ago that my aunt – Ted's sister – thought they were mad and tried to talk Ted out of it. I remember relations being a bit frosty. But Mary's won her over and she told Mary that adopting me and marrying her are the two best things Ted ever did.'

'And they never had any children of their own?'

'No. You must have found them very different from your parents. Didn't you find them rather quiet?'

'It was rather a relief, actually. They have a… a dignity about them.'

'Is that damning with faint praise? You have to get to know them better, I suppose, to find out what they're really like.'

'What are they really like?'

'It's hard to put into words, and any I use sound so old-fashioned and stuffy, like your saying "dignified". I could say kind, decent, hardworking, honest but it sounds like a politician flattering some section of the electorate. They don't like a fuss, not at all showy. In that respect chalk and cheese compared to my grandparents – Art's parents, that is.'

'Go on.'

'Well, as I told you, Max and Annie live in a huge flat, stuffed full of expensive furniture and paintings. They have a coloured maid, you know. She was called Estelle, she was really nice to me. She said why shouldn't they spend money, they'd made it themselves. They'd come to America with nothing and done well. So what. But over here, people would say that they were flashy, they'd want to put them down, especially because they were Jewish. Who likes rich Jews? And then Estelle said how well they treated her, not like a servant. She called them Max and Annie, and Annie probably worked harder than she did in the kitchen.'

'So?'

'So, underneath maybe they weren't so different to Ted and Mary.'

'I thought you just said they were chalk and cheese.'

'I know. But like your parents, maybe the important thing is just whether they're kind, *good*, I suppose, and the rest doesn't matter. Just a question of luck, the accident of who you were born.'

'You are a funny boy sometimes.'

THE FILM IS about Billy Fisher, about my age, in a dead-end job up north, who nearly runs away with his girlfriend to start a new life in London but chickens out at the last moment.

As we leave the cinema I ask, 'So, what did you think of the film? Did you like it?'

'It was great. It was just so annoying that he didn't go to London with Liz. Apart from the fact that it was Julie Christie and she's so gorgeous…'

'Not as gorgeous as you.'

'Shut up. Now I've forgotten what I was going to say. Oh yes; it was so annoying he didn't break free and do something about the ghastly boring life that was stretching ahead of him.'

'So you think that if you're offered the chance to do something new and exciting, you should always take it?'

'Well I suppose it depends on the circumstances, but generally, yes.'

Now is the time to tell her about getting a job with Boeing and living with Art in America, but somehow the moment passes.

# DECEMBER 1963

I'M BACK HOME for the Christmas holidays. I've got up rather late and pass the ringing phone on my way down to breakfast.

'Riverside double four, one, two.'

'Geoff? I've got in!'

'Julia?'

'Of course it's me. Newnham. I've got in.'

'Fantastic!'

'Not a scholarship, of course, but that doesn't matter.'

'No, of course it doesn't. God, you must have done terribly well. The competition's much tougher for girls.'

'I know.'

'What do your parents think?'

'Oh well, Daddy did they usual stuff of commiserating with me for going to a second-rate institution, and all that rubbish, but I know he's really pleased. They'll want you to come up, I expect, for another congratulatory dinner.'

'Have you decided what you're going to do for the rest of the year?'

'Yes, I'm definitely going to get a job as an au pair in France. I want to get my spoken French up to as high a standard as I can. Mummy's going to put out feelers. She's very good at that sort of thing.'

'So you'd be away most of next year.'

'Oh, does that make you glum?'

'Yes.'

'I've got to do it, you do understand that.'

'Of course I do. But it'll be so hard not being able to see you.'

'You are sweet, Geoff. I promise I'll stay faithful to you.'

'You don't have to.'

'Do you mean you want me to go off and have lots of affairs

with glamourous Frenchmen?'

'No, of course not, but, well, we've only being going out since the May Ball, I don't have any claim on you. That's why I'm glum.'

'Well, you could always find another girlfriend.'

'You know I'm not interested in anyone else. Sorry, we shouldn't have got on to the subject. The main thing is I'm so pleased you've got in.'

# MARCH 1964

I ARRIVE HOME for the Easter vacation at teatime and I'm keen to tell Ted and Mary how the term has gone. I've been working hard, but I'm also now president of the University Jazz Club. 'I booked Les Bunting's septet and we played the *Liner Notes* stuff. Apparently it's one of the biggest crowds we've ever had.' After tea, I get up to help Mary with the washing up but she says I should sit down as Ted wants to tell me something.

'I'm afraid it's bad news, old chap. About your mother.'

'My mother?' I automatically turn towards Mary.

'Sheila, I mean. Sorry, I realise this is completely out of the blue.' He then tells me that he had a call from Phil Vine, the RAF policeman who'd told him about Frank's death and Sheila's disappearance. 'Course, he's retired now but asked his successor to tell him if there were any developments as he felt personally connected. He asked me to meet him for lunch at the RAF Club in Piccadilly as he didn't want to tell me on the phone.'

'And?'

'They've found her body, you see.' Ted sees the colour drain from my cheeks. 'Are you all right? I can tell you the rest later. It must be a terrible shock. I'm so sorry.' He stretches out his arm and puts his hand on mine.

'No, it's all right. I'd rather hear everything now.'

'It's hard to believe actually, it sounds so far-fetched. Apparently some Greek Cypriot militants were experimenting with bomb-making somewhere in the hills about twenty miles from Akrotiri. The police were alerted and went up to investigate, and amongst the mess the bomb had made they found some human remains.'

'She was killed by a bomb?'

'No, it wasn't like that. The remains had been there for years.

They must have been buried but the bomb exposed them. They also found a suitcase, which was fairly well preserved, with Sheila's passport inside it. They checked their missing persons records and found the original investigation and the detective who'd been on the case. He contacted the RAF police and they contacted Phil. He said there was no doubt it was her and the forensics suggested she'd been there for at least ten years.'

'But why was she buried? Does it mean Frank killed her?'

'I asked the same thing but Phil said that actually all the evidence points to it being the Greek chap. Frank didn't have a car, and if he'd borrowed one they would have known about it at the time. On the other hand, the Greek had a car and local knowledge. He'd apparently cleared out his bank account and left Cyprus sharpish very soon after he was questioned about Sheila's disappearance, so that fits too.'

'But why did he do it? I thought they were running off together.'

'Unless they find him – which Phil said doesn't look likely – we'll never know. Phil thinks maybe he hadn't been bargaining on Sheila leaving Frank and panicked when she turned up on his doorstep with her suitcase. Might have had a girl in every port; perhaps it didn't suit him to have Sheila tagging along.'

'But killing her?'

'Maybe they argued and it got out of hand. Phil said these things happen. I'm terribly sorry, it's a horrible thing.'

Mary comes in and puts her arm around my shoulder. 'Oh Geoff, I know you hadn't seen her in years, but to lose your mother is still a terrible thing. We can't tell you how sorry we are.'

'It's so hard to take in.'

'I know, I know,' says Mary. 'You must take your time. It's a shock. You'll need time.'

I don't get to sleep till after three. For most of the last ten years or so I've pretty much blocked her out of my mind, apart from trying to picture her and Art together, especially when he showed me her letter. I think of her as Sheila rather than my mother, as if we're not really related. The years I spent living with her are now hazy anyway. I only remember inconsequential occurrences, brief vignettes like film trailers: her asking me to open a jam jar for her, watching her apply lipstick with a small brush, the smell of nail varnish as she fanned her hands to get the nails to dry, an argument with Frank. I'm not even sure if they're real or imagined.

But do I feel anything, apart from shock? Am I sad? Do I feel connected in any way? There must have been times when she laughed with me, when she smiled at me. Surely every mother shares moments of affection with her child? Maybe not.

There's a noise outside – a delivery van or something – and I see shafts of light are already escaping from the curtains. I've been having a dream that I haven't had for years. It started after Ted told me that Sheila had run off with a Greek man, and I used to have it two or three times a week when I was eight or nine. He hadn't said 'run off' to me of course, but I overheard him saying it. I used to go shopping with Sheila sometimes in the town near the RAF station and there was a greengrocer's we'd stop at. The greengrocer was a jolly man, and he'd kneel down next to me and pat my head and say something like 'How's my little friend today?' and then he'd give me a piece of fruit. And in my dream, I was here, at Ted's house, and the bell would ring and I'd go to the front door and Sheila would be there with the greengrocer – maybe it was because green sounded like Greek – and then they'd each take one of my hands and we'd run down the street, laughing and laughing. I liked having the dream, it made me feel happy. And then, at last, some tears come.

At breakfast I ask, 'Do her parents know?'

'Parents?' Ted looks confused.

'Yes. Sheila's parents.'

'I've no idea. I don't even know if they're still alive. I could ask Phil Vine, I suppose. Why do you ask?'

'I don't know. It just came into my head. Don't you think they ought to know?'

Ted refills his teacup. 'When we adopted you, the children's officer did contact them. She reported that an "estrangement" between parents and daughter had occurred and that as far as the parents were concerned they no longer had a daughter and, by extension, they had no grandson either.'

'You'd more or less told me that before, although you hadn't put it quite that way.'

'Sorry. But now you're older perhaps it's better to tell you exactly how it was.'

'But still.'

Like other things from my childhood, the subject of Sheila's parents has also been buried. Art Shiner was a much more intriguing and attractive area of exploration for my boyhood imagination than the grandparents who abandoned their daughter – or vice-versa – and whom I never met. But now, finding out that she's dead, I have an overwhelming urge to find out about them, for them to acknowledge my existence, to validate my birth, to make amends. Rationally, I realise that they may not be alive anyway, and if they are, how unlikely it is that they will welcome me with open arms, but I can't stop myself imagining some touching scene of reconciliation.

Ted rings Phil, who says he will check with his Cyprus contact. Some hours later he calls back to say that there had been no next of kin listed other than Frank, who was recorded as deceased. Without Phil's personal connection with the case, Ted and I would never even have found out about Sheila's death.

'I think I'd like to try to find Sheila's parents and tell them,' I say.

'Oh.' I can sense Ted's discomfort.

'I know it sounds mad. I've never met them and they've never made the least effort to find out about me. It's just that they're my only connection with her.'

'It's all right. I understand. It's just that I'm worried it might be…' I watch him searching for the right word, 'that it might be distressing for you. That's even if they're alive and you can find them, of course.'

'Yes, I realise all that, but it's something I feel I've got to do.' All I know is that Sheila's maiden name was White and that her parents lived in Oldham, unless they've moved or died. 'Can you think of any way I might be able to get their address?'

'The LCC children's office might have it still. Otherwise, if they've got a telephone they would be in the directory. I think Hammersmith library has directories for the whole country. You could try there.'

STRAIGHT AFTER BREAKFAST on Monday morning, I ring the London County Council offices at County Hall and am put through to the Children's Department. I explain what I need and they say that they will need some time to find my file and that I should call in later that morning. I go straight away anyway and then have to wait for half an hour in a drab waiting room. Finally a young woman calls my name and we go into a small interview room.

'We've found your file, Mr Cunningham, but I'm afraid that we are not at liberty to give you any information about your mother's parents. There is a note saying that they specifically do not want any contact with you. I'm sorry.'

'Is there nothing I can do? Write to them, maybe, via you?'

'I'm sorry, but that would not be possible.'

'What about if I try to find them off my own bat?'

'That's up to you. We can't stop you, but given what they've said about contact, I wouldn't advise it.'

'Even to tell them my mother's dead?'

'I know it sounds inhumane, but there are strict rules in place and there really is nothing I can do to help. I am sorry… really.'

Feeling angrier than is justified, I take the tube back to Hammersmith. Sure enough, in the library's reference section there are shelves containing phone directories for the entire country. I find the directory which covers Oldham. There are about forty listings for the name White, and what if they don't have a telephone? I go to the librarians' desk where a middle-aged woman is filing cards into small drawers. She sees me waiting there. 'Yes?'

'I wonder if you can give me some help. I'm looking for someone's address but I'm not sure where to start. I've tried the telephone directory but I'm not sure it's the best way.'

'Do you have their full name?'

'Not really.' I realise this sounds stupid and decide to take the librarian into my confidence. She looks friendly. 'I'm trying to find my grandparents actually.' I see her doubtful expression. 'You see, I never knew them. They and my mother fell out before I was born, but she died recently and I wanted to let them know.'

'Oh, I'm sorry about your mother. I see. Let me think.' She raises her head in thought. 'You don't know their names.'

'Only the surname. And they did live in Oldham, but they might have moved.'

'Do you have your mother's birth certificate? That would have her parents' full names and address when she was born.'

'No.'

'Well then, I think Somerset House would be your best bet. They have copies of all birth certificates. You could find your mother's and then start from there.'

'Oh, yes. I see what you mean. Thanks.'

'Do you know where it is?'

'Sorry, no.'

'I'll write it down.' She gives me a card. 'Just next to Waterloo Bridge.'

I start walking away from the desk and then walk back. 'I'm really sorry to bother you again, but I just thought, if I found their address would there be any way of finding out if they still lived there?'

'The local library – was it Oldham, you said? Well, they'd have a copy of the electoral register. That would tell you who's living at the address.'

ANNOYINGLY I WOULD only have had to cross Waterloo Bridge to get from County Hall to Somerset House. I take the tube back into town. Somerset House is grand but rather shabby. I follow the signs to the General Register Office and enter the dark pillared hall with its long wooden counter, like a bank. There are wooden boxes above the counter containing search forms. I take one out and fill in my name and address and that I am looking for the birth certificate of Sheila White born on twenty-first of January 1921, and then take it to a window underneath a sign which says 'Births K-Z' and hand it under the metal grille. 'That'll be two shillings, please.' I pass over the coin, I am handed back the form and directed to the Search Room. Inside there are shelves of large ledgers ordered by year and month. I find January 1921 and there, sure enough, I find the entry for Sheila White. There is a number next to the entry, I write this on the form and then return to the Births grille where I hand it in and pay another five shillings and eightpence. 'It'll be about four hours, sir,' says the man behind the counter. 'We shut at five. It should be ready by then, but I can't promise. Otherwise you can come back tomorrow.'

'I'll come back at ten to five and take a chance.'

I walk to Fleet Street and find an A.B.C. where I get a sandwich and tea. I still have hours to kill so I wander into the Middle Temple. I could almost be back in Cambridge as I walk through archways into courtyards and pass old buildings with the names of the occupants sign-written on the doorways. I then remember that Ted told me that he'd seen a barrister here about my adoption, the name 'Crempel of the Temple' had stuck in my mind. I look on the doorways for 'Crempel' but can't find it anywhere.

It's beginning to rain, so although it isn't four yet, I go back to Somerset House anyway and wait on one of the uncomfortable wooden benches next to the entrance to the Search Room. At 4.30 I go to the grille. 'You're in luck, sir. Just came up,' and I'm handed the typed copy of the original certificate. *Father's name:*

*Percival Albert White; Mother's name: Edith Susan White. Address: 18 Palmerston Street, Oldham, Lancs.*

On the tube home I think about what I will do next, now I'm on the trail, and wonder how Art's detective found me. Next morning, I phone my college. 'This is Geoff Cunningham, em, second year, engineering, Dr Seaton is my tutor. There's a chap in my year, Nigel Higgs, reading economics, he's a friend of mine but I've lost his address and phone number. I was wondering if you could give them to me.' I take down the details and immediately ring the number. By chance it's Nigel who answers the phone.

'Hello, is that Nigel? This is Geoff, Geoff Cunningham from St Christopher's.'

'Geoff Cunningham! This is a surprise. What's it all about?'

'Look, I know this is out of the blue, but is there any chance I could come up and stay with you for a couple of days? There's something I need to do in Oldham – I can explain when I see you, it's a bit complicated – but as you're in Manchester, I wondered if I could sleep on your floor or something.'

'I'm sure that would be fine. When were you thinking?'

'Well I know it's terribly short notice but I was thinking of coming up tomorrow and then staying tomorrow night and possibly Thursday. It certainly wouldn't be more than two nights.'

'I didn't realise that "oop north" had such an allure for you. Tomorrow and Thursday then. Hold on, I'd better just check with my mum.'

There is the sound of a distant conversation. 'My mum says you'd be very welcome.'

'Are you sure?'

'Sure.' We arrange that I'll ring again when I know my train and Nigel will meet me at the station.

Ted and Mary are a bit taken aback when I tell them. 'You think I'm mad.'

'No, of course not,' says Ted. 'It's just a bit sudden. I thought you might want to wait a bit.'

'I don't really know why, but I just want to get on with it. Get it over, maybe. I've got to try to find them, you see. Now I'm on Easter vac, I don't want to waste any time.'

'Are you sure your friend's mother didn't mind you staying?' asks Mary.

'He said not. Actually I don't even know him that well. We're part of the same gang who sit together in hall. He's more of a friend of a friend.'

Mary and Ted glance at each other. 'You'll need to take something with you. A gift. For staying there,' says Mary. 'I'll bake a cake, you could take that.'

'And a bottle of something,' says Ted. He gets out his wallet. 'How much is the train?'

'Not sure yet.'

'Well, here's three pounds. That should cover the ticket with enough over to get them a bottle of sherry.'

'Thanks Ted. And you too, Mary. A cake would be great.' I pause. 'I don't deserve you, you know. Or you don't deserve me anyway.'

'Don't talk such nonsense,' says Mary.


I ARRIVE AT Manchester in the late afternoon and Nigel and I take the bus back to Didsbury. Nigel's father is a GP and they live in a comfortable 1930s detached house with mock Tudor beams on the front. 'You're in the spare room,' says Nigel as he shows me upstairs to a neat room with a single bed and a washbasin.

'It's awfully decent of you, Nigel, to put me up like this. I do hope it didn't put anyone to any trouble.'

'No trouble at all. My mum's always asking about my Cambridge friends. She's terribly excited to have you.'

'I hope I live up to expectations.'

'Don't worry, her standards are pretty low.'

'Thanks!'

We go down to the kitchen, where the tea things are laid out on place mats of hunting scenes. Mary's cake is on a glass cake stand.

Mrs Higgs has swept back hair in a bun and glasses with corners that curve up. 'So, Geoffrey, are you enjoying it at St Christopher's?'

'It's terrific, Mrs Higgs. Quite a lot of work, but it's all very interesting.'

'Nigel says you're quite a musician.'

'Well, I don't know about that, but I try to play when I can and there are some excellent chaps to play with.'

'Now, you're being modest,' says Nigel, 'you know you're the best saxophone player in the university.'

'No really, Mrs Higgs, it's not true. It's the chaps I'm playing with who are carrying me along.'

Nigel laughs. 'He's too modest, Mum, but let's not embarrass him. What about a slice of this lovely cake you brought?'

'Oh, yes please.'

'So what brings you to Manchester?' asks Mrs Higgs. 'Nigel says something about your wanting to go to Oldham.'

I've been dreading this question, but as they're putting me up I owe them an explanation. 'It's a bit complicated, I'm afraid. Em, my mother was estranged from her parents so I've never met them. They live in Oldham – or at least I think they might still live there, that is if they're still alive – and I wanted to meet them.'

'Gosh,' says Nigel, 'sounds like a mystery novel.

'And what does your mother think?' asks Mrs Higgs.

'Well that's part of the reason I want to see them. You see I was adopted when I was eight and haven't seen her since then, but now it turns out she died not long after that and I wanted to tell them.'

'Oh, that's sad. I'm so sorry Geoffrey.'

'I've got an address in Oldham from my mother's birth certificate and have been told I can check the electoral register in Oldham library to see if they still live there.'

'How are you planning to get to Oldham?' asks Nigel.

'Train?'

'It'll take you ages,' says Mrs Higgs. 'Nigel, you must borrow my car and take Geoffrey. It's only a half-hour drive.'

'Oh really, I couldn't put you to all that trouble, Mrs Higgs.'

'It's no trouble at all. I'm not using the car tomorrow anyway.'

We make a plan. We'll leave at half past nine tomorrow morning and while I do my detective work, Nigel will work in the library. 'I've got masses of stuff to read for next term. I usually leave it till the last minute so this will get me started in good time for a change.'

'I know what you mean.'

Dr Higgs comes home at seven and the four of us sit in the lounge and have a glass of sherry. 'Sorry I'm back so late. Had a couple of visits to do. Poor old Mrs Badcott has taken a turn for the worse and the Perry boy's got mumps. You know his older sister, don't you, Nigel?'

'Not that well. Mind you I wouldn't mind getting to know her better, she's a real cracker.'

'Nigel,' says his mother. 'Inappropriate.'

'Sorry.'

'So, are you enjoying life at Cambridge?' asks Dr Higgs.

Nigel laughs. 'Mum asked almost the identical question.'

'Oh, sorry.'

'Really, it doesn't matter. Yes, I'm enjoying it a lot. There's a very good crowd of chaps. St Christopher's is a very friendly college, friendlier than some of the others, I think. After all, here I am staying with you, just because Nigel and I are at St Christopher's. It's awfully kind of you to have me, Dr Higgs… and Mrs Higgs, of course.'

'You're extremely welcome,' says Dr Higgs.

'I just need to get something ready in the kitchen,' says Mrs Higgs. 'Angus, could you give me a hand?'

'Can I do anything, Mrs Higgs?'

'That's very kind of you to offer, Geoffrey, but no, you stay here with Nigel and finish your sherry.'

I imagine Mrs Higgs telling her husband why I want to go to Oldham. Will they think it's a very odd thing?

After we've eaten, Nigel rings two of his local friends and

arranges to meet them for a drink at a nearby pub. It's a barn of a place, decorated inside like a hunting lodge, with stuffed animal heads on the walls and deer antlers as coat hooks. Nigel won't hear of me buying the drinks. 'Manchester hospitality. My treat.' Confusingly both his friends are called, Neil. They'd been at school with Nigel and one is in the same year at Oxford and the other is at Bristol. 'What's brought you up to Manchester, then?' asks the Oxford Neil. Nigel jumps in before I can answer.

'Oh, he's just looking up some long lost relative. Aren't you, Geoff? Very boring. But much more important, he's the best jazz saxophone player in the university. Neil's quite a jazz buff, you know.' Conversation now flows on this safer ground and it turns out that Neil (Bristol) has even heard of Les Bunting and has been to one of his gigs.

On our walk back home, I thank Nigel for diverting the talk away from why I was going to Oldham. 'That's all right. I can see it must be, well, a bit bothersome to go through the story every time.'

'Thanks, Nigel. It's just that as soon as I say I'm adopted and that my mother's dead, it's as though I'd had some dreadful disease, like cancer or malaria, and I might somehow be contagious.'

'Now, you're being over-sensitive. Cancer and malaria aren't contagious anyway.'

'You know what I mean.'

'Sorry, comes of being a doctor's son. Yes, I sort of understand. People think you're carrying a big burden around and feel sorry for you.'

'Yes, that's it. And I don't want people to feel sorry for me because there's nothing to be sorry about. As far as I'm concerned, my adopted parents are the best people in the world. Nobody could wish for better parents. I've wanted for nothing, had a great education and now I'm up at Cambridge. I certainly don't deserve any sympathy.'

'But still, you want to find your grandparents in Oldham.

Doesn't that mean something's missing? Sorry, that's out of order. Forget that.'

I sigh. 'No. That's a fair enough question. Ted, who adopted me, thinks more-or-less the same. Better to leave well alone. I don't even know myself why I'm doing this. Is it just curiosity? Trying to find the last piece of a jigsaw? Or more than that? I don't suppose I'll know till I've done it.'

'What about your father? You've said your mother's dead, but nothing about him.'

'Oh.' I take a deep breath. 'That's another story. I don't usually tell people about this, but – will you keep it under you hat?'

'Of course. But you don't need to tell me anything you don't want to. I'm being nosy.'

'No, I'd like to tell you. Given I've billeted myself on you and you're taking me to Oldham tomorrow, I owe it to you. Here goes.'


OLDHAM CENTRAL LIBRARY is a solid building reflecting nineteenth-century civic pride and bears a strong resemblance to Cowling Court at St Christopher's. A librarian shows me the shelves where the electoral registers are kept, while Nigel finds a table where he can do his work. I look up Palmerston Street in the large cloth-bound volume and scan the list for number eighteen. And there it is: *Edith S White*, but no other names. I wander over to Nigel.

'She's still living at the same address – my grandmother that is, no mention of anyone else. I've looked on the map, it's only half a mile away. I'll walk. I'll see you back here later.'

'Are you sure you'll be OK?'

'Sure. Thanks.'

'Good luck.'

The larger civic buildings, shops and offices soon give way to warehouses and industrial buildings and then rows of red-brick terraces, of which Palmerston Street is a nondescript example. Number eighteen has faded net curtains, a front door where the brown paint is dull and cracked in places, and no bell. I knock on the black knocker and hear a chain being put on and the door opens a chink.

'Who is it?' It's a woman's voice.

'I'm looking for Mrs White. Edith White.'

'Who wants her?'

'Could I talk to her?

'What about?'

'It's a personal matter.' No response. 'About her daughter. Sheila.'

'Don't know anything about any daughter.'

'Please. I'm her son. Sheila's son. Please.'

I hear a long sigh. 'You'd best come in.' The chain is unhooked and the door opened. A small woman stands in the tiny hallway. She's wearing a faded housecoat, grey curled hair over a grey lined face. But there's something in the eyes and the set of the mouth, and I know it's my mother's mother. I squeeze around the door and put out my hand but she stands there impassively.

'I'm Geoffrey. Geoff.'

She gives a weary sigh. 'Come through, then.' I follow her into the small front room. It smells of cat, sour milk, disinfectant, coal and human waste. There's a small round table in the middle of the room with a cream crocheted table cloth. It sits on a square of faded Axminster carpet, a small island in a pond of cracked brown lino. The only other items of furniture are three brown armchairs. In one of them sits an odd-looking woman. Her head is resting on her shoulder looking up at the ceiling, and her arm and hand stick out stiffly. She has a young face but is dressed in what look like the dregs of a jumble sale: a baggy knitted cardigan, a voluminous tartan skirt and beige socks. As I come in she moans in a guttural monotone. My grandmother points me to one of the chairs. As soon as I sit down a thin cat comes from nowhere and jumps on my lap with a painful insertion of claws.

The old woman sits down too. 'Well then?'

I've planned what I'm going to say, but now my mind goes

blank and I stare at her helplessly.

'Cat got your tongue?' she cackles. It seems to me a spark of humanity and I smile. The woman in the other chair makes a sort of squeaking noise.

'Sorry. It's a bit difficult. Not sure where to start.' My grandmother says nothing. 'I wanted to come to tell you that Sheila died. My mother, that is. I thought you ought to know.'

'Why should I care? She's nothing to me.'

'But she was your daughter.'

'What makes you think that?'

'I looked it up. You're on her birth certificate. That's how I found you.'

'You shouldn't have bothered. She were no daughter of mine.'

'I don't understand.'

'Course you don't.'

'But why? Why do you say she wasn't your daughter?'

Now the other woman starts to moan, an unintelligible sound of distress. 'You've gone and upset her, you have. Why couldn't you leave well alone?' She goes over to her and starts stroking her hair, saying 'There, there, no need to fret,' with great tenderness.

I'm on the verge of tears. 'Please help me. Other people have said that – better to leave well alone – but it's not better. She was my mother. She abandoned me when I was eight. You're my grandmother. I want to know. About her, about you. Please.'

She strokes her nose. 'Mebbe. But then you're to go and never come back. I'll make some tea. Meanwhile you can get acquainted with Catherine. Your sister.' And then she hurries off into the back room and I hear a kettle being filled and the pop of the gas being lit. My sister? I look at Catherine, but have no idea whether she can see me or not. The cat stands up, digging its claws into my thighs again, and then skulks off.

Edith comes back with a tray of tea things including a folded tea towel and a bottle of sterilised milk. She pours three cups and gives one to me. 'I'll give Catherine hers when it's cooled down.' She looks around the room. 'Your mother; she always

255

thought she were better than the rest of us. So, what she die of?'

'Nobody knows for sure. Her body was only found a few months ago, in Cyprus. They think she died in 1952. She'd left Frank for a Greek man and either he killed her or possibly Frank did. Most likely it was the Greek.'

'Doesn't surprise me either way. She had it coming to her.'

'You speak as if you hated her.'

'And why shouldn't I? I knew about you. They came to see me and her father – the Welfare. Asked could we take you. Take *you*. When we already had *her*,' and she nods towards Catherine.

I give her a questioning look.

'You weren't the first baby. The little tart. Who knows who the father was? Might even have been that clever dick Frank. She went with loads of different men. Then she got in the club and we let her stay here. Then she had the baby, took one look, and were off. That's the last we ever saw of her. Killed her father it did. And then I'm left with *her*.' Another nod to Catherine. 'Aren't I, my love. Here's your tea.' She takes the tea towel from the tray and ties it around Catherine's neck and slowly feeds her the tea, drips running down from the sides of her mouth. 'This is your brother, love. Your little brother come to visit us. Say hello to him.'

Catherine moans.

'Can she understand?'

'Course you can understand, can't you, my love?' She strokes her hand and then kisses her. Then, turning to me, 'Like the cat can understand. Who knows what's going on in her head?'

'How do you manage? Do you have any help?'

'We manage all right, don't we Cath? Don't worry about us.'

'And my grandfather?'

'Percy. He died eight years ago. They said Bronchitis. But after Sheila left he were never the same, lost the will to carry on. Broke his heart she did.'

'I'm sorry.'

'Sorry? You don't need to be sorry. Weren't your fault.

256

Anyroad, you seem to have landed on your feet. Adopted, weren't you? Welfare said something about it.'

'Yes. Someone who knew my parents in the air force. He taught me singing to get into a choir school. Then he looked after me when they went to Cyprus. He and his wife are my adopted parents. If it hadn't been for Ted and Mary I don't know what would have happened to me. They've been amazing.'

'Well, that's all right then.'

'Yes, in some ways. But my mother and Frank left me, you see. I realise now that they didn't love me. It turned out Frank wasn't my real father anyway...'

'Oh yeah, doesn't surprise me.'

'But they were all I had. I was eight. Just left. With no one. Except Ted.'

Edith shrugs. 'Well, turned out all right, din't it? Seems to me you've got nothing to complain about.'

'No. I suppose you're right.'

'So, now you know why your mother were nothing to me.'

I take some sips of the disgusting tea with its sickly taste from the sterilised milk. I look around the room and notice the gas mantles on either side of the chimney breast and then see that there are no electric lights or table lamps. 'Are those gas lights?'

Edith nods.

'Don't you have electricity?'

'Why would I need that? We've always had the gas. Does for us. Landlord wouldn't want to spend the money on this old house. Talk is they're going to knock them down soon.'

'Where will you go?'

'We'll be all right.'

I want to know so much. About my mother. About Edith and Percy. But I can't bring myself to ask, and doubt anyway whether I would get any answers.

'I suppose I should go then.'

'Mm,' grunts Edith followed by a moaning echo from Catherine.

I go over to Catherine and kiss her on her cheek and stroke her hand. 'Oh, just a sec.' I find the scrap of paper I've written Edith's address on and write my own address on the back. 'In case you ever need to contact me.' I put it on the table and go over to kiss Edith, but she turns her head away from me.

'Bye then,' I say. There's no response.

I get as far as the end of Palmerston Street and then break down in uncontrollable sobs, bent double, holding on to a lamp post for support. An elderly gentlemen in a cloth cap and a suit that's too big for him passes by and asks me if I'm all right. I straighten up.

'Sorry. Thanks. Yes, I'm OK now. Just had a bit of a shock.'

'Bad news, were it?'

'Yup. Just some bad news.'


I FIND NIGEL back at the library. 'How'd it go then?'

'Not sure.'

'You don't look too clever. What about finding a pub and getting a pint and a sandwich, and you can tell me all about it?'

There's a pub across the road from the library, where we find a quiet corner in the saloon bar. Nigel brings over a couple of pints. 'Bill of fare on the limited side. Hope cheese and onion sandwich is OK – a couple are on their way.'

'Thanks.'

'So?'

I describe my meeting with Edith. 'Perhaps it would have been better if I hadn't gone to see her.'

'Rubbish. You had to do it. Anyone would have done the same. You had to know, didn't you?'

'I suppose so. But now what? And that poor girl. My sister.' We sip our beers.

'Look, the library's not bad at all. What about checking their engineering section, finding something to read that'll take your mind off things? Surprisingly I've been able to get quite a bit done, and if we stayed till about four I think I could knock

Schumpeter on the head.'

Looking through some engineering textbooks is not what I feel I want to do, but I'm already indebted to Nigel so go along with this suggestion. He turns out to be right and it clears my mind, for the time being, of the images of my grandmother, half-sister and their grim front room.

We get back to Didsbury at five and it's decided that I should stay another night and then take the train back to London tomorrow. At supper, Nigel's parents ask how the day has gone and I'm able to unburden myself, giving all the details of my meeting with Edith. Perhaps it's easier because Nigel's parents are strangers and I doubt I'll ever see them again. 'I can't see how they manage. My sister must need lots of looking after and my grandmother must be over sixty. It's too much for her on her own, surely?'

'Look,' says Nigel's father, 'I don't mean to interfere, but I know one or two of the Oldham GPs. You are next of kin so I don't think it would be unethical if I made a few enquiries on your behalf. Would you like me to?'

'I'd be tremendously grateful. But I don't want to put you to any trouble. You've already been so hospitable and helpful to me. I'm sure you have better things to do with your time.'

'Nonsense. I'd be delighted to help if I can. But no promises. Quite likely I won't be able to find out anything about them at all.'

I FEEL PRETTY miserable as the train draws into King's Cross. The feeling of mission that I had when I left London has completely gone and the rows of grimy houses that back onto the railway line have depressed me further. Each one holds so many stories, so many minute preoccupations. I feel utterly insignificant. There's nobody in when I get home so I go straight to my room and write a thank-you letter to Nigel's mother and then a letter to Julia in France, then go out to post them. At the post box the thought strikes me that I should probably write to Art too, to tell him about Sheila and meeting Edith and Catherine. Mary is home when I get back and I tell her about what had happened.

'Oh, Geoff, I am sorry. It wasn't what you'd hoped for.'

'It's just that I thought that because I was her grandson, there would be some spark, a bond of some kind, I don't know…'

'I understand, but people can be funny that way. It sounds like she's got a lot on her plate and didn't want to get involved with anyone else.'

'But I could have helped. I keep thinking about my sister. I feel responsible. Who'll look after her if anything happens to Edith?'

'Try not to worry about it. In a few days things will have settled down and then we can decide what's best. Ted is the wisest man I know. He'll know what to do.'

'He said meeting her might be – what was his exact word? Oh yes, "distressing" and of course he was right.'

'But he knew you had to see it through. He understood that, but he just didn't want to see you upset.'

'Think, it might have been me up there in Oldham, living with Edith, with no electricity, it was so grim. But instead I've got you and Ted and all this,' I spread out my arms, 'and Cambridge, and "prospects", and they've got nothing. It seems so unfair.'

'Life may not be so bad for them as you think. You said Edith was very gentle with your sister. They have each other. Plenty of people are poor – you should have seen how I lived when I was a girl in Ireland – but there's more to life than money.'

'We were poor, but we were happy.'

'Now, Geoffrey Cunningham, you're not to make fun of me.'

'Sorry.'

'You say it seems unfair, but you had your own share of unfairness when you were a boy. And look what came out of it. You were the best thing that ever happened to Ted, and because of that, I met you both. So three people's lives were changed immeasurably for the better.'

When Ted comes home, just as I start to recount the events of the last two days, the phone rings. It's Dr Higgs. 'Ah, I'm glad I've caught you, Geoffrey. I've had a bit of luck. I said I knew some of the Oldham GPs and it turns out that your grandmother's doctor is one of them and I've just finished speaking to him. I explained your concern and he said that the welfare people keep a pretty close eye on them and you shouldn't worry on that front. Your sister goes to a day centre most days and she's well looked after by your grandmother when she's at home.'

'Oh. That's a relief. Thank you. But what if something happened to Edith, my grandmother that is?'

'Well, if she couldn't look after your sister, then your sister would go into a council home.'

'Wouldn't that be very, em, distressing for her?'

'Not necessarily. They're generally quite reasonable places with very dedicated staff. It wouldn't be easy for her without your grandmother, but that would be the case wherever she goes.'

'Yes, I see. I don't know how to thank you Dr Higgs. You and Mrs Higgs and Nigel, you've all been so kind.'

'That's quite all right. We're more than happy to help.'

I tell Ted and Mary what Dr Higgs has said. 'Well, there you are,' says Mary, 'I told you things might not be as bad you thought.'

'Maybe.'


A WEEK LATER it's my birthday. Art's present is Frank Sinatra's *Come Fly With Me*. Not strictly jazz, but still great. Frank is on the record sleeve, holding an alluring woman's outstretched hand, his other thumb pointing to the planes on the runway behind him as if he's thumbing a lift. He's smiling, the sky is blue. I get the message.

I write to thank him and also tell him about Sheila and going to see Edith. I keep the letter very matter-of-fact and leave out that Edith's reception of me was far from welcoming. I hope that Art will understand my compulsion to find my grandmother as being similar to his search to find me. His reply comes two weeks later:

*Too bad to hear about Sheila. I can't help thinking*

*how things might have turned out so differently for her if I'd never met her, or you hadn't come along, or I hadn't been shot down, or a million other 'ifs'. I guess that's life though. Sure must have been quite a surprise to find you had a sister. I didn't see that one coming.*

# APRIL 1964

I'M BACK AT Cambridge, revising hard for my end-of-year exams. I check my pigeon-hole after lunch and find a letter to my home address which has been readdressed to me in Cambridge in Mary's handwriting.

I open it and pull out several sheets of cheap paper filled with a neat copperplate. I flick to the end and it's signed Edith.

*Dear Geoffrey,*

*I have been thinking a lot about your visit and now regret that I was not very friendly. Your grandfather would have told me to behave myself but I am afraid that this has become my normal behaviour with strangers after being alone with just Catherine for so many years. Your mother broke our hearts and when I am reminded of her I become a bitter old woman. I have been trying to think back to when I was a girl. My father was a cold man. Perhaps that is where I get it from. My mother had a hard life but despite everything, one thing I was sure of was that she loved us, us being me and my two brothers. I think you said that your mother didn't love you. I'm not surprised because she was always a selfish person, but I see it must have been very hard for you as a boy and I am sorry for that and pleased that you found some new parents who could love you and look after you. Your grandfather and I both loved your mother. But maybe I wasn't very good at showing it and I can't remember her showing any love back to us, even when she was a little girl.*

*A few days after you came, Catherine became*

*unwell and the doctor came to see her. He said that*
*he had heard I had a grandson who had been worried*
*about me. I was quite angry about that and told the*
*doctor to mind his own business but I see now that you*
*were only trying to help and I'm sorry I was rude to the*
*doctor. He was also just trying to help. He said that he*
*would have to take her into hospital and she died the*
*next night. It is probably for the best as hers was not*
*much of a life, but I loved her and I know she loved*
*me.*

*If you wanted to visit me again, I would be pleased*
*to see you and would try to be friendlier than last time.*
*Yours truly,*
*Edith*

I take some deep breaths. My hand is shaking which makes the letter flutter. I go outside and walk through the two courts down to the river, then over the bridge and into the Scholars' Garden, where I sit on a bench. Weak sunlight is trying to break through the white sky. I sit there for about five minutes, then get up and go back to Old Court. My tutor's rooms are on C staircase. The air is noticeably chillier through the stone arch and I climb to the first floor where the sliding wooden indicator shows that Dr Seaton is in and the outer door to his room is ajar. I knock and a muffled 'Come' issues forth. I pick my way through the foot-high piles of books neatly stacked on the floor, with slips of pink and yellow paper sticking out of them. Dr Seaton swivels around on a large leather-upholstered chair beside a dining table piled with yet more volumes.

'Cunningham? What brings you here?'

'Sorry to disturb you, Dr Seaton, but I need an *exeat*, please.'

'Tell.'

'I've just got a letter saying that a half-sister I had in Oldham has died. She lived with my grandmother and I'd like to go up tomorrow to see her.'

'Sorry to hear that. Were you close?'

'It's a bit complicated. I'd only recently met her actually. There'd been an, er, estrangement with that side of the family.'

'Oh. Sorry, I don't mean to pry. Just for one night is it?'

'Yes, I'll be back for hall on Thursday evening.'

'Good.' He fishes out a sheet of headed writing paper from a drawer and writes a brief note which he blots with a rocking blotter. 'I think there might be some form I'm supposed to use nowadays, but this will do. Show it to the porters and remind them to let your bedder know. Everything else all right? Revising for Tripos I suppose. Dr Massey tells me he has high hopes.'

'I'm not sure if he's justified there.'

'Oh well, do your best.'

After seeing the porters, I go to the public phone outside the JCR and ring Ted at work.

'Shall I ring you back?' asks Ted.

'No, it's all right I've put a shilling in pennies in. That should last long enough.' I read out Edith's letter and tell him that I have decided to go up to Oldham tomorrow. 'I'll reply this afternoon to tell her I'm coming up.'

'Will you stay with her, do you think?'

'I don't know, but I'll bring money for a B and B in case.'

'I think it's the right thing to see her. It must have taken quite a lot for her to write to you and say what she said.'

'I know.'

'I'm sorry about Catherine.'

'I feel I should have done more. I feel guilty.'

'You mustn't feel that way. It wasn't remotely your fault. There was nothing you could have done.'

'Maybe. But I still feel bad about it, and about not knowing her. I should have tried to look for Edith before. Why did I wait so long?'

'Geoff, you mustn't think like that. You knew nothing about them. I'm not blaming her, but it was Edith who decided she didn't want to have any contact with you, not the other way around.'

'Yes, but I just can't help feeling that I'm somehow to blame.'

I write a postcard to Edith telling her I'll be coming up tomorrow and post it in the box in the porters' lodge, then I cycle to the station to check what route I can take to Oldham and what time the train leaves. The booking clerk leafs through a huge timetable. I'll have to change at Ely, Peterborough, Leeds and Manchester. If I take the 6.35 I should be in Oldham by noon. Back at college I try to do some work but can't get my mind away from the recurring image of Edith and Catherine in the dingy sitting room in Palmerston Street.

THERE IS A slight drizzle when I get to Edith's house which adds to its depressing aspect. She opens the door to my knock and unhooks the chain when she sees it's me. 'I got your postcard. You didn't need to come.'

'I wanted to.'

'Come in then. I'll put on the kettle.'

Everything is pretty much as last time, except Catherine's chair is empty and her absence hangs in the air. The cat skulks in and jumps onto my lap, pricking my thighs as before. Edith comes in with the tea tray. I desperately try to think of something to say. All that comes out is, 'Are you all right?'

'Course I'm all right. Why shouldn't I be?'

'I don't know. I just thought it might be difficult for you to get used to life without Catherine after so many years, and that being on your own might be a bit lonely.'

'I can manage very well, thank you.'

'Thank you for your letter and for saying that you'd be pleased to see me if I came again.'

'Did I say that?'

'Yes.'

Edith looks away from me and stares at Catherine's empty chair. 'I've done it again. Can't help it I suppose. It's the way I am.' She turns back to face me. 'Sorry for being so short with you just now. You meant well. I know you did.' She sits down and then begins to weep. First just sniffs, then sobs which shake her whole body and whimpers from the back of her throat. I painfully push the cat off my lap and go to kneel on the floor next to her chair and put my arm around her shoulder. To my surprise she leans into me and holds me tight, sobbing into my neck. It seems that minutes go by until she pulls back and wipes her eyes with a handkerchief from her sleeve. 'I'm sorry.'

'You don't need to be.' And then I realise that my eyes are also wet. 'It's sad. Something very, very sad. It's OK to cry.'

'Mebbe.' She tightens her lips and holds her breath and then breathes out. 'Look at me. I haven't even poured the tea.'

'I'll do it.' Still on my knees, I shuffle over to the table and fill the two cups, bringing one over to Edith.

'Thank you.' She takes a sip. 'You're a good boy.' Her tears well up again, and now my eyes start streaming too.

'And you're a good gran,' I manage to say through my sniffs, and then we both begin to laugh.

'Do you have a biscuit, by any chance? I'm starving.'

'Might have. They'd be in the cupboard in the kitchen. Top shelf on the right.'

The kitchen is very bare. An old-fashioned gas stove, a small table covered with a faded oilcloth and a wooden cupboard with round ventilation grilles in the doors. I look inside but there are no biscuits, in fact there is very little at all, just a few tins – peaches, corned beef, evaporated milk – some eggs, a couple of nearly-empty jam jars and a glass dish containing margarine.

'I couldn't find any. You seem a bit low on things. Could I go out and buy something for lunch? Some bread and cheese, perhaps?'

'I'm not hungry myself. I had bread and jam for breakfast. But you go out and get something. You're a growing boy. What time did you leave to get here?'

'I got a train at 6.35.'

'And have you eaten anything?'

'I had a quick cup of tea and a biscuit at Leeds station in-between trains.'

'No wonder you're hungry. Here, pass me my bag,' and she points to a scuffed beige leather handbag hanging from the door handle.

'It's OK, I've got money.'

'I'll pay. You're my guest. I've got enough you know. I get my old age pension and a widow's pension. And I used to get extra for Catherine. Here's a ten bob note. Be sure to bring me back the change.' She glances at the square wooden clock on the mantelpiece. 'It's nearly twenty to one. They shut at one, you'd better go now. The shops are just up the road, two minutes away.'

'Can I get you anything else? What will you eat tonight?'

'I've got plenty.'

Much as this seems to contradict the contents of the cupboard, I don't argue and just gulp my tea down and go out. I'm back ten minutes later with a packet of sliced bread, a block of cheddar, some tomatoes, apples and a packet of digestive biscuits. Edith comes into the kitchen and watches me make a cheese and tomato sandwich. She won't let me make one for her but agrees to have a small piece of cheese with a digestive biscuit. 'What time do you have to leave?' she asks me.

'I told them I'd be back for hall tomorrow. It's at seven.'

'What's hall?'

I explain, which provokes more questions about the college and my life at Cambridge. 'You could come and visit and I could show you around. It's very beautiful.'

I expect a flat rejection, but to my surprise she answers, 'You wouldn't want me down there. And anyroad, how would I get there?'

'Well, maybe Ted and I could drive up and fetch you. One weekend. And then you could stay with us in London. Have you ever been to London?'

'Years ago, when I were a girl. We all went to the Crystal Palace. 1911, just after the coronation. Dad had an idea about emigrating to Canada or Australia, and there were a big show at the Crystal Palace where you could see about it. There were so many people. That's mainly what I remember. We went there on the top of a bus, that's all I really got to see of London.'

'But you didn't emigrate.'

'No. He couldn't make up his mind, I suppose. But my brothers both went to Australia. Maybe that's where they got the idea from, the Crystal Palace.'

'So I've got two great-uncles in Australia?'

'Yeh, they're still there. We send Christmas cards.'

As with Art's family, it seems so strange that there are all these relatives I know nothing about. Normally prior generations exist and new generations come along, but in my case, I existed first and only later do I acquire father, brother, sisters, and the others. And this on top of Ted and Mary.

'And did my grandfather also have brothers and sisters?'

'Percy? Yes, he had a younger brother, Gus. He were a lovely chap. He helped in the Sunday school, you see. Percy were older, he'd long gone, but Gus were still there when I started and then he carried on, helping the teacher. I always liked Gus,' and she smiles, 'had a bit of a pash for him, I suppose. All the girls did.' She sighs. 'Killed in the war, 1917.'

'In France?'

'No. Preston. Run over by a staff car. Percy were in France. Never got a scratch. He used to say that God had protected him. Shame he didn't protect Gus too.'

And then the family history begins in earnest, as Edith turns from a dour and guarded old woman to someone reliving her younger days with a sparkiness which Sheila had also sparingly displayed on odd occasions. I assumed that all my Oldham family worked in dark satanic mills but it turns out that both Edith's father and Percy had been postmen. Chapel was their social hub and Percy and Edith had been identified by their parents as a good match. Edith's father used his influence to get Percy the job which provided the suitable 'prospects' on which the marriage could proceed. Edith herself was good with figures and before marrying had worked as a wages clerk at a local dairy, but that had ended with marriage. 'And then I had your mother.'

'What was she like, as a child, I mean?' Edith sighs, rests one elbow on the kitchen table and cups her chin in her hand. 'I know in your letter you said she was selfish, but…' I tail off.

'She were a beautiful baby. No two ways about it. Everybody cooed over her, said how pretty she were. I don't know how, but even then she seemed to know what they were saying. And when she were old enough to sit up, there were this mirror we had on the table in our bedroom, and I'd put it on the floor and she'd spend hours looking at herself. Almost her first words were when she were looking in the mirror: "Seila," – she couldn't say Sheila – "Seila pretty, Seila pretty." And then when she went to school everyone wanted to be her friend. You know what children are like, I suppose they thought her prettiness would rub off on them. And she didn't even have to be nice to them, they still wanted to be her friend, almost more, in a funny kind of way. So most of the time she didn't even bother to be nice to them, it weren't worth the trouble. Hold on, I've got a snapshot of her somewhere.' She gets up from the table and I follow her to the front room. There's a small cupboard in the corner that I haven't noticed before. She kneels down and rummages around and then takes out a metal tin which says *Milady – Toffee of Quality* on the side and has a painting of a country scene on the lid in the style of Gainsborough, faded and rubbed through in parts. Inside is a pile of old photos: women in long skirts and hats, in formal sepia poses mounted on dark cardboard; a man in a bowler hat holding a bicycle; family groups with children cross-legged on the floor and adults sitting on chairs or standing, potted plants on stands beside them. Edith sorts through them quickly as if she's dealing cards. 'Here we are.' These were unmounted snapshots. 'My brother took these.'

I last saw my mother when I was eight, but I instantly recognise the little girl of four of five, with ringlets and what must have been a party dress, looking straight at the camera, not with a childish smile but with an angelic look of composure and confidence.

'Would it be OK if I stayed the night here? Only if it's no trouble. I could always find a B and B.'

'Well, I suppose it would be all right. You can sleep in Catherine's room.'

The thought flashes through my mind that this would be in the bed that she died in, but then I remember that she died in hospital. 'Thanks. That'd be great.'

The room smells of disinfectant. The brown linoleum floor has been scrubbed clean and the bed, with its dark brown headboard and footboard, has been stripped, leaving just the mattress covered with a maroon rubber sheet, just like the one I was given when I wet the bed at St Christopher's. There's a wooden chair and a chest of drawers, but otherwise the room is completely bare apart from some chintz curtains with a motif of pink and red roses. Rather than cheering up the room, they only highlight its drabness. I fold up the rubber sheet and put on the sheets and blankets that Edith has given me.

I know that there is no food in the house apart from what I'd bought for lunch and I'm mystified as to what, if anything, Edith eats. 'What about if I got fish and chips for us tonight? There must be a fish shop nearby.'

She looks at me as though I'm mad, but then tosses her head back. 'I suppose you could. I'm not hungry myself. It would just be for you.'

'We'll see about that.'

The fish shop is in a parallel street. The window is steamed up and there's a crowd of people at the counter. I feel incredibly self-conscious as I ask for two plaice and chips in my BBC English and feel sure that a couple of small girls are smirking at me. I want to tell them that I'm just like them, that my *nan* lives around the corner, that I was orphaned and I've only become different because I was adopted by a man in London, like Oliver Twist.

Despite her protestations that she can't possibly eat the portion I've bought for her, Edith makes surprisingly good work of most of it. I do the washing-up in the butler's sink. There's only a cold-water tap and hot water comes from the kettle, boiled up on the ancient stove. It's dark now and Edith has lit the gas mantles. 'There's no gas in the privy, so you'll need this if you want to go.' She points to a candle in a jam jar, which she then lights and takes with her through the back door to the small paved yard where the outside lavatory is housed in a wooden lean-to. When she comes back she shows me how to turn off the gaslights and then she goes to bed. There's a chill in the air now as I take my turn in the privy, which smells of rotting wood and rusty ironwork. What a contrast: the luxury of Max and Annie's apartment compared to an Oldham privy in candlelight.

Despite the bond that I now feel exists between us, there is an awkwardness when I leave her the next morning; not knowing quite how to say goodbye, how to indicate our affection for each other, on what terms we are parting, what will be the next steps. We kiss and hug, but both of us seem wooden. I thank her and promise to write. And I do write, to my surprise almost every fortnight, with everyday news about my studies, goings-on in college, my jazz gigs, working for Ted in the vacation and so on. She writes back too. The demolition of her street is going ahead but she will be given a new council flat nearby and she will receive a compensation payment for the inconvenience. She has moved into the new flat – it has hot water, electricity, a bathroom, central heating. It has two bedrooms so I can come and stay if I want. She has become friendly with a gentleman neighbour.

# OCTOBER 1964

'HAVE YOU DONE it before?' asks Julia. We're lying naked in my single bed, trying not to fall off the sides. I've smuggled her into my room, but assure her that as it's now the swinging sixties, in the unlikely event of discovery, the outcome would be a five-pound bribe to the porter rather than rustication.

'Done it?'

'You know, fucked a girl before?'

'Yes.'

'Have you... slept with a boy before?'

'Course not.'

'Why, "course not"? You know you'd only have to say the word and you'd have any number of boys at your command. And I can't believe that you weren't seduced by some smarmy Frog?'

'I told you, I spent the whole time looking after the ghastly brats and as far as I can remember I didn't see one solitary man between the ages of twelve and forty while I was there. Mind you, the Monsieur did make a pass at me.'

'What? You never told me that in your letters. If I'd known I would have come over on the next boat and knocked his block off.'

'Don't be absurd. You know you couldn't say boo to a goose. It would probably have ended up with him taking you out for a drink and betrothing you to his ten-year-old daughter.'

'So what happened?'

'I smacked his hand and told him that if he tried it again I'd tell the Madame. He was very apologetic and said that he'd just thought I might be lonely away from home. Anyway, who was it? The girl you fucked before?'

'Please stop saying "fucked", it sounds so animal.'

'Well, that's what it is. Anyway, who was it?'

'Do I have to tell you?'

'Of course you do. It's only fair. If you want to f… sleep with me, then I have a right to know.'

'I don't think you have any *right* to know, Julia, but I will tell you because, I don't know, I suppose I quite like your being my confessor.'

'*Confessor*! Like some deaf old priest. Thanks.'

'Julia! It just that there's actually something incredibly sexy about not having any secrets from you, of being able to tell you anything.'

'God, you're sounding like a complete pervert. Anyway, tell me about her.'

'Well, actually there was more than one.'

'What, at the same time.'

'No!'

'Well, what then?'

'Do you remember I told you that when I first went to America to meet Art, I worked my passage as a band musician on a liner?'

'It sounded so romantic.'

'It wasn't, but anyway, to get the job on the liner I had to notch up some professional experience, so Les found me a job playing at Butlins in Bognor. I had no idea, but it turned out that half the people who go there are going for sex, not the children or the parents of course, but pretty much everyone else. People who work there, like the redcoats or the musicians, are strictly forbidden to consort with the guests, but that apparently increases their allure, and there are simply dozens of girls who are desperate to sleep with them.'

'Sleep? Don't you mean *fuck?*

'Julia! Anyway, as I said, I didn't have any idea about this, but two slightly older chaps in the band rather took me under their wing and almost forced me to join in.'

'Join in! You mean an orgy?'

'No! If you're going to carry on being silly about this, I won't tell you any more.'

'Sorry, I won't interrupt, I promise.'

'We did the first night's dance and then at the end, one of the chaps had three girls waiting for us outside and we each went off with one of them. And that was my first time.'

'Where did you go?'

'Well it was in the bushes behind the dance hall that night.'

'God, that sounds disgusting. And who was your girl? What was she like?'

'That night it was Jean, she sounded like she was from Bristol. That's all I really know about her.'

'Was she pretty?'

'I'm not really sure. It was dark you see, but she was perfectly nice.'

'Perfectly nice? It sounds like a tea dance.'

'But that was the thing. It was all very polite and just a bit of fun and nobody took it very seriously. We knew we'd never see each other again, and it was just about physical pleasure, nothing remotely emotional.'

'And was it physically pleasurable?'

'Well, yes, in its way.'

'And then there were others?'

'Only two. I was there nearly a week. Maggie and Susan.'

'God, Geoff. I don't know what to say.'

'Well, you did ask. But the thing is, it meant nothing. The four Fs, Art called it.'

'The four Fs?'

'It's pretty coarse I'm afraid. Find 'em, Feel 'em, Fuck 'em and Forget 'em.'

'Ouch. And why Art, what did he have to do with it?'

'God, Julia, I thought we were going to have a night of passion and now you've opened up a whole can of worms.'

'Can of worms. You do know how to charm the ladies.'

'Sorry, but you started it. Anyway, I'll have to tell you everything now.'

'Go on.'

'Well when I went to see Art in Seattle, we played together one night in a jazz club – not really a jazz club, just a bar with a music room – but anyway while I was doing my ballad number he went backstage to a little dressing room, and then halfway through, when the pianist was playing his solo, I went backstage to get a new reed and I found Art and the singer, Donna, having it away in the little dressing room.'

'Fucking?'

'Yes.'

'Seriously? What did you do?'

'Well I just turned round and went back to the bandstand, but later on I had a bit of an argument about it with Art.'

'Why?'

'Why do you think? He's married to Beth, has two children and I was angry with him.'

'What did he say?'

'That it didn't mean anything and so where was the harm. And then he asked me about whether I had a girlfriend or anything and I told him about the girls at Butlins, and he told me about the four Fs and what was the difference between him and Donna, and me and Jean.'

'And Maggie and Susan.'

'All right, and Maggie and Susan. But I didn't agree with him because he was married, which made it different.'

'God, it's quite a story. Catching them "at it",' and she begins to giggle.

'It's not funny. You're as bad as Eric.'

'You told Eric?'

'He's my best friend, who else could I tell? I needed to unburden myself.'

'I love Eric.'

'Shut up, Julia, you're supposed to love me.'

'So how did it end then, with Art?'

'Well, I said I forgave him – what else could I say? – he'd begged me, but I still felt angry about it. And, I think in his heart of hearts he felt bad about it too. In fact last year when I went over for his fortieth birthday he told me that he'd stopped being unfaithful.'

'Did you believe him?'

'I really want to.' I could tell her now about going to live with Art in America, but it hardly seems the right moment. Instead I say, 'But, Julia, if we were married, and I was, well you know, having a bit on the side with some other woman, what would you think?'

'Is that a proposal?'

'I'll rephrase that. If you were married and you found out that your husband was…'

'I get the picture. Let me think about it for a moment.' I start kissing her neck. 'Stop it, you're putting me off, I'm thinking… I'd certainly be bloody, bloody angry, and hurt, but if he promised me he'd never do it again, I might take him back. But I don't think it would ever be quite the same after that. What about if it was the other way around and it was me, sorry, *your* wife, who took a handsome lover? What would you do?'

'I expect I'd kill her or myself or probably both of us. And the handsome lover too, of course.'

'You are an idiot.'

'But seriously, let's say you go to France in your third year, and you meet a French boy who you like, and you go to bed with him. I would mind terribly, but I wouldn't want you not to do it. You might find you loved him and you'd be much happier with him than me. But of course I'd hope that you'd prefer me, so then at least I'd know that you'd *chosen* me. Sorry, I haven't put it very well.'

'You needn't worry, Geoff, I've chosen you already. What about you, after all you could still go back to Jean, Maggie or Susan?'

'Can we stop talking now. I'm desperate for you.'

'So I can feel.'

'Only if you want to. I don't want to force you.'

'I want to.'

# JANUARY 1965

THE CHRISTMAS VACATION is nearly finished, Ted is at work and Mary is out when the call comes. 'May I speak with Geoffrey Cunning-ham?'

'Speaking.'

'This is Murray Hickman. You won't know me but I've been given your number by Art Shiner. I work for Boeing. He told me that you might be interested in working for us, and as I was coming to London he thought maybe I could look you up. You still there?'

'Yes, sorry, em… yes, I'm very interested in working for Boeing.'

'Great. I have quite a tight schedule but I could fit you in tomorrow morning at nine. For an informal chat. I'm staying at the Cumberland, Marble Arch. I'll be waiting in reception. Just ask for me at the desk, oh and bring your resumé.'

My hand is shaking when I put the receiver down. 'Resumé' – what on earth does he mean? Who the hell can I ask? I take some deep breaths and call Directory Enquiries for the number of the University Careers Service. Luckily there's someone there who tells me what to do. 'Typed is better, but if your handwriting's OK, that should do.'

I TELL TED and Mary that I'm going to town first thing to get in a good day's revision at the Science Reference Library in Chancery Lane. I wear a jacket and trousers but don't put my tie on till I've left the house. I ask for Murray Hickman at the hotel lobby desk and the receptionist points to a man sitting a few yards away. His hair is greying but his tanned face still looks young. We shake hands and he motions me to an adjacent armchair. 'It's pretty quiet here, if it's OK with you.'

'Yes, of course.'

He hands me his card: *Murray Hickman, Senior Recruitment Manager.* 'Did you bring your resumé?' he asks.

'I'm afraid it isn't typed. I didn't expect I'd need it quite as soon in the year as this.'

'No problem.' He scans through it. 'Good. Yes, it's pretty much what Art told me. So you'd like to work for Boeing.'

'Well… I suppose, yes. But I wasn't sure whether you take British trainees.'

'Not as a rule, but as I understand it, you're something of a special case.' He leans closer to me. 'See, Art's explained to me that he's your father, so as long as we can show you're a family member, we should be OK. It's not so much an immigration thing. Right now it's not too hard for Brits to come over to work in the US, but Boeing policy is to give preference to Americans.' I nod and he carries on, 'So tell me why you want to work in the aero industry.'

We talk for another twenty minutes or so, then we shake hands again and he says he'll be writing to me with further details. 'We have to go through the company procedures of course, but Geoffrey, all I can say is, I like what I see.'

I go to Chancery Lane anyway, the library is a good place to think. I feel just like I do before a gig: keyed up, eager to start, but also with butterflies in my stomach. I picture myself. I'm Frank Sinatra on the cover of *Come Fly With Me*, I'm surrounded by jets, the sun is shining and the sky is blue. I get into a big American car and drive over to Art and Beth's house. The children run out as I walk up to the front door. Then Art comes out and we embrace.

I wonder why I've said nothing to anyone about Art's invitation. What is there to be frightened about? Why have I made it a secret? He's my father. This is my chance.

WHEN I GET home I ring Julia. 'I've got to see you. I need to talk to you about something.'

'You sound excited.'

'Well yes, sort of. When can I see you?'

'I could come down to London tomorrow if you want. Or you could come up to Oxford.'

'No, let's meet here. We could get lunch somewhere, and then maybe do something in town.

I WAVE TO Julia as she walks down the platform and then we hug and kiss. 'What's happened?' she asks.

'We need to sit down somewhere and talk properly.'

'My mother says we must go to see the Peggy Guggenheim collection at the Tate. We could eat in their cafeteria first.' We get the tube to St James's Park but when we get to the Tate there are people queuing for the exhibition all the way down the Embankment. It's cold and drizzling.

'Bugger,' I say, 'let's just find somewhere else. I don't have the patience for this today.' We find a café.

'So?' says Julia.

I tell her about Art inviting me to live in Seattle and my meeting with Murray Hickman. 'Do you remember when we went to see *Billy Liar* and I asked whether you should always take an opportunity like he had – to change his life – and you said "generally yes"? You see I was thinking about Boeing and Seattle then, and your words have been echoing in my head ever since.'

'You never said anything.'

'No, it never seemed the right time. But I'm telling you now. What do you think?'

She leans over the table and puts her arm on my mine. 'It sounds brilliant.'

'I sort of imagined that later you'd come out there and live with me.'

'That's harder. I mean, I've only done one term. If you went out next year I'd still have three more years including a year in France or Italy. How can I know exactly what I'll want to do then?' Her eyes meet mine. 'Sorry, is that the wrong answer?'

'No, er, course not, you've got your life to live too. It's only the thought of being apart for all that time. We might only see each other once a year, if that. Seriously, Julia, I love you so much I'm not sure how I'd manage that.'

'And I love you too. So we would manage it if we had to.'

'And then there's Ted and Mary. I'm trying to work out how I can break the news to them.'

'You say they always support you in what you want to do.'

'It almost makes it worse. I can hear Ted saying "well done old boy – great opportunity" but really they'd be utterly miserable. I'm all they have. It would be so cruel. And if I had to become Art's son officially, it would be as if I'm dumping them after everything they've done for me. After that, how would they be able to think of me in the same way?'

'But they've had you for all these years. Maybe you owe some years to Art.'

'Do I? He could have taken me with him when I was nine, but he left me with Ted.'

'Because they thought it was best for you. Art was thinking of you and made the sacrifice.'

'When I came back from seeing him the first time in America and told Ted and Mary, Mary said something about not being sure she trusted him.'

'Maybe she was just jealous.'

'No, it was more than that. Of course she doesn't know about him and that singer…'

'The four Fs.'

'Yes. But even without knowing anything about that, she sensed something about him.'

'But you said he's changed his ways now.'

'That's what he said, but…'

'Look, Art's invited you to America, you're on the point of being offered a dream job, I've said that even if it means we're apart for a bit, we'll manage. You've said that Ted and Mary would think it was a great opportunity, and you know that Art had good reasons for not taking you with him when you were nine. And of course Mary would have been protective of you and would have been worried about your going with Art. But you keep on finding counter-arguments. Can't you see? It's obvious. You don't want to go.'

I hear the clatter of the cups and plates in the café, the voices of the other customers, the waitress shouting orders. I see an image of my mother going to Art's base and finding out that he's missing in action. So many hopes crushed in a moment. Seconds pass. I know Julia's watching me but she says nothing. Eventually I say, 'So, I am just like *Billy Liar.*'

'Geoff, forget about *Billy Liar*. You're nothing like him. You're not a fantasist, you don't go round lying to people, you're not in a crumby job with no prospects. You've a great career ahead of you whether you go to America or stay in England. And Ted and Mary love you. And if he really wants to be a good father, Art will love you whatever you decide. And so will I.' And she holds my arm again.

I'm in a bit of a state for the next two days. I'm all right when I'm doing maths problems or practising the sax, but the rest of the time I can only think about Art, and Ted and Mary, and about what Julia said. On the third day, I wake up and decide that I can't procrastinate any longer. I have no idea what I'm going to say but as soon as I start writing, it turns out to be easy.

> *Dear Art,*
>
> *Since I last saw you at your 40th birthday celebration, not a single day has gone by without my thinking of what you said to me about coming to live with you in Seattle, working for Boeing and becoming your legal son. I was deeply touched by your invitation and thank you from the bottom of my heart.*
>
> *I have recently seen Murray Hickman and I realise that time is running out and I need to make a decision.*

*When I came to Seattle, I told you about how connected to you I felt, and now I've met my grandparents and the rest of my American family, I feel that even more. I'm so proud to be your son and so grateful for what I have inherited from you, and it would be wonderful to catch up on all those lost years we've spent apart. Yet I also feel so many ties to England, which after all has always been my home. I know that Ted and Mary would always back me in anything I wanted to do and would never attempt to persuade me to stay here, but I also know that they would be heartbroken if I left them. It's not just that I owe them so much, it's that I am their only son, and love them too much to abandon them.*

*I'm sure that there will be lots of future opportunities for us to get together both here in and the States, and that the distance in miles between us will never affect the emotional closeness I feel for you and all my American family.*

*Your loving son,*
*Geoff*

I ring Julia and read her the letter.

'It's beautiful,' she says.

'He won't be hurt?'

'He'll understand.'

'God, I hope so. I really hope so. And Julia?'

'Yes?'

'I didn't say anything about you, because you were right, we would have managed, but I don't think Ted and Mary would have done. So although I could have said that I'd also met you and fallen in love with you and didn't want to be apart from you for all that time, it wouldn't have been the true reason I'd decided not to go.'

'I know.

'But I will write to him soon about you. I promise.'

'I know you will.'

'God, I don't deserve you.'

'Am I much to deserve?'

'You know you are.'

'Well then, you are too… Geoff, are you still there?'

'Sorry, I was just thinking about what might have happened if I hadn't spoken to you, or even worse, if I'd never met you in the first place. I can't believe how lucky I am. You said it was obvious I didn't want to go. And it was. But I just couldn't see it. I suppose I was sort of trying to show that I could make a choice for myself. Other people had made the choice for me when I was nine, now it was my turn. It's so hard to explain. When Art came to see us, he was like a fairy-tale hero. And when I worked out he was my father, it just felt so amazing. Then when we first played jazz together, it was like everything I'd dreamed of. I felt so close to him. But then there was the Donna thing, and I know I was judging him far too harshly, but it was because I'd wanted him to be perfect.'

'Anyone in your position would have felt the same.'

'Maybe. But the thing is, later I saw that I was wrong: it wasn't such a big deal, and anyway he'd said he was sorry and he'd changed his ways. So I know he's human, just like the rest of us. So what? But I think that some bit of the dream was still there, and I thought that if I went to live in Seattle it would be as if I could turn back the clock and he really had taken me with him when I was nine.'

'Oh, Geoff, it's so sad thinking about that abandoned little boy.'

'But that's the point. I wasn't sad. For a moment when I was nine, I'd wondered what it would be like to have someone like Art as a dad, but it didn't matter because I had Ted and Mary.'

# NOVEMBER 1965

'Hello Ted, just ringing to see how you both are.' It's Thursday evening. I've started at Hawker Siddeley, renting a one-bedroom flat in Hatfield and enjoying the luxury of having my own phone.

'Geoff? Oh I was just about to ring you.'

'Oh?'

'It's about Mary actually. She got a letter this morning from Ireland, from her brother saying that her mother was very ill and had asked to see her.'

'From Ireland? But I thought they'd completely written her out of history.'

'And she'd pretty much written them out too.'

'So what's she going to do?'

'Well, she had to go, so she found a flight this afternoon and should be in Dublin by now. She thinks she'll be able to find a bus or a train or something to where her mother is. I offered to go with her, of course, but she said she wanted to do it on her own. I would have liked to have been there for moral support but I can see that maybe it's easier for her not to have the complication of introducing me to her family.'

'Will she be all right? After all these years?'

'You know Mary. She's strong, she'll manage all right but it won't be easy. It was always at the back of my mind that something like this might happen. Between you and me, I never liked her having this rift. You only have one life, it seems a shame to cut yourself off from people who should really matter to you, but I can see that her family treated her very badly. Anyway I'm pleased that this might mend some bridges, even at this late stage.'

'What was the rift all about in the first place?'

'Oh, some family thing. Probably all out of proportion now when people look back.'

I can't help thinking there must have been more to it. I've always wondered, but this is the furthest I've ever gone in asking about it. 'Will you be OK, on your own?'

'Good Lord, yes, of course. Don't forget I was bachelor for all those years. I'll look after myself very well, don't worry.'

'If you're sure.'

'Course.'

'And you'll keep me up to date.'

'I'll ring you when I get more news.'

TED RINGS ME the next evening. 'It's bad. Her mother has cancer, seems to have spread pretty well everywhere. She's at home on morphine – in and out a bit, but she and Mary have been able to talk and it sounds like they've made their peace.'

'What about the rest of the family? What about Mary's father?'

'It turns out he hasn't been on the scene for some time. Apparently he went off to Australia with another woman. Mary'll tell us more when she gets back. Two of the brothers and Mary's younger sister are there. I get the feeling that relations are strained but they are talking to each other at least.'

'How long will Mary stay there?'

'For the duration, she says. I don't think it will be long, but she wants to stay on for the wake and the funeral.'

TEN DAYS LATER, instead of visiting Julia in Cambridge, I come down to London to stay the weekend with Ted and Mary. I arrive only a few minutes after they've got back from the airport. I let myself in and find them having whiskies in the sitting room. Mary rushes up and hugs me. 'Oh, my boy, my boy,' she repeats as the tears flow freely on to my shoulder. She pulls away, wiping her face and holding her eyes clenched shut. 'Sorry, I'm all right now. I'll just get my breath back.' She breathes deeply and then sits down and takes a sip of whisky. 'That's better. So Geoff, how's work?'

'Oh, everything's going well, thanks.' Ted and Mary continue looking at me expectantly, so I give them a detailed description of the project I'm working on, answering their questions about technical points and the characters of my colleagues and what I've eaten in the canteen that week. Then they ask about Julia and I relay similar minutiae.

'Well that all sounds very nice,' says Mary. 'Now Ted, have we any food in the house?'

'I've decided we all need a treat…'

'Does that mean you're cooking?' and Mary and I exchange smiles.

'Enough of that. I've booked a restaurant – the Italian place in King Street.'

'Grand idea, Ted. I'd forgotten just how awful the food is in Ireland, now we're all Fanny Craddocks over here.'

ONLY ON SUNDAY morning is Mary ready to talk. We've finished a late breakfast and Ted is aimlessly leafing through the *Observer*. 'Princess Margaret seems to be going down well in New York.'

'You've both been very good,' says Mary, 'not asking me about what happened in Ireland. You know me, I like to get everything sorted out in my head, but I'm ready now.' Ted puts down the newspaper and I stop doing the washing up and come and sit down at the table. 'I'll start at the beginning. I was lucky and just managed to get a train to Roscommon and then found a taxi to the village, so it was nearly ten when I got there. It's all changed more than I expected. Mam had moved out of the old house and was living in the twentieth century now in a place with "the light" as we used to call electricity and an inside bathroom with hot water. To his credit, it's Eamon's doing. He lives next door with his wife and four children and they got her to move when Bridget got married last year, but she wasn't long in there before she became ill. My daddy had gone seven years ago. He'd stopped sending money over from England and Eamon had gone over to look for him and it turned out he'd met another woman and they'd taken one of those ten pound ships to Australia. Nobody's heard a word from him, he could be on the moon for all the difference it would make. Mam had found work as a cleaner and they'd managed somehow, what with Eamon and Eugene both working on farms. Then Eugene met a girl, married her and they decided they'd had enough of Ireland and went off to Canada and he started in the building trade and said there was plenty of work so Pat joined him – they were always close. So there's only Eamon, Liam and Bridget left now. Eamon's doing well it seems – agricultural machinery I think he said. His wife would hardly say hello to me when I arrived, Rose her name is, but later on she became a bit friendlier. She has a younger brother who wants to come to London to work on that new tube line they're building…'

'The Victoria line,' says Ted.

'Yes, that's the one. She said they're desperate for strong Irishmen to do the hard work and it's good money and I said he could stay with us if he wanted, while he found his feet, and she was much nicer to me after that. Is that all right, Ted? He came to the wake and seemed like a good boy.'

'Course.'

'Where was I? Oh yes, well Mam was terribly bad. She'd gone to the doctor more than a year ago, and at first he didn't think it was anything serious, so she just carried on feeling unwell until Eamon told her she must go back. And then she went to the hospital for tests and they found cancer in so many places they said it was too late to do anything and she must prepare for the worst, as they say.' She takes a handkerchief from her sleeve and dabs her eyes and blows her nose. 'I'm all right, I just need a moment.'

Ted gets up and puts the cereal and marmalade away in the larder.

'After the diagnosis Mam tried to carry on working, but it was soon too much for her, and then she took to her bed and the doctor would come in and give her morphine injections and Eamon and Rose have been looking after her, and, well you know

Eamon and me don't get on, but they have been wonderful to her. And of course, when she asked to see me, she told me he was angry, but she said she had to set things straight between us before she went.' She pauses and stares into an empty corner of the room. 'And she did. We set things straight between us and I'm so pleased.' Her eyes fill with tears again. We wait for her to recover.

'She wanted to know all about both of you. We talked for hours, but with the morphine, I'm not sure what she took in, but when she was alert she asked questions and – oh she was very interested when I told her you'd gone to Boston, Geoff, she said she'd a cousin there and what a shame, if she'd known you were going you could have looked him up. Imagine. He would certainly have got a surprise!' We all laugh. 'Course it was too late and expensive for Eugene and Pat to come back from Canada, so it was Eamon and Rose and Liam – he's living in Dublin now, working for the water board and married too with three little ones – and Bridget – she's seven months pregnant of course – and her husband, Donal, just a boy,' she turns to me, 'younger than you; and it was very peaceful, she was in no pain. She'd had a hard life, she had no fight left in her. She was only fifty-seven you know.'

Eamon hadn't wanted Mary to stay for the wake and the burial, but she'd insisted. 'The old faces, girls I'd been at school with, their mothers and fathers, the shopkeepers, the farmer I used to help with the milking. Some of them cutting me dead, but some of them friendly, too. I couldn't tell whether it was because they'd forgotten why I'd left or didn't care anymore. Even Ireland's changing. Course, Eamon couldn't bring himself to say anything civil to me when I left, but Rose whispered that it was a good thing that I'd come.'

# JUNE 1966

My boss asks me to go with him to a meeting in London at the Royal Aeronautical Society near Hyde Park Corner. I'm there to take notes and he tells me that I'm not supposed to say anything. We finish at four and he says I can go home as he is staying in London, which gives me time to take a bus down Piccadilly and pop into Dobell's jazz record shop in Charing Cross Road.

'Hello, young man, haven't seen you in a bit,' says John behind the counter, who knows me from Les's band. 'Still playing I hope.'

'Now and again with Les, but it's getting hard to find the time. I'm working in Hatfield now. What's that you're playing? Sounds good.'

'Hang on,' says John, 'I'll put it on from the beginning. You can listen in the booth.'

I listen to the first track and go back to the counter. 'It's brilliant.'

'Any guesses?'

John's knowledge is legendary and I don't want to make a fool of myself. 'The only one I think I know is the pianist. Is it Horace Silver?'

'Spot on.' He hands over the record sleeve; the LP is called *Song For My Father*.

'I'll take it.' I pause. 'Actually can I have two? I'd like to get one for a friend.' He pulls two copies out from the shelf behind him. 'And John, I'd like to send it to America. Do you have anything I could wrap it in to keep it safe?'

'America? Coals to Newcastle.'

'I know, but it's a birthday present you see.' He takes out two sheets of thick card from under the counter.

'We normally charge, but seeing it's you I'll make an exception. Gawd knows what the postage is going to cost you.'

He puts the record between the two sheets and wraps it in brown paper and then points me in the direction of the Trafalgar Square post office. He's right, the postage is more than the record, but with luck it should get there in time for Art's birthday. I realise that there's no card or note with it, but he'll know who it's from.

# JULY 1969

THE REGISTER OFFICE ceremony is supposed to be just for immediate family, but that still means quite a lot of people. There are Ted and Mary, Julia's parents and her brother Peter, Ted's sister Barbara and her husband George. To our surprise and delight, Edith agreed to come down from Oldham and is looking very smart in a white hat and blue suit with white piping. All the American family have come over: Art, Charlie and Carol; Max and Annie; Joan and Gersh and their two boys. We asked Beth, but she wrote a very nice letter wishing us congratulations but declining the invitation. Mike and Georgie Denston's two children are bridesmaid and page, and as Eric is best man, his parents are there too. Julia and I wanted something informal, but Julia's father was disappointed that we weren't getting married in the college chapel so we compensated by agreeing to morning suits for the men. After the ceremony, we walk over the road from City Hall to Radnor College where glasses of champagne and cups of tea are waiting and more guests have already assembled. There are speeches from Julia's father, me – I was dreading it but it doesn't go too badly, Eric – who is hilarious, and finally Julia, who has insisted that it is only fair that she says something and makes the best speech of all. We can't stop Max from making an impromptu contribution, in which he recommends everyone to watch the Laurel and Hardy film *A Chump at Oxford* to find out what it's really like, and how surprised he was when his son-in-law Gersh told him that one of his colleagues at the Harvard Medical School had been a Rhodes Scholar at Oxford. What was a medical doctor doing, going to Oxford, England to study highways? 'I thought he meant roads, R O A D S!'

Weddings at the college normally end there, but because of the Americans, we decide there should be dinner too – in the hall – and then I find out that Max and Annie can't understand how you can have a wedding without any dancing, so after much negotiation with the Governing Body of the college, Julia's father manages to get them to agree that we can have a small (not loud) band in the senior combination room until no later than ten. I ask Les if his band can play, and they are all invited to the dinner too.

As the guests mill about in the hall while the band's getting ready, I see Art and Ted chatting to each other. I wander over to them. 'I was just saying to Art,' says Ted, 'we did pretty well, didn't we? Our boy, he's turned out all right.'

'He's our boy, but it's you who did it, Ted. I had nothing to do with how's he turned out, that's all down to you and Mary. I don't know if I ever even thanked you properly. If I didn't, let me say now, that I thank you more than words can express.'

Ted goes over to talk to Julia's parents leaving Art and me alone. This is the first chance we've had to talk. 'I was sorry to hear about you and Beth,' I say.

'Yeh, I sure screwed up. I really wanted to stay together with her, but I don't blame her. I'm a bad boy, but I don't seem to be able to change however hard I try. Just a sucker for the ladies. Dad won't talk to me. I only hope the children don't hate me too much for it. That includes you. When you're a child you think your parents are judging you the whole time, but when your children grow up, then it's the other way round.'

'Of course I don't hate you. These things happen. It's not for me to judge.'

'You'd have every right. I haven't been a great husband. Not sure if I've even been much of a father.'

'You know that's not true. I've seen you with Charlie and Carol, you're a tremendous father.' A little late, I add, 'And to me too.'

'Come on Geoff, I've been no father to you. You might have got the jazz from me, but the way you are, you got that from Ted, and Mary too. I try to be good, sure, but I never quite make it. But you're like Ted. You know how to do the right thing and you stick to it. Maybe I knew that all the time, in the back of my mind, and that's why I left you with Ted. And you were right to stay in England and not come out to work for Boeing. I respect you for that.'

Julia comes over and Art kisses her. He puts his arms around both of us. 'You two are great together,' he says. 'You gotta hold on to what you got and never let go of it.'

When we're all in the SCR, the first dance is announced and then after doing the usual embarrassing shuffle, the others join us. Next, Art, Les and I play a number together to riotous applause. Then Les announces that a special guest singer is joining them for the next song. To my amazement, Julia goes up to the bandstand and takes the microphone. Everyone goes quiet and she nods to the pianist, who strikes a dramatic first chord.

'Someday he'll come along, the man I love…' Her voice is clear and pure, not a full-bodied jazz voice, but instantly engaging and moving. Everyone is spellbound. At the end of the applause the calls for 'more' are so insistent that Les hushes the room again and the drummer comes in with a bossa nova beat, and the piano starts a vamp – a chord moving up a semitone and then back down again. Then Julia comes in: 'Tall and tan and young and handsome, The boy called Geoffrey he goes walking…'

In the taxi after the wedding, I say, 'Julia, you never said you could sing. You stole the show, you were sensational.'

'I've been rehearsing every week with Les and the pianist for the last five weeks.'

'What? I had no idea.'

'A bride's got to save some secrets for her wedding night.'

# MARCH 1987

'I'LL GET IT,' calls Julia. 'Hello.'

'Hello, is that Julia? Mary here.'

'Oh Mary, how nice. We so enjoyed seeing you and Ted on Sunday.'

'Oh, we loved having you. The children, every time I see them they seem to have grown another few inches. Jack is a real young man now, and Alice, she's a sweetheart.'

'Thanks, I'm not going to disagree but I think we might be a bit biased.'

'Of course not. It's only the truth. Now, I wonder if I could have a word with Geoff.'

'Yes, of course. I'll just get him.'

I come to the phone. 'Hello Mary. How's everything? It was lovely seeing you on Sunday.'

'That's just what Julia said and I said how much we loved having you.' She pauses. 'Geoff, I have some news I need to talk to you about.'

'Oh? Talk away.'

'It's not very good news, I'm afraid. It's Ted. He doesn't want to say anything – you know what he's like, he hates having a fuss made – and he doesn't know I'm ringing you, but I had to tell you.'

'What is it?'

'Well, he went to the doctor and he sent him in for some tests, and… and they say it's cancer.'

'Cancer?'

'Of the prostate. He's got to go in for deep X-ray, oh what do they call it now? Radiotherapy, that's it.'

'Oh. Have they said any more than that?'

'Well, you see, he took a long time to see the doctor about it and they think it's already quite advanced. Of course, they don't know… they can't say anything for sure, the consultant told him that the success rate for the treatment is very good now, getting better all the time he said, but the way he said it, it didn't sound good to me.'

'Oh. How's Ted?'

'Well he says he's fine, but… didn't you think he looked thinner when you saw him on Sunday?'

'Maybe.'

'Well he is. He's lost weight and… he puts on a good face, especially when he's with other people, but I know, I know he's not himself.' There's another pause. 'Are you there?'

'Sorry, yes.'

'I didn't want to scare you, but I had to tell you, I had to talk to someone.' She sniffs.

'Of course. You did absolutely right.'

'I would have told you before, but I knew Ted didn't want me to say anything, and on Sunday, when we were all enjoying ourselves, it wouldn't have been right.'

'Can I talk to Ted?'

'Yes, but maybe right now isn't such a good time.'

'What about if I came to see you both, say, tomorrow evening?'

'But it's a long way for you.'

'No it is isn't. It's only an hour or so. I could get to you at about seven.'

'Oh, that would be great, Geoff. You're a good boy.'

'OK, I'll see you tomorrow at about seven, then. In the meantime send my love to Ted.'

Julia has been listening to my side of the conversation. 'What was all that about?' I tell her what Mary's said. 'But he seemed fine on Sunday.'

'That's what I thought, but you know what Ted's like, he would never let on if anything was wrong.'

'Dunkirk spirit.'

'More like just how he is. He wouldn't want to make other people unhappy and he wouldn't want to draw attention to himself.

'I know. He's the sweetest man. Shall I come too, tomorrow?'

'That would be fantastic, you know they think the world of you. But can you spare the time? I thought you had loads of marking to do.'

'I want to come. I can make time.'

# JUNE 1987

THE FUNERAL GOES as well as can be expected. As Ted isn't a churchgoer, he said that he just wanted a simple service at the crematorium. Considering that Ted and Mary lived 'quietly', there's a good turn-out: most of the old hands from P V Cunningham, some of Ted's choir friends, Julia's parents, Eric and his parents, various neighbours and acquaintances. I ask Michael Denston to say a few words about Ted as a boy. Although they hadn't known each other that well at school, as Julia's uncle it seems appropriate and he does it well. Then I tell my story. Most of the people there know that I was adopted but few know much more than that. I avoid the more lurid details about Frank and Sheila and what happened at St Christopher's Choir School, just explaining that Ted rescued me from an unfortunate set of circumstances. I pretty much keep my composure, while Mary weeps quietly in the front row. The choir friends sing one of Ted's favourite Bach chorales and then everyone's invited back to Hammersmith for tea and sandwiches. As arranged, Julia goes back home with the children and I am staying at the house tonight with Mary. I help her clear up and put everything back.

I say, 'I think it went well, didn't it?'

'You did a grand job. What you said... it couldn't have been said better. He would have been so proud of you. Well, he always was, anyway... now look at me...' She gets out her handkerchief. 'Sorry, whenever I think of him I just can't stop myself.'

'Me too,' and we hold each other tight.

In time-honoured fashion, Mary insists we need another cup of tea.

'Mary, there's something I want to ask you, and if I don't ask now I probably never will.'

'You know you can ask me anything. Is it about Ted?'

298

'Sort of. It's just that I've always wondered why you didn't have any children, well, apart from me.'

'Have you been thinking about it for all these years?'

'Not really, but sometimes just curious to know. You both gave so much love to me and you absolutely dote on Jack and Alice. Did you not want children of your own?' Mary looks away and stares into the distance. 'Oh, I'm such an idiot. I should never have asked. Forget I said anything, it's none of my business. I'm just an insensitive oaf.'

Mary turns back to me. 'No, you've every right. It's a perfectly reasonable thing to ask. We should talk about these things. Everything used to be shut away when I was a girl, it's right to get things into the open. P'raps we should have told you long ago. The answer is that we tried. We tried and we tried, but I could never get pregnant. I thought it was because of me, you see – I've never told this to anyone except Ted – when I was a girl in Ireland I got pregnant and had to have my baby in a terrible place run by vicious hateful women who claimed to be the brides of Christ; I'll not tell you now about all that, it's for another time, but I had my baby and he – it was a boy, you see – was born dead, stillborn. That's why I left Ireland and my family cut me off. And because he was stillborn I thought that was why I couldn't get pregnant again. But in the end I went and had some tests and they told me that there was nothing wrong and they suggested Ted have some tests. And that was it. Low sperm count they said. It sometimes happens, for all sorts of reasons. And then, I remember it so well, Ted and I both said the same thing, you know how you do sometimes, the exact same words came out of our mouths at the same time. We said: "It was meant to be," and we both knew exactly that it was because we had you and that was more than enough.'

# ACKNOWLEDGEMENTS

IT ALL STARTED with inspiring tutor, Shelley Harris's *Writing Fiction* at the Oxford University Department for Continuing Education. More insights and encouragement came from other Oxford courses led by Noel White and Morag Joss, and at the informal writing groups some of us formed after the courses had finished. Particular thanks must go to Judy Bastin, Jenny Perkins and Gay Mallam who read my early drafts and gave such valuable feedback. I would never have completed my novel had I not attending a writing retreat at the beautiful Casa Ana, so thanks to Anne Hunt and my fellow writers for their *esprit de corps*, and tutor Tom Bromley for his wise and perceptive advice. Sadly my uncle, His Honour Judge Leonard Krikler, died before completion but I gratefully acknowledge his invaluable input on the legal aspects of adoption in the 1950s. Similarly, *In The Family Way* (Penguin/Viking 2015), written by friend and neighbour, Jane Robinson, was a great help in revealing the plight of single mothers during this period. Most important of all, I could never have done any of this without the love, support, advice and encouragement of Sara Stoll.

Printed in Great Britain
by Amazon